TITLES BY NADIA LEE

A HOLLYWOOD DEAL
THE BILLIONAIRE'S FORBIDDEN DESIRE
THE BILLIONAIRE'S FORGOTTEN FIANCÉE
THE BILLIONAIRE'S SECRET WIFE
THE BILLIONAIRE'S HOLIDAY OBSESSION
MERRY IN LOVE
THE BILLIONAIRE'S COUNTERFEIT GIRLFRIEND
MERRY IN LOVE
FOREVER IN LOVE
SWEET IN LOVE
REDEMPTION IN LOVE
REUNITED IN LOVE
VENGEFUL IN LOVE

The Billionaire's Forbidden Desire

The Pryce Family Book Five

nadia lee

The Billionaire's Forbidden Desire

For Darryl Lawrence.
Thank you for the best gumbo I've ever had.

PART I
The Beginning

ONE

Three years ago

DANE PRYCE ENTERED A STERILE PRIVATE room at the hospital. The air was comfortably warm, the light semi-dim. He inhaled sharply. All the disinfectant and flowers in the world couldn't disguise the cloying scent of the dying.

In the center of the bed lay his grandmother—Shirley Pryce, the matriarch of the family. Her body seemed to have shrunk since the last time he'd seen her, the thin white skin hanging over her protruding bones like a cheap tent. Even her hair, usually the color of polished steel, looked dull. Tubes and wires covered her, monitoring her condition and giving her the fluids and medicines she needed to stay alive.

The doctor had said she'd had two cardiac arrests. Given her advanced age and generally poor health, she wasn't going to last long. Dane clenched his hands. If it weren't for the beeps from the machines, he might have thought she'd passed away already.

Why didn't anybody contact me after her first heart attack?

He stood by the door, unable to take another step. He didn't know how to behave before death. And he didn't know if he could get through it without breaking down.

Being vulnerable.

Shirley was the only one he cared about. The only person from his family who'd ever given a damn about him.

"Dane…" came a whispery voice.

He stepped over and carefully, gently took her brittle hand in his. "Grandma."

Her murky eyes turned to him, and she gave him a soft smile. "They said you were busy in London… but I knew you'd come."

"Of course." He kissed her knuckles, ruthlessly reining in his fury at whichever bastard had told her he was too busy. That was for later. "Of course I came. Where is everyone?"

Didn't his family think she deserved that much? *Fucking assholes.* The fact that they could be this unfeeling stunned him. She wasn't even inconveniencing them by dying in some foreign city. He knew firsthand how something like that could get in the way of his family's "caring." He'd experienced it when he'd been in a car wreck in Paris and the only people who'd visited him were Shirley and the lawyers the family had sent over to deal with the matter.

Sick as she was, a glimmer of fire appeared in her eye. "I told them to get out. Useless bunch, all of them." She coughed weakly. "Geraldine's still stuck at the airport. Some mechanical delay."

Geraldine was Shirley's favorite child.

Dane swallowed an unfamiliar lump in his throat. "I'll send my jet immediately. She'll be here soon, so just…hang in there."

Her fingers tightened around his. "You're such a good boy. Always were." She wheezed, the sound sending a ripple of terror through his heart. "Don't be sad. It's only natural that an old woman like me die. It's what the Lord intended."

"Don't say that." The skin around Dane's eyes grew hot, and he blinked rapidly. The last thing his grandmother needed was his tears. "You're going to outlive us all."

She chuckled weakly. "No woman wants to outlive her grandchildren."

"Well, then live as long as I do at least. I'm your favorite anyway."

"Wishful and fanciful. Always are. Doesn't work that way." She squeezed his hand with surprising strength. "Now, promise me something."

"Anything."

"Don't marry someone like your mother. She never had the courage. Never deserved Salazar."

Shirley's thin mouth twisted into a scornful line. "Although he isn't any better, letting his emotions rule his head. Don't be like him. Weak. Pathetic. He let her use him, and for what? I taught him better, but the moment he saw her..."

"I promise."

"Still, he's your father—save him from himself if you can. I've done what I could, but... I'm afraid he won't know what to do with himself after I'm gone."

"You're not going anywhere. But I'll keep an eye on him."

"Your siblings, too. They aren't strong like you. Especially Shane, that poor child. So needy."

"I will."

Shirley drew in a labored breath. "Be kind to Geraldine. She has no one. Those children of hers...horribly misguided. Worthless...every single one of them."

His throat tightened. He rasped, "I will."

"And one last thing."

"Anything," he said, putting both of his hands around hers. If he held on tight, maybe she would stay, at least until he was ready to accept the inevitable.

"Let it go."

"What?"

She dragged in air, the sound loud and shuddery. "I know you think about Paris. Stop it. Get rid of that damn Lamborghini. That whole thing is in the past, and we took care of it."

Dane almost froze.

The incident didn't plague him the way it used to, but he still thought of it from time to time. It had been his fault—he'd caused the crash due to carelessness. He'd never told anybody how he'd felt, not even his best friend. Still, he should've guessed Shirley would know. She seemed to know everything about him.

"Not your fault…just bad luck. Five million dollars is more than enough to make up for it."

Dane recoiled, his heart thudding. He'd never asked the lawyers how much the accident had cost. Money had never been an object in his family, but five million? What the hell could have happened to the other party? The family lawyers were ruthless, and would never have allowed that kind of payout unless there was no other way to reduce the damage.

Shirley squeezed his hand again. This time, her grip was so feeble he could barely breathe. "You're the best thing that's happened to this family. Don't ever forget it."

She was the only one who thought that, his stern but loving grandmother. Everyone else in his family probably wished he'd never been born. He knew his parents did.

She let out a soft sigh, her grip loosening. And then Shirley Pryce was no more.

Dane swallowed hard, his eyes burning with unshed tears.

Intellectually he knew Shirley was old and had lived a full life, but emotionally…

He looked around. If he hadn't made it in time, she would've died alone.

He fell to his knees and pressed his forehead against her papery knuckles. If he stayed like this she might just reach over and caress his head, tell him everything was going to be fine the way she'd done so many times when he'd been a child.

"Sir?"

A soft touch on his shoulder startled him. He blinked.

"Sir, are you all right?" the nurse asked again.

"I'm fine," he answered automatically. His legs felt rubbery, but he stood up anyway.

The grandson that Shirley Pryce had been so proud of would never show vulnerability to another.

His family dutifully showed up at the funeral, even though the weather sucked—skies the color of granite and rain, the bane of all Californians. Stoic and serious in their black suits and dresses, they stood under umbrellas in the drizzle like so many mushrooms.

Dane curled his lip at how ridiculous they sounded as they read scripted eulogies. His mother even held a pristine silk handkerchief in her perfectly manicured hand…as though she were actually planning to cry at some point.

When it was his turn, he got behind the microphone and looked at the small crowd for a few moments. Then he said, "Shirley Price had more balls than all of you put together, and I can never hope to meet the high expectations she set for me."

Gasps could be heard over the rain. His mother turned pale with embarrassment. She was always embarrassed about him for not being the kind of son she'd needed to keep his father from straying.

When the funeral ended, a few sycophants came over to say a few words of faux condolence. But not one of them had felt anything for Shirley. How dare they show their faces?

"You know I'm here for you," one of them said.

It was all he could do to not spit on the man. "Fuck off," he snarled.

Dane spun on his heel and walked away fast, away from the farce before he did something he might regret later. He dug his phone out of his pocket and dialed his office.

"Cancel all my appointments for the next three weeks."

There was an infinitesimal pause. "Understood," his assistant said. "Where can—"

He hung up and turned off the phone. He was finished.

TWO

Sophia Reed drew warm, salty air into her lungs. The pristine beach called out to her, its waves gentle and edged with light white foam. Still, the knot in her chest wouldn't ease.

"You okay, champ?" came a low, gruff male voice.

She forced a smile. "Fine, Chad. I'm just enjoying being here again. It's nice to escape the cold." Mexico was where she'd come to recuperate after the accident a few years before. "Why don't you go on ahead? I know you're tired from the flight. I'll take a short walk and then head back."

Her bodyguard-slash-chaperone looked around, brows furrowing. Sunlight reflected off his head, which was as dark and as shiny as a bowling ball. "You shouldn't be out here alone."

"You think my stalkers are hiding behind there,"—she gestured at a nearby palm tree—"waiting to pounce?" She'd been having stalker issues for years. "I doubt they're still interested now that I'm too..." She waved a hand, unwilling to say the rest—*too damaged to be in the spotlight.*

"Not just the stalkers. You've been kind of blue lately."

She forced a carefree laugh. Sweet of him to be concerned, and most people wouldn't have unexpected it from a man built like a tank. A couple of long, jagged scars marred his left cheek. She was sure they were from a knife or something, even though he hadn't ever talked about it. *Too rough a story for a pretty girl like you*, he'd said.

"I'm not going to swim out to sea if that's what you're worried about," she said.

He pursed his mouth, and she knew what he was thinking: *It should've been me.*

He'd said that to her when she'd opened her eyes in the hospital, and every time the doctors had wheeled her into surgery to put her back together. He'd only stopped because she'd asked him to.

It shouldn't have been anybody.

But she could tell he was still feeling it from the way his eyes darkened every time he thought she wasn't looking. She gave him a serene smile and made a gentle shooing motion.

"All right," he finally said. "But if you're not back in an hour, I'm coming looking for you."

"I promise." She watched until he vanished into the vacation rental, then started walking down the beach. Sun-warmed sand tickled her toes. She took off her flat, sling-back sandals and carried them in one hand.

The sea-salted air was refreshing, but the change of scenery hadn't eased the pain in her heart. *Four years.* Everyone had told her that was enough time to accept the possibility of never achieving her dream, but they weren't the ones who'd worked tirelessly since the age of five. Fourteen years of relentless, bone-cracking work, and then an accident at nineteen had derailed everything she'd been working for.

Life isn't fair. She'd heard that a lot as well.

The knot in her chest grew bigger.

She'd sought out the best surgeons in the world, done all the rehab. She'd pushed herself hard, determined to get back on the ice, healthier and stronger than ever before. Kept her weight under control; every extra ounce helped gravity pull her down. Only the most nutritious food, carefully calibrated to create optimal health and an optimal bodyweight for figure skating, ended up in her belly.

Twenty-three wasn't young in her sport. Actually it was sort of on the old side, what with new teenage sensations popping up every season, but she knew she could do it if her shoulder and hip would just cooperate.

She closed her eyes. It'd been so long, but her muscles still remembered what it was like to fly across a rink at full speed. She didn't believe in slowing down or hesitating before executing her elements: a powerful takeoff on the outside edge as her free foot's toe-pick hit the ice, pulling in her limbs and rotating in the air: one...two...three. Then a perfect landing on one foot for a split-second as she launched herself into the air again for a triple loop—three tight revolutions. And before she knew it her blade would be gliding across the ice again, creating a smooth, clean line, the combination jump completed as she transitioned into another element of her program.

But now...now her reality was different. Her body might remember, but it could no longer perform any of her key jumps with the consistency she needed. She could deal with the aching shoulder, but her hip couldn't seem to handle loops at all. The surgeries and endless physical therapy just hadn't been able to fix all the damage.

And there was absolutely no one she could talk to. Her father didn't really understand what it meant to her, even though he'd had no problem forking over the money for her training, and her mother was too busy being a trophy wife. Her figure skating friends were single-mindedly focused on getting ready for the Olympic season. They were also avoiding her—she could tell. Not that she blamed them. Athletes were superstitious, and it probably made them feel uncomfortable to be around her, a former star who was now just a has-been. She would've felt the same if the situation had been reversed.

And Libby Grudin... Her best friend commiserated, but she also saw the accident as an opportunity for Sophia to live her life.

"There's something so...*cloistered* about being twenty-three and never having been on a date," Libby had said. "Look at you. You're gorgeous! It's about time you get out and experience the world. Do the kind of stuff women our age do."

Sophia sighed and resumed her walk. Maybe Libby had a point. On the other hand, nothing had made Sophia feel alive like being on the ice. Every beat and strain of the music would reverberate through her, and it was like her soul was free.

To be free again like that…

She stopped walking and leaped vertically in the air, rotated a couple of times and landed on one foot, her arms outstretched and her free leg raised behind her. So long as she landed on her uninjured side it wasn't so bad…except that wasn't her landing foot. She dropped her shoes and tried it again. Then again. And again. Sweat beaded on her skin, blood pumping through her body.

She tried a small, single-rotation jump on her bad side, keeping it low. *No problem.*

Encouraged, she tried for a double, getting some air under her. When she came down, a numbing pain shot from her hip through her entire body. The sand seemed to shift underneath, and she crumpled with a cry.

Until a strong hand caught her.

She gasped, clutching at the hard, muscled arm and trying to get her balance. Then looked up at the owner of the heroic limb. He stared back at her, his eyes hidden behind a pair of reflective sunglasses.

Her skin tingled like she was only a second away

from competing, her heart knocking against her ribs. She licked her lips and studied the stranger. A few days' growth of beard couldn't hide the clean, bold lines of a face that ought to be on glossy magazine covers. The clothes on him had exceptional stitching and material, although they weren't fresh. She could tell that the body was lean under the shirt, his shoulders broad and hips narrow. The rolled up sleeves revealed forearms carved with muscle.

"Who are you?" she rasped, her throat dry. "Are you lost?" This was a private beach. The real estate agent had sworn she'd be the only one there.

"Lost...?" He rolled the word on his tongue.

She frowned. Maybe he didn't speak English. After all, they were in Mexico...

"Um, no español," she said, suddenly flustered.

"'No español' is fine. I'm not lost," he said in perfect English, his diction precise.

His deep voice washed over her like the summer sun, and she leaned a tiny bit closer. Maybe...just maybe the warmth it generated could thaw the cold knot in her chest.

Suddenly he shook his head and gave a short laugh. There was a hint of harsh derision underneath. "Or maybe I am. I walked for quite a while."

Embarrassed, she pulled away from him. As he dropped his hand, cold seeped through her despite the tropical sun. She shivered and cleared her throat. "Thanks for the help."

"You're welcome."

Then it finally registered in her frazzled brain that he smelled like alcohol. For the first time she noticed a half-full bottle clutched in his other hand.

She tilted her head. Being short, she was used to looking up at people, but for some reason, he seemed taller than most. "Have you been drinking?" she asked almost stupidly. She'd never seen anybody indulge this early. Her parents might've had their issues, but substance abuse wasn't one of them.

He cocked an eyebrow, and she got an impression of arrogance. "What if I have?"

"Just..." She frowned, not sure what to say or why she felt so defensive. Even though they weren't standing close, the skin around her spine was prickling like tiny needles were being pressed against her. "Isn't it a little early?"

"It's never too early to drink when the occasion calls for it." He flashed her a roguish smile, a dimple popping on his cheek.

She blinked at how unexpected that was. How could a hard and unyielding man like him have something as innocuous as a dimple?

"You should try it some time. In fact, why not now?" He shoved the bottle at her. "Here."

"Uh..." She stared, unsure what to do with it. People never offered her drinks. They gave her water, tonics and smoothies and various green concoctions—things designed to make her body healthy.

He smirked. "Are you underage? Worried about what your parents might say?"

That stung, especially the crack about her parents. She could shoot heroin and they wouldn't say anything. They'd just give more money to Chad and ask him to deal with it.

"No and no. I'm twenty-three." Far too old to care about what her parents would think anymore.

She took the bottle from him. She'd never, ever touched alcohol—¬¬it wasn't good for performance—but what the heck. *It's just a sip*. She would never compete again. Why should she sacrifice anymore? Why should she be this perfect girl who did everything she was supposed to do?

She took a fast swig. Fire exploded in her nose and mouth. She choked, her eyes watering, her throat hot and smoky.

He laughed, and she frowned at him. "Ugh! What is this stuff?"

"Scotch. First time drinking it?"

She nodded before she could catch herself.

"Figures." He chuckled.

There was something bleak in his laugh. Nothing about him indicated he was a bum or an alcoholic. The watch on his wrist was fairly new and expensive, and there was a vitality to him that said he didn't indulge in vices that could hurt his health. So what could make somebody like him drink so early?

Probably something as bad as what she was going through.

His belly growled, dragging her attention back to the present.

"When was the last time you ate?" she asked.

He shrugged. "Don't remember. It's not important."

Not important? Hunger was a nasty companion, always gnawing at your gut. She knew because she'd been hungry for years in order to keep her weight down. She ate better during the off-season, but even then she'd never allowed herself to really cut loose. "Can you make it back to your hotel?"

His eyes swept around their surroundings. "Probably."

She worried her lower lip. "Want to have dinner at my place?" She almost smacked herself as soon as she asked. It wasn't like her to be so impulsive, especially with men she didn't know very well.

"Depends."

That wasn't the response she'd expected. "On what?"

"On whether you're going to serve rabbit food."

She choked back a laugh. The stuff she generally ate would probably be considered rabbit food by this man's standards. But why should she continue to live on salads? Her competitive career was officially over. She didn't have to diet anymore.

"No," she said, making up her mind. "No rabbit food." She could do whatever she wanted.

"Well then." His dimple showed again. "I'll take you up on it."

She nodded, picking up her shoes. "I'm Sophia."

"Dane."

THREE

THEY WALKED TO THE VACATION RENTAL IN silence. He didn't try to touch her or stay too close to her, although her whole body was sizzling with electric excitement.

She wasn't sure why she was so hyperaware of him. Was it because he didn't treat her like she was made of eggshells? Everyone, including Chad, tiptoed around her. It was actually nice to be with a person who didn't know her history and treated her normally.

Like she wasn't damaged.

It didn't take long before they reached the rental house. It was a two-story structure with panorama windows and yawning decks that faced the beach. The modern design showed off its clean and minimalist lines.

Dane stopped in front of the door. "You sure about this?"

"What do you mean?"

"What if I'm a serial killer?"

She laughed. "I'll take my chances."

Right on cue, the glass door to the house opened. Chad stood at the threshold, glaring at both of them. The muscles in his arms bulged as he crossed them.

Dane let out a low whistle. "I take back my previous assessment. You're not dumb."

Chad eyed him. "What the heck is this thing?"

She rolled her eyes. "He is a person, not a 'thing.' We met on the beach. He helped me, so don't be mad."

"Helped you with what?"

"She was jumping and spinning and almost fell," Dane said before she could give Chad some made-up story.

Chad's face softened. "Aw, Sophia."

"I was just having fun, running around in the sand, and lost my balance. It's nice out here," she said quickly. He'd seen her do her vertical leaps, and she didn't want him to feel sorry for her. She was sick of people feeling sorry for her.

Dane's gaze bored into her. Her mouth dried, but thankfully he didn't contradict her, and she let herself relax as much as she could. Inside she felt like someone had tightened a corset around her lungs, and she didn't know why except that it had something to do with Dane.

Sighing, Chad moved aside to let them in.

She walked past him, not meeting his eyes. He worried about her—he'd been more like a parent than her real father and mother, who'd never had the time.

He was the one who'd taken her to every practice,

every competition, every training session since she'd started skating. He was the one who'd sat by the rink, brought her tissues and water, and did all the things skating moms did for their daughters. Plus he'd scared the crap out of would-be stalkers with his flat stare, even though that hadn't discouraged every creep. Some had perversely considered it a challenge, an opportunity to prove their dedication to her… although none had ever tried twice.

"Dane will be joining me for dinner," Sophia said.

Chad made a sound that could have been a growl. "I'll cook something up. What are you in the mood for?"

"How about…something fried?"

His eyes almost bugged out. "Something *fried?*"

She shrugged. "It's not like I need to watch my weight anymore."

He gave her a bemused look, then disappeared into the kitchen, muttering under his breath. "There's some shrimp in the fridge," he called out.

"That works." She turned to Dane. "There's a guest bathroom at the end of the hall there if you want to freshen up. It should have everything you need. You can leave your scotch on the coffee table…unless you want to drink it in the shower."

"You sure he can cook?"

"He's a great cook." Who'd often despaired that she would eat only the most boring food. She couldn't remember ever having had fried shrimp, but found she was looking forward to it.

She went to the master suite and showered, washing away the sand and sweat and grime of airline travel off her body. Hot water sluiced down her soapy skin, and she closed her eyes.

This was it for her. She felt like she was at a crossroads and should just accept that her dream was dead, no matter how much it hurt.

Time to start a new chapter in my life. She should just cling to the thought and move on, for her own sake. It would be terrible to end up bitter and angry, like some of the competitors who'd never reached the pinnacle they'd wanted.

She stepped out of the shower, put her hair up in a messy bun and pulled out a fitted magenta tank top and loose gray cotton pants, her favorite outfit when she just wanted to relax and unwind.

On the other hand…

She hesitated, thinking about the magnetic man she'd picked up at the beach.

Dane.

It was a strong name, simple and blunt. It rolled smoothly off her tongue like a cool marble.

What did it matter? It wasn't like she wanted to impress anybody…did she?

She suddenly stopped in the middle of putting on a pink lipstick. It wasn't like her to fuss over the way she looked. The only time she cared about that was before press conferences or competitions.

What the heck was she doing? Trying to look pretty for Dane? It wasn't like they were going to have a date.

Then…what was it?

She finished running the tube over her lips. She was just lonely and wanted to have a meal with somebody, that was all. Besides, it seemed like he was hurting for some reason. People didn't usually drink scotch straight from the bottle during the day.

What was wrong with two unhappy people sharing a nice, companionable dinner?

Chad was standing in the hall on the way to the dining area. He had his arms crossed, which meant he was about to say something she didn't want to hear.

Sure enough, he didn't disappoint her. "I don't like him, Sophia."

"Why not?"

"He's got that look."

"What look?"

"That asshole look. The type of person who doesn't give a damn about anybody but himself."

Sophia tilted her head. "That's pretty cynical."

"Hard not to be when you've had so many creeps. I've lost faith in my gender."

"Well, he's not a creep. I can tell. Besides, we're not getting married here, Chad. It's just dinner."

"Uh-huh. You're too sweet for your own good, you know that?"

She rolled her eyes. "Yeah, right. Look, I don't want to argue. I just want to relax and forget about…things." She forced a small smile. "It'll be nice to be able to eat with somebody who doesn't know who I am."

He grimaced. "I set the table for two. Enjoy.

Holler if you need anything or if he does something you don't like."

"Don't worry."

She wouldn't even have to scream before Chad would show up. Her heart-shaped garnet necklace came with a panic button. It had been Chad's idea, since he couldn't keep an eye on her all the time, especially during competitions when things were hectic.

She went to the dining room. Dane was already seated at the round glass-top table. A bit of his torso showed through the V of the white robe he wore. He'd also shaved, revealing an incredible jaw line. His profile was so perfect she couldn't believe he was actually a living, breathing person rather than a sculpture. Then, as though he'd sensed her, he turned, regarding her with eyes so blue and direct it felt like a lance through the center of her chest.

Suddenly she couldn't move, transfixed by that gaze. Her heart pounded like a captured bird's as heat spread through her body.

He rose and pulled out a chair for her, the gesture surprisingly gallant and elegant. She walked slowly over, feeling like she was dreaming. Men were generally nice to her—she was young and pretty and had a bit of fame. But none of them…*intensified* her like Dane did. The blood in her veins seemed thicker and hotter, her pulse louder and more pronounced.

Why now? Why this man?

"Your nanny isn't joining us?" Dane asked, returning to his seat.

She choked back a laugh. "His name is Chad. He doesn't eat after flying. It upsets his stomach."

A corner of Dane's mouth curled. "How unexpectedly delicate."

Her voice warm, she said, "Chad is special." He had never complained about having to travel with her, and they'd had to travel often, at least four or five times a year when she was competing.

"Hang onto him, then. Special people are rare." Dane reached for his scotch, ignoring the baskets of bread and fried shrimp and sauces and fresh salad on the table.

"You should eat first."

He cocked an eyebrow. "Certainly, mother."

Her cheeks heated. Looking away, she reached for a dinner roll. The scent of fresh yeast and flour made her mouth water. She sighed softly at the texture and buttery flavor. She hadn't touched bread in… She couldn't even remember. Before she knew it, the roll was gone and she was reaching for another.

Dane bit into a shrimp. "When was the last time you ate?" he asked, his eyes on her. There was something dark and primitive lurking in their depths.

She licked her suddenly parched lips. "I don't know. A few hours ago?"

"You sure? You eat like it's been ages."

"Oh." She stared at the second, already decimated bread roll. Had she really eaten all that? "Well, um… I was dieting." She laughed at how absurd her effort had been. "Been dieting since forever."

He frowned slightly. "Whatever for? You can't weigh more than a hundred pounds soaking wet."

"That was the point. To maintain the most optimal weight." Light and strong. That had been the goal. "It doesn't matter now."

She bit into a shrimp and almost moaned at the crisp texture of the spiced breading. Jeez. Why hadn't she had any before? Why had she denied herself every little pleasure in life when it was going to end up like this anyway?

She shoved an empty glass his way and gestured at the scotch. "Pour me some of that?"

Quirking an eyebrow, Dane put half an inch into the glass. She sipped it carefully. The liquor still burned, but it was more manageable now.

"Is this supposed to be a good brand?"

"The very best. I don't touch bad stuff—or even mediocre stuff. Ruins the palette."

"I'm such a pleb, I can't tell." She gestured at the bottle. "Have much have you had?"

"This is my third bottle."

"And you aren't even tipsy."

"I don't get drunk easily."

"Must be nice."

"What it is is expensive." His mouth twisted into a sardonic smile. "Can you hold your liquor?"

"I don't know. I've never tried." The scotch seemed kind of nice with her seafood. She pushed the glass toward him again. "Can I have some more?"

"I don't want you getting drunk."

"I'm fine." She smiled at him. "Besides, you had two full bottles to yourself. I think you can share a third."

He gave her a bit more.

"Come on," she said, crooking her fingers. "A full glass. Don't be stingy."

He stared at her. Grinning, she drank the scotch slowly. It would be embarrassing to start slurring words after only two tiny glasses.

"What are you doing in Mexico?" he asked.

She considered. *I'm running away from my troubles, trying to scrub them from my head* seemed a little melodramatic. In the end, she simply said, "Vacation. You?"

"The same."

"Do you come here a lot?"

"No. I rarely vacation," he said. "No time."

"Me either," she said. "Although I think that's about to change."

"You like it here that much?"

She shrugged. "Not just here. There are lots of places I haven't been yet." Cities she'd visited for competitions didn't count, since she'd never had the time or mental energy to enjoy them. "Maybe I'll tour them all. I've got nothing but time now." And broken dreams.

FOUR

DANE REGARDED HIS DINNER COMPANION. How did a woman go from not having any time to having too much of it? Or from dieting to maintain the "perfect weight" to eating whatever she wanted?

The cynical side of him said she was trying to snag herself a sugar daddy. If so, Chad was doing a pretty shitty job of protecting his territory. Or maybe he was too pussy-whipped to assert himself. After all, he hadn't even joined them for dinner, letting his woman share a meal with a strange man she'd picked up from the beach.

Dane should've left already. Picking up random women wasn't why he was in Mexico. But maybe he was more like his father than he wanted to believe. How mistaken Shirley had been to say he was different.

A fresh wave of pain rolled over him, and he pushed it away. He didn't want to dwell on it, especially not in front of others who didn't give a damn. Pain and regrets were only indulged in private.

"Is your boyfriend okay with your plan?" he asked.

"Huh? My boyfriend?"

"Chad."

She choked on her bread. He pushed a glass of water over, but she didn't touch it. "He's not my boyfriend." She laughed, her slender shoulders shaking. "Oh my gosh. I think you're the first person who thought that."

"Really?" Dane poured himself some scotch. The tension around his neck and the base of his skull was beginning to ease. *The alcohol must be finally working.*

"He's actually somebody my parents hired."

"Bodyguard?"

"Well...sort of. He's more like a chaperone...and everything else my parents couldn't be for me."

Dane understood that part. His parents had dumped him on nannies as soon as they realized he wasn't going to play the role they'd assigned for him. But her parents' choice was a bit odd. Most of the people he knew chose young, fresh-faced women as caretakers for their children.

But then her parents might be the type who just didn't give a damn so long as they thought they'd thrown enough money at a problem. And to such parents, a child who needed time and attention was a *problem*.

"Aren't you a bit old for a nanny?" he asked.

"Yes, but I couldn't let him go." She bit into her chicken.

"So he tagged along with you, on campus and everywhere else too?"

She shook her head. "I didn't go to college. Actually, I didn't really go to school at all."

He cocked an eyebrow. "Why not?" Not even *his* parents thought it was okay for their children to skip education. Certain appearances had to be maintained.

"I just…had other things I had to do. I generally had tutors to help me, and college wasn't something I was thinking about going to for a while, and then…" She shrugged, her eyes dark now. She pressed her lips together, then shook her head. "It just…happened that way." Shrugging, she looked away with an awkward smile.

Her obvious embarrassment bugged him. "Private tutoring is better than most schools, and college is nothing but an overpriced four year-long vacation." His mouth twisted. "My biggest regret is that I didn't choose better."

"What was wrong with your college?"

"Too damn cold. Should've picked somewhere with a beach."

Her lips twitched then slowly curved into a big, glorious smile. It was the first real smile he'd seen from her. Her green eyes glittered until they looked like immaculately cut emeralds, and a hot shade of pink crept into her cheeks.

His mouth dried, and he found himself staring at her lips, wondering what they would feel li—

What the hell? He didn't... He didn't want her, did he?

She was entirely too young—twenty-three by her own admission although she looked quite a bit younger—and she wasn't his usual type. Even putting aside his requirement about the dumber the better, she was too skinny. He liked his women with tits and ass. Although Sophia's ass was quite gorgeous—firm and round—she had virtually no tits and she certainly didn't have the kind of worldly, easy sex vibe going for her that he was usually attracted to. On the other hand, that thick golden hair was just begging to be wrapped around his hand.

He drank more scotch. Shirley's death must've affected him more than he'd thought.

"When I decide on a school, I'll take that into consideration," she said softly, then finished her scotch. "Would you like anything else? Dessert?"

You.

The thought came to him unbidden, and he pushed it away forcibly. "Got any cake or pie?"

"Ha. Not likely. We have fruit though."

Dane didn't like fruit that much. He should just decline and go back to his hotel. So long as he waved some money, any cab driver would take him there. But for some reason he couldn't get up. So he nodded instead. "Sure. I love fruit."

SOPHIA WATCHED HIM UNDER HER LASHES AS HE picked at his dessert. The fresh-cut pineapples and mangos were so sweet and ripe that they melted in her mouth, but Dane didn't seem too interested.

Either he didn't care for fruit or he'd already eaten more than he'd realized. He had an incredible appetite. She knew guys could put it away, but it still amazed her sometimes. Dane had polished off five times as much food as she had, and she was eating a lot more than her usual.

As he pierced another chunk of mango, he watched her, his gaze dark and unreadable. Maybe he was worried she'd get drunk and make a mess. She knew what happened to people who couldn't hold their liquor…and it *was* her first time.

But her gut told her he wasn't that worried about her passing out or puking. Something about the way he looked at her made her skin so hot she wanted to take her glass of ice water and press it against her cheek.

The knot in her chest was gone, now replaced by a deep pulsing ball in her belly. It was similar to the need and hunger that had driven her all these years, and it centered around Dane—his very presence and vitality. She felt the tug, pulling her closer to him.

Did he feel it too?

Maybe not. He seemed entirely too poised. Maybe a lot of women invited him to dinner. That wouldn't surprise her, given how magnetic he was. For the first time in her life, she wished she were a little bit more like her mother. Betsy Reed would know exactly what to do. There was no man-situation she couldn't handle with ease.

After they finished their fruit, Sophia took dirty plates into the kitchen. She rinsed them in the sink, turned to load them into the dishwasher and almost yelped when she bumped into Dane. "What are you doing?"

"Helping you clean up," he said matter-of-factly. He was standing right behind her. "That seems like the least I can do."

"You don't have to," she murmured, flustered.

She was somewhat trapped between Dane, the sink and the open dishwasher, which was pressing into her calf. She tried to reach around him, but somehow couldn't. Her limbs felt too heavy, and she couldn't look away.

He took the plates, leaning past her to put them into the washer rack. Although he'd claimed to have had three bottles of scotch, he moved with such cool control she couldn't help but wonder if he'd miscounted or exaggerated. He loaded the plates and shut the appliance.

He was only a few inches away, and she could see every long, gorgeous eyelash around his stunning blue eyes. He smelled amazing this close, like scotch and something else she'd never smelled before. If she had to put a word to it, she'd say it was masculine and… irresistible.

Her insides turned soft and gooey, and something hot and needy coursed through her veins. She looked at his mouth, set in a firm flat line. A crazy impulse to press hers against it crashed through her, and before the rational side of her brain could kick in, she rose on her toes and pressed her lips against his.

They were unexpectedly soft. A sweet ache knotted in her belly, and she clenched her hands, gripping the edge of the counter. Her heart hammered as though she were suspended in the air, just nanoseconds away from landing a jump.

He didn't move, and suddenly embarrassment hit her. It wasn't like her to be so forward. Besides, his being helpful didn't mean he was inviting her in for a kiss.

She pulled back.

Dane's strong arm snaked around her waist, keeping her close. His eyes glittered like dark sapphires as he studied her. Her face grew hot, but she couldn't look away. She swallowed, licking her lips for the lingering taste of him. "I, ah… Sorry—"

"Don't be," he rasped, his breath brushing over her cheek. "Now. My turn."

FIVE

BEFORE SOPHIA COULD PROCESS ANYTHING, Dane cupped her face and kissed her. His mouth was insistent and persuasive as he explored her lips—their texture and shape. He seemed to know just where she was most vulnerable, and he licked along the line where they joined, probing gently.

Acting on her instinct now, she opened her mouth and let him in. He plundered her, his tongue and teeth and lips relentless. Blood roared through her, and her knees grew weak. Before she could fall, she wrapped her arms around his neck. Pleasure curled in her belly then spread through her body like the sweetest of drugs.

He gripped her ass and pulled her closer. His thick erection pushed against her, and she moaned with want. Her panties were already damp.

"Which way is your bedroom?" he asked between kisses.

Unable to speak, she gestured behind her. He picked her up and carried her without breaking the kiss. Every step rubbed her against him, and she whimpered at the maddening friction. Heady need swept through her, and she hung onto Dane's unyielding body, knowing he was the only one who could ease the throbbing knot in her belly and below.

He set her down in front of the giant bed and pushed the tank top straps down her arms. "You aren't wearing a bra."

"I…don't really need to," she said, almost apologetically. Was he disappointed that she was so small? She'd never worried about it before. Actually she preferred that her breasts were next to nonexistent, but now she couldn't help but be self-conscious. She crossed her arms over them.

"Don't." His order shot out like a crack of a whip. He took her wrists and lowered them to her sides. "Don't ever cover yourself in front of me."

He fell to his knees, pulling her down until she was perched at the edge of the bed. His warm breath blew over a nipple, and she bit back a moan as sharp pleasure shot through her.

"Gorgeous," he murmured before taking it into his mouth.

Her thoughts scattered, and it was all she could do to hold onto him as he suckled it hard. His teeth scraped it, and she could barely drag in air. Restlessness grew, coiling tightly inside her. She dug her hands into his hair as electric pleasure streaked through her body, and she heard herself whimper *please* over and over again...although she wasn't sure what she was asking for. She just knew he was the only one who could give it to her.

He cupped her other breast in his large hand, pinching the nipple with just enough force to make her back arch. When he pulled away from her chest, she groaned loudly with protest until she found his lips trailing down her belly, leaving wet kisses behind.

Her body quivered as he pulled down her pants and panties. She should be embarrassed, but she was past caring as he breathed softly over her inner thighs. He pressed his mouth against her calves, and she bit her lower lip, hoping he wouldn't notice her ankles weren't quite perfectly straight or that her feet had suffered years of abuse inside ice-skates.

She didn't even know why his opinion mattered when tens of thousands of people had seen her flaws already, but it did. She'd never felt more vulnerable and nervous.

"Perfect," he whispered.

The tension eased, and she let out a shuddering breath. He nibbled on her skin, his lips and tongue and teeth moving expertly to set her nerves on fire. Cool air brushed between her slick folds, and she flushed, although she was too turned on to care much.

"You're so wet, love." His eyes glittered.

"I can't help it."

He growled, the sound reverberating deep in his chest. "I don't want you to."

She swallowed, waiting and wanting and…

His mouth closed over her sex.

Her head fell back. He lapped her up, like she were a peach dripping with juices. His hands pushed her thighs wider apart, and she let him, willing to do anything so long as he didn't stop. He sucked her clit hard, then pushed a finger inside her.

She clenched around the sudden invasion. It felt so good as he stretched her, but somehow it wasn't enough. She wanted to beg for more, but something held her back. He plunged his finger in and out, then a second one joined.

Something bright and wondrous formed inside her. He increased the pressure of his movements, then curled his digits, hitting just the right spot. "I want to taste your orgasm on my tongue."

The dark whisper rippled over her senses just before he licked and sucked between her legs. Fiery pleasure exploded inside her, ecstasy overloading her. Her back arched as she screamed. She put a palm over her mouth, biting the heel of her hand to muffle the sound.

Dane pulled her up the bed, setting her in the center. He was already nude, having shrugged off his robe. He twisted her hair in his hand, holding her head tightly, and kissed her mouth. He tasted salty, like her, and she welcomed him into her mouth, sucking him and moaning against him. His thick erection nestled between her folds, and he rocked sweetly, bumping into her clit. She shuddered as the familiar tight ball formed in her belly.

He lined his cock so the head could dip in and out of her, teasing her with shallow thrusts. She angled her pelvis for a deeper penetration, but he adjusted himself, frustrating her.

She clutched him to her, her hands clumsy. "Please… Don't deny me."

He groaned. "I don't have a condom."

"It doesn't matter. I can't get pregnant." Her periods were extremely irregular, and when she had them, they were more like light spotting. Her doctor had said she wouldn't be fertile until she gained at least thirty pounds.

"You're so small and tight." The muscles in his jaw bunched. "I don't want to hurt you."

"You can't hurt me." He'd already given her more pleasure than she'd ever experienced. "Please."

He took both of her wrists in his hands, pushing her arms up, imprisoning her in his grip. "You're so damn beautiful. Hot."

He plunged in, burying himself deep inside her. She cried out at the stunning invasion. It felt like he'd split her open.

Strain and tension deepened the lines around his mouth and corners of his eyes. He cursed and held himself still. "Why didn't you tell me?"

"Wha—what?"

"That it was your first time." He choked out the words between clenched teeth.

She blinked away tears. Was it something she should've discussed earlier? It had never occurred to her, but then what did she know about relationships anyway? She'd never had time to even look at boys while growing up. "Sorry. I didn't think it was important."

"Don't ever apologize," he said, his forehead resting against hers. "Especially when you did nothing wrong."

"But—"

"I would've been able to make it better for you if I'd known." He brushed his thumbs over her tears. "You're killing me here, do you know that?"

He kissed her, his mouth gentle and sweet. She kissed him back, loving the texture and taste of him, the way he changed the angle of his head for a deeper connection.

The kiss seemed to last forever. All of her senses were drenched in him—his scent, his taste, his heat and solid presence. His callused fingers caressed her sensitive skin with a delicacy she hadn't expected from a man so large and physical.

He seemed to know exactly where to touch and just the right amount of pressure to exert. She was already so sensitive from the previous orgasm, it didn't take long before a knot of pleasure throbbed to the fast beating of her heart. She cried out, her whole body arching with the need to reach for more.

Only then did he move, slow and steady. His gaze focused on her, making sure she was all right. The delicious friction sent shivers along her spine, and she gripped his shoulders.

It was too much—the steady, hard strokes of his cock and the hot intensity of his eyes. She'd never experienced anything like it, not even when she was competing for a world title.

Her heart thundered, and she couldn't draw in air. The bitter disappointment that had been her constant companion for the past four years was gone, replaced by Dane and the searing pleasure he was giving her.

When the second wave of climax crashed into her, she let go, drowning in electric feeling. His arms wrapped around her, and he groaned, biting out a harsh word, before he joined her in the sea of mind-obliterating sensation.

SIX

When Sophia could breathe normally again, she looked at Dane through her lashes. He was absolutely gorgeous naked, his shoulders wide, muscles lean and beautifully defined all along his tall body. She reached over to run her hand along his ribcage, then stopped. It was ridiculous for her to feel shy now, but…

"I don't bite." Amusement lightened his voice.

She flushed.

"I don't know how you can blush now." He propped his head on a hand and looked at her. His finger grazed her cheek. "You weren't shy when I had your legs spread and was—"

She put a hand over his mouth. "Oh my god, stop." Her face felt hot enough to fry eggs.

He fell back on the bed, laughing. He looked so carefree and happy that moment, she couldn't muster even a bit of annoyance at his amusement.

Suddenly, he sobered. "Still, I meant what I said. You should've said something."

She gave him a sidelong glance. "Do you normally discuss your sexual history before you sleep with someone?"

"If it's relevant, yes. And this being your first time, it was. By the way, you should also have asked me if I was clean before you told me I could forgo the condom, and yes, I am clean," he said.

Oh jeez. That thought had never even crossed her mind. Crazy how little she knew about real life while knowing more than almost everyone on competition prep, jump technique and edge control.

Sophia couldn't tell what Dane was thinking as he gazed at her. Was that also a side effect of her lack of experience or something else?

Finally, dark regret flitted through his eyes. "Not that I'm complaining, but you should've done it with somebody you've dated for a while, not some random stranger you picked up off the beach."

"I don't have a boyfriend." Suddenly she couldn't face him anymore. She lay on her back and stared at the ceiling. "Didn't think I needed one to, you know… do that."

"No, you don't." He ran a finger down her shoulder. "I just…" He sighed. "Never mind."

His lips brushed where his finger had been, and the tension drained from her muscles. "I don't want to talk about 'should've'. It is what it is." The mantra she'd told herself over and over again to push aside disappointment. She curled toward him. "And I wanted to…experience something other than my troubles. Didn't you?"

"What makes you think I have troubles?"

"You were drinking, and you don't really seem like an alcoholic, so…" She cleared her throat, looking away. "It looked like you had something painful you wanted to either forget about or run from."

Silence stretched, and he didn't move. Sophia winced. Maybe it was presumptuous or something to talk that way after sex?

"Go to sleep," he said softly, his voice oddly lacking inflection. He pulled the covers over her.

Something was off, but her tired mind couldn't quite grasp it. She let her heavy eyelids fall. She could sort it out tomorrow.

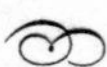

DANE LOOKED AT THE SLIM BLONDE CURLED NEXT to him. She was breathing evenly now, her body relaxed in sleep. What the hell had he been thinking?

Nothing. That was the problem. Drinking for the last four—or was it five?—days hadn't done a thing to make him any sharper. And he'd had more than three bottles of scotch, despite what he'd told her. He'd just lost count after the second day, but he was going through more than three a day.

Something painful he wanted to either forget about or run from…

Damn it.

How weak and vulnerable that sounded. He wasn't running from anything. Every shitty memory was a life lesson. Every harsh word he'd heard stripped another blindfold from his eyes.

Dane studied her face. He wished he could trace the delicate line of her nose…the smooth curve of her lower lip…the stubborn sharp tip of her chin. But he didn't dare do anything that could wake her up. If she opened those honest, perceptive eyes of hers and looked at him, his resolve to leave might crumble. So instead he drew in close and inhaled her sweet scent one last time, etching every subtle fragrant layer into his memory.

He went to the dresser and found a memo pad and a pen. He scrawled ten digits, all neat and legible. Then he added: *Call in case of unintended consequences.*

She'd been sure she wouldn't get pregnant, but nothing was one hundred percent certain in life. He should've never given in to the urge when he didn't have a condom, but he hadn't been able to resist.

Probably a five percent chance she'll dial the number. That was five percent too high, but somehow he couldn't bring himself to regret spending the night with her.

And precisely for that reason, he got dressed and left.

SEVEN

It had been two months, but Sophia couldn't stop looking at the memo from time to time. There was no signature, but she didn't need one to feel Dane's touch on it.

"Girl, you have it bad," Libby said, stepping onto the deck in a sky-blue bikini that brought out her eyes.

Her best friend had arrived the previous week. Sophia had already told her everything over the phone, but Libby had made her go over it all again face-to-face.

Sophia folded the memo. "It's nothing."

Libby plopped herself down on a lounge chair and smoothed her curly brown hair behind her. "So throw it away." She sucked down a juice drink, her bright pink lipstick smearing the straw.

"Maybe later." Sophia still couldn't figure out why he'd just…vanished. She'd racked her brain, thinking about everything that had happened, but still couldn't come up with a reason.

"Don't let it get to you. Some men take advantage. But that's on him, not you. We'll find you a nice guy when you get back in town."

"But I told you he didn't. I started it, and I'm pretty sure that if I hadn't, he wouldn't have done anything."

"Oh, come on. He's a man, and you're gorgeous." Libby frowned. "You think maybe he was scared of Chad?"

Sophia shook her head. "Doubt it. He's not the type to be intimidated."

"How do you know?"

"Because he didn't, you know, shrink back when Chad gave him the once-over. It wasn't an entirely friendly appraisal."

"Fine. So call him."

Sophia flushed. "For what? I'm not pregnant." There was no other interpretation of "unintended consequences," was there?

"Yeah, but what if he changed his mind? He wouldn't know how to get in touch with you or want to drop everything and come back here on the small chance that you might still be around." Libby pursed her mouth. "I just hate seeing you being indecisive. I know he was your first, but…" She sighed. "It looks like you need some kind of closure. So go get some."

Biting her lower lip, Sophia unfolded the memo and stared at the ten neatly written numbers again. She recognized the area code as L.A. She and Dane were in the same time zone, and it was only eleven in the morning. "You know what? You're right."

She pulled out her phone from her tote bag and dialed. As her phone rang, she waited, her heart pounding in her ears. Da-dum, da-dum.

After the third ring, it clicked. "Rosenbaum, McCracken, Wagner, and Associates. How may I direct your call?" came a modulated, professional female voice.

"Uh…" Sophia swallowed. "Sorry, wrong number." She hung up.

"What?" Libby asked.

"I think I misdialed," Sophia said, her mouth dry. "Let me try again."

The second time also got her the same, professional voice. "Rosenbaum, McCracken, Wagner, and—"

Sophia hung up again. Embarrassment heated her face.

"What is it?" Libby asked.

"It's not his cell phone."

"What then? His office?"

Sophia shook her head. "I don't know. Maybe. It's a place called Rosenbaum, McCracken, Wagner, and Associates."

"Sounds like a law firm. Lemme check." Libby pulled out her phone and tapped away. "Yup. A law firm in L.A. Found their website." She scowled. "You think he works there?"

Sophia shrugged helplessly. "Maybe."

"What a dickhead. He could've at least given you his direct line. Let's see… Oh, they have a section on their lawyers." She tapped a few times. "You said his name was Dane, right?"

"Uh-huh."

There was a pause as Libby tapped. "He's not listed anywhere."

"He's not?"

"No. But maybe he gave you a fake name. Does anyone here look familiar to you?" Libby handed over the phone.

Sophia scrolled down, looking at a series of professional headshots of lawyers. None of them was Dane. Her stomach twisted. "No."

"What the hell?"

Dane never wanted to see her again. That much was clear. She didn't even know why she cared—it was just a one-night stand, and they hadn't made any promises to each other. Given how gorgeous he was, he probably had plenty of women throwing themselves at him, all of them undoubtedly far more sexually experienced and skilled than she was.

She gave the phone back to Libby. "Well, there's my closure."

They sat for a few moments, watching the waves crash and ebb along the beach.

"This sucks," Libby said.

"Hey, at least I'm not pregnant," Sophia said, forcing some cheeriness into her voice.

She crumpled the paper and tossed it into the trash. Mexico was supposed to be about letting go of her past and planning her future. She shouldn't be wasting even a moment moping on a stranger who'd never wanted anything but sex from her.

Spinning his pen absent-mindedly, Dane stared out the window. A new tech guy was blabbering on about some business idea or other.

Normally Dane would give the man his undivided attention, but somehow he couldn't. His thoughts kept wandering back to Mexico. Or more precisely, what had happened there. Maybe it was the view from the conference room that got in the way of his focus. It was bright and sunny in L.A., the sun reflecting off the metal and glass skyscrapers. And somehow it reminded him of sun reflecting off the sea…

And the pen… He clenched his hand around it. Every time he saw something spin, his mind drifted to the first time he'd noticed Sophia—leaping and spinning in the air and landing on one foot. She'd looked so graceful and powerful, her lithe body taut and in control. She'd seemed like some kind of goddess… until she'd lost her balance and stumbled.

It'd been two months, and his lawyers hadn't contacted him, which meant Sophia hadn't called. He was certain she'd seen his note. And apparently there was no reason for her to reach out.

He should be relieved. He *was* relieved. And yet…

Her face kept flashing through his mind at the most inopportune moments. And it wasn't even the sublime expression of bliss as she'd come. No, it was her gorgeous, bright smile. Or that sweetly earnest look she'd had when she'd asked him not to be upset for not telling him she'd been a virgin. Or the soft empathy in her eyes when she'd told him about how vulnerable he'd been…

He licked his lower lip. Sometimes he thought he could taste her there…but that was ridiculous. It had been months. There was nothing left.

Perhaps he should've given her his personal number. If he could go back in time to that moment, he would have. Not that it would've made a particle of difference since she wasn't pregnant and didn't have any reason to call. But he wished he could've left her his mobile—

He shook himself mentally. What did it matter? Who gave a damn what number he'd jotted down on the piece of paper when the outcome was the same? And surely he didn't hope she'd gotten pregnant. What a disaster that would have been. He had zero interest in becoming a father. There was already enough on his plate.

"Sir?"

"Yes?"

"We were wondering—" the entrepreneur said hesitantly.

"The idea may have potential, assuming the costs can be kept down." It was a stock answer. "Send me the slides and let me study them again before making up my mind."

"Yes, of course." Everyone scribbled on their notepads.

Dane glanced at his watch. Two p.m. "Anything else?"

"I don't believe so."

"Well then." He got up and left, his wide strides eating up the distance between the conference room and his office. Restlessness rode him, and he resisted the urge to rub the back of his neck.

His assistant straightened at the sight of him. She was impeccably put together with a sleek French twist and a neat dark navy blue skirt suit. Anything less wouldn't be tolerated in his office. "Good afternoon, sir," she said.

"Anything from my lawyers?"

"No." She frowned. "Would you like me to call them?"

He shook his head. "Clear my calendar for the weekend. I'm going to—" He caught himself before he said too much. He wasn't going back to that beach in Mexico. Sophia probably wasn't even there anymore.

And even if he were to go, and she was still there…then what?

"Sir…?"

"Never mind. Leave my weekend as is."

"Yes, sir."

EIGHT

DANE GRIMACED AS HE MADE HIS WAY TO the cemetery. The only thing worse than attending a funeral was attending one in the Pacific Northwest. The weather there was disgusting. Gray. Rain. And more rain. Fog. The dead deserved a courtesy of sunshine on their way to the other world.

He'd meant to arrive earlier, but the traffic had been horrendous. Some idiot had skidded off the road and of course everyone else had slowed down to rubberneck. You would think that they'd be more blasé, not to mention better drivers, living in a water-drenched area like this.

The shitty weather made him think of Mexico… which was ridiculous. He had no idea why everything these days kept reminding him of it. What possible feelings could he have for Sophia when it'd been almost three years now? It wasn't like him to let his mind linger over a woman.

Was it because she'd been a virgin?

As quickly as the thought came, he dismissed it. That couldn't be. He'd had virgins before. And his interest had always soon waned.

If he wanted, he could probably find Sophia again. The place where she'd stayed undoubtedly had a record of its renters. But then what? How ridiculously awkward would it be for him to just show up at her doorstep like some stalker—or worse, a lovesick fool.

Hi! You didn't get pregnant, so I thought we should have a three-year anniversary meet.

He shoved his thoughts of her aside and focused on why he'd come to this god-forsaken location in the first place: Rick Reed's funeral.

It wasn't difficult to spot the plot set aside for the man. Dane was the sole Pryce to attend, but only because he was in Seattle and Salazar thought he should for the sake of appearances. Geraldine had also agreed, albeit grudgingly. Rick wasn't the one who'd wronged her, even if he had married Betsy Ford, who had taken Geraldine's husband Julian Reed from her all those years ago.

Geraldine hid it well, but she was still bitter about the way Julian had dumped her for Betsy. Three beautiful children hadn't been enough to ensure that he wouldn't stray. In Dane's opinion their parting was a blessing in that it freed Geraldine from a crappy marriage, but women could be irrational about stuff like that. And that was the only explanation for the simmering anger his aunt still harbored against Betsy and her children.

The Pryce family never associated very closely with the other Reeds—there was never a reason to—and thankfully they weren't a prolific lot. Rick had been Julian's half-brother and had a serious inferiority complex, but for some reason he'd decide to marry Julian's second wife Betsy within a month of their divorce. The idiot had apparently never realized he was taking his brother's leftovers.

Dane stopped at the sight of the grieving family. Betsy was there, of course, and somewhat familiar—a trim blonde with a beautiful face kept young by an abundance of Botox and surgical help. She stood with a hip cocked, feet encased in a pair of fashionable high-heel boots. She dabbed at her eyes daintily with a handkerchief and let out an occasional sob, like she was a star in a tragic movie.

Next to her was a younger woman who barely reached Betsy's neck. Unlike Betsy she wore a black one-piece dress that reached an inch below her knees and sensible flat booties. Her shaking hands covered her face, and Dane tilted his head. Something about her tugged at his memory, and he had the most absurd urge to go put his arms around her.

A large, dark-skinned man in a suit was holding an umbrella over her, his body positioned like a shield between her and the crowd. A brown-haired fellow in his late twenties came over from the knot of people standing behind them and squeezed the girl's shoulder—the gesture overly familiar in Dane's opinion. The umbrella holder shot the other man a look sharp enough to draw blood and shifted closer to her. The younger man's mouth twisted into an ugly line, but he didn't back off.

She finally dropped her hands.

Sophia.

The sight sucker-punched him; all the breath rushed out of Dane's lungs as he stared at her. Tears dripped from her pain-filled green eyes, staining her colorless cheeks. She looked small and forlorn standing in the rain. The man next to her whispered something in her ear, and she nodded.

Dane's hand tensed around the umbrella handle.

What the hell? The Sophia from Mexico was Rick Reed's only child?

He closed his eyes as everything inside him clenched tightly. She was the only woman he'd ever slept with who'd seen him appear weak. He didn't believe in giving anybody a glimpse of his vulnerable moments. The death of his grandmother had hit him hard—she was the only person he'd really loved—and the fact that Sophia *Reed* was the one who'd seen him in his lowest moment made his head buzz with conflicting thoughts and feelings.

The strongest and loudest of them was that he should go over there, squeeze her hand and comfort her.

Except that would be an utter disaster.

Without a word, he turned back. No more indulging in his ridiculous sentimental moments, thinking about their night in Mexico. He was scrubbing her out of his memory, starting now.

Even if she hadn't witnessed him at his most vulnerable, she would still be off limits. She was Betsy Ford's daughter. Geraldine would never stand for it, and she was the only person Shirley had asked him to be kind to.

SOPHIA WIPED HER TEARS WITH THE HEEL OF ONE hand, heedless of appearances. She couldn't believe her father was truly gone. Nor could she believe some of the whispers she'd overheard.

Drunk all the time. Obnoxious. Erratic. Probably doing drugs.

There were even rumors that he'd taken one too many sleeping pills on purpose, although the coroner hadn't declared the death suicide—just an accidental overdose.

I should've been there for him.

She'd had no idea he'd had problems, but they explained why he'd been so distant in the last two years. Since her return from Mexico, she'd been so busy wrapped up in her disappointment, and with college… And there was the memory of Dane too…

The coffin was lowered to the dark, wet hole, and she swallowed. This was it. This horrible finality.

Her heart twisted painfully.

"Hey, hang in there, champ." It was George, Libby's older brother and her father's protégé, squeezing her shoulder. Still quite young, he was an angel investor who funded promising startups, and he credited her father for helping him get started.

She managed a nod and dragged in some rain-cooled air. Clearing his throat, Chad stepped closer. She looked up, her neck muscles tensing. He never positioned himself in that particular way unless he'd noticed something that seemed off. It seemed—

Goose bumps rose all over her body, stealing her breath, and her nerve endings electrified. It wasn't the creepy sensation she'd gotten when she'd had stalker problems. This was just like the moment she'd been caught by...

Dane.

She snapped her head up, looking around for a sign of him. Maybe he was a family friend. Her father knew lots of people. A sea of solemn faces surrounded her, their attire stark and black, but none of them had the unforgettable blue eyes or the unsmiling mouth that tormented her in her dreams.

"What's wrong?" Libby said.

"I thought...I thought I saw someone."

George stepped forward and almost bumped into Chad. "Who?"

"I..." She couldn't explain it, not without sounding like she'd lost it. "I need to use the ladies' room. I'll be right back. Excuse me."

She ran as hard as she could. Chad shouted and ran after her. The cold rain drenched her. Her hip ached, but she ignored the pain as she dashed across the meticulously maintained grounds.

But no matter which way she looked, there was no sign of Dane.

"Ladies room, my ass," Chad said, finally catching up and putting the umbrella over her. "What's wrong?"

"I thought I saw..." She shook her head. How crazy and pathetic would it sound to say that she was looking for the man she'd had a one-night stand three years ago? Chad knew the score: Dane never wanted to see her again.

She was the only one who cared. And even if she were to see him again, what was she going to do? What was she going to say?

"What?" Chad prompted, when she didn't continue.

She shook her head. "Nothing. I must've just imagined it."

He let out a sigh. "Let's get this over with and get you dry. I don't want you getting sick."

"Okay."

Even as she let him lead her back to the crowd, she couldn't help but take another look over her shoulder, just in case.

But the only things there were the rain-soaked trees.

NINE

"Hey, listen. I have to leave."

Sophia glanced up at Chad's voice. She put the day's mail down on the dining table. "Okay. You going to run some errands, or…?"

He was looking at her sorrowfully. "No. I mean *leave* leave."

"What? You're…quitting?"

"Yeah." He cleared his throat, shifting his weight. "Just wanted to say goodbye before I took off."

"But why?" She frowned, then suddenly a realization dawned on her. "Oh no. Is your sister okay?" His sister's cancer had gone into remission a few years ago, but there was always the chance it could come back.

"Uh, no, she's fine." Chad cleared his throat again.

"Then…?"

"Can't really talk about it." A frown fleeted across his face, then a small smile replaced it. "Ask George." Chad stepped forward and hugged her tightly. "Sorry. This is awkward, and I don't want to make you feel uncomfortable or anything, but I couldn't leave without seeing you one last time."

She hugged him back even as her internal alarm went off, the same one that had gone off when her doctors had hemmed and hawed before telling her she'd never compete again.

Brisk and efficient as always, Chad didn't linger after they were finished with their hug. She watched him go, knowing that he'd never tell her anything. She'd have to talk to George.

The drive took about half an hour from her place. She parked her car haphazardly in front of George's pricey mansion. He almost always telecommuted unless he had meetings, and he never scheduled a meeting for the afternoon.

The house was tastefully decorated with expensive leather furniture and dark wood. She inhaled beeswax and paper, and let her slippered feet sink into the thick rug as she marched into his home office. George had been helping her figure out her father's estate since her mother wasn't interested. Within a month of the funeral, Betsy had remarried, this time to a wealthy Russian businessman. They'd just finished their honeymoon in the south of France and gone to Moscow to start their new lives.

Sophia pushed down the familiar resentment bubbling inside her. Betsy was the official executor, and she knew the most about how things lay with the estate. But somehow it was too much for her to stay put for a few months to help out. Every time Sophia met with George, she couldn't decide if she should cringe or try for a smile…even though it would probably come off as a horrible mixture of embarrassment and gratitude.

But still… If he'd had anything to do with dismissing Chad, she wasn't going to sit back and pretend not to notice.

"Sophia. What a surprise," George said, rising from behind his large desk. He looked good in a crisp white dress shirt and charcoal gray slacks.

"Hi. We need to talk."

"I agree. Please." George gestured at a couch in front of a huge bookcase full of heavy leather-bound tomes.

She perched at the edge of the soft cushion, her back straight. The heavy faux-bronze lamp on a table next to her cast a cool glow about the room. She adjusted her skirt and waited for him to retake his seat at the desk.

Instead, the couch dipped under his weight and she tensed slightly. He'd never done anything inappropriate, but her instincts had been tickling her with a warning every time he got too close over the past few weeks. She squashed the feeling. It was unfair to be skittish and stiff around a man who'd done so much to help. Besides, he was Libby's older brother.

"What is it you'd like to talk about?" George said.

"Did you let Chad go?" she asked. "He said he had to leave and asked me to talk to you if I had any questions."

He pursed his lips. "I did. But I had no choice."

"What are you talking about?"

"Do you think he would stay without getting paid?"

"Why wouldn't he get paid? Is there a problem?"

George watched her, his eyes hooded. "I'm sorry, but your father's estate is broke."

"I don't understand."

"There's no money. He left you penniless, which explains why your mother was in such a hurry to remarry."

She stared at him. Words like "broke" and "penniless" didn't apply to her family. "Dad had five vacation homes alone."

"Mortgaged to the hilt. The debtors were notified of his death, of course, and now everyone wants their money back. It's pretty bad."

She clasped her shaking hands together. "How bad?"

"Net negative, really. Thankfully, you aren't responsible for his debt. But…" Letting out a heavy sigh, George reached over and took her hand. "Unless you have your own income, keeping Chad isn't an option." He leaned forward. "The man can't work for free. You know that."

Did she ever. It had been seven years since Chad's sister had been diagnosed with breast cancer, and he'd been helping her out financially ever since.

Biting her lip, she rested her forehead against her palm. She had no income. She'd only completed two years of college, so she didn't qualify for any job except flipping burgers…unless she found a way to get a coaching or choreography job with figure skaters. But she hadn't kept in touch with anybody from that world. And it wasn't like there were lots of promising skaters just dying to get a new, untried coach.

"Don't." George put a hand on her shoulder and turned until he was almost embracing her. "It's not that bad."

"How can it not be bad?" Sophia said, looking at him.

"I can take care of you. That's the least I owe Rick." His hand tightened around hers like a lasso while his eyes glittered. "And Libby would want that too."

"I can't let you do that. I'll just call my mom and see if she can help out."

"Her new husband won't be thrilled to have to fund another man's grown-up daughter."

"What choice do I have?" she snapped, suddenly furious with her situation. Her world was falling apart, piece by piece, and she couldn't imagine what else could possibly go wrong now.

"Me."

"You?"

She didn't get a chance to resist as he suddenly pulled her forward, crushing her to him in a python embrace. He shoved his mouth against hers, his lips cool and damp. Her heart knocked against her ribcage so hard she thought she might faint. Clenching her teeth, she turned her head away. "No, don't!"

"Come on. You know you want this," he ground out. "You have no idea how long I've waited. I've been watching you for years."

Cold panic froze her.

This wasn't just any man, but *George*. How could this happen?

Then her competitive spirit kicked in. She wasn't going down without a fight.

She twisted, and they crashed onto the floor. He landed on top of her with a grunt, and she bucked against him, trying to get him off her.

"Stronger than you look," he grated.

"Get off me!"

"Stop it," he said. "I don't want to have to hurt you."

"Are you crazy? You're hurting me right now! Stop!"

His erection rubbed against her, and bile rose in her throat. She twisted and turned and bucked, trying to claw away from him. But George wasn't some couch potato whose only strenuous activity involved going to a fridge for more beer. His fingers dug into her thighs as he pushed them apart. Then before she could pull them together, he pressed himself between her legs.

Terror clogged her throat, and she could barely draw in any air. She searched for anything she could use as a weapon. So many heavy books but they were all out of reach.

Come on, come on! There had to be something...

The lamp!

He was kissing her neck as she snaked a hand out and yanked on the rubber-coated wire. The lamp crashed to the floor, and she grabbed it and smashed it against his head.

He yelled, pulling back. She kicked him away, jumped to her feet and swung again. Blood spread on his head instantly, matting his hair. He was on his hands and knees, but she didn't trust him to stay down. Clenching her teeth, she stepped forward and hit him a third time, hoping she wouldn't kill him by accident. She wouldn't be able to deal with that even if he tried to…

Finally he groaned and collapsed on the floor. The sound of her own harsh breathing filled the room as she stared at him. His back rose and fell slowly. He was still alive, at least for the moment.

The lamp fell from her shaking hand. Covering her mouth to contain a sob, she grabbed her purse and fled downstairs, stumbling and bumping against the walls. She wanted to get as far from the place as possible.

What to do? What to do now?

She accelerated out of the mansion grounds and onto the road. There was nobody to turn to—Libby was out of the question now, Chad was gone, and her mother was not only not interested, she was half a world away.

Still, Betsy was her only option now. Sophia pulled over and dialed the number with trembling fingers.

Her mother picked up after what seemed like forever. "Hello?"

"Mom!"

"Sophia. My lord, what on earth has you calling at this hour?"

"I need help," she said, trying to draw in air more evenly. "I need a place to stay."

"Isn't there a hotel...?"

"There's no money in the estate. Dad was broke."

A beat of silence. "You just figured that out?"

"You *knew?*" Sophia hadn't really believed George about her mom, especially after the attack.

"Of course I knew. Your father was a lot of things, but good with money wasn't one of them. He only got to enjoy the lifestyle he did because he was lucky." Betsy sighed. "I can send you a bit to tide you over, but only this one time. Dimitri doesn't like it when I'm frivolous with his money."

Sophia covered her mouth and swallowed a hysterical laugh. "This isn't about money. I need a *safe place to stay.*"

"Can't believe the banks got to all your father's houses already. Damn vultures."

"Not one of Dad's places." George would know all of those. "Someplace else. Outside the family."

Betsy sighed. "Well, what about Chad? He has his own place."

"He's gone. He can't stay with me if I can't pay him."

Betsy tsked. "Disloyal of him. Won't Libby—?"

"No!" How was she going to tell her best friend about what had happened? "She's out of—"

"Then try Salazar."

"Who?"

"Salazar Pryce. He's related, but only distantly. He's your uncle Julian's in-law, and lives in L.A. Not far from Seattle, really. He has a reputation for being kind to women."

Now she remembered. "Are you kidding? Geraldine's brother? You stole her husband!"

"I did no such thing."

"But from their point of view, you did. Salazar would never help me."

"Beggars can't be choosers, sweetie, and you're mistaken. He *will* help you—he owes us."

Sophia's jaw dropped. Her mother had always had a wacky way of looking at the world, but this was too much. That man didn't owe them anything!

"No matter what, you're still my daughter and I love you. I'm hanging up now, but I'll call him and arrange things, all right? And I'll text you his address. You have enough cash to get out there, don't you? If not, use the credit card before the vultures cut it off."

"*Mom!*"

It was already too late. Her mother had hung up.

PART II

The Present

TEN

The Pryce mansion

STANDING IN THE MIDDLE OF THE STUDY, DANE looked dispassionately at his father. *How the mighty have fallen…*

It wasn't even ten in the morning, but Salazar Pryce was already semi-drunk. At least he had the taste to get plastered on good booze, but still, the study stank, and the custom-tailored Italian shirt on Salazar had lost all its starchy crispness. Dane wouldn't be surprised if his father hadn't touched a razor…or soap…in the last four days or so.

"What do you want, Dane?" Salazar's words were slurred. Sloppy.

"Stop moping," Dane said coldly. "This isn't like you."

"I'm not moping. What do you know about what I'm like?" Salazar poured more scotch. "Want some?"

"No."

"Then get out. I don't want to hear your whining."

"I do not whine," Dane said, his diction sharp enough to draw blood. "Your lawyer called."

"What the hell for?"

"If you'd answer your phone, you'd know." He tossed an envelope on the desk. "Sign. It's the divorce papers."

Salazar's knuckles turned white.

"Need a pen?" Dane asked, ignoring his father's reaction.

"I don't need a fucking pen," Salazar snarled.

"She only wants fifty million, the same amount you've given every one of us, including your by-blow."

"Blaine is your *brother*."

Dane smiled slightly. "Doesn't change the fact."

"She doesn't deserve it," Salazar mumbled. "It's not in the prenup."

His parents and their damn prenup. "*I'll* pay her then. Just sign it."

Salazar threw his glass. Dane didn't even flinch. The intricately designed crystal sailed by his head, missing him by a couple of inches at the most, and shattered against the wall. "*Shut the hell up!*"

"If you don't want to sign it, then fight. She's out there, happy, carefree…and look at you." Dane curled his lip. "Go screw a pretty young thing or two. They're a dime a dozen in the city. That'll cheer you up. It always did."

"How dare you." Salazar's face turned bloodless. His cheeks quivered slightly as he glared at his oldest.

The sight of Salazar being laid so low tightened Dane's chest, but he couldn't deny it also tasted like the finest champagne. If Dane had been a better man, he would've walked away at this point, but he couldn't help himself.

"Upset that you can't use your pawns anymore?" he asked softly.

"What?"

"I know we've just been minor pieces in your sick game with Mom." Dane tilted his head. "But now your pawns are all grown up, and the other side doesn't want to play anymore. What are you going to do to continue the game?"

Salazar's mouth parted, his eyes wide.

Dane almost laughed at his father's utter shock. Did he think Dane was too dumb to figure it out? He'd known it since forever… since the time Ceinlys had put the best clothes on him so he'd "look good for Daddy," and Salazar had smiled down at him as his gaze slid away from Dane's and crashed into hers.

"Don't make me come out here again," Dane said. "And clean yourself up for Mark's wedding. You don't want to embarrass yourself, do you?"

Then he turned, his movements precise, and left his father spluttering.

THE TUNE FROM *DANSE MACABRE* BY SAINT-SAËNS blaring from her earphones, Sophia dragged her lone suitcase up the winding road to the Pryce mansion. Her apricot-colored toy poodle Roco trotted in front of her, tail wagging in delight at finally being off the bus. Sweat beaded on her hairline, and her hip and knees hurt from walking the long distance. But she gritted her teeth and kept on moving.

Thankfully the gardener had seen her at the gates and let her through when she'd said she was there to see Mr. Pryce. She'd always hated the fact that she was small and younger-looking than her age, but right now, she was grateful those two attributes had gotten her past the first hurdle in seeing Salazar Pryce.

He had to at least hear her out.

Finally. She reached the door and rang the bell once. She pulled out the earphones with sweat-dampened hands, then swallowed a curse as she almost dropped them before shoving them into her purse.

Desperation and foreboding curdled in her belly like old milk. Despite Betsy's reassurance via text that Salazar would help, Sophia was fairly certain she'd wasted her last fifty bucks on the bus trip to L.A. She didn't know the man, and he wasn't close to her family. He hadn't even bothered to come to her father's funeral. Not surprising since her mother had wrecked his sister Geraldine's marriage.

If Sophia had any other choice, she wouldn't be here. But she couldn't go back to Seattle and risk running into George again. In retrospect, she should've called the cops even if he was her best friend's older brother, but she hadn't been thinking clearly. And now it was probably too late to call and file a formal complaint.

Besides, what would the police do except talk to George? There had been no witnesses, no real physical evidence, other than the injuries she'd inflicted. It would be his word against hers, and he had expensive lawyers, while she probably couldn't get anyone to return a call.

And she knew how the game would be played. She'd seen how every innocent thing she'd said was scrutinized and blown out of proportion by fans and the media during her competitive years. She'd accepted it as the price of success, but this was different. If she called the cops, George's lawyers would smear her with a whole new level of aggression. They would be getting *paid* to rip her apart.

It was probably better for her just to stay away from Seattle. She doubted he'd call the cops on her for hitting him since that'd only make them ask *why* she'd done it.

Her only regret was that she'd lost her best friend. She had no idea how to tell Libby the truth, and didn't want to imagine how she'd react if she knew. Nobody wanted to believe they had a monster in the family.

Sophia inhaled, breathing deeply. She was a fighter—she always got back up. She could survive this, just as she'd survived the death of her dreams. She could survive anything.

Biting her lower lip, she looked around while waiting for someone to answer the door. The mansion was absolutely stunning and so much bigger than any of the giant houses her father had owned. The classic architecture and landscape complete with an aged bronze fountain and perfectly groomed topiaries hinted at old money. The late afternoon sun tinted everything golden, making the place look almost magical, like a castle from a fairy tale.

The only question was… Did it hide a savior or a beast?

The door opened finally, revealing an elderly man in a crisp suit. Rail thin, he had an oddly stiff way of standing, all his joints set at tight angles.

Just be aware that he's too good-looking and charming for his own good.

Her mother's texted advice came back to Sophia, and she squinted a bit. Betsy could be accused of a lot of things, but having low standards wasn't one of them. Not that the man in front of her was ugly or anything, but he was extremely…average.

He looked at Roco, gamboling around her feet, then at her. She couldn't read anything in his placid face. "Yes?"

She swallowed. "Mr. Pryce?"

The man's forehead creased. "Mr. Pryce…?"

"Mr. Salazar Pryce."

"He's not receiving any visitors."

She blinked. "You aren't…?"

"I'm the butler."

Oh wow. She'd never seen a butler in real life. "I'm Sophia Reed. Could you just ask if he'd see me please?

My mom, Betsy Reed, called yesterday." Or at least that was what she had promised to do.

The man ran his gaze over her from head to toe. She knew she looked presentable in her favorite white blouse and gray pencil skirt paired with pink ballet flats; she'd checked after she'd gotten off the bus.

She straightened to ensure she looked as tall as possible. She was barely five four, the perfect candidate for a little help from the shoes department. But heels hurt her hip too much.

"Please wait a moment," the man said and disappeared.

She let out a soft breath. She needed to project the proper confidence. Nobody wanted to be around the downtrodden.

The butler reappeared. "This way, miss."

She started to drag her suitcase along, but he waved a hand. "Leave it in the foyer, please. I'll have it looked after."

"Thank you, sir."

"You needn't be so formal, miss. Call me Al. Regrettably, your dog should remain here. Animals aren't allowed in the study."

"Sorry, boy," she whispered at Roco, leashing him to the suitcase. She didn't like leaving him behind—it felt like he was the only one she had left—but she had no choice if she wanted a roof over their heads.

Al led her up the winding stairs, his head held high. She followed him, doing her best not to wince or drag her feet as her hip and knees ached. They only bothered her when she overdid it, and the hike from the bus stop had definitely done that.

The inside of the Pryce mansion was just as stunning as the outside with gorgeous portraits—done with actual paint—on the paper-covered walls. Everything was gleaming marble, hardwood and plushy rugs. Chandeliers dripped with fat crystals hung from the ceiling, and Sophia couldn't help but admire the beautiful home. The display of wealth should've been gaudy, but there was just enough restraint to keep it classy somehow.

Al stopped in the middle of the hall and opened a door to his right. "Miss Sophia Reed, sir."

"Thanks, Al," came a soft voice.

She went inside; the door closed with a loud click behind her. Al had disappeared, leaving her alone with Salazar Pryce.

His dark hair was slicked back, damp from a recent shower. Silver streaked his temples, and he watched her with polite curiosity.

Her mother hadn't exaggerated at all. He had to be at least sixty, but he was still extremely handsome. His skin was even and smooth except for some small lines around his eyes and mouth, and his blue gaze was steady and sharp.

Something about his appearance tickled her memory. He seemed familiar somehow, but she had to be imagining things. She'd never met him before.

He adjusted his starch-stiffened collar and flashed

her a quick grin. "Sophia Reed, huh? Nice to finally meet you in person. How are you?"

"Good, thanks."

"Please, sit down." He waved at an empty chair.

She sat with her knees pressed together. This was it.

"What can I do for you?"

"Um, well..." Her cheeks grew hot, and she found that she didn't know how to broach the subject. How much had Betsy told him?

He laughed. "Shall I help you out? I'm sure Rick could've left his estate in better financial health. Is that why you're here?"

She parted her mouth, then shut it. What was there to say?

"Have I embarrassed you, dear? If so, I apologize." He spread his hands. "But why else would a distant relative—are we even considered relatives?—show up on my doorstep a few months after her father's death?"

If only the ground would open up and swallow her whole... "Didn't my mom call?"

"She might have. But I haven't been answering any calls for the last several days."

She cringed. Most likely he was just trying to be kind, and her mother as usual had forgotten. Sophia had never been a priority for Betsy. "I'm sorry, but... I need some help getting back on my feet."

"Help, huh?" Salazar rested his chin on one hand. "Are you here to proposition me?"

The question sucker punched her, leaving her gaping at him. Finally she said, "*Excuse me?*"

"What? It's a perfectly reasonable question. A lot of women have tried..." he gave her a gleaming, good-humored smile, "...most of them not as pretty as you."

She clenched her hands as humiliation coursed through her. She should've known better than to listen to her mother's advice. Hoping Salazar wouldn't try to force himself on her with his butler in the house, she got up stiffly. "Sorry for wasting both of our time. I'm not at all interested."

He waved her back into the chair. "Sit down, for christssake. I'm not going to grab you. Jeez. I do have some standards, and I never had anything against your father. He's not the one who hurt my sister." He gestured at the chair again. "Please." He waited until she perched gingerly back on the edge of her seat. "Of course I'll help. After all, you're family. I just wanted to make sure we were on the same page."

She studied him, looking for any clues of sarcasm or insincerity. The talk of "family" rang hollow when he hadn't bothered to come to her father's funeral. On the other hand, he had offered to help. "Thank you."

"Least I can do. You have a place to stay in the city?"

"No, but—"

"I'll have Al prepare one of the guest wings for your use." When she opened her mouth, he raised a hand. "No, you won't say anything except 'thank you.'

This house has over twenty bedrooms, and I'm the only one living here. I'm sure we can spare one of them for you. Maybe even two."

She didn't want to stay in this house, no matter how many bedrooms it had, after the mention of propositioning. Salazar might still try something. Without Chad, she was in a vulnerable position…just like she'd been with George.

"I have a dog." She tilted her chin up, watching for Salazar's response. Chad had always said that being mean to animals was the surest sign a person was a jerk. If Salazar reacted badly to Roco, she'd leave and take her chances at a homeless shelter for the night and figure something out later.

"Is it with you?"

"*He*. And yes, he's downstairs. Your butler said he couldn't come up here with me." Now that she thought about it, that might have been some kind of sign already.

He shrugged. "As long as he doesn't bark all night."

She cleared her throat. "Thank you for your hospitality."

Salazar nodded. "You're too skinny. How bad is your situation, really? You look like you haven't seen food in weeks."

"I'm not…" She pulled her lips in, embarrassed. She hadn't eaten since she'd fled Seattle, saving her money for Roco. "I haven't had much appetite lately."

"Well, that's understandable. Why don't we get

you fed? One of my sons—Mark? Ring any bells?—owns a couple of restaurants in town. I'm sure he can give us a table, and we can do a quick, early supper."

"Sure. I'd like that," she said, her shoulders sagging a bit. She'd noticed Salazar hadn't said anything about not having a grudge against Betsy, but right at the moment she wasn't going to bring it up.

One step at a time.

"Afterward, I need to stop by a charity auction. You should come along. It's Elizabeth's gig. You know her, right? Elizabeth Pryce-Reed?"

Sophia nodded gamely, although she had a slightly sinking feeling in the pit of her stomach. Elizabeth was Salazar's sister's only daughter. This could get awkward.

"Don't look so torn. It's going to be a grand affair. I'm getting old, so I gotta do my good deeds while I can. You know, to be able to sneak my way past the Pearly Gates when it's my time." Salazar laughed. "She's going to hit me up to feed some children somewhere. No matter how much she raises every year, there're always more hungry people somewhere in the world." Salazar slapped both palms on his desk and stood up. "Okay! Why don't you freshen up and change into something a little dressier? If you don't have anything, Al can find you something acceptable. God knows the boys' girlfriends have left enough clothes here over the years. And we can discuss how we can help you get back on your feet."

ELEVEN

Dane looked out his office window. On this day, three years ago, Shirley had died.

Probably nobody else remembered. Nobody had been upset about her death but him anyway. *But the circus of grief was astounding*, he thought sourly. If it had been a movie, everyone would've gotten Oscars.

Suddenly images of Sophia at her father's funeral flashed through Dane's mind. Her tears and open expression of loss. She'd dashed off all of a sudden, right in the middle of the ceremony, and Dane had hidden himself among the trees. Desperation and something else had driven her that day, but he still didn't know what it was.

And he had no idea why he'd felt the almost overwhelming urge to show himself and embrace her, tell her everything was going to be all right.

A part of him wanted to check up on her, see how she was doing. He wouldn't have to do it himself. The family's PI on retainer, Benjamin Clark, would be more than happy to put a man on her.

Except that would be so damn stalkerish.

Dane grimaced.

Besides, what was there to check? Given how well off Rick Reed had been, she was going to be fine. She'd find some nice schmuck to marry and live happily ever after with two point three children…

He shook his head as bitterness churned in his gut. It wasn't like him to feel like this about a woman. Any woman, really, much less one he'd slept with only once.

If she'd been just slightly less perceptive…seen him as a guy who drank because he liked to drink and fucked her because he was doing what men naturally liked to do, then he might not have ended it in Mexico the way he had. On the other hand, she might not have lingered in his mind either.

There was a knock at the door, and he said, "Come in."

He tapped his fingers as the HR director sat across from him and crossed her legs. In her mid-forties, Patty Peterson projected a polished professional image in her pale beige blouse and skinny skirt. She was great at her job, completely no-nonsense, although she knew how to lay it on thick with the workforce when necessary. Amazing that his workers couldn't see what was in her steel-gray eyes.

"It's already seven. You going to spend the night here again?" she said.

"Maybe not, if you get to the point fast."

She shook her head, the tip of her brown bob swishing around her neck. She was one of a few people who didn't seem bothered by his directness, and he respected that about her. "Normally I wouldn't bother you with something like this, but we just heard from JJ's lawyer." She leaned closer, her expression turning even more serious than usual. "She wants to sue for wrongful termination, sexual harassment and gender discrimination. Oh and she's mad that you deducted the cost of a new desk and couch from her last paycheck."

He smiled. "Tell her I don't keep office furniture that people have fucked on. Also tell her I look forward to being served because I'd love an excuse to release the tape."

Patty raised one sculptured eyebrow slightly. "What tape?"

"The sex tape. JJ screwing her boyfriend right here in my office. It's very explicit."

"She's claiming you tried to have sex with her."

"In her dreams. But if she's honestly going to try that tack I can bring the pictures of the women I've dated in the last twelve months. JJ doesn't measure up to any of them, in any way, and nobody's going to believe I'd want to force myself on an average-looking brunette when I've had all these stunning blondes in my bed. By the time I'm through with her, she'll never get another job in this state."

Patty looked at him with a glint of respect in her eyes. "Remind me never to cross you."

"I believe I just did. Also, Patty?"

"Yes?"

"I needed a new assistant yesterday. See that I have one tomorrow."

She nodded crisply. "Got it."

His mobile phone rang. The screen flashed VANESSA. Normally he'd let it go to voice mail, but she was hugely pregnant. Possibly it was some kind of emergency.

He dismissed Patty with a finger-wave and swiped the phone screen. "I'm busy, make it quick." He needed to change and make an appearance at Elizabeth's charity function. Another hundred thousand bucks or so in tax deductions would be helpful this year.

"Do you know what Dad's doing right now?"

Dane started removing his tie. "No."

"He's at Éternité, with some young thing that looks like she's barely out of high school."

"And?"

"'And?' He's been flaunting her, claiming he's only doing what you advised him to! Do you have any idea what it was like running into him and *her*?"

So Salazar wasn't beyond help. "What's wrong with that? It keeps him young and happy. He isn't going to be married much longer. For all we know, he's signed the papers already."

Vanessa made a choking sound. "That's precisely what's wrong with it! Him being single soon, and we both know Dad doesn't do single even if he can't be faithful. I do not want my son to have a grandmother who's younger than his mommy."

So that was the issue. "Dad probably won't be so eager to remarry, now that he knows a prenup can't keep him safe." On the other hand...if the woman in question was exceptionally clever, she might be able to ensnare him in an ill-advised second marriage. Thankfully, Salazar had never particularly valued women for their intellect.

Vanessa was sputtering, so Dane took a breath and made a concerted effort to be nice. "Don't worry," he said. "She won't be your stepmom since Salazar isn't your dad." *Easy*. He smiled, pleased with his finesse.

"What about *our* mom? It's going to hurt *her*."

"The divorce was her idea. It's not like she didn't know what would happen once he was single again. If she doesn't like it, she can always get herself a younger man. She's still beautiful."

"*Are you absolutely crazy?*"

She hadn't said anything worth acknowledging, so he went on. "Being upset over something this inconsequential isn't like you."

"Dane!"

He was about to hang up, then stopped. His sister was pregnant after all. "Eat for two, relax and fantasize about spending all that Sterling money."

He hit the red button and tossed the phone on the desk. Two seconds later the thing buzzed again like an angry hornet, but he ignored it. Let her complain to Justin Sterling if she was still upset. That was what husbands were for.

Dane got up and changed into a tux. As he was leaving his office, a blonde walked into the elevator, her golden hair reminding him of Sophia again.

Damn it.

He looked away from the woman. There were plenty of pretty blondes to be had in the city. There was no reason to keep thinking about Sophia Reed. As a matter of fact, he was going to have one in his bed as soon as the damn charity function was over.

TWELVE

ELIZABETH'S CHARITY FUNCTION WAS AS grand as expected. Nothing but polished marble floors, giant chandeliers and a live orchestra for his cousin's events. Dane hadn't been able to attend the past few times, but it was good form to go when one could. After all, somebody had to think about the starving, under-educated children of the world…even while worrying about their tax bracket for the year.

He sipped champagne as his date clung to his arm. Her hair was sculpted into some kind of towering…thing on her head. She wore too much makeup and her dress was inadequate to cover her surgically enhanced tits. None of that was really relevant, though; she was vapid and blonde, just the way he liked.

He would have bet his Lamborghini she didn't remember his name. Not that he knew her name either—didn't care and didn't want to know.

"You made it!" Elizabeth came over and gave him a big hug. "I wasn't sure if you could."

"I told you I would." He hugged her in return; anything else would have been awkward and rude.

She pulled back, looking up at him with a smile. Her golden curls were pulled back in a manner that made him think of ancient Greece. Unlike his date, Elizabeth was adequately covered in a red Versace. "Still. I know you're busy."

"Remember that next time you decide to invite me. I can just write you a check."

"But it's nice to see you and catch up. Even Ryder showed up."

Dane cocked an eyebrow. Elizabeth's older brother Ryder hated this kind of gig. He was more of a rowdy party type. The more half-naked women the better. Coke and other drugs were de rigueur although Dane didn't know if his cousin indulged. "You sure it's not an impersonator?"

Someone slapped Dane on the shoulder. "Nobody can impersonate my good looks."

Dane managed to not roll his eyes too hard as he turned to greet his cousin. Ryder Pryce-Reed was an actor and a notorious playboy—the black sheep, the one who deserved every ounce of derision Shirley had felt for the Pryce-Reed children.

"Showing unusual restraint tonight I see," Dane said. "Only two women?"

"One for each arm," Ryder cheerfully agreed. "But I had to come. Charity event, right? And just by walking in the door I upped the average handsomeness of the men at this party by at least twenty percent."

Dane snorted. "And reduced the collective intelligence by twice that."

"Don't hate the player," Ryder said, impervious. He waggled some fingers at Dane's date. "Hey, beautiful. Wanna hang out with us rather than this humorless ogre?"

She giggled, and Dane gave Ryder a cool look. There was no point in indulging his cousin, who was hopelessly inappropriate. "You can have her after I'm finished."

Elizabeth covered her ears. "Oh my god, I did *not* hear that." She walked away.

"Prude." Ryder chuckled. "Well, gotta go see and be seen. I was told to be good."

"Faint hope."

"Very."

As Ryder disappeared into the crowd, Dane shook his head. No wonder Shirley had been worried about Geraldine. Her oldest child, Blake, was the only one with a decent head on his shoulders, but he was too busy to humor his mother.

Dane mingled, saying hello and making small talk as needed. He could play the part as well as anyone, even if he thought it was pointless. He even managed to be polite to a fat politician who bored him with empty talk about "bettering the community." It was obvious the entire world would be a better place if he were abducted by aliens, but Dane refrained from saying as much.

Finally somebody else distracted the self-deluded man, and Dane turned around to locate his date. She'd left a few moments earlier to freshen up, but hadn't come back yet. He was finished for the evening and wanted to leave before the bachelorette auction started. A hundred thousand bucks in donation was more than sufficient to make up for his refusal to bid on women who didn't appeal to him.

As he scanned the crowd, the hair on the back of his neck stood up. The right side of his face suddenly felt over-sensitive, like somebody was dragging needle tips across his cheek. The sensation reminded him of Mexico—god, he really needed to stop thinking about that damned place—but it seemed like he couldn't help himself. Very slowly he turned, then sucked in air.

There, barely five feet away, was Sophia. And she was looking right at him.

She had on a classy black dress that deepened her eyes to dark emerald, and high heels added several inches to her stature. Soft pink lipstick glistened on her plump mouth, which was slightly parted as she stared at him over her champagne glass.

He blinked. He had to be seeing things. He'd been thinking about her earlier and that had to be the reason…except she didn't vanish.

A sensual *zing* went through him. His entire body responded, alert and vibrating with anticipation.

Everything around them seemed to fade away, leaving only her. Damn, she looked amazing. He could make out every detail, including a slight tremor in the way her delicate throat worked.

And she kept staring back at him, those green eyes dark and direct, like she could pierce through all the outer layers and reach the core of him.

His insides went hot and cold at the same time. Her ability to see through his armor was the reason why he'd left her the way he had.

How the hell had she gotten invited? Elizabeth would've never asked her to come, given the ugly history between their mothers. His cousin wasn't a shit stirrer.

Sophia's slim fingers shook, even as her eyes held his. The skin on his shoulders grew hot at the memory of her nails digging in as he drove into her. His blood roared and went south, straight to his dick.

Damn it.

The flute slipped from her grip. Before it could shatter on the floor, Dane lunged and grabbed it, the cold liquid sloshing over his hand.

She blinked as if a spell had been broken.

"I'm sorry," she said, her voice low and husky.

He handed the glass to a waiter who'd appeared unobtrusively. Sophia's gaze roamed all over his face, her gaze like a feather brushing his skin.

"How did you get invited?" he asked.

"I didn't. I came here with somebody." Her fingers toyed with her choker.

Dane glanced at the bauble…and then took a second, longer look. Triple-stranded with diamond accents, it was just like one that used to belong to his grandmother. He studied it, then hissed out a breath as he saw the initials S J P.

It *was* his grandmother's. And she'd left it to Salazar, so…

How the hell had Sophia gotten it? Or should the question be, *what had she done to earn it?*

Something dark and ugly unfurled in Dane's belly. It was all he could do to stand there like a civilized human being.

Vanessa's call came back to him. So. This was the stepmother candidate his sister had been worried about.

Technically there was nothing that would stop Salazar and Sophia from marrying; they weren't blood relations. And normally Dane wouldn't have given a fuck who his dad screwed around with.

But this wasn't a normal situation, and Sophia wasn't just any woman.

Dane had a feeling that she would be able to accomplish what other women before her had not—getting Salazar to put a ring on her finger. After all, she'd already managed to get Shirley's choker.

"We need to talk." Dane took Sophia's elbow and looked around. The area was too crowded. "This way."

He led her toward a pair of French doors. The garden would provide better privacy. He had no desire to become somebody's gossip for the week.

As he pulled her past the doors, she stumbled and cried out. He stopped instantly, biting back a curse. "Don't tell me you can't walk in those heels."

"It's not that. They hurt."

"Then why are you wearing—? Never mind. Why do women choose their clothes and shoes so poorly?"

"I couldn't put on flats."

"Of course." Salazar liked his women in heels.

Dane let go and waited as she arranged herself. The outside lamps illuminated the wince on her face, and something like sympathy stirred inside him.

Damn it. This wasn't what he needed. He knew better than anybody how well people could pretend. Innocents didn't just gravitate toward people like his father or swindle valuable chokers from them.

And not just any choker, but one of Shirley's. Dane clenched his jaw. Technically it was Salazar's now, and he could do whatever he wanted. But given its history, it should've stayed in the family. There were other baubles, meaningless ones, that could serve as… incentives.

"So where do you want to talk?" Sophia asked.

He motioned with his chin toward a bench in the shadows. "Over there. We should have some privacy."

She nodded and followed. They didn't touch, but he felt her anyway across the small distance between their bodies.

"Sit."

He waited until she settled on one side of the bench. He didn't take the spot next to her. He was so restless, he could barely stand still. But he knew better than to let her see his agitation.

"What are you doing with Salazar?" he asked.

Her mouth parted. "You know him?"

Dane laughed. "You could say that. Now what the hell kind of game are you playing, Sophia?"

"Game? I'm not playing any game."

"Right." She opened her mouth but he waved a hand dismissively. No longwinded explanations. "Fine, let's play it your way. Salazar is my father. Now answer my question."

THIRTEEN

SOPHIA GASPED AND BLINKED A FEW TIMES. "I had no idea."

Dane smiled. *And I'm the king of England.* "Did he promise to marry you as soon as the divorce is final?"

"What?"

"Surely you've heard about his marital situation. Come on. You didn't get this far"—Dane gestured at the choker—"without doing some research."

"Dane, what are you talking about? There was no 'research.'"

Uh-huh. Women ran into Salazar and ended up with family heirlooms all the time.

"I had to come to L.A.," she continued. "I have nobody back home."

"You could've called me."

"You mean your lawyers," she said, her voice sharp.

"So you called after all."

"Don't worry." Her mouth tightened. "I was never pregnant."

"That wasn't what I was thinking." If she'd called the lawyers, she must've discovered who he was. And since they weren't idiots, whatever they'd offered probably hadn't been satisfactory for her, assuming that they'd bothered. They'd most likely laughed at her for wanting anything when she wasn't even pregnant with his kid. He should've left her his private number after all. "What's your endgame here, Sophia?"

"Oh for…! I keep telling you, there is no game."

Typical denial. Wasn't even worth acknowledging. "Do you think you're too smart to be played by Salazar?" He tilted his head. "Did your father not leave you enough money?"

She choked back a bitter laugh. "Enough money… How would you define that?"

He narrowed his eyes. "A couple of million at least." Which wouldn't have been a lot for Rick. He'd inherited over a hundred million dollars.

"And you're acting like I'm the crazy one." She laughed, this time not bothering to keep it quiet. The sound was full of derision. "Two million dollars? Really?"

"Chump change for you?"

"I would've been happy if his estate was worth two hundred dollars." She gave him a long, level look. "Listen to me carefully, Dane. There's nothing. Zero. No money."

Despite himself, Dane believed her. He pulled back. *How could Rick have died broke?*

And why was Sophia being so candid about her money situation? Most gold diggers didn't like to talk about their poor finances. They preferred not to give any *wrong* impression, like people were too stupid to figure it out.

"I needed a safe place to stay, and Salazar was the only candidate. If you wanted me to contact you, maybe you shouldn't have snuck out in the middle of the night."

Touché, and he hated her for putting him on the defensive. The women he associated with didn't do that. They were either too busy fawning over him or following his instructions. Any other kind were ruthlessly cut from his life, the only exception being his family. "I left a number," he gritted out.

"To your lawyers. You might as well have told me to go fuck myself." Her hand flew to her mouth and she shook her head slightly. Then she got up, chin high. "Excuse me. I think we're done here, and I need to get back inside."

He gripped her wrist. "Not to him." He could stand anything but her going back to his father.

Her eyes glittered in the dark. "Why would you care? You never wanted me more than once."

The cynicism ate at him like acid. It didn't belong on the perfectly formed lips that had haunted his memories over the past three years.

A sudden fury seared him. Did she have any idea how much he hated himself right at the moment? Even knowing who and what she was, something inside him warmed at the sight of her, and he craved that warmth with the desperation of a man lost in the long Arctic winter.

She had no right to look at him like he was some pathetic pawn she found wanting.

You should've never been born. Then none of us would have to suffer through this ridiculous game.

Each softly spoken word stabbed into him like an ice pick. Her pulse leaped, beating against his hand. There was a small tremor in her breathing, on her lips that softened ever so slightly.

It was an Oscar-worthy performance. It had to be. But even knowing that, he couldn't stop himself.

He crushed his mouth against hers.

She made a small sound and melted under him. His tongue flicked over her mouth, then invaded aggressively. He'd show her he wasn't fooled by her clever games. He'd played with best of the best—his parents.

Her pulse fluttered faster against his palm. The heady, sweet taste of her filled his mouth, her body pliant. She met his tongue with her own. Her free hand reached over and grabbed his shoulder; her body arched into his.

A pulse of desire reverberated through him, making every cell edgy with anticipation. His cock hardened, stabbing at her belly. She merely moaned and rocked, their mouths still fused.

Their breaths mingled, their lungs breathing the same air. Sophia flooded his senses, and his heart thudded like it existed only for that moment. He still couldn't figure out what it was about her that drew him like this, and he wanted to unravel her so he could stop this madness.

He pulled her wrist behind her. Her back arched further against his chest, her breasts flush against his torso. He palmed her small tit, and she mewled, the sound muffled against his mouth. Even through the layers of clothing, he could feel her pebbled nipple.

She became bolder, her teeth nipping at him to give her more, eroding his control. Damn it. Every drop of blood in his veins seemed to rush south. There was nothing but desire pounding in his temples. He wanted nothing more than to rip her panties off and take her in the garden. To show her how stupid it'd been for her to go to his father when he made her scream his name while his cock was buried deep inside her.

A small rational voice in his head said this was wrong, that he was letting her use sex to manipulate him. The kiss should've been a punishment for both of them, not something he got a sick kick out of.

He quashed the voice.

Dane's fingers slid under her skirt and touched her drenched panties. She cried out as he ran his knuckles along the wet strip of lace, then bumped lightly against her swollen clit. Her breath became erratic pants. Sexual need glittered in her green eyes, and he pulled her even closer. He circled his thumb against the nub, while breathing in the sweet scent of her—all that luscious female aroma.

Tremors ran through her. He could feel her pulsing against his hand, and he knew she was close.

"Dane, please."

"Please what, sweetheart?" he asked tauntingly, unwilling to give in. She'd been inexperienced before, but she wasn't anymore. He wanted her to show him how much she'd learned since then.

When she stayed quiet, he dipped the first knuckle of his forefinger into her dripping pussy, grinding the heel of his hand against her clit. She bit her lower lip, a sublime expression settling over her gorgeous face. But it wasn't enough. He made sure it wasn't enough.

She clutched him to her, nails digging into his muscles. Her moist mouth parted, and he had to rein himself in. Thrusting into her throat would be incredible, but this wasn't about that.

"Say it," he whispered hotly against her ear, making her shiver. "Tell me what you want." He deepened the penetration, pushing to the second knuckle.

She gasped, tilting her pelvis in silent supplication for more, but he retreated slowly. "Please—"

"Sophia? Where are you?"

Shit.

Dane pulled back, pulled out, pushed Sophia away until she was at arm's length. She whimpered, her eyes glazed with frustrated need. "Elizabeth," he whispered.

Sophia flinched as if she'd been slapped. Her hands trembled as she smoothed her dress and checked her hair.

Dane closed his eyes briefly. His cousin had some of the shittiest timing in the world. He hadn't meant to leave Sophia on the edge and frustrated, but now… He adjusted his jacket and waited until Sophia dropped her hands to her sides.

"Over here," he called out.

Seconds later, Elizabeth appeared. "My goodness, I panicked a little when I couldn't find you."

"What do you need her for?" Dane said, his voice colder and harder than usual.

Elizabeth blinked. "What's gotten into you?"

"You've interrupted a conversation."

"Well, sorry about that, but it'll have to wait. Sophia, you need to get out there for the bachelorette auction. You're up soon. And Dane, your date's been looking for you. You might want to go back inside and find her." She smiled slyly. "Unless you want to bid?"

"You know I don't do auctions of this kind. If you want more money, just ask."

"Oh, yes, I know, but hope springs eternal. First time for everything, and all that. Maybe you can win Sophia and continue your conversation while helping some under-privileged children."

Then she smiled, took Sophia by the hand and led her away.

Pressing the tip of his middle finger against the spot between his eyebrows, he watched them disappear. Various contradictory emotions tangled and knotted until they were an ugly ball in his chest. Then he suddenly chuckled.

Buy Sophia and continue their conversation.

If only Elizabeth knew.

SOPHIA WAS SHAKING INSIDE, BUT SHE DIDN'T LET it show. It wasn't that difficult; she'd had years of experience controlling her nerves for competitions.

But Dane…

He was something else. How could he act so nonchalant and unaffected?

"Was the conversation unpleasant?" Elizabeth asked.

"What?" *Oh, that's right.* "No, just…unsettling." In fact, it had been shockingly pleasurable and frustrating. Her panties were soaked through, and unfulfilled need throbbed between her legs. She was so swollen and slick down there, even the slight friction of the lace was setting her nerves on edge.

"That's good. Dane can be…difficult. We all say that ice water flows in his veins."

That didn't sound at all like the man she'd met three years ago, but perhaps something had happened to him since then. "Has he been like this for long?"

"Ever since I can remember. Which is why he has no friends. Well, except for my oldest brother. They're like two peas in a pod."

"Are they?" She'd heard of Blake Pryce-Reed—impossible not to, since he was Uncle Julian's heir—but she didn't know anything about him.

A tall blonde woman came up to them. "Have you found my date?" Her dress was so tiny, it looked as though her breasts would pop out if she sneezed.

Elizabeth nodded. "Out in the garden. If you go that way, you might run into him."

Sophia watched the blonde walk away on a pair of impossibly high heels, hips swaying in an exaggerated manner. "Who's that?"

"Dane's date."

"Oh." Jealousy knotted in Sophia's gut. Suddenly the things she and Dane had done felt wrong and sordid. "How long have they been dating?"

"No idea, but it wouldn't surprise me if it's their first date. Dane doesn't usually do more than one. Two is like this huge commitment from him." Elizabeth pursed her lips. "He has a type."

"I see." *Big-breasted. Long-legged. Sophisticated.* None of which described Sophia.

"Dumb and blonde. At least he's discreet, unlike Ryder." Elizabeth made a face. "Let's get you ready for the auction. You're going to rock, and by the way, thank you so much for doing this. I know I sprung it on you."

"Happy to help out." Sophia smiled warmly.

She didn't think she was much of an attraction. However, Elizabeth had gushed that having a famous athlete would bring in more money and said the fund would help build schools for young children. Sophia couldn't pretend she didn't care enough to do it. It was a small and brief discomfort for her, but a lifetime of opportunity for children somewhere. And now that she'd stopped competing, she didn't have stalker problems anymore. So there was really no excuse for turning it down.

They went to the backstage to get ready, Sophia focusing on calming her nerves. She didn't know why she felt so jittery. It wasn't like she had to move elegantly on a pair of razor-thin blades over a field of ice or anything.

"Your turn." Elizabeth squeezed her hand. "Good luck! You'll be awesome!"

Sophia drew in a deep breath and pasted on a smile. This was simply performing, just like she'd done hundreds of times before in rinks. She didn't even have to worry about executing difficult jumps or falling on an unforgiving surface.

Widening her smile, she strutted onto the stage. So what if her joints hurt? She'd done much more, winning competitions while her knees felt like they'd burst into flame. The emcee blabbered a few factoids about "tonight's special surprise bachelorette."

Sophia tuned her out and tried to see who was in the audience. Spotlights got in the way, keeping non-stage areas dark. Still, she thought she spotted the blonde—Dane's date. Was he still out there or had he left already?

But then there it was again—a familiar tingling sensation that rippled over her. Dane was in the audience. She knew it. He was the only one who could make her feel this way.

Suddenly something that had been bugging her for a while clicked. He'd been at her father's funeral… but chosen not to approach her.

Why not?

Hadn't he thought she deserved a few words of comfort?

Bitterness tightened her chest. How little did she mean to him, anyway? Or the night that they'd had? Maybe she was stupid for thinking that it should mean more than it did. After all, it had been *her* first time, not his. Maybe leaving quickly after sex was par for the course for men like him.

Besides, Elizabeth had said one date was his style. He was sticking to his MO.

The emcee's squeal jerked Sophia back to the present. "Five hundred thousand dollars! Ladies and gentlemen, a new record!"

Sophia blinked, dumbfounded. Who on earth would pay that much for a date with her? It was insane.

Then her old training kicked in. She'd managed to smile like everything was fine after a fall from a botched jump. She could control herself here too. She waved and blew a kiss to the audience before leaving the stage.

Elizabeth hugged her. "Did you *hear* that?"

"Yes," Sophia said, almost numbly. "I had no idea people spent so much money."

"They don't. But I knew you'd be special!"

Sophia smiled ruefully. Despite her initial doubts, Elizabeth had turned out to be just as sweet as everyone had said. Even Betsy thought Elizabeth was perfect and saintly. "If she were Catholic, they'd've made her a saint."

"I mean it's already unbelievable that he stayed because he absolutely loathes auctions like this," Elizabeth went on. "He usually just writes a fat check and splits, but for you, cousin, he stayed. And bid, and bid, and bid."

Sophia grinned. As shallow as it sounded, it felt great to be wanted. Dane might not have thought she was worth his time or attention, but she shouldn't let that bother her so much. Obviously there was someone who thought the exact opposite…and had showed it to everyone with half a million dollars! "So who's the winner?"

"Dane."

Sophia's jaw slackened. "Dane?" she repeated faintly.

Elizabeth glowed. "The one and only."

FOURTEEN

SOPHIA WALKED OUT TO THE FLOOR. PEOPLE beamed at her, gushing with congratulations. She smiled back and said all the right, polite words on autopilot.

The only thing on her mind was: why on earth had Dane bid so much money for her?

He'd made it clear he didn't like her. Wanting her physically didn't mean anything, not to a man like him who could have sex with any woman he wanted.

Salazar found her and handed her a glass of champagne. "Fabulous, my dear! What a way to make an impression." He rested a fatherly hand on her shoulder, giving her a warm glow.

She smiled. "Thank you."

"I was just telling Dane he did a good thing."

"Well, I'd hate to embarrass a relative. It is her first social scene in L.A., after all."

Sophia snapped her head around. Some parts of Dane were just like before—the stunning harshness of his beauty, the directness of his gaze, the large imposing body. She responded to them all, heat and nerves rolling and twisting in her gut as she recalled what had happened earlier outside. But there was something about him that was also very different now—he was harder, colder, infinitely less approachable. His formal clothes seemed to accentuate those qualities.

The blonde from earlier was clinging to him like an octopus, arms like tentacles and one breast flattened from pressing into his bicep. Dane made no move to discourage her. Instead he studied Sophia, his eyes steady.

Anger lanced through her, the earlier sexual frustration fueling her temper. How dare he stand there, cool as a cucumber, like nothing had happened between them? Or was it a regular thing for him to drag a woman outside and take her to third base at a public event?

"If that was your concern, you didn't have to bother," she said, her words clipped. "I'm sure somebody else would've bid a decent amount...without creating a spectacle."

"A spectacle?"

"The excessive amount will only create unnecessary gossip. I prefer to remain more anonymous." George wasn't the type to read tabloids, but she didn't want him to get even a whiff of where she was. She didn't think he'd try to confront her, but then again she hadn't thought he was capable of attacking her.

"You gave up any expectation of anonymity when you started coming to events like this. Especially on his arm." Dane's gaze raked over his father, then Sophia.

"Pshhh. Don't be ridiculous," Salazar said. "I'm old news. Boring."

"People are still speculating that The Eternal Couple won't split after all," Dane said. "There's a betting pool."

"Really? I had no idea." Salazar seemed oddly energized by the thought. "Did you put some money down?"

"No."

"Should've, since you were the one who delivered the papers. You know the odds better than anyone." Salazar yawned. "I think I'm done for the evening. Not as young as I used to be."

"None of us are," Sophia said quickly.

"You ready to exit in triumph?" he said.

"Sure." She was wiped out from the long trip and the impromptu auction, and her hip was killing her. Also, her nerves were too frayed to deal with a disapproving Dane...especially when Malibu Barbie was all over him. "Completely, totally ready."

Salazar turned to his son. "Well, good night." He gave the blonde a rakish smile, then offered his arm to Sophia.

She looked at it, hesitating. She could feel Dane's gaze. He looked even colder and more remote.

Her mouth tightened. *You know what? You aren't the only one upset here, buddy.*

She put her hand on Salazar's arm.

DANE WATCHED THEM LEAVE, THE MUSCLES IN HIS jaw bunching.

Son of a bitch.

Salazar had bid heavily on Sophia, and so had other men. She was an incredible prize. When Dane had gotten tired of the incremental bidding, he'd tossed out half a million to end the bullshit. He didn't give a damn who the other women belonged to for an evening, but not Sophia. He'd be damned if his father would win her.

On the other hand…

Dane forcibly relaxed his fingers to avoid shattering his flute of champagne. He'd probably tipped his hand. Salazar wasn't an idiot, especially when it came to women and sex.

This was why Dane was careful not to let his emotions show. Every time he got careless, he had to deal with an unpleasant aftermath with his family. Even his mistake of three years ago was coming back to haunt him.

"Honey, you all right?" his date said.

"Fine."

"You wanna get going?" She pressed a huge

plastic tit against his arm again. "I've been thinking of some…fun things," she whispered into his ear.

Normally he'd like nothing more than to let her exercise what imagination she had, but the only thing he wanted right now was Sophia.

Sophia…

His possible future stepmom if Vanessa was to be believed.

Damn it.

Dane drove to his date's place at exactly one mile per hour under the speed limit. It wasn't far from his penthouse. He parked in front of the luxury condo building and stared straight ahead. He had to get ahold of himself before he did something he'd regret. Like speeding over to his father's house, dragging Sophia out and finishing what they'd started in the garden.

"You want to come in for a nightcap?" the blonde said, dragging her fingernails lightly along his thigh.

He picked up the offending hand and dropped it in her lap. "No. And if you don't get out in the next three seconds, I'm going to start driving."

She gasped. "You can be *such* an asshole."

"So I hear. Now get out."

"Fine!" She climbed out and slammed the door.

His hands flexed around the steering wheel as he maneuvered the Lamborghini toward his penthouse. A ball of pressure was bearing down on his rib cage. He took a couple of deep breaths and flexed his shoulders, trying to relieve it.

An urge to push the car to its limit and speed down the highway hit him, but he resisted, grinding his teeth. He hadn't indulged in the last seven years, and he wasn't going to start now. Not over Salazar. Not over Sophia.

Then what? Go home and drink?

Dane shook his head. That wasn't enough.

He needed to run.

FIFTEEN

PLEASANTLY COOL EVENING AIR CARESSED HER bare butt, causing goose bumps to rise, but hot hands soon covered her naked skin. They pulled her closer until she could feel the long, thick erection against her belly. Strong fingers brushed tantalizingly close to her already soaking folds.

Yes, yes, yes.

She moaned into his mouth, begging for more. Her legs spread as wide as possible, seemingly on their own volition. She arched her back, pressed into his big hard body.

Still he maintained control over himself, and she bit back a frustrated groan. If she could just make him let go a little… If Dane would just—

"Sophia?"

She woke with a start and blinked as her eyes focused on Salazar. "Uh…hi," she said.

They were inside his car, which was currently parked in front of his house.

"Hi yourself. You must be pretty tired."

She forced a smile, her lips feeling rubbery. *How do you deal with the father of the man who just starred in your dirty dream?* "It's been a long day."

The driver opened the door. The interior lights illuminated Salazar's face, and she looked for any hint of an ulterior motive. Dane had been so certain that either she wanted to marry his father—which she absolutely did not—or that Salazar was planning to marry her for some weird, messed up reason. Some… game he was playing with his wife.

Dane knew his father better than she did, so was he right? But no matter how hard she searched, there was no hint of malice or ill-intent in Salazar. He seemed genuinely interested in helping her.

"Thank you," she said, taking a chance, squeezing his hand and watching for the reaction. "For everything."

He shrugged and smiled. "Hey, everyone can use a hand sometimes. Am I right?"

She laughed as they walked up to the mansion. Al greeted them at the door, crisp in his suit despite the late hour. Maybe the man was some kind of cyborg that didn't need to sleep or rest.

"Your suite is ready. I had the housekeeper unpack your things. Also, your dog has been walked and brought in for the evening."

"Thank you," Sophia said, slightly stunned.

She said goodnight to Salazar and let Al lead her down a long corridor. Oil portraits of men and women looked down at her from the cream and sage walls. Every alcove had a giant vase with fresh flowers.

Al finally stopped and opened double doors made of pale wood. Sophia gaped at the sumptuously appointed room.

"Will this be satisfactory?"

"It's…gorgeous."

"Your dog is in a special nook I prepared for him. I hope that's acceptable."

"Thank you. You've thought of everything."

"He deserves his own place." Al's tone was as placid as an autumn lake. "If you need anything else, please let me know. I took the liberty of stocking some toiletries for you. They're Miss Vanessa's favorites."

"Vanessa?" The name sounded familiar, but Sophia couldn't place it.

"Mr. Pryce's daughter," the butler said, face completely impassive. "If that's all, I shall bid you good night."

Sophia murmured a good night. The doors shut silently behind her.

Her suite looked like something out of a fairy princess's castle. The hardwood floor gleamed with a fresh coat of wax, and the ceiling fans spun lazily. Pale cream and gold paper covered the walls, and a few rugs lay on the floor in a seemingly careless fashion. The only thing that took away from the effect were a few oddly ugly paintings, but Sophia shrugged it off. Maybe they had been gifts from a relative or something.

A canopy made entirely of gold, pink and lavender lace covered a huge bed in the center, and a cream-colored love seat and a matching armchair occupied the living room. The bathroom had a sparkling Jacuzzi bath and a multi-head shower and double vanity. It was better than any hotel she'd ever stayed at.

Roco let out a soft sleepy yip, wagging his tail. Al had set him up with a small doggie bed in a corner of the living room where, amazingly enough, Roco seemed content to stay. Maybe the house and its staff intimidated even her incorrigible dog. Sophia bit her lower lip. She hoped the bed was something that the family had used for a previous pet, but it looked brand new.

"This is all entirely too generous, isn't it?" she said to Roco as she undid the clasp on the choker. She stared at the gorgeous piece. Dane had been upset at seeing her at the charity event, but the pearls had somehow tipped him over the edge. She palmed the cool strands and studied them. There were small initials, S J P, on one of the platinum links in front.

The P must have stood for Pryce, but she didn't know what the S was for. She was certain it wasn't Salazar.

Another mystery about Dane, but she didn't dare ask anyone directly. As nice as Salazar was, she'd sensed tension between him and Dane. He'd want to know why she was curious, and she didn't want to tell him about Dane's reaction to the choker. Al was out of the question. Even though she was certain he knew, he was loyal to Salazar. She didn't want to put him in an awkward situation or make him think she was being nosy. He probably didn't know the history between her and Dane, and she didn't want to have to tell him.

Shaking her head, she put the choker into an ornate white jewelry box on the vanity. Her instincts had been right. Staying at Salazar's house was a mistake. Thank god it was temporary.

She took off her dress and hung it in the huge walk-in closet. The housekeeper hadn't just unpacked her things. Everything was laundered and pressed.

Sophia tossed her panties into the laundry basket and threw herself on the bed. Her skin was so sensitized even the five hundred thread-count sheets felt coarse. Sexual frustration simmered as she lay in the dark, unable to sleep. At this rate, she might never get any rest.

But why suffer when she could take the matter into her own hands…literally?

She moved her hands over her body, cupping her small breasts. Closing her eyes, she tweaked her nipples, gasped as pleasure rippled outward. Slowly she dragged one hand down until it hit the flesh between her legs. She stroked her moist folds. A warm tingling sensation curled in her belly and spread to her limbs, but it wasn't enough to get her off. She needed something more.

Her mind focused on Dane. The spicy scent of him, the heady taste of him mingled with a hint of champagne. He'd been incredibly magnetic three years ago. He was more dangerous now but at the same time more thrilling and irresistible. His unpredictable actions made her unable to gauge him, and she couldn't fully figure out what he wanted with her.

He wants your body for sure. He was rock hard against you.

She held her breast in her hand the way he'd held it—firm and confident with just the right amount of pressure. Her thumb brushed over the tip, then she rolled the tight peak between her fingers. A moan rose up in her throat, and she swallowed it.

She remembered how his hand had felt between her legs earlier. He'd teased her, running his knuckles along her clit and folds as though he was waking her senses, readying them for the ecstasy only he could give. She did the same to herself now, even though her senses were already quivering, ready to go.

Tell me what you want, he'd demanded as he dipped his finger in and out of her, the penetration shallow and frustrating but also unbelievably pleasurable.

She'd wanted him to plunge his fingers into her, fuck her with his hand in the garden, even though anybody could've walked in and discovered them in the compromising position. Then, as her orgasm built, she'd bury her face against his neck and scream against his bare skin. It would muffle the sound, but he'd know how hot she was from the strong vibration, the desperate, rough breathing.

Her fingers thrust in and out of her, her pelvis moving in sync. She was so close, so close.

She imagined Dane driving into her, his thick length unforgiving and relentless, his hips grinding against hers and bumping into her clit—

Her pleasure crested and she bit her lower lip, arching her back, trying not to make any sound.

By the time her breathing returned to normal, her body felt like warm wax, soft and pliant. Just as she was about to drift off, the memory of the blonde slipped into her mind. Sophia scowled. Dane had undoubtedly gone home with his date. By now they were probably done screwing each other's brains out.

Damn it.

Bitterness tightened her muscles, and Sophia let out a frustrated growl. So what if she'd been pathetic enough to masturbate to a man who didn't want her anymore? Given how badly her life had gone in the last few months, this was nothing. There was no physical danger. Nobody had to know but her, so there wasn't even public humiliation. People masturbated to improbable fantasies all the time.

Still, her heart felt heavy and off-kilter. And she hated herself for letting Dane affect her like this.

OVER AN HOUR OF HARD RUNNING DIDN'T DO ANYthing to lessen the horrible restlessness riding Dane. Finished, he stood in front of his penthouse window, wiped the sweat off his face and torso with disgust and swigged a sports drink. The city glittered on the other side of the glass—a pretty, sparkling veneer without substance.

He'd started running as a kind of therapy after the accident in Paris. It helped him chase away the nasty memories—the horrible sound of metal crashing into metal and the smell of blood and burnt rubber.

Shirley had said the victims were given five million dollars. *Five million.* A life-changing amount, far too much for a mere accident. Dane had never tried to find out what had happened to them that would warrant such a payment. He'd been too afraid to ask. Still was.

Now that visions of Sophia and Salazar had entered the toxic attic of his brain, running until his leg muscles were about to explode didn't do the trick anymore.

Maybe he should try smashing his head against the wall a few times, see if that would help him forget. Inducing amnesia seemed like a great idea.

But given his luck, he'd probably forget everything but the shit he didn't want to remember.

His mobile vibrated on the counter. Dane glared at it. Who could be calling? It was already well past one.

His eyebrows pinched together when he saw his father's name on the screen. Why the hell was he calling instead of doing what he did best with Sophia?

To gloat, undoubtedly.

Despite his better judgment, Dane set it on speaker. "What do you want?"

"I'm firing Kim," Salazar said without a preamble.

That made Dane pause. His father only hired the prettiest girls he could find as assistants, regardless of their suitability, then let them go after a few months so that, having gotten to know the women, he could fuck them without worrying about sexual harassment lawsuits. Dane considered that to be the height of stupidity, but so far it'd worked for Salazar.

But Kimberly Sanford was different. She'd lasted for years despite the fact that she was objectively hot, and that meant the woman had to be damn good at her job. And she'd never struck Dane as the type to succumb to Salazar's charm.

"Why are you telling me this?"

"I want you to hire her," Salazar said like it was the most obvious thing.

"And why would I do that?"

"Because you got rid of your assistant. Kim's good at her job, and it'd be a shame to put her on unemployment."

"Then don't fire her."

"Have to. I told somebody else I'd give her a job."

"Really?" Dane's mouth twisted into an ugly smile. It was probably some dumb but pretty bimbo who couldn't type her name without breaking her fingernails. "Before or after you slept with her?"

"Don't be crude."

"I learned from the best. Who's going to be your new assistant?"

"Sophia."

The sports drink bottle crunched as Dane clenched his hand.

"What was that?" Salazar asked.

Dane ignored his father. "Is she actually any good?"

"No idea. But who cares? She said she wanted a job."

Wanted a job, did she? For what? If she became the second Mrs. Salazar Pryce, she wouldn't need to work. His father had more money than Rick Reed had ever dreamed of. "Why does she want to work?"

"Why does anybody work? Boredom? Shits and giggles?"

"Instead of playing musical jobs, it might be better if I just hired Sophia directly."

"So you can scare the shit out of her like you do with all your assistants? Or is it because you want to fuck her?"

"Unlike you, I don't fuck my employees, terminated or otherwise."

"Ah, but you want to. I saw the way you were looking at her."

Dane breathed deeply, controlling his temper.

"Too bad she came home with me."

"Is there a point to this conversation?"

"Just letting you know I took your advice about sleeping with pretty young things very seriously. Because you were right. It's just the thing to get me out of my funk." A short pause and a smug chuckle. "What does it feel like to want my leftovers?"

Fury seared through Dane—his whole body throbbed with it. *You're with* my *fucking leftovers* was on the tip of his tongue, but he swallowed it. It would've been satisfying for him, but Sophia…

Shit. He didn't even know why he gave a damn about her. He'd warned her, but she'd made her choice clear by going home with his father, hadn't she?

Salazar laughed. "I'm sending her tomorrow at eleven. She doesn't have a résumé, but I guess you'll do what you need to do. By the way… This is how you continue a game nobody else wants to play." He hung up.

Dane threw the empty bottle at the wall. If Salazar hadn't been his father…if Shirley hadn't asked Dane to keep an eye on him, he would've destroyed the son of a bitch.

Just because Sophia had given him her virginity didn't mean Dane should let his dick do all the thinking. *Somebody* was going to be her first, and it had just happened to be him. It didn't mean anything.

Sophia could come work for him, and he'd make sure she quit in tears, or better yet fled the damn state.

SIXTEEN

Despite the late night, Sophia got up at seven sharp. It was an old habit—one that she could never seem to shake off.

After showering and getting dressed for the day, she took Roco for his morning walk. He enjoyed exploring the new area. The garden was much bigger than she'd expected. It was more like a small forest, complete with its own little pond and tennis courts.

Despite its size and display of wealth, the Pryce family mansion didn't have the flashy veneer of nouveau Hollywood money. It might have been the landscaping and architecture, but the place felt…dignified. If it were a person, it would have been the sort who kept their chin raised and upper lip stiff no matter what.

When Sophia came back to the house, a uniformed housekeeper said, "Good morning, miss. Your breakfast is ready." She looked down at Roco. "And his too, although it's in the kitchen. I'll take him."

"Thank you," she said, surprised. Her family had never been waited on hand and foot.

The breakfast room was made of glass walls that let the sun pour in. Oblong, sand-colored tiles formed interesting patterns on the floor. A blue crystal vase full of freshly cut tiger lilies sat in the middle of a round table large enough to seat ten. Oddly enough, there were only two chairs. Salazar was already in one, going through some newspapers.

"Did you sleep well?" Salazar said, snapping the gray sheets closed and putting them next to his coffee cup.

"I did, thanks." Before she could move, Al appeared and pulled out the remaining chair for her. He then produced a silver tray with eggs, bacon, toast and chunks of fruit.

"Help yourself," Salazar said. "And if you want anything else, just say the word."

"No, it's…more than enough."

As she served herself and started in on her eggs, Salazar said, "By the way, I got you a job interview. It's at eleven. That should give you plenty of time to eat and get out there."

Sophia blinked. "So soon?"

He got a slightly cocky look. "Hey. Told you I'd help you get back on your feet."

"What kind of job?"

"It's an assistant position. So you assist. Basically do whatever your boss wants. Nothing too intellectually taxing or physically demanding. But I gotta warn you. I know the guy you're going to be working for. He's kind of an asshole."

"Um..." She reached for her tea, not knowing whether to laugh or be worried. "I see."

Salazar chuckled. "No need to look so concerned. I'm not sending you to work for a psychopath. Do you have a car you can drive?"

"Uh, no." She flushed. "I had one, but it wasn't under my name. So..." She shrugged delicately, clearing her throat.

"I understand. No sweat, you can take one of mine."

"Oh, I can't possi—"

He waved her away. "I have so many cars, it's a chore to have to choose one. And it's not good to let vehicles rot in the garage. You'll be doing me a favor."

She ran her thumb along the rough edge of her whole-wheat toast. She didn't know anything about cars and maintenance, but she should just accept the offer. There wasn't any decent public transportation near the mansion. She'd had to walk quite a while to reach his place from the closest bus stop on the map. "Thank you."

"Great!" He smiled. "Let me give you my number so you can call if you need anything." He gave her a card that only said SALAZAR PRYCE and had a phone number underneath.

"Is this your...business card?"

"In a manner of speaking. Sometimes it's just handy to be able to give someone your number."

She took the card, then finished her meal and returned to her room to make sure she looked professional and presentable for the job interview. Even though Salazar had acted like it was a done deal, she didn't want to embarrass him.

Roco watched as she got ready. She dug out a navy skirt suit and nude ballet flats. Her hair went up, then a pair of pearl studs completed her look. She fingered her heart-shaped garnet necklace with the panic button. It was just plain jewelry without Chad, but she couldn't bring herself to remove it. She'd wanted to call him more than once, but hadn't been able to. She didn't want to complicate his life with her problems when she knew he needed to earn a living. It was ironic, but taking care of herself was the best thing she could do for him.

She picked Roco up and touched his nose with hers. "Wish me luck. If all goes well, we'll have a place of our own soon."

He licked her nose and squirmed, wagging his tail. Smiling, she put him down, gave him a scratch behind the ears and left.

Al was waiting for her downstairs with a car key. "This is yours to drive, miss," he said, gesturing at a green Aston Martin convertible that had been brought around to the front of the mansion. The car gleamed in the morning sunlight. The license tag read 2HOT4U.

"Oh no, that's too…too…" She swallowed the rest. She didn't want to seem like she was complaining, but the car's flashiness made her squirm. When

Salazar had offered, she'd assumed he'd lend her a station-wagon or something.

"The location of your interview has been programmed into the vehicle's GPS. If you get lost or need assistance, please call this number." Al handed her a card. It felt smooth and expensive in her hand. "Good luck, miss."

She took the keys with a murmured thanks and climbed in, feeling like she was in some kind of trance. The engine roared to life, and she carefully pulled out.

The traffic wasn't as bad as she'd feared. The GPS led her to a downtown skyscraper. She parked her car in the underground garage and started toward the elevator.

On the way up she clenched and unclenched her hands and took a few calming breaths. She could do this. She absolutely could. If there was one thing she knew how to do it was control her nerves. That was the reason why she'd been so good at skating—while others crumpled under the pressures of competition, she stayed calm and composed. She could handle a job interview.

The elevator opened up to a wide reception area. A sleek company logo read Digital Angel Capital in strong, unembellished block letters.

A slim brunette in a pale gray suit peered at Sophia through a pair of fashionable glasses. "Sophia Reed?"

"Yes."

"Please follow me."

She rose and escorted her down a long corridor. The office was stately with pale earth-tone carpet, dark furniture and frosted glass partitions. Everything hinted at wealth and elegance. What kind of company was this?

Now that Sophia thought about it, she probably should've researched that before showing up. It was too late to pull out her phone and google, especially not when the receptionist was moving full speed ahead in a pair of pricey pumps that, Sophia noted, she walked in with a sophisticated ease.

The receptionist opened the door at the end of the hall. "Here you are."

The inside was surprisingly spacious with a couple of leather benches. A curved desk sat to one side, on the right of double doors. Sophia looked back at the receptionist.

"There's an adjoining office. He's waiting for you on the other side," she said, then vanished.

Sophia licked dry lips and breathed deeply. *I got this.*

She pushed the doors by the desk open and walked inside.

It was a huge corner office with a stunning view of the city. The space was minimalist and museum clean. A large black executive desk predominated, completely devoid of clutter. Only one sleek laptop and a phone sat on the shiny surface.

To the left of the desk, near the floor-to-ceiling glass wall, was a mini-bar stocked with bottles of amber liquor. A couple of chairs and a couch that were arranged around a coffee table took up the space on her side of the office. There wasn't a single plant or photo in the austere space.

She hesitated, unsure what to do next. No one else was in the room…but the receptionist had acted like somebody was waiting for her.

Then a door on the other side of the office opened, and Dane walked in. Her mouth parted as shock rippled through her.

Dane was in a gray suit and pearl-colored tie; the flash impression was of a great white shark. He strode purposefully over to his desk and took a seat.

Despite the energy he radiated, the small lines around his eyes seemed more pronounced than the night before. *Maybe that blonde kept him up late.* Her mouth flattened at the thought.

"Sit down," he said quietly, indicating a chair in front of the desk. Despite his calm demeanor, something dangerous lurked in his eyes.

She sat, knees and ankles pressed together.

"I hear you're looking for a job. Why?"

"To earn an honest living."

"I see. Did Salazar encourage you to look for work?"

She tilted her head. Dane was watching her like a lion would an impala. Did he still think she was out for his father's money? "No. It's something I want."

"Of course." He leaned back in his seat. A bemused smile curled his lips, but his eyes remained cool. "So you won't object if I ask you to move out of Salazar's house as a condition of your employment?"

"If you can wait a couple of months, no."

"Why the delay?"

"I don't have the money for a deposit or—"

He flicked away her explanation. "I can advance you the money. And my staff can find you a temporary place to stay."

"That's very generous, but I'd hate to impose."

"Unless it's on my father."

His superior expression made her hands clench. "There's absolutely nothing good about my situation. Do you think I want to take someone else's charity?" She shook her head. "The only difference between you and me is that you didn't spend all your life pursuing something highly uneconomical out of love and passion, and your father's better at managing his money than mine was. If what you're really worried about is protecting your inheritance, don't worry. I won't be a leech."

"This isn't about any inheritance. I don't want his money, and in any case I'm already quite wealthy."

"Then what's the problem?"

"There are two. One, you pretending to want to share his bed because he's such a great guy. And two, you becoming my stepmother, which I find singularly distasteful." He paused for a moment, his eyes narrow. "I know what you sound like when you come."

The gall! "Your dad said you were an asshole, and I thought he was mistaken. But it's obvious I'm the one who was wrong. You *are* an asshole."

"And proud of it. I suppose he forgot to mention that."

"He did. I guess he didn't want to paint his son too badly."

Dane laughed out loud. "*Right.*"

"For your information, I actually *do* like him. He's charming, and he's nice to me without expecting anything in return. He's made sure that my dog and I are comfortable while I try to find a way to get back on my feet."

"Next you're going to tell me he loves you and you love him."

She fumed. Was his mind too broken to think of anything but that? "Obviously you're one of those people who can't accept kindness at face value. There has to be some ulterior motive, right?" She shook her head. "Now I see why you left the way you did. Despite what you think, all I wanted back then was dinner and sex, and the only thing Salazar's been offering is assistance, because he realizes I need it. So when your brain starts coming up with all the horrible reasons people might have for being nice to each other, maybe you should reflect on your own soul. Ask yourself why you have to be so cynical when you've lived all your life in absolute privilege."

Dane didn't respond in any outward way except for an almost imperceptible tightening of his mouth. She swallowed. She didn't know what made her just say all that. Generally she avoided confrontations, but she simply couldn't keep her mouth shut with Dane. He pressed every single one of her buttons.

Finally, he got up and walked around the desk, stopping in front of her. Probably a deliberate move to make her tilt her head back to look up at him.

He leaned forward until his nose almost touched hers. His scent—some luxurious aftershave and pure male—enveloped her until her senses drowned in it. Her pulse leaped.

"Are you finished?" His near-whisper was hot against her cheek.

She shivered despite herself. "Yes."

"Then listen very carefully, Sophia. I'm about to give you an important lesson in surviving my family. It's precisely *because* of the way my life has gone that I've become so cynical. Kindness can be kindness, or it can be a weapon. And when it's a weapon, it can be deadlier than a gun. Don't take anything at face value."

Her heart thudded, not just from the proximity to him. Dane seemed genuine. Just how messed up had his life been that he believed this? She'd always thought she'd had a less than ideal childhood with her oblivious and negligent parents and her single-minded focus on her sport career. But nothing had damaged her to the point that she equated kindness to something worse than guns. "I see. Well, I'm sorry for wasting both of our time."

He cocked an eyebrow. "What makes you say that?"

"Salazar said you needed an assistant. Obviously I'm not suitable for that position."

His mouth quirked. "Are you turning down a job I haven't even offered?"

She flushed. "You weren't going to, so don't pretend."

"One thing you need to know about me is that I don't pretend. I say what I mean, and I do what I say." He straightened. "You're to start immediately. Fill out whatever paperwork HR throws at you and then come back here."

"Excuse me?"

"Unless you think you can do better elsewhere, I suggest you hurry. My offer has a rather tight expiration date."

DANE STARED AT THE CLOSED DOOR. SOPHIA'S FEMinine scent lingered, making his body practically vibrate with need. Shit.

Desire still simmered, unfulfilled from the night before. He'd come, his hand fisted around his dick, but that was a poor substitute for her. He remembered—clearly—how sweet her body was, how wet and welcoming. And he still hadn't felt what her lips felt like around his cock.

Perched at the edge of his desk, he put his fingertips together. He'd thought to intimidate her. Most people would've sweated and stammered when he'd gotten in their face, even without raising his voice.

But not her.

She'd stood her ground, told him what she thought. Called him an entitled asshole. He could respect that in spite of himself.

Still, that didn't mean he was deviating from his plan. He hadn't been kidding when he'd said he didn't want her as his stepmother. Who would want to call a woman they'd slept with "Mom"?

Not to mention, despite her insistence to the contrary, he knew Salazar's transformation had something to do with her. Dane had seen how perceptive she was regarding other people's vulnerabilities. And people like that were also great at using them to their advantage. Just look how Salazar had done it to the ones around him, and the same for his mother, Ceinlys.

People were no different from wild animals—it was all about survival of the fittest. Sure, they wore nice clothes and pretty smiles and spouted polite words. Sort of like the way predators looked innocuous until they pounced. Dane had no interest in becoming the prey. Nor did he have any interest in masking himself just to make everyone else around him feel safe. It wasn't his job. Besides, everyone already knew what a bastard he was anyway.

Better to be an asshole than a failure…or worse, a pawn.

He dialed a number from memory. His brother

Mark was getting married soon, and Dane needed to speak to his fiancée. When she picked up, he didn't wait for a greeting. "My assistant's going to call you to help with your wedding plans. Keep her busy."

A short pause. Then Hilary Rosenberg said, "That's nice of you, but I'm already covered with Jo, and Vanessa is helping too."

Dane felt his mouth tighten. Josephine Martinez was the maid of honor, and not only did she have great taste, she was superbly organized to boot. "Still. If you do this for me, I'll skip the wedding."

This time there was a long pause. "Um…what?"

"It's not like you want me at the ceremony." He was well aware of how he ranked.

"Don't be ridiculous. You're family."

Cynicism tugged at a corner of his mouth. "Don't worry, I'll still send a wedding gift."

"Dane, you have to be at the wedding if I do this. That's my price."

"Fine. I'll be there."

"Good. I think I can keep her busy. Things always come up at the last minute with weddings."

"Surprising." Hilary was one of the most efficient people he knew. "I thought you had everything figured out."

"I do. It's other people who don't."

Of course. Dane hesitated for a moment. "Thanks."

SEVENTEEN

Dane glanced at the clock. It was already three in the afternoon, and Sophia hadn't been by since she'd left earlier to help Hilary. So his future sister-in-law was making good on her promise.

He poured himself a scotch and savored it. He'd be surprised if Sophia would last the day. On the other hand… She seemed like a fighter. So it might take two days before she cried uncle.

His mobile buzzed. Vanessa again. She should really call her husband if she found her life so unsatisfying. This was getting ridiculous. He ignored it.

A few minutes later Hilary called. Curious about how things had gone with Sophia, he answered. "Dane Pry—"

"*Oh my* GOD*! I cannot believe you gave her a* JOB*!*"

He jerked the phone away from his ear. Vanessa deserved her own Guinness record for her screeching. Wasn't pregnancy supposed to mellow women out, making them all warm and fuzzy thinking about their babies? Apparently not…at least not with his sister.

"I give a lot of people jobs," he said. "Got a problem with that? Sue me."

"She's not 'people'!"

"Calm down, Vanessa," came Mark's voice. "Just so you know, we're on speaker right now."

Dane rolled his eyes. How many times had his siblings gathered to worry themselves sick over immaterial stuff? "Anyone else there?"

"Just me, Hilary and Vanessa. I got here right around the time your assistant left."

"Good. Can you or some other rational human talk to me?" Dane said. "I'm tired of hysteria."

"Vanessa's upset because she's driving Dad's car."

He scowled. "Who?"

"Sophia!" Vanessa said, breathing hard. "Your new 'assistant'! She's driving Dad's 2HOT4U 1965 Aston Martin DB5 convertible, which he never lets anyone else even *sit in*, much less take out on the road."

"What the hell?" Dane sat up straighter.

Salazar loved that convertible more than any of his children…or even his own mother. Shirley had often lamented about his ridiculous obsession with "that car." Sophia had said there was nothing going on between her and Salazar. If that were true, she wouldn't be allowed anywhere near the vehicle.

Vanessa lowered her voice, but it was no less forceful. "By the way, she's the one I saw at Éternité. He had his hands all over her. It wouldn't surprise me if they went home together." She made a gagging noise. "Mark my words, she's aiming to be Dad's next wife. Our stepmom."

Dane breathed deeply, forcibly reining himself in. "I'm well aware of that. I saw them with my own eyes at Elizabeth's function. Which, by the way, you skipped."

"I wasn't feeling well," Vanessa said defensively. "Besides, I heard you spent half a million on her at the bachelorette auction."

Elizabeth had wasted no time spreading that piece of gossip. "I needed a bigger tax deduction for the year."

"But you had to bid on *her?*"

"Dad was bidding too. Would you have preferred him to win?"

That shut Vanessa up for a moment, but then she started again. "I don't understand why she bothered to get a job at your company. Every pretty thing that approaches Dad always has the same objective—to replace Mom."

"She denies it," Dane said, then paused. It was out of character for him to toss something like that out. But he'd wanted to voice Sophia's point of view for some reason.

Probably because she wasn't around to do it herself. He might be an asshole, but he wasn't unfair.

"Wait, you believe her?" Vanessa asked, suddenly getting quiet. "Because if you do… I don't know. I guess I'll back off then."

Dane poured himself another finger of scotch.

"No, but I've half a mind to let him have her. It'd serve him right."

But the image of Sophia, naked and moaning, on the pristine sheets on Salazar's bed preyed on Dane's mind. His skin suddenly felt too small, and he clenched his teeth to contain an uncharacteristic snarl.

"She might not want to marry Salazar," Hilary said. "She seemed…uh…nice."

"Your unflinching faith in humanity is admirable, but quite unfounded," Dane said. "She's my employee. I'll deal with her."

"Are you going to fire her?" Mark asked. "That doesn't solve the problem of her being with Dad."

"Amateur. My methods are far more effective than that."

Dane hung up and turned off the phone before anybody could waste any more of his time. He leaned back in his seat and set the tips of his steepled hands against his lips.

Salazar had made it clear he was playing a game. Sophia had denied it, and very convincingly. Dane would've believed her, except there was too much evidence pointing the other way. First Shirley's choker… and now the *Aston Martin?*

If she honestly didn't want to get sucked into the drama, she could've moved out of Salazar's house. If she didn't want to impose on Dane, she could've crashed with a friend. Everybody had a friend. Even Dane himself had one he could count on…despite his family thinking he was the biggest asshole in the universe.

The fact that Salazar was letting her drive the Aston Martin changed everything. Dane had assumed she'd have her own car or borrowed one of Salazar's lesser cars, like a Mercedes. Or perhaps an Audi.

He'd underestimated the situation. It was about time he gave it the attention it deserved.

SOPHIA RETURNED TO THE OFFICE A LITTLE BEFORE five. Helping Hilary had turned out to be much more complicated than she'd expected. But that wasn't the bad part. The real difficulty had been the emotional strain of dealing with Vanessa, who was obviously unhappy. Sophia still wasn't sure why the redhead was so upset, but she knew it had something to do with her.

Or to be specific, the car Salazar had lent her.

She should've told him it was too flashy and ostentatious. She didn't know a thing about cars, but from the way people had stared at the Aston Martin, she knew it had to be very rare and expensive.

Sighing, she stretched her neck. She wanted to check in and make sure Dane didn't need anything else before she went back home. No, not "home". Salazar's house. Dane seemed to think she enjoyed staying there, but that couldn't be further from the truth. It was a grand place, but it wasn't her home. She could never forget that she was just a guest there, a poor relative who had nowhere else to go.

A charity case.

She knocked on Dane's door and poked her head in. "Do you need anything else for the evening before you head out?"

"Come in and shut the door." He waited until she followed his instructions before saying, "Where have you been all this time?"

She looked puzzled. "Helping Hilary. She needed—"

"You do not work for Hilary. I said to assist her, not spend your entire working day with her. I still need the items on this list done." He pushed a sheet of paper across the desk.

"I'll get to them—"

"Today," he added.

Her jaw slackened. "But you never said—"

"It's your job to anticipate my needs, not vice versa. If that's too much, you're free to quit. I won't even ask for two weeks' notice."

She clicked her mouth shut as anger knotted in her belly. It wasn't that hard to figure out what was going on—he was setting her up to fail. Well, he'd picked the wrong victim. She'd suffered much worse in the form of unfair calls and biased judging when she was competing.

She curled her hands, itching to wipe that condescending look from his handsome face. His looks were the only evidence she needed to know the world was an unfair place. If it were, he would've been born ugly. "Understood. I'll get them done."

"Excellent." He got up from his seat and walked past her.

They didn't touch, but even so she could feel an electric charge pass between them, an inexplicable voltaic link that made her skin tingle like he'd run his hands over her. And she didn't seem to be the only one sensing it. She followed him to the door; Dane's shoulders were set in a tense line as he walked down the hall and into a waiting elevator that had been held by an office worker.

Sophia went to her desk and took a deep breath.

A few moments later, the same woman who had held the elevator stuck her head around the door and knocked softly. "Sorry about all that," she said with a sympathetic cringe. "I'm Roxie Rodriguez, by the way. Mr. Pryce's assistant." Her gorgeous glossy black hair framed a friendly round face. She had dramatic makeup with little glittery highlights around her eyes that made her look like she was about to jump on a stage and start belting out a Broadway tune. However, her teal blue tunic and white skirt were conservative and office-appropriate.

Sophia forced a smile. "Do I look that bad?"

"You looked a bit shell-shocked when you walked out of his office. He's been sort of moody recently. If he doesn't change soon, it's not going to be fun for you here."

"Thanks for the warning. I'm sure I can manage."

Even if it killed her. She wasn't going to let Dane win.

EIGHTEEN

As Dane pulled into the driveway of the Pryce family mansion, he spotted the green Aston Martin, parked in the shadows. The infamous 2HOT4U.

The top was up, windows closed. Guess Sophia had finished her tasks faster than he'd expected. It wouldn't have bothered him if she had to pull an all-nighter while he implemented his plan.

He got out quietly with a small suitcase. As he started toward the house, he caught something in his peripheral vision. He turned around and looked more carefully into the convertible.

Ah there. The unforgettable golden head, shining even in the dim light. The back of her skull was round and had fit perfectly into his hand as he'd kissed her. His right palm twitched as if it too remembered.

Sophia was still in the driver's seat. She'd draped her arms around the steering wheel and was resting her face on them.

Placing his suitcase in front of the door, he went to the car. He started to knock on the window, then stopped. Her shoulders drooped, and her body seemed to have deflated like a day-old balloon. Something that felt suspiciously like sympathy stirred in his heart. Had he been too harsh with her earlier?

Don't second-guess yourself.

Salazar might think she was his pawn, but the reality wasn't that simple. Sophia was also playing a game of her own. Dane wanted them both to lose.

His mouth set in a flat line, he knocked on the window.

She blinked, then stirred and got her purse. A bit of her hair had escaped the tidy bun, and it floated around her face like wisps of cloud. Dane kept his hands by his side, so he didn't do something stupid, like pull the pins out to watch the chignon come undone.

He would have loved nothing more than to unravel her right there, right that moment.

"What are you doing here?" she asked, opening the door.

The sleepy husky tone sent heat straight to his cock. Damn it. "Fixing the situation you've created."

"Which is…?"

"Your refusal to move out."

She shook her head. "If you're here to ask Salazar to make me leave, don't bother. I'm going to do that as soon as I can find a place."

When? danced on the tip of his tongue, but he

resisted saying it. "I'm not here to ask him to toss you out on the streets." That would be pointless. Even if Salazar had thought about doing exactly that, he wouldn't, just to spite Dane.

"Then what?"

"I'm moving in."

Shock replaced fatigue in Sophia's eyes. Her jaw dropped.

Dane shot her a triumphant smirk, then walked up the few steps to the main entrance to the house.

Within seconds of knocking, Al answered the door. "Sir?"

"Good evening, Al."

"Good evening." The butler frowned. "Is that a suitcase?"

"Very astute. In fact, it is." Dane smiled. "I'm moving back."

"Sir." Al blinked twice, then opened his mouth and closed it. "You haven't lived here since you turned sixteen."

Shirley had gotten him an apartment in the city in addition to a car on his sixteenth birthday. Ceinlys had objected at first, but not many people could bend Shirley to their will. "Yes, I'm aware of that."

"So..." Al cleared his throat. "I—"

Dane almost laughed. He'd never seen the family butler flustered before. "Where's my father?"

"Resting in his room. I'll let him know you're planning to move back home."

"Yes, you do that."

"And I'll take care of your bag. Will you be taking your old room?"

"No." He hated that horrible place. There were no good memories. He pretended to consider, then said, "I'll take the guest suite next to whichever one Sophia is using."

Al's gaze flickered behind Dane, and he could feel Sophia's stare on his back. *Yes, my dear, take that!* It was about time he got involved even if he didn't want to.

The butler nodded. "Of course, sir." He pulled out a phone and spoke discreetly into it. "Please follow me." He led Dane and Sophia up to the second floor, walking a bit more slowly than usual, probably to give the staff time to ready the room. Not that there would be much to do.

As they mounted the staircase, a maid passed them going down. Her eyebrows rose slightly when she saw Dane. "Oh! Good to see you, sir."

"Thanks." Dane gave her a small smile. *Good to see you*. Right. That was the last thing she was thinking, since every staff member was well aware of the tension between him and his father.

They got to the top of the staircase; Dane's eyes narrowed slightly as Al directed them away from the master bedroom suite that Salazar used. When they reached the end of the hall, Al stopped. "Here you are."

The suite's double doors opened, and a housekeeper walked out. "All ready for you, sir."

Dane turned to the butler, about to ask if he hadn't understood Dane's instructions about wanting a room next to Sophia's. Then he saw that Sophia had peeled off from the small party and opened the next door along the hall. "Good night, everyone," she said, and slipped inside.

Dane tilted his head. Interesting. He'd assumed she'd be sharing his father's room, or the one right next to it. Was this distance simply for the sake of appearances? If so, who would talk? Al would never gossip about it, and the housekeeper knew better than to tell anyone who Salazar slept with. The only possible exceptions might be other family members.

Possibly.

"That's her room?" Dane asked.

"Yes, sir."

"Been hers all along?"

"Of course." Al hesitated, then added, "If you're worried about Miss Sophia, there's really no need. She's been treated with every bit of decorum and respect she is due."

Dane shook his head as he entered his own suite. Al had no idea how *un*reassuring his words were. Sophia was Betsy's daughter, and it was true that Geraldine hated Betsy. But Salazar wasn't particularly close to his sister, and his idea of the level of "decorum and respect" Sophia was due was probably very different from Al's. The butler should've known better.

After all, he'd been with Salazar for decades. Just like Dane.

NINETEEN

THE NEXT MORNING, SOPHIA WALKED ROCO and went to the breakfast room. There was only Salazar at the table. She glanced at the clock. If Dane didn't join them soon, he'd be late for work. He didn't seem like the type to be tardy.

Salazar set aside his newspaper and smiled. "Good morning, dear. How did you enjoy your first day at work?"

"It was great. Thank you."

"Any difficulties and you let me know."

"Of course," she lied. She had no intention of involving Salazar.

Al set her breakfast of scrambled eggs and fruit salad and yogurt. She murmured her thanks. When he was finished pouring her morning tea, she turned to Salazar. "There's something I need to talk to you about. I hope you don't take it the wrong way."

"What is it?" Salazar peered at her over a fine, bone-china coffee cup.

"I'm afraid I won't be able to drive your car anymore."

"Not dri—? What do you mean? It's a great car!"

"Oh, I know. It *is* a great car…but it's too much."

"In what way?"

"It just…draws too much attention. And it's too valuable. What if I get into an accident?"

He shrugged. "I'm sure the other driver will have a heart attack, wondering how he's going to pay for it."

She choked on her tea, but managed to not spit any of it out. "Yes, well… Now that Dane's here, it'll be easy enough to carpool." If he could invade her space, she could return the favor. She didn't want him thinking he could intimidate her that easily.

"Ride with Dane? He drives slower than my dead mother."

"Observing the speed limit is hardly a flaw."

Sophia turned in the direction of the cold voice and almost swallowed her tongue. Dane stood at the doorway, topless. Sweat beaded on his tanned skin and rolled down the hard planes. She'd seen a lot of good bodies—after all, she'd been surrounded by young athletes in their prime—but Dane's physique redefined greatness. So much power leashed in those big muscles. Not an ounce of fat on him anywhere.

She remembered how strong he'd been. He'd caught her like she weighed nothing. Carried her to the bedroom effortlessly. Pulled her close to his body.

Heat curled in her belly.

It was unfair. If a man spent most of his time in the office, he should have a soft, pale body that didn't make her mouth water or cheeks flush.

"Are you joining us?" Salazar said.

"I don't have much appetite."

"Didn't you just go for a run?"

"Should I feel like eating, I'll grab something in the office cafeteria."

"Suit yourself. You always do."

"Learned from the best." Dane went upstairs.

Sophia turned her head to watch him climb the stairs. The workout shorts showed off his tight butt.

"Asshole," Salazar muttered.

"Excuse me?" Sophia said.

"Nothing." Salazar smiled, but his eyes stayed cold. "Nothing at all."

SOPHIA WAITED FOR DANE TO SHOW UP IN THE foyer. It didn't take long.

He came down in a suit, hair still slightly damp from a shower. He smelled like spicy aftershave, soap and clean male flesh.

A small frown creased his eyebrows when he noticed her, but he walked past, his thumb scrolling the screen of his phone. Without looking up, he opened the door and walked down a few steps to the cars waiting outside.

"I need a ride," she said, following him out.

He paused, then turned around. "Are you talking to me?"

"Of course I'm talking to you."

"What happened to the Aston Martin?"

She shrugged. "I decided not to drive it anymore."

"Why not?"

"I don't want any misunderstanding."

He gestured at a red Lamborghini. "You think carpooling is going to prevent a misunderstanding?"

She sucked in a breath. She hadn't realized it was his car. She hated red sports cars, and Lamborghinis in particular. It was a red Lamborghini that had crashed into her taxi and ended her career.

So what? This isn't the same car. It happened in Paris. Do you really want to go back to Salazar and ask him for a key to one of his cars because you can't deal with Dane's over something that happened seven years ago?

He climbed behind the steering wheel without waiting for her. Her mind made up, she got inside quickly before he could say no. She wasn't letting the accident hold her back. *It was a long time ago. I have to think about now.*

"Misunderstandings aren't limited to cars," he said as he pulled away from the Pryce family mansion.

"There's more?"

"Your dog. I saw him in the kitchen this morning."

She blinked. That was the last thing she'd expected him to bring up. "What about Roco?"

"My father has never allowed any of us to have a pet, especially a dog. My grandmother bought one for us, but she had to take it back because he wouldn't bend the rule. It upset her, since he used to like dogs, but what could she do? His house, his rules."

"I didn't know. I guess he let Roco stay since sending him away wasn't an option for me." She would've risked sleeping on the streets than give up Roco.

"Right."

She gritted her teeth. She was beginning to hate that word, especially when spoken with such cynicism. "He's just being nice."

Dane snorted. "One thing you have to understand about my father is that he's never 'just' nice. I told you that already. I meant it."

"So what do you suggest I do? Be suspicious of everyone around me? Doesn't that get tiring?"

"At least you won't get fucked over."

I give up, Sophia thought. It was impossible to talk to a man who was determined to see the worst in everyone. What had made him so harsh? She'd meant what she'd said about the privilege he must've taken for granted.

On the other hand, he might also have experienced some emotional hardships she knew nothing about. Salazar had been kind to her, but he might've been a difficult to please father, harsh with his children.

She stared at the traffic. It looked like a parking lot rather than a highway. She counted the number of blue cars…then the hybrids. It wasn't a bad game to distract herself.

"You can relax," Dane said suddenly. "I'm not going to fuck you over."

She turned to him. "Am I supposed to take that at face value?"

He chuckled. The sound was genuine, void of malice or derision. "Not bad."

"Why did you get a Lamborghini if you drive like an old woman?" she asked.

"Says who?"

"Salazar. Actually, he said a dead woman. And you didn't disagree."

Dane paused, his knuckles whitening briefly. "I bought a red Lamborghini because my father didn't like it."

"Really?"

"The Lamborghini part was fine, but according to him it should have been anything other than red."

She shook her head. "Was he worried about getting tickets?"

His mouth curled into a smile. "We don't worry about things like that."

"You don't?"

"It's just money. No, the problem was the color itself. Heresy to drive a red Lamborghini. He can be a bit of a stickler for things like that, mostly because he has no imagination or taste when it comes to colors. Or art for that matter."

"You don't like your father, do you?"

"No." A beat of pause. "He's an asshole."

She frowned. She felt disloyal for even listening to Dane talk about Salazar like this.

Dane's gaze darted toward her before it focused back on the road. "Where did you think I got my sparkling personality from?"

Not touching that one. "Are you going to give me more busy work, like helping people who obviously don't need my help?"

"She's a bride-to-be. People like her always need help."

"And I'm the queen of France."

"You're my assistant. It's your job to do what I tell you."

"There are limits."

"Yes, to my forbearance with recalcitrant employees." He tapped his fingers on the steering wheel. "But I'll make you a deal. A bet."

"A bet?"

"If I win, you move out of the family house. Actually you leave the city entirely. Maybe even the state."

Her chest felt like someone had driven a spear into it, but she didn't know why what he was proposing hurt. He'd never implied that he saw her as anything other than an intruder. "What do I get if I win?"

"You won't."

"Let's say I do."

He shrugged. "Fine. What if you win?"

"You owe me two hundred bucks, plus you're to

treat me fairly, instead of like I'm the antichrist or something."

He snorted. "I've never treated you that badly."

"Yes, you have. So what are we betting on?"

"Something that requires skill. I hate games of chance."

"All right."

He gazed out the windshield, his eyes narrowed. "How about a race?"

"You mean like a sprint?"

"Distance. A few miles."

"You're a foot taller than I am, and besides, you run all the time."

He considered. "Swimming?"

"Can't. Bad shoulder. And you're still taller."

"Hmm. Something that will negate the height advantage," he said, thinking about it. "How about ice-skating?"

Ice-skating? She pretended to mull the idea over. "That would be…acceptable."

"Then why don't we go a few laps at a rink? Whoever's faster wins."

She gave him a sidelong look. "You're going to embarrass yourself."

"I doubt that very much. I used to play hockey." His smile was full of superiority and insolence. "Can you even skate?"

She pressed her lips together so she wouldn't laugh. He was delusional if he honestly believed hockey would give him better speed and edge control than she had. "I've been known to strap on a pair every now and then."

He arched a skeptical eyebrow.

Yeah, keep that eyebrow cocked while you still can. You're going down. "Let's make it challenging. Twenty laps forward, twenty backward."

"Fine."

She grinned. "You're on."

DANE GRABBED A BUTTERY BACON-AND-EGG-stuffed croissant and a giant, extra-espresso latte from the cafeteria and went into his office. *Artery clogging be damned*, he thought. Given the kind of night he'd had, he deserved it.

Sleeping in the room next to Sophia's turned out to be a challenge. It would have been nice to blame his lack of sleep on the fact that he was under his father's roof, but he hated lying to himself.

It was her.

At least she hadn't snuck down the hall to Salazar's room at night. He was a light sleeper. He would've heard it.

But the nightmare would be over soon enough. He settled at his desk and went over the agenda for the day, then checked his emails.

As soon as he finished his croissant—which coincided with the simultaneous deletion of over two hundred messages he wasn't even going to acknowledge—Blake came in. He was the oldest of the Pryce-Reed cousins, a partner at the firm, and the only person Dane considered a friend. The shape of Blake's eyes was much like his father's, but he had the famous Pryce profile, something he'd inherited from Geraldine. Combine that with his dark hair, he looked more like a Pryce than a Reed, which probably soothed Geraldine.

"Do you know who your new assistant is?" Taking a seat, Blake gestured at the door with a huge tumbler that read, *Want a piece of me?*

"Of course I know. I hired her."

Blake blinked. "You're kidding. She's *the* Sophia."

"The one and only."

"You know it's going to upset my mom. She still hasn't forgiven Betsy."

"It would've upset her more if Salazar had hired her instead."

"Salazar? What's the story there?"

Dane leaned back in his seat. "What are you doing in L.A.? I'm sure you didn't fly out here from Boston just to talk about my new assistant."

His cousin had an office in the city, but didn't spend much time there. He was too busy splitting his time between Boston and Washington D.C.

Blake sipped his coffee. "I was, but then I figured I should be in L.A. Mark's wedding and all."

"That's not for another two weeks."

"Yeah, but Dad's getting married again. Being on the east coast means having to watch him with Future

Wife Number Six. I'd rather not." Blake shuddered. "I'm not even sure she's finished high school."

"I sympathize." Of all the shit Dane had had to deal with, watching his father with numerous wives younger than his children wasn't one. "He wants all the Pryce-Reeds to attend the ceremony?"

"Yes, plus the twins. They're looking for a reason to stay away." They were the children Betsy had given Julian—another slap in the face as far as Geraldine was concerned.

"So. When are you moving out?" Blake asked.

Gossip traveled fast. Didn't his family have more productive things to do? "Who told you?"

"Iain." Blake regarded the lettering on his mug. "Technically."

"Technically?"

"He called Elizabeth, which is how I heard."

Iain couldn't have found out that fast. He generally kept to himself. So that meant Al must've called… and he wouldn't have done that without a direct order from Salazar.

"What's going on?" Blake asked. "I thought you were dying from some kind of inoperable tumor when I heard you'd moved back in…although Elizabeth assured me you were perfectly healthy."

"As a horse. I'm there because of Sophia."

"This same Sophia?"

Dane nodded.

"So what's the problem?"

"Are you joking? A young, nubile woman under

Salazar's roof? With no chaperone? I don't want to end up with a stepmom who's younger than Vanessa."

"Ah, the old guy's getting divorced. It's a rebound thing. He's not going to marry her."

"You don't get it. He let her drive the Aston Martin."

Blake sat up straighter. "No way." He shook his head. "I guess he must be serious then. But really, why do you care? It's not like you spend a lot of time with your dad or anything. If Salazar wants to remarry, he isn't going to settle for less than younger and prettier. And—no offense—your mom's friggin' hot. She sets the bar pretty high."

"You remember that time after Shirley's funeral? When I disappeared for a while?"

Blake nodded.

"I met Sophia then."

"Okay, so? That was, what, three years ag—" Realization dawned on his face. "You slept with her."

"Yes."

"Well, all right, but still. Why not let Salazar have his fun"—once again Blake stopped in mid-sentence—"You still want her."

Dane didn't say anything.

"Dude. So do something about it."

"Such as?"

"Fuck her until you get your fill. It's not like you to let a woman mess with your head."

"I don't fuck my employees."

"Then fire her first."

"I'm not emulating Salazar." *Fire 'em and fuck 'em* was his MO. Dane raised a finger when Blake opened his mouth. "Not anymore than you're going to emulate Julian."

"Okay, okay. Point made."

"In any case, I have a plan to get rid of her by the end of the week at the latest."

"You sure it's going to work?"

Dane nodded. He'd only played hockey for a few years, but his coach had remarked on his speed and power. "Believe me. She won't know what hit her."

TWENTY

Sophia worked well past six. Since Dane didn't look like he was about to leave, and she didn't have a ride, she was stuck. Roxie had offered, but Sophia didn't think it was prudent to reveal she was staying with the boss's father. Of course she still had tons of work left to do. It was incredible how much got piled on. But at the same time she was learning what Dane did—finding and funding promising startups in the technology sector.

She didn't understand how he chose what startups to invest in or why he was so successful. Digital Angel didn't fit her image of a big, bustling corporation with thousands of busy workers. On the other hand, maybe you didn't need a lot of staff to be successful. What did she know about the business world anyway?

The door to Dane's office opened. "You ready for our competition?"

She frowned. "What competition?"

"You've forgotten already?"

Oh. That. "Now?"

"I found a suitable rink. Pack your things."

She bit her lower lip. She hadn't finished one of the reports he wanted, but she could probably work on that afterward. "Okay."

He drove them to a humble rink not too far from the office. Outside a sign read, "Closed." She pointed to it with an enquiring look.

"Doesn't matter, " Dane said. "The owner owes me a favor."

A ropey older gentleman came out and greeted them. He introduced himself as Timothy. He looked at Sophia for a moment too long, then muttered something under his breath. She smiled at him, unsure what he was about.

"The locker rooms are that way, skates over here," he said.

"Are there any pants I can borrow?" she asked. "I can't really skate in my skirt."

He gestured at a small shop. "There's plenty for sale."

"Oh." She hesitated. She didn't have any money.

"I need a pair too," Dane said, handing over his plastic. "I'm not skating in dress pants. Put everything on my card."

She gave him a look. He didn't have to buy a new pair unless he was going to fall over and rip his clothes, which she doubted he'd do. "Thanks."

"Don't thank me. I don't want to give you any reason to cry foul."

Oh, this is going to be good. "I'll try not to lose *too* ungraciously."

She selected a pair of black workout pants and went to the locker room to change. The scene felt so familiar, her eyes prickled with moisture. This had been her life for so long.

After warming up and stretching quickly, she picked out a pair of figure skating skates. They weren't as nice as her old ones, of course, but they would do for forty laps. Dane had changed into a black workout shirt and matching pants. He looked great, the fitted top showing off the lean, strong lines of his entirely too lickable body. Predictably, he was in a pair of hockey skates.

It was too bad that he wasn't the kind of man she'd thought he was. She could see herself being in a relationship with that man, but not this cynical person.

"You're going to trip and fall," he said, pointing at the toe picks.

"Why Dane, are you worried about me? I thought you wanted me gone."

He looked down at her. "Regardless, I don't want you injured."

She smiled with bemusement. He always denied that he was capable of being nice, but then he had to ruin it by saying he didn't want bad things to happen to her. If he just wouldn't do that, she would've found it easier to dislike him. "I'll be fine."

He shrugged. "Suit yourself. But don't expect me to take you to the hospital if you break something."

"You won't have to." She looked at the rink. There was a single line running around the edge. "So how's this going to work? There's only one lane."

"Hmm. I suppose we'll have to go one at a time."

"Okay. You can go first if you want," she said.

"Nervous?"

She shrugged.

He studied her expression, but she knew he wouldn't pick up anything. She'd perfected her game face when she'd been ten. Her competitors had never gotten a good reading on her.

"Fine. I'll have Timothy time us."

Dane went around the rink a few times. He was better than she expected, sure on his skates. She didn't know how long he'd played hockey, but it couldn't have been more than a few years when he was in school.

When Timothy was ready with his stopwatch, Dane started in earnest. He was quite fast. Men generally had the advantage of power, and given that he ran and kept himself in great shape, forty laps was nothing to him.

He grinned when he finished and Timothy read him his time. "Damn, I'm good."

"I have to admit, it's an impressive time." She smiled, said, "Guess it's my turn," and stepped onto the ice.

It felt strange to be back on it. She'd been convinced she would never return when she'd realized she could no longer skate like she used to. But there was an odd sense of serenity and comfort as she glided across the ice. After all, she'd literally spent more waking hours on the ice than off. It felt so effortless to push herself forward, knees soft and edges precise.

Forty laps was child's play. Her coach—the sadist—had often made her do over a hundred laps at full speed. No longer in competition shape, she still had the muscle memory and technique that had been drilled into her since childhood. She went around and around, then switched directions easily as Timothy called out the twentieth lap. Everything became a blur of smooth, sustained effort. Her heart thundered, and the good, clean fire of exertion burned in her legs.

She was going to beat Dane. And not just because of the bet. She hated losing. There was no feeling worse than not being at the top of the podium, and she wanted the euphoria of victory. She deserved that much after the mess her life had become.

Timothy whistled as he clicked the stopwatch on her final lap. "Wow. She beat you by more than thirty seconds."

Dane scowled. "Are you sure?"

Sophia came to a full stop in front of them. "I told you you were going to get embarrassed."

"But thirty seconds? Let me see that stopwatch."

Timothy showed it to him, but was looking at her. "Miss, I have to ask… Are you Sophia Reed?"

She made a small curtsy. "I am."

His face split into a huge smile. "I thought you looked familiar. Knew for sure when I saw them edges. You always had the best ones."

Her cheeks heated at the unexpected compliment. "Thank you."

Dane slowly turned to look at the older man. "You *know* her?"

"Sure. She was a world champion in figure skating. Ladies singles." Timothy turned to Sophia. "Would you mind signing an autograph? I'd love to hang it in the shop."

"Of course." She smiled.

After Timothy left to get a pen and paper, Dane gave her a look. "A world champion?"

"Well. That was years ago."

"And you've been known to 'strap on a pair of skates every now and then,'" he said in a slow, sardonic voice.

She spread her hands. "You didn't ask me if I was a world champion."

Before she could say anything else, Timothy returned. She gave him an autograph, and did her best to hide her amusement when he prevailed upon Dane to take a picture of the two of them together. His excitement at meeting her was genuine, and she couldn't be impatient with him even though she was tired and starving.

They walked out to the car after changing back into their regular clothes. "Hungry?" Dane asked.

"Yes," she said emphatically. "I can't wait to see what Al's prepared for us."

"I'm not eating anything at that house." He opened the car door for her. "Get in. We're having burgers and fries."

Dane took them to his favorite bar. It was a hole in a wall kind of place—small and tidy and nothing that caught your attention when you passed by. But it served the best burgers and fries in the city. The place was always busy, thanks to word of mouth, but Wayne, the owner, always made sure Dane got a table. He'd invested in the business after Wayne's manager had embezzled funds. Although Dane wasn't into restaurants—that was his brother Mark's thing—he didn't mind throwing seventy or eighty thousand bucks at a worthy eatery.

"Two cheeseburgers and fries," Dane ordered. "The beer of the day for me and…?" He cocked an eyebrow at Sophia.

"A margarita," Sophia said. When the waiter left, she turned to him. "A bit presumptuous of you."

"I'm a presumptuous kind of guy. And you didn't object."

"Only because I like cheeseburgers." She peered at him through her eyelashes. "How good is this place?"

"The very best."

"Huh. I pegged you as the caviar type."

"I'm not a cat."

She snickered. "You know what I mean. The kind of people who frequent restaurants like the one your brother owns."

"You've been to Éternité, right?"

"Yeah. It was stunning."

"It's a good place, but I prefer not to dine at my brother's restaurants unless I can't get a reservation elsewhere."

Her eyes sparkled. "Too much like eating at your father's house?"

He laughed, then stopped when he realized it was springing from genuine humor. He couldn't remember the last time that had happened. "No, but it is a family thing. I prefer to limit my dealings with them. However, I'll take you to La Mer. It's one of those restaurants you have to go to at least once if you're in L.A."

"Also your brother's?"

He nodded. "Mark. He's the restaurateur."

"Then it must be amazing."

Their waiter plunked down their drinks and disappeared, promising to bring out their burgers soon.

"So. I won," Sophia said.

"That you did." Dane sipped his beer. Wayne brewed his own, and the beer of the day was excellent as usual, with a faint hint of raspberries. "Go ahead and gloat if you want. I won't hold it against you."

"Not really good sportsmanship to gloat." She toyed with her straw.

"What about withholding material facts about your skill?"

"Hey. I told you I was going to beat you." She sucked down the margarita. "Now tell me: if you'd known, would you have made a different bet?"

He considered. "No."

"Are you going to honor the terms?"

He frowned. "Of course." It hadn't crossed his mind that he wouldn't. "I'm a man of my word. Speaking of which…" He peeled two hundred-dollar bills and pushed them across the booth toward her.

Her shoulders relaxed as she pocketed the money. "I'm glad. Thank you."

"Don't thank me. You earned it. Have you lived your whole life surrounded by liars?"

She hesitated. "Not everyone's honest."

Who had betrayed her? The idea tasted bitter, and he washed it down with some more beer. It was irrational for him to react this way. "If you weren't sure, why did you bet?"

"Just in case." She shrugged. "You might be that one in a million."

Their food arrived. Dane dug in, grateful he had something else to focus on. He didn't want to think about some asshole hurting Sophia or analyze why that made his chest feel funny.

Sophia took a small bite, then moaned. "Oh my *god*. I can see why you didn't want to eat at home."

He smiled. "Can you?"

"It's incredible."

"And unlikely to cause indigestion." He stopped. That was more than he would've normally revealed. His dates never had any clue how he felt about his family. *Or anything else, really.*

"You should give Salazar a chance," she said softly. "He's actually not a bad guy."

Dane felt his mouth curl. *Not a bad guy*. Sure. He merely wished Dane had never been born, used his children in a "game" to hurt his wife, and cheated on her. Not that Dane held Ceinlys blameless—she too had used her children in a bid to control Salazar, and she'd taken her share of lovers. Moving deliberately, Dane dunked a fry in ketchup. "Some things are irreversible."

"What happened between the two of you?"

"Something too boring and pointless for me to remember now." He wolfed down more than half his burger, not wanting to talk about it. "So, Miss Former World Champion, why aren't you coaching or something instead of working in my office?"

"I didn't go into coaching because I was getting my college degree. And it's not like there are tons of job openings for figure skating coaching."

"Mm." Dane chewed contemplatively for a moment. "You know, I never really followed skating, but I do watch the Olympics. Don't remember ever seeing you."

She dropped the fry she was holding and looked away. "No. It wasn't meant to be."

"Your bad shoulder?"

A curt nod. "Among other things."

"How? Did you fall while skating?"

"Boring and pointless to talk about now," she said, throwing his words back at him. "It's been years."

But pain darkened her eyes. Going to the Olympics was a skater's lifelong dream. For somebody like Sophia, who'd been good enough to be a world champion, not going would've gutted her.

His heart squeezed. He wanted to call it pity, but it wasn't. He reserved that for pathetic people, and she was anything but.

No matter the sport, to be world class took unspeakable amounts of dedication and effort. And to be a world champion people remembered years later… Dane couldn't imagine how hard she must've worked for it.

People like that didn't go around expecting others to hand them what they wanted. Anybody without the work ethic would've given up long before they could be any good, much less reached the top.

Had he misjudged her? Twisted everything to fit the most logical worldview for him?

People around him generally thought him too cold and cynical. He'd never had reason to be anything else since people never gave him a cause to doubt his beliefs. But Sophia was different.

She kept challenging him, making him think about things he'd been certain he already knew very well.

"Why are you looking at me like that?" she asked.

The question startled him. He couldn't remember the last time he'd dined with a woman who actually noticed anything except how much money it cost to buy the latest fashion items. He shifted, suddenly uncomfortable, then picked up a napkin and dabbed a corner of her mouth. "You had a little ketchup."

"Really?"

"Didn't know, did you? I told you the burgers here are great."

"That you did." She finished the last bite. "Thank you."

"For what?"

"Dinner. It's nice to be out."

Her smile, full of gratitude and joy, made him feel like he was going to fall off his chair. He pressed his fingers onto the table, dazzled by the brilliance of her expression.

Apprehension uncurled in his belly. After Shirley had died, he'd been so certain nobody would ever breach the walls around his heart. But now, he knew, they were cracking. All because of a smile.

TWENTY-ONE

DANE HAD KEPT HIS PROMISE, BUT BEING fair didn't mean being easy on Sophia. He'd dumped a giant list of tasks on her the next morning before disappearing into his office. Sophia sighed. At least it was real work, not some stuff he'd made up just to keep her busy. Around ten o'clock, Roxie went into his office.

When she reappeared her eyes were glassy and wide. She was walking stiffly, like she'd aged twenty years in the ten minutes she'd spent in Dane's office.

Sophia got up and reached out for the other assistant's hand. "You all right?"

Roxie blinked. "Uh. Yeah. I'm fine."

"Did something happen?"

"Nothing. I'm going to help you transition until you get the hang of things around here."

"Oh." Sophia wasn't quite sure what to say. "Well…thank you."

"No problem."

And true to her word, she spent the rest of the morning helping out. Sophia couldn't believe how smart and efficient Roxie was. Everything she'd struggled with for hours the day before, Roxie got done in half an hour or less.

After they finished a memo on some biotech ideas, Roxie said, "Want to grab lunch with me and Amy? It's almost noon."

"Sure. Who's Amy?"

"She's the receptionist."

Ah. Sophia remembered a super elegant-looking brunette. "Okay."

The three of them went to a sandwich shop a couple of blocks away. It served food made with local, organic ingredients. Sophia breathed out a sigh. Thank god Dane had remembered the money part of the prize the night before. She hadn't because she'd been too excited about winning in the first place. The two hundred bucks had been something extra she'd tossed in there. She really needed some spending money, and she hadn't been able to bring herself to ask Salazar to advance her some until she got paid.

After they grabbed their food, they took a table in the corner. Roxie took a long sip of her iced latte, then said, "You have to tell me what you did to him."

"Who?"

"The boss."

Sophia blinked. "What do you mean?"

"He asked me to mentor you. He's never asked anybody to do anything like that before."

Amy leaned closer. "Does he like you?"

An alarm bell went off. Sophia didn't want to be the center of any office gossip. She snorted. "I don't think so."

Roxie and Amy raised their eyebrows and exchanged a quick glance.

"What? Why are you guys looking at me like that?" Sophia asked. Did they not believe her?

Amy smoothed her napkin. "It's just that you don't seem affected by him."

"Like how?"

"He's so cold, you know? Every time he looks at me, I feel like my whole body's gonna freeze solid."

"Me, too." Roxie shuddered. "I can feel my blood going sluggish."

Sophia chuckled. "You're exaggerating."

"I'm not. Most people coming in to pitch act like the office's twenty degrees too cold. Don't you feel even a little chilled, Sophia?"

"Um…not really." What she'd felt was complicated and conflicting, but there had always been warmth underneath—the kind of soft gooey warmth that spread all over her body in languid pleasure, making her pulse with longing. *And that makes me dumb, because he doesn't want me like that. Not really.*

"It's too bad, because he's so good looking. When I see his picture somewhere, I think, 'Hot, hot *hot*,'… and then I get to the office and see him for real and it's like cold, cold *cold*." Roxie shivered. "I still can't decide if I should call him Dane or Mr. Pryce or sir. And the bastard knows I'm unsure, but he's never said anything one way or the other."

"You're lucky that's your reaction though," Amy said to Roxie. "Otherwise you would've ended up like JJ."

"Who's JJ?" Sophia said.

"His previous assistant."

"What happened to her?"

"The rumor is…" Amy lowered her voice. "She propositioned him."

Sophia gasped. "Really? So what happened?"

"Got canned the next day. The boss does *not* mix business and pleasure. You can say a lot about the man, but he isn't inappropriate."

"The complete opposite of his horn-dog father," Roxie said.

Sophia chewed on that. Dane had said Salazar had a certain reputation. So had Betsy. "Is his father as bad as I heard?"

"Probably worse," Amy said. "I mean, you know, don't always believe everything you see on the Internet and all that, but…" She shrugged.

Had Dane moved into the Pryce mansion because he was that upset about the situation with his father? Sophia considered. The mansion was grand, and it had staff, but his own place was probably just as grand and closer to work.

"He used to be nicer when his grandmother was alive," Roxie said.

"Salazar?" Sophia asked, momentarily confused.

"No, the boss. Ever since she passed away three years ago, he hasn't been the same."

Three years ago. That explained Mexico.

Sophia thought back to meeting Dane for the first time. He'd been quiet…and hurting. And he hadn't sought solace with his family or friends. Bottles of scotch, no matter how expensive and soothing, couldn't compare.

Maybe he hadn't had anybody he could turn to. Maybe he still didn't, as he'd grown colder and more aloof since then.

Crazily enough, she wanted him to be able to turn to her. She didn't know why—she wasn't the type who opened up to people easily, and most people didn't confide in her, probably because she didn't invite them to do so. Libby and Chad were the only confidants she had, but it'd taken her years to warm up to them.

Roxie sucked down the last of her latte. "Ladies, are you finished? If so, we need to get back." She looked at Sophia. "We have those reports and statistics for the latest portfolio to organize before COB today. I'd hate to make him wait."

"Me too." Sophia dabbed her mouth with her napkin. "Ready whenever you are."

DANE REVIEWED THE SLIDES AND MEMOS FROM THE morning's presentation. The concept was excellent, and the man behind it was smart, driven and ambitious.

It was a sizzling proposal with incredible, industry-changing potential. Dane should be excited.

Except he wasn't.

His thoughts kept drifting to the woman sitting outside his office, and it irritated him that his attention was wandering. Normally a woman would never have disrupted his focus.

But Sophia wasn't just any woman, was she?

His mobile rang. Glad for the interruption, he answered without checking to see who it was.

"Is it true you've moved back in with your father?" came Ceinlys's voice.

Damn it. He put a hand behind his neck. The muscles there felt like rocks under his fingers. He really should be screening his calls.

Just hang up? The idea was seductively appealing. "Yes."

"But why?"

"Haven't you heard?"

"The Reed girl?"

"The Reed girl."

His mother sighed. "What does it matter who your father dates? And when did you start caring? Once he signs the papers, he's free to do what he wants."

"So you aren't even slightly jealous of this younger, prettier woman?"

A slight pause. "Are you certain you're well? It's not like you to worry about my feelings."

"I'm fine." He wasn't acknowledging the second part of her statement.

"Dear, I know being near your father makes you uncomfortable. There's really no need to linger around on my account. I'm not at all bothered by his little houseguest. It's not as though I expected him to remain celibate after our divorce. He"—her voice cracked for a moment before it returned to normal—"he couldn't even stay faithful during our marriage."

Dane leaned back in his seat. She was saying the same things he'd told Vanessa when she'd freaked out about their "stepmom." Somehow, hearing Ceinlys say them made the whole situation sound much worse.

Like she'd simply given up.

Well, she didn't get to give up now, not after putting him and his siblings through any number of ringers. "Don't even pretend you're hurt. Every year your men got younger, like you wanted to signal to the world how older men just didn't have what it took to keep you happy in bed. You're no better than Dad, and I wouldn't lift a finger on your behalf."

She gasped. "How could you say such a thing?"

Suddenly he couldn't stand it anymore. "Why do you care what I do, *Mother?*" he asked. "You stopped playing the game with him. Gave up your seat and walked away from the board. Who gives a damn what happens to the pawns?"

"What on earth are you talking about?"

"Isn't that what I was? A pawn? Except I disappointed you because I didn't get Dad to do what you wanted him to." Dane breathed roughly through his nose and kept his voice down. "It didn't take me long to figure out what my purpose was, and how I failed miserably in my role. He hated the fact that I was ever born, and you were embarrassed about me."

"That is absolutely not tr—"

"Admit it. Neither of you thought I should've ever been born."

Ceinlys gasped. "Dane!"

"Why did you keep having children while your marriage was falling apart, if not to create new pawns?"

"It wasn't like that. You have to understand."

"Oh, I understand quite well. I've had decades to understand."

"I thought maybe if we had enough children, created a large and loyal family, he'd change." Her voice sounded wet and thick. "I was young and foolish... and, quite frankly, desperate."

Goddamn it. Was he supposed to feel sorry for her now?

"Dane, don't make the same mistake I made. Don't do things because of your father or for Shirley or anyone else."

"Believe me, I don't."

She went on like he hadn't spoken. "Do them because they're what *you* want to do. That's all I called to tell you." She exhaled, the sound tinged with defeat. "I'm sure you're very busy. I have to go." She hung up.

He tossed the phone on the desk and pressed his thumbs over his eyes. Easy for her to say. She hadn't been created to serve her parents' need for control, or to hurt each other.

He slumped in his seat and stared at the ceiling. Lashing out at her had been a mistake. All that was in the past, and he'd told himself numerous times that he wouldn't let his parents get to him. Not worth his mental energy.

Still… Her parting remark wouldn't leave his mind.

If he really could do whatever he wanted, consequences be damned…

He spun his chair around. The sun shone through his ceiling-high windows; outside the city of Los Angeles winked and sparkled, from the chrome-and-glass office towers to the shimmering sea beyond. It seemed like a vista of possibilities.

What would he have done with Sophia if Salazar hadn't been in the picture?

If Sophia had come to Dane and asked for help, he would've given her money. Maybe even found a place for her to stay. Her father had apparently left her broke, and Dane had more money than he could spend in ten lifetimes. She hadn't finished college—she'd said she hadn't even started when they'd met three years ago—so he would have helped her graduate.

Her ability to see through his layers always made him apprehensive. He didn't want her to get too close, unveil too much, but she intrigued him like no one else and had lingered in his mind for three years. That was an awfully long time…especially for someone like him.

So his reaction to her had been tainted by Salazar's presence. The comment about "leftovers" had goaded him. But there hadn't been any hint of impropriety between Salazar and Sophia at the family mansion. Dane squinted into the sun, considering. If he had to put a word on the way his father was treating her, it would be "fatherly"…even if Salazar *had* let her drive the Aston Martin.

Salazar had said he was continuing a game nobody else wanted to play. And he knew the power of perception better than anybody. Dane could very well be dancing to his father's tune.

Dane stood up, running a hand over his mouth. Then he turned and looked at his austere, utilitarian office. On the other side of the right-hand wall was Sophia.

Fuck Salazar. It was about time he started doing what the hell he wanted.

TWENTY-TWO

HEART POUNDING, SOPHIA TIPTOED BACK to her desk. The memo in her hand trembled; she realized it was actually her hands that were shaking.

She plopped into her seat.

She hadn't meant to overhear the conversation, but she hadn't been able to stop herself either. The furious, barely controlled voice had made it impossible to move. She'd never heard Dane sound like that before.

If she hadn't heard it with her own ears, she wouldn't have believed his parents had treated him with such calculated cruelty, but Dane hadn't been lying about the way he'd grown up. There had been an ocean of raw hurt beneath his contemptuous words.

She placed the memo on her desk and took a deep breath. Dane mustn't know she'd overheard the phone call. It would only upset him, and there was no telling how he'd react. He seemed to have a knack for putting the worst spin on everything—not surprising, given what she'd just heard—and she didn't want any misunderstandings between them.

The intercom buzzed. "Sophia, can you come into my office for a moment?"

She composed her features before entering. Dane's face was as calm and placid as if he'd just come from having a pleasant afternoon tea with someone. If she hadn't heard the conversation, she would've never known he'd just had a knock-down drag-out with his mother.

Ice water flows in his veins.

Elizabeth's words came back to her. That was one interpretation for his reaction. Or maybe he'd forced himself to be cold and unfeeling so nothing could touch him. A man with ice water for blood wouldn't have drunk all that scotch over the death of his grandmother.

"I need the memo on yesterday's pitches."

She'd left it on her desk. "I'll bring it right away."

"Also make dinner reservations for the rest of this week and next, but not tonight."

"For how many people and do you have any preferences?"

"Two. There should be a list of acceptable restaurants filed under F for 'Favorite Restaurants.' Pick whichever look good to you."

She nodded.

"And make sure to have everything finished by six sharp. I need to leave the office by then."

"Okay."

"Excellent. See you at six."

SOPHIA HAD LUNCH AT HER DESK, TRYING TO GET everything done. Before coming to work at the company, she'd assumed Dane had cruised through life using his family's wealth and connections. But he worked harder and more efficiently than anyone she'd ever seen, and he demanded the very best from all his employees.

No wonder most people tiptoed around him. The only exception was Blake, but he didn't work out of the L.A. office much or answer to anyone.

Dane finally emerged from a series of meetings and came over to her desk. Sophia glanced at the clock on her laptop. Exactly six o'clock.

"Ready?" he asked.

She got up, grabbing her purse and briefcase, which was stuffed with documents she wanted to go over after dinner.

Dane drove them, coping with hellish traffic. Unlike most of the other drivers on the road, he didn't look like he was on the verge of losing his patience. His expression betrayed very little.

She stared outside, pretending she was in a different kind of car. Maybe a Ferrari or Mustang. Anything but a Lamborghini.

"Why don't you like being in a car?" he asked.

Startled, she swiveled her head his way. "What?"

"You're always tense. I've seen people react the way you do when they fly, but not in a car."

"Oh. It's just... Traffic makes me nervous."

"No one will hit us, don't worry." He checked the time. "Six thirty. Dinner before heading back to the family mansion."

"Don't worry about it. I'm fine." She added, "I don't need dinner."

He cocked an eyebrow. "I thought you didn't have to diet anymore."

She blinked. When had she said that? Oh wait... in Mexico. She couldn't believe he still remembered. "I don't, but I'm sure the housekeeper made something nice. I don't want to disappoint her." *I have to stretch the two hundred bucks I won from you, and I don't think I can afford the kind of restaurants you go to.*

"She's used to it. It won't be the first meal the family ended up not eating. And don't worry about the money either," he said. "I'll pay."

Her cheeks heated. "Do you ever think about how rude you sound?"

"What's wrong with what I said?"

"Pointing out that you have money and I don't? Kind of not cool."

"You're over-thinking it like most people. I never pointed out that you didn't have any, even though I know that's true. Money is something people use at their pleasure. It would please me very much to buy you dinner."

"Why? You don't even like me that much."

"That's not true. I like you well enough. And I certainly like your body. I liked it in Mexico. I like it more now." His gaze lingered over her. "It's fuller...softer."

She sputtered at his bluntness. It was that or melt, and she didn't want to embarrass herself. From anybody else the comment would've been offensive, even creepy. She'd had her share of stalkerish emails and notes. But when Dane said it, need pulsed through her. Suddenly it felt too warm in the car.

"Isn't this some kind of sexual harassment?" she said. Any excuse to make him stop before she did something stupid, like throw herself at him again. That hadn't ended so well three years ago.

"I suppose"—a corner of Dane's mouth crooked up—"unless the woman likes it. If you can swear under oath that you found something I said objectionable, I'll stop this instant."

That was unfair. He'd made her feel a lot of things with what he'd said, but objectionable wasn't one of them. Intellectually she felt like she should be at least annoyed or scandalized that he could talk so baldly. But she couldn't deny a part of her was thrilled to hear him say he wanted her.

Thankfully, they arrived at the restaurant. She focused on the line of people outside. "Unless you have a reservation—"

"Which I don't need."

"—we won't get a table here."

Dane gave her a superior smile. "Watch."

A valet hurried over to take his key, and an attendant opened the door for her. The exterior had oddly shaped trees and shrubs that looked like a topiary seascape, especially with colored lights beaming on them from the ground. A sign with swoopy, elegant writing read *La Mer*. The name seemed familiar.

The maître d' in a perfectly pressed tux greeted Dane as they walked inside. "Good evening, Mr. Pryce."

"A table for two."

"Certainly."

A tall blonde in a black dress came out and led them to a table. As they walked into the main area of the restaurant, Sophia felt her jaw go slack.

Dane leaned over. "You're going to catch flies."

She flushed.

They wove their way through aquarium walls full of exotic tropical fish. Unlike some restaurants that showcased fish destined to be made into meals, none of the specimens were for consumption. The bluish light and gentle movements of the fish were soothing, and the restaurant glowed like a magical underwater world.

Diners in the latest fashions and bedecked with jewelry conversed softly as they ate, their silverware clinking. The perfume in the air alone was probably worth more than a brand new Mercedes. Chopin played from speakers embedded in the ceiling and columns.

The woman stopped at a private booth. "I hope you find this acceptable, Mr. Pryce."

"It is," Dane said.

Sophia sat down and looked around, trying not to seem too overwhelmed. "I can see why you said it's one of those places you have to come see. Is this"—she gestured at their booth—"a perk of being Mark's brother? Or does he owe you a favor too?"

"Both, actually. But if you ask he'll deny that he owes me anything."

"Why? Is he the ungrateful type?"

"He thinks I tried to sabotage his relationship by giving his girlfriend a ride into the city once. Never mind that she climbed into my car without asking. It's not my fault he can't control his woman."

Just then a waiter appeared. Dane ordered a five-course meal featuring lightly seared sea bream and green sauce. She hadn't been sure what to get—the menu didn't have prices or even much information—so at the end, she followed Dane's lead.

The service was fast and efficient without being intrusive. The waiter seemed to be invisible until he was needed. The sea bream melted in her mouth, the sauce just right to compliment the flavor of the meat without overwhelming it with herbs.

"This is amazing," she commented, savoring each bite.

"Worth skipping dinner at home, isn't it?"

"Yes. And I feel kind of disloyal."

"Why? This is better and that's the truth."

"But I feel like I shouldn't say it out loud, you know?" She licked the sauce on her lips, and his gaze dropped to her mouth. She looked away as her face warmed. She shouldn't put much stock into this dinner. It undoubtedly meant nothing to him. "There's something about you that makes me more direct than I would normally be."

"Do you prefer lies?"

"Of course not."

He tilted his head, studying her. "Does honesty make you uncomfortable?"

"Sometimes, but it's preferable. And refreshing."

"So my guess was right. You have been surrounded by liars."

"I've been surrounded by...doublespeak." She'd loved competition, but she didn't like confrontation. Skate federation officials and the media had always been careful to ensure that either they could cover their butt or elicit certain juicy responses out of her. She'd learned to be circumspect about what she'd said to avoid unnecessary drama.

"Is that how people excuse lying these days?"

"Easy for you to say. Who's going to ding you for being blunt? Unless I'm mistaken, people want you to like them, not vice versa. I've seen people trying to get you to buy into their business ideas."

Dane shook his head. "They're wrong about that. I don't need to like them to invest in their ideas. All they need to do is convince me that their business is going to add value to human lives, and therefore be profitable."

That was probably true. He always seemed cold and remote in the office, prompting the complaints she'd heard from his staff. Would they have found him more human if their first interaction had been in Mexico or something similar?

She moved a piece of sea bream around, gathering up sauce, then chewed it thoughtfully. "So when are you moving out?"

He cocked an eyebrow. "Moving out?"

"You lost the bet. I thought you'd give up and move back to your place."

"The deal never said I had to leave."

She gave him a skeptical look. "Don't tell me you enjoy living at home."

"I wouldn't use the word 'enjoy.' But it has its benefits."

"If you still think I have ulterior motives—"

"I don't trust Salazar." Before she could say anything, he raised a hand. "I know you like him, but I don't. He raised me, and I know what kind of a man he is. I don't believe for a moment he's going to be different with you. And there's a further benefit…or torture, depending on how you look at it."

"Which is?"

"You and I only have one wall between us." He sipped his white wine. "Feel free to come by whenever you're in the mood for a little dirty fun."

TWENTY-THREE

Dane should've never been allowed to say things like that. Sophia flipped over—again—in her bed, unable to stop thinking about sneaking into his room, which was ridiculous and juvenile. Even though she hadn't really dated while growing up, she knew that much.

Does it matter? Nobody's going to know but you and him, and he's not going to tell.

Her conscience really had no morals whatsoever. Skank.

She sat up and stared at the door. Maybe her coming over had been just a suggestion. What he'd really meant was that he'd love to come over.

Annoyed she tossed herself back on the bed. She absolutely *had* to get some sleep if she wanted to be sharp the next day.

The next morning, he didn't join her and Salazar for breakfast. But he paraded by topless again, sweat glistening on his exquisitely sculpted torso. She choked on her tea, and Al discreetly handed her a napkin.

Dane flashed her a grin, filched a croissant from her plate and vanished upstairs.

Bastard.

"I taught him better than that," Salazar muttered, then turned to Sophia. "One of my sons is getting married next weekend, and I think you should come."

"Are you sure that's a good idea? I wasn't invited."

"You can come as my guest. They're expecting me to bring someone. Be good for you to meet the family anyway."

"Let me think about it."

"Make sure to take Friday afternoon off. The entire family's going to the grove for dinner."

She nodded noncommittally.

By the time she needed to leave for work, Dane was already at his car. He watched her climb in with a travel mug. "Coffee for me?" he said, his voice inscrutable.

"It's actually green tea. Al said I should. If you want, I can go back—"

"Forget it." Dane pulled away from the mansion. "We'll be late if we let him make it. He's too traditional."

She frowned. "It's just hot water and a tea bag."

"Don't say that in front of him. He'll collapse from shock." A small smile curved his mouth. "He brews it with clay pots and wooden scoops and everything. Watch him do it sometime. You'll be amazed at the man's patience."

She sipped the tea. It did taste a bit different—grassier and more fragrant. Maybe Al really was a zen master of green tea.

"My brother Mark is getting married next weekend. You should go."

She looked over at him. "I should?"

"It's a good idea to meet the Pryces in the area, figure out who's who. You are related to us, after all... even though it's by marriage and in a fairly convoluted way."

True enough. Maybe she really *should* go if Dane thought so as well.

"I know Mark didn't invite you, so you can come as my guest."

Uh oh. She hadn't seen that one coming. She cleared her throat and took another sip of her tea. "Um...yeah. Your father already asked."

"He *what?*"

"Asked me. To the wedding."

"Asshole," he muttered under his breath.

She blinked. *Asshole?*

When she got settled at her desk and checked Dane's agenda for the morning, a delivery came. Surprisingly, it was for her. She signed for it, then opened the package. It was a gorgeous bouquet of white tiger lilies.

She read the accompanying card.

Hope you like lilies.

– D

Roxie came in with some papers. "Nice flowers! Who're they from?"

Sophia shrugged, smiling for her coworker's sake. "Not really sure. Excuse me, I need to brief Dane on the day's agenda." She stuck the card in the stack in her arm and went inside his office before Roxie could pepper her with more questions.

Dane looked up from his coffee mug. "Yes?"

"Your morning agenda." She gave him the list.

Dane ran his eyes rapidly down the page. "Tell Stevenson I'm not going to meet him after all."

"Got it." She jotted a note down on her pad. "Before I go, I can ask you something?"

He nodded.

She showed him the card. "Is this 'D' you?"

"Yes."

"Why?"

A smile curled his lips. "I always sign cards that way, because 'DP' would send the wrong signal. I never, ever share."

She stood nonplussed for a moment before deciding that he'd misunderstood her question on purpose. But pressing him would be futile, especially since she had no idea what he was talking about. She nodded and returned to her desk, then googled "DP."

The search results made her jaw drop. *Double penetration.*

The entry also included "related acronyms," all designed to inform the naïve like her. DAP, double anal penetration. DVA—

Heat flooded her cheeks, and she closed the browser, holding her forehead in one hand.

Later that day, when she went to give him his afternoon coffee, she said, "You could've used your full name."

"I could have." His tone was as grave as a minister's, but his eyes twinkled. "But that would make it even more inappropriate. My middle name is Adam."

Her mouth formed an O as her cheeks grew hot.

"Don't worry. I'm not the only one in the family with shitty initials."

Was this one of the ways his parents had fought each other?

Sophia had been neglected, but none of her parents had actively used her to make a point with each other. Shame surged at the way she'd called him an entitled jerk who'd had too much privilege. Material abundance could never make up for emotional scars. She shouldn't have judged him without knowing anything about his personal struggles.

At six thirty, Dane pulled up at the restaurant where she'd made his reservation for that evening. "Let's go."

"Aren't you meeting someone?" she asked.

"Why would you think that?"

She looked at him. "You can't possibly mean to buy me dinner for the next two weeks."

"Of course I'm going to buy you dinner. It would be cruel to have you wait in the car while I eat." His voice dropped half an octave. "Like I said before, I don't like to eat with my family."

He meant he didn't like to eat with Salazar. Knowing what she knew, she couldn't blame him. She nodded and they went inside.

And so the rest of the week went. Roxie and Amy wanted to know who kept sending flowers to her in the morning, but Sophia demurred, not wanting to be the center of office gossip. She might not have much corporate work experience, but she knew any kind of romantic entanglement with a boss was a big deal.

Thankfully he was always so cold and formally polite that nobody in the office suspected he was the one behind all the bouquets. But he was impossible at the family house. He paraded around topless, stole danishes and slices of bacon from her plate every morning—making sure to somehow brush her with his arm or hand each time—and made double-entendres when saying good night. If all that wasn't bad enough, he spoiled Roco by sneaking him treats and taking him out for runs. She could withstand a lot, but kindness to Roco…

On Sunday, Dane was out playing fetch with her dog. Sophia went up to him, determined to put an end to the whole thing.

Her traitorous heart picked up its tempo at the sight of him scratching Roco behind the ears. The poodle's eyes had turned into slits of bliss. Then Dane stood and threw a stick halfway across the field they were in. Roco dashed off.

"Okay, you have to stop."

"Roco will be disappointed," he said, taking off his shirt and pretending to wipe imaginary sweat from his lean, muscular torso.

She flushed in spite of herself, and tried clearing her throat authoritatively. "I'm not talking about my dog, and you know it. What kind of game are you playing?"

"What makes you think it's a game?"

"You promised to treat me fairly, and now you're sending me flowers, playing with Roco..."

"Is it working?"

"If you're trying to drive me crazy, yes."

Dane laughed. "I'm treating you the way I would have if my father weren't in the picture. You should appreciate the time and effort I'm putting in. I've never bought flowers for a woman I wanted to sleep with."

His bald confession took her breath away. Her body tingled, and heat gathered between her thighs. "Is that what this is about? You're trying to get me to sleep with you?"

"I'm not trying to get you to do anything." Dane crouched and patted Roco as he brought the stick back. "The ball's entirely in your court. Yes, I want to sleep with you, but I'm not sure what you want." He threw the stick again, and Roco charged off, barking excitedly. Dane straightened and faced her. "You lost a lot after your father passed away, mostly the ability to do as you please. Your choices became limited. I don't want you to be pushed into something you aren't sure about." He rested a large, warm hand on the juncture of her neck and shoulder. "There are a lot of things we have no say in. Sex shouldn't be one of them."

"Then stop sending me flowers and taking me out to dinner."

"No. Flowers signal to other men that you already have someone who's very interested, and they cheer you up." He tilted his head. "Unless I've misjudged. Are diamonds more your thing?"

"Absolutely not!" she sputtered, thinking, *Better nip this in the bud.*

He moved the hand down and rubbed her back, the gesture comforting and caring. And suddenly she couldn't remember why she'd been upset with him. She hadn't been touched like this in so long that she hadn't even realized she missed it.

"Finally," he continued, "I don't eat with my family because I don't particularly enjoy indigestion. So the dinners aren't all for your sake."

"I don't understand you," she said. "It wasn't just your dad that made you change. You left without a word in Mexico."

Something in his expression shifted. "It's complicated."

"Complicated doesn't mean I won't understand. I'm not stupid."

"I never said you were." He took the stick from Roco and threw it again.

She narrowed her eyes when he didn't elaborate. All this mysterious behavior and lack of explanation was getting old. "Why didn't you say hello at Dad's funeral?"

His eyebrows rose. "You knew I was there?"

"I felt it."

"I didn't want to stir anything up." He looked at the wildflowers they were standing in. "Geraldine can hold a grudge for life. She married Julian despite her mother's opposition, and she's still angry that she proved Shirley right." Pain flitted through his gaze. "I promised Shirley I'd be kind to her. Her deathbed wish. Couldn't break it."

Sophia bit her lower lip, then tentatively put an arm around his waist and rested her head on his shoulder. He took her hand and squeezed. Elizabeth had been mistaken. Ice water didn't flow in his veins. He cared a great deal about his family; he'd just chosen not to show it.

Sweetness as thick as honey seeped through her, and she closed her eyes. She'd never been this emotionally in tune with another person before, and she didn't want anything to shatter the fragility of the moment.

On Wednesday morning, two bouquets arrived just as she returned to her desk from the break-room. Sophia signed for the one from "D" and then studied another one.

"You sure about this?" she asked the delivery man.

The guy snapped his gum. "Says two for Sophia Reed."

Why would Dane send two? It must've been a mistake. She opened the card on the other one—a bouquet of yellow chrysanthemums. Her heart started slamming against her chest, but she calmed herself. She'd been out of the spotlight long enough that it couldn't possibly be—

Hope you're doing well.
- Your greatest fan.

Her fingers shook. There was only one person who signed his cards that way. He had been one of her most persistent stalkers. Chad had spent a lot of time and money trying to find out who he really was, but everything had led to a dead end.

Goosebumps rose along her spine. *He* knew where she was, and now she no longer had Chad to keep her safe.

"These aren't mine," she said, pushing the chrysanthemums back at the delivery man.

"You sure? Aren't you Sophia Reed?"

"Doesn't matter." She hugged herself. "Look, they aren't mine. Take them back." Just then her mobile buzzed. "I have to answer this. Just...please. I can't sign for them."

"All right." He shrugged but took the flowers.

Taking a deep breath to calm herself, Sophia checked her phone. *Oh no*, she thought as she saw the new text.

It was from George.

She deleted it, unread. Why was he contacting her now? They had nothing to say to each other. It'd be better if they could pretend they didn't know each other.

"Hello? Earth to Sophia."

She snapped her head around. Roxie was peering at her. "Are you okay?"

Sophia managed a smile. "Yeah. Fine."

"You look like you saw a ghost. Why don't you sit down?" Roxie pulled a chair over.

Sophia didn't object. Her legs felt like pasta noodles. When her phone buzzed again, she turned it off.

"Are you sure you're okay?" Roxie asked.

"Yes, I'm fine. Do you have time to go over the Havergill memo?" Sophia said, desperate to not think about George or the stalker. "I want to make sure it looks okay."

Roxie gave her a couple of raised eyebrows, but nodded. "Okay. Let's check it over."

TWENTY-FOUR

Sophia kept herself busy all day long. She didn't want even a second of down time to dwell on the incidents that morning.

Dane finally emerged from a series of meetings and came over to her desk. Sophia glanced at the clock on her laptop. Six thirty sharp.

"Ready to head out?" he asked.

She nodded, and they left together. If her coworkers noticed that she always left with him, they didn't comment.

She still couldn't get used to the Lamborghini, although she was better at controlling her nerves.

"You're extra tense today," he said, his voice casual.

"Before you start, it's not the car," she said. "I was just thinking about something."

The stalker and George had been leering at her from the back of her mind no matter how she tried to not let them. She didn't know how to shove them out of her head. Before, she'd had Chad to handle stuff like this. Most people didn't want to mess with him, and his menacing glare had been enough to keep almost everyone away.

The fact that the stalker had found where she worked made her palms slick. *It's okay*, she told herself. He'd never get to her so long as she wasn't alone. She knew Dane would keep her safe.

As for George, he probably didn't know where she was. And that was good enough.

She pulled out her phone and stared at the dark screen. She hadn't turned it back on since the morning. Maybe…just possibly…he'd texted to say he was sorry. He knew she was his sister's best friend. He'd also looked up to her father.

Keep dreaming. He knew all that before he tried to rape you.

The engine died; the interior of the car plunged into silence. She looked up and blinked at the underground parking garage. She dropped her phone into her purse. "Where are we?"

"At my penthouse," he said. "I need to get something."

She considered waiting for him in the car for about a nano-second, then climbed out. The last thing she wanted to do was stay in this concrete, tomb-like place alone. And she had to admit she was curious about his home. Was it as dignified as the family mansion, or was it more contemporary and chic? Maybe it was like an igloo, since he wanted people to think he was cold and unfeeling.

He entered his key code, and the lock mechanism clicked and opened. He went inside and checked an electric panel. "Feel free to look around." He slipped into a room.

Okay, so I'll look around. The wraparound floor-to-ceiling glass panes provided a stunning view of the city, just like he had at the office. Buildings shone like jewels while the traffic streaked the dark with bright reds and whites.

The penthouse was mostly a frosty white, with some pale blue and a dark wood that reminded her of teak flooring she'd seen overseas. There was a bare mantle over an unused gas fireplace. An enormous TV occupied most of the wall facing a couple of white leather couches. A series of glass sculptures in various vivid colors sat in niches.

As she leaned closer to examine them, Dane emerged. She almost couldn't breathe at how amazing he looked. He'd lost his suit jacket and cufflinks; his sleeves were rolled all the way to his elbows. He'd undone a couple of buttons of his shirt, creating a V that framed his throat and chest.

She'd always thought he was way too tempting in the morning, all topless and bare muscles glistening with sweat. But this semi-casual look was even more lethal. She knew exactly what was under the shirt, and her fingers itched to undo the rest of the buttons and push the snowy fabric aside to reveal the entirety of him.

Don't even go there. She gestured at the glass

pieces. "Original?" she asked, her voice somewhat hoarse.

"Commissioned pieces." He went to a kitchen that was all fancy stainless steel appliances and marble countertops. "Help yourself to whatever's in the bar."

Glad for something to do, she went over and poured herself some cold orange juice.

There was nothing personal about the space other than the sculptures. They were modern, abstract with no discernible, easy-to-describe shape. But they made her feel something—a tight restraint over overwhelming emotions.

Dane checked his oven. "Has it been on all day?" she asked, noticing the light.

"Just for the last twenty minutes or so. I can control it remotely." He heated a big stainless steel pan on the gas stove and pulled out a package of beef from the fridge. There was also a bottle of wine that he opened and started to decant.

She sipped her juice. "What are you doing?"

"Isn't it obvious?"

Okay. "Let me rephrase. I thought you just wanted to pick something up. Why are you cooking? We have a reservation."

"No, we don't. I canceled it. I didn't want to drag you to the oyster house because it's overly crowded, and the oysters aren't that good this time of year."

"Do you need some help?" she asked, even though the only thing she could cook was cheese omelets. Chad had taught her how to make them, saying they were versatile enough to be served as any meal of the day.

A corner of Dane's mouth lifted. "Don't worry. I've yet to poison anyone."

"That's reassuring."

"Medium rare?" he asked.

"Please."

She took a seat at the big dining table. It was set for two people, with heavy silverware and linen napkins. A clear vase of pale pink roses and baby's breath occupied the center.

"Nice flowers, but…they don't seem like your thing."

"No. But I thought they might be yours."

Somehow it was the perfect comment, and she found herself relaxing. She pulled out a stem. What *was* it about him that got to her like this? Was it the talk he'd given her about choices? She'd had very little freedom. She'd gone where people had told her to, kept to herself more than she might have because of stalkers. No one, not even Chad, had worried about her prerogatives. As long as she'd skated well, they hadn't cared.

A sliver of apprehension pierced her heart. *Careful, Sophia*. Dane had so much power over her. She didn't think he would deliberately abuse it, but at the same time he wouldn't be gentle either. That just… wasn't his style.

The meat was sizzling on the pan, and Dane checked the timer. "It's come to my attention that you haven't finished college."

Sophia buried her nose in the rose, inhaled its fragrance. "Um…no, I haven't. Going back to school wasn't an option. Is that a problem?"

"Could be. I don't hire dropouts."

Her mouth dried. She'd asked him to treat her fairly. He might've decided that she should have the same qualifications as everyone else at the company.

"Of course, you could finish while working."

"I plan to go back," she said quickly.

"When?"

"When I have some money saved and…stuff." She forced a smile. "I'll need to transfer."

The timer beeped, and he flipped the meat. "What's wrong with your old school?"

"Wasn't the right program for me. Also, it's in Seattle."

She didn't want to be in the same state as George, much less the same town. She'd assumed he'd given up. Why now…what had changed? She hated how he'd contacted her on the exact same day her stalker had sent flowers. It made her feel doubly vulnerable.

She hugged herself. It was her responsibility to keep herself safe.

Dane looked up from the meat. "Did something happen in Seattle?"

"No." She forced a smile. "Why would you think that?"

"Because it seems odd to leave the one place where you're most likely to have friends and people who could help you."

She shrugged. "I was always at rinks and competitions. Didn't really spend much time in Seattle." That was true enough, and she hoped he wouldn't catch on what hadn't been said. Dane seemed to have a very accurate internal lie detector.

He put the entire pan in the oven, then brought the bottle of wine over to the table. The label said *Mouton, 1959.*

"If you want, I can arrange to have you transferred to UCLA. It's close, and it's a great school."

It didn't seem like he was going to make a big deal about it, and the sense of gratitude that suddenly flooded her gave her pause. "You don't have to."

"I know that. But I want to." He poured the wine into the two glasses set on the table.

"Why? Do you want me to be as employable as possible so you can get rid of me?" she half-joked. If she wasn't working for him, it might make it easier for him to seduce her.

"I'm not trying to get rid of you. But it's a good idea to have something other than figure skating on your résumé if you plan to work in the corporate world. College dropouts look sexy if you're a tech genius, but otherwise they're pretty pathetic."

"You're right. I'll think about it." She took one of the glasses and breathed in the wine. "Wow. This is… complex."

Dane stuck his nose in the glass and inhaled slowly. "There are a lot of elements. Cassis, chocolate…cedar…a hint of flowers."

She sampled it slowly. She wasn't too crazy about red wine, but this was excellent, with just the right balance of fruit and spice. "I meant what I said. I plan to move out as soon as I can. I may need help finding a safe apartment, that's all."

"I'd be happy to help if you want." He laid out a basket of bread and grabbed a bowl of salad from the fridge.

"When did you make that?" she asked.

"I didn't."

The oven dinged, and Dane went to check up on the meat. Soon he came back with two plates of steak.

He dipped his head and pressed a kiss to her mouth. The feel of his lips on hers sent a *zing* through her body. Before she could do more than gasp, he pulled back. "Happy birthday, Sophia."

He placed a plate in front of her, and she shook herself mentally. "How did you know?" she asked, her voice scratchy.

"The HR file. Surprised you haven't said anything about it."

"I didn't even realize."

He gave her a skeptical look. "You're still young enough for birthdays to be special. You just don't want to remember."

Wow. Talk about hitting the bull's eye. "What's so special about it?" she said, trying to act nonchalant. "Today's just like any other day."

The only person who'd ever bothered to remember had been Chad. She'd preferred to focus on her training or something—anything to distract herself on the day that reminded her how insignificant she was to her parents. Competitions always came first, of course, but other skaters at the rink had still gotten presents from their parents or spent time with them. Not her.

She didn't have to turn on the phone to know Betsy hadn't bothered with a text.

"Still. Thank you." She cut into her steak. There wasn't any fancy sauce, and the seasoning consisted of simple salt and pepper. But the meat was tender and juicy, and nothing got in the way of its natural flavor. "This is excellent."

"It's one of the few things I can make well."

"You don't strike me as the domestic type."

"I'm not, but there are times I want to eat alone, and I absolutely despise birthday meals in restaurants."

She watched him over the rim of her glass. "You don't like the production. The waiters all singing."

"If I want to hear people sing something they don't believe, I prefer to spend my money on people who can sing well."

"I don't like it either."

"Not for the same reasons," he mused. "I'd say you don't like the attention."

Another point for Dane. "You're right."

"It's a bit surprising, actually."

"Why?"

"Most women love being in the spotlight. At least for a day."

"Spotlights are *hot*. And overrated. Might as well tattoo 'stalk me' on my forehead." She knew the price of fame all too well. She took a slow sip of her drink. "It's interesting how nice and charming you can be."

"Nice and charming? Oh, good." Dane actually looked slightly gratified. "I wasn't sure if I was pulling it off. I never had to be either. Men only care about what I can do for their careers, and women are only interested in what I can buy them. I could look like a cross between Quasimodo and a rabid hyena, and women would still want me."

His words were flat, almost factual, like he was reading the label of an aspirin bottle. But a corner of his mouth curled, his eyes hooded.

She reached over and held his hand. "I'd treat you the same even if you didn't have any money at all."

DANE LOOKED DOWN. SOPHIA'S HAND WAS MUCH smaller than his, and much more delicate, but somehow it seemed to be more powerful. "I know."

What was it about this woman that made him believe? If anybody else had said it, he would've laughed in their face for the obvious lie.

He'd never felt any compulsion to go out of his way to care for someone. He'd watched over his siblings because that had been Shirley's wish. He'd made sure Salazar didn't kill himself with booze over the divorce because, again, Shirley had wanted it. But he'd never, ever felt the innate need to think of someone until Sophia. Maybe that was the reason he hadn't been able to shrug it off when Salazar had acted like he and Sophia were an item.

And Dane still didn't know what to do about the fact that she made him want to be sweeter and gentler, two things he considered pointless and had sworn he'd never be. But when Sophia softened her gaze or held his hand or smiled at him, everything inside him warmed. It wasn't just sexual—he knew how he felt when he wanted sex. This was far more complex.

He shook himself mentally.

Life was far simpler and easier to compartmentalize when he dealt with facts and numbers. Seeking approval and acceptance from others was the surest way to living in a kind of hell. He'd wasted the first six years of his life on that sort of thing, and he didn't plan on repeating the mistake.

Suddenly uncomfortable, he put his utensils down. He had finished his steak anyway, and wasn't interested in the salad. "More wine?"

"Sure." She smiled. "It's my birthday. I'll splurge."

He poured her another glass. "You should splurge every day. Life's short."

"That it is." She sighed, then took a long swallow of her wine. "This is a perfect birthday dinner. Thank you."

She leaned over, her mouth about to brush his cheek. *Keep it platonic*, he thought, *just like with the earlier birthday kiss*. He'd told her he'd let her decide.

But he couldn't resist. He turned and their lips met.

Instead of pulling away, she pressed closer, her flesh soft and sweet. He ran his tongue over her lips, tasting the glorious wine and even more glorious flavor of her.

His heart pounded. He deepened the kiss, and she devoured him back, her mouth turning aggressive on his.

Blood throbbed, a sharp need gripping his entire body. *Jesus.* He needed to rein in the situation before things got out of hand.

"Sophia. Don't do this if you're going to regret it tomorrow," he whispered against her cheek.

She pulled back, her eyes searching his. "Are you going to regret it?"

There were so many reasons why he should. She was his employee, and he never, ever crossed that line. In addition, she was in a vulnerable situation—poor, homeless…no friends she could turn to. Unlike the other women he'd fucked and dumped, Sophia didn't understand his MO. If he took her again, he'd be responsible for her in ways that he'd never been for anyone else before.

The last thought should've killed his libido. The idea of signaling anything even remotely serious and long-term had always made him cut a relationship short. But none of the other women had been Sophia.

"No," he said.

"Then I won't regret it either."

"Thank god you aren't sensible," he muttered before reclaiming her luscious lips.

He devoured them, hungry for every inch, all the texture, every taste. Sharp need streaked through him. His senses hyper-focused on her reactions. Her hands clutched him, almost clumsy with desperation.

Their mouths still fused, he stood, drawing her up with him, and cupped her ass. She wrapped her strong skater's legs around his waist, and he could feel the damp heat through their clothes. Desire pounded through him, and it was all he could do to not rip their clothes off, shove her up against the wall and have her right there.

He carried her, every step making his cock rub against her folds. Her chest vibrated with a suppressed moan. Heat flushed her cheeks and neck, and her eyes sparkled with excitement and need.

He paused at the stairs. He'd never taken a woman into his bedroom—that was what the guest suite was for. But he didn't want her where all the other women had been.

He went into the master suite. The dim lights came on at their entrance, and Sophia reached for his shirt buttons.

"Patience," he muttered.

"I've waited long enough."

"It hasn't even been half an hour."

"Wrong. It's been weeks." She scraped her teeth over his earlobe. "I made myself come with my fingers after the charity function," she whispered, lips next to his ear. "But it was nowhere near enough."

Fuck. The image of her, naked and writhing while masturbating to him was nearly his undoing. *What a waste.* She should've called him. They would've had a much more satisfying time together.

He reined himself in. He'd never lost control over a woman, and he didn't plan to start now, especially not with Sophia. Women were all the same once he'd had them undressed and on their knees with their mouths wrapped around his dick. But somehow Sophia was different. She was the first one to make him want more than easy, uncomplicated sex.

Deliberately, he undid the buttons on her top and let it drop to the floor with a whisper. The skirt was next. She stood before him, so delicious and ready, with nothing but a lacy pink bra and matching panties. Small tremors went through every creamy dip and mound. She was softer and fuller than three years ago, her body ripe.

Unhooking her bra, he kissed her shoulder. Despite her strong muscles and athletic achievements, everything about her was fine and delicate. Her injuries spoke volumes about how fragile she could be.

His lips trailed down her body, his tongue flickering over a pebbled nipple. He pulled down her panties, then pressed his mouth against her hip.

She dug her hands into his hair. "Are you kissing all my owies?"

"Mmm-hmm." He looked into her eyes. "I don't think anybody has, and every owie deserves a kiss."

TWENTY-FIVE

Sophia blinked as a hot lump clogged her throat. Nobody had ever said that to her. She was the girl who got up every time she fell, who pasted on a smile and moved on like nothing had happened. She wasn't supposed to hurt or shed tears.

But somehow this man, who people said had ice water in his veins, seemed to know what outwardly sympathetic people didn't.

Her legs grew shaky, and she fell to her knees, bringing their bodies closer. Her small hands cradled his cheeks, and she sought his mouth. Her hard nipples stabbed against his chest, and her fingers undid his shirt buttons, pushing the garment out of the way. Electric shocks went through her body when her hands touched his bare chest. Who would've thought that simple skin-to-skin contact could feel this good?

He dragged his hand along the smooth line of her body until his fingers brushed between her legs. She was unbelievably wet and hot down there, but she didn't feel any shame, not when he looked at her with such naked desire.

His thumb circled over her swollen clit. A small cry tore from her, her teeth biting into her lower lip.

"You're fucking gorgeous," he whispered against her jaw line as he peppered it with feathery kisses.

"You make me feel gorgeous. Whole."

With him, she wasn't the damaged girl with broken dreams. She was a woman desired, a woman on her way to figuring out the rest of her life.

He picked her up and deposited her in the center of the bed. Impatiently he shrugged out of his shirt. The rest of his clothes received the same careless treatment. He kneeled on the bed and picked her foot up.

Self-consciousness suddenly shot through her. Her feet had gotten better, but they were awful from years of abuse. And she hated the thought of having them compared to his other women, who undoubtedly had soft, well-cared for feet—

Dane pressed a thumb into her instep. "Relax," he murmured.

Sophia bit back a moan. That felt amazing.

"I like everything about you."

"You're such a liar," she said, her voice breathless. "I'm not blind to my...deficiencies."

"You've done interesting things with your life. It's no shame your body bears the marks." He pressed a hot kiss against her not-so-straight ankle.

Her heart knocked against its ribcage. How could he talk to her like this? He was the last one she'd expected to say something so sweet. Knowing how he hated lies and pretenses, she knew he meant everything.

He showed the same tender, sexy care to her other leg, then slowly moved upward, her ankles resting on his shoulders, then her knees, licking and loving every inch of her along the way.

Her nerves jittered in anticipation.

His breath fanned over her clit, and she bit her lower lip. She didn't dare move or make any sound lest this was a dream. This might be the part where she woke up.

He covered her with his mouth and her body surged with pleasure. Before she could muffle herself with a hand, he gripped her wrists.

"Let me hear you," he said, then pulled her clit into his mouth.

She was completely exposed, her legs wide apart. His wicked mouth and tongue moved along her dripping flesh, lapping up every drop. Her hands twisted around the sheets underneath. She couldn't stop her breathless whimpers.

"Please—"

"Don't waste your hands," he said. "Play with your tits. Make yourself feel even better."

Heat suffused her face and torso, and at first she didn't move. But when he merely waited while gently breathing over her, she couldn't help herself. She cupped her breasts, kneading them. "Dane..."

"Pinch your nipples," he ordered as he pushed a

finger into her. When she hesitated, he stopped, making her cry out in protest. "Show me how you pleasure your body. Now."

DANE HELD HIMSELF BACK. THE SWEET TASTE OF her on his tongue was urging him to go back down on her, but he wanted to see how she'd made herself come that night.

It was her birthday, for fuck's sake, and he should just give her everything now, but he was a selfish bastard.

She squeezed her breasts, then pinched the tips with her forefinger and thumb. The nipples reddened, and when she let go, they stayed tightly puckered.

Her dark and lust-glazed eyes made his blood boil. Unable to wait even a moment longer, he devoured her flesh. A delicious gasp from her parted lips drove him forward, and he fucked her with his tongue while using a slick finger to press against her tight rosette.

She let out a sharp cry, her back arching. Her muscles contracted tightly around him. Blood pounded in his cock, so hard he could have used it to hammer railroad spikes.

She pulled him up for a kiss, gripping him with desperation. "I want to feel you inside me," she whispered. "*Now*. I feel like I've waited forever."

When she arched and twisted in wanton

invitation, he couldn't hold back. He put on a condom and sank into her swollen, juicy depths. She trembled around him, her inner muscles like a slick fist around his cock.

He cursed under his breath. "You feel amazing."

"So do you."

His control slipped. All he wanted to do was pound into her, rut like an animal. But she deserved so much better. He held back and pulled her nipple into his mouth, trapping and suckling it. She whimpered, then cried out.

"Please," she begged. "I want you so much."

Damn it. He squeezed his eyes shut as the tight reins of self-control snapped. He'd meant to go slowly, steadily, so their breaths mingled and bodies glided along each other until they went crazy. But he couldn't resist her impassioned urging.

He pulled out until only the tip of his cock remained, then slammed into her, hilting himself. He watched carefully, making sure he wasn't hurting her—he was so much larger—but she merely clutched him and met his thrust with a sharp inhalation that he knew wasn't from pain.

All right.

He drove into her over and over again, angling himself to make sure he hit her most sensitive spots. He wanted to make her come with a hard, primal fucking, with his dick buried deep inside her. He wanted her to become addicted to him, just like he was to her. He couldn't even pretend he'd been doing things for a reason other than his desire for her.

Even with her under him and crying out with pleasure, he wasn't fully satisfied. He wanted her in ways that made his heart twist, like there was a shard digging into it.

A strong climax gripped her, and she shattered in his arms, her inner muscles milking him. He was so damn close; all he had to do was let go, but he couldn't. He wanted to see her come again.

Before she could descend from her high, he increased the speed and depth of his thrusts, angling up so he rubbed her G-spot every time. When another orgasm crashed through her, he finally emptied himself inside her.

Even as physical fulfillment burned through him, another kind of hunger gnawed in his gut. And he knew he'd finally done something he'd sworn never to do—want someone's heart.

When Dane returned to bed after cleaning up in the bathroom, Sophia curled around him, wrapping him in her arms and resting her head over his heart. He generally didn't care for women clinging to him after sex, but somehow it was okay—even enjoyable—with Sophia.

He pulled her closer; she pressed a kiss to his

chest. His heart was still beating too fast. Or maybe it was the effect of having her near him like this. He'd assumed that she was like a splinter under his fingernail—something that nagged at his attention but would be easy enough to get rid of. Now he knew that wasn't true.

"Do you want to go on a getaway this weekend? We can stay until the end of the next week," he asked, drawing a sheet over them. His calendar was full for the coming week, but he didn't give a damn. He wanted to go away, just her and him, with no one else in the way.

"Mmm, sounds nice." She looked up at him. "Where?"

"Paris, maybe?"

The skin between her eyebrows furrowed, and she lowered her eyes. But then she laughed. "We can't go that far. Don't you have to go to Mark's wedding?"

"They don't want me there, trust me."

"Who said that? Mark or Hilary?"

He frowned. "Oh, they're *saying* they want me there, but trust me, they don't. Paris is vastly more entertaining. Food. Culture. History." He paused. "Romance," he added, with an exaggerated French accent.

She giggled. "Come on. You can't skip your brother's wedding."

"Sure I can. They're used to it."

"How many weddings have you skipped?"

"No actual weddings so far, but I don't bother to

attend most of the family stuff. They don't expect me to show these days."

"That's sad," Sophia said quietly. "I don't have siblings, but if I did, I'd spend as much time as I could with them."

"Forget siblings." He kissed her, trying to drag her mind away from his family. "You. Me. Paris. Didn't you say you wanted to travel? I don't think you've had much time to do that over the last three years."

"No, but I've been to Paris already. I don't really want to go back."

He had an odd feeling she hadn't meant to say the last part. "Why not?"

She sighed. "That's where I had the car accident that ended my competitive career."

"I'm sorry."

"It was a long time ago." She forced a smile.

"Wanna talk about it?" The question slipped from him before he could think it through. He never invited women to talk about their problems. He never cared, never wanted to know.

She was quiet for so long, he thought she didn't. And strangely enough it bothered him that she didn't want to talk about it.

"The Trophée Éric Bompard. It's a skating competition, one of the top ones. Usually happens in the fall, and that year it was in early November. I entered and I won. It was thrilling because it was the first competition of the Olympic season, and it was important to start on the right foot. Afterwards, I was on my way to the airport. The cabbie was speeding. I think he was impatient because I told him I was running late and I'd promised him a big tip if he could get me there fast. I didn't want to miss my flight home. Then we were hit by some rich guy in a red Lamborghini, which was also speeding from what I understand. I don't really remember…everything after the accident is sort of hazy."

Dane's mouth went dry. "Did you say a red Lamborghini?"

She nodded. "I saw it. It T-boned the taxi."

"Jesus." Apprehension cut through him. He'd been driving a red Lamborghini when he'd gotten into his accident in Paris.

Five million dollars. Nobody paid that kind of money unless it was death or something similar. But five million could've been the price for killing her Olympic dream.

Stop jumping to conclusions, he told himself. It could've been some other driver. He wasn't the only person in Paris who had a red Lamborghini. It could all just have been a coincidence.

"Hey, it's okay." She forced a smile. "It was a long time ago."

"How long?" he asked, unable to help himself.

"Seven years."

He swallowed, light-headed. It couldn't possibly be…

"I don't really think about it," she added.

Not much more than him, undoubtedly.

He shook himself and spooned her, kissing her shoulder. "Get some sleep. We still have to get up early tomorrow."

"Shouldn't we call or something? Let them know we aren't coming home?"

The last thing he wanted to do was call Al. "They're used to me doing whatever I want. We're fine."

She nodded, stretched, and soon drifted to sleep. When he was sure she was dead to the world, he slipped out of bed.

Restlessness rode him. He dragged his hands through his hair.

Okay, let's not get ahead of ourselves here. He didn't *know* anything. It could be just a coincidence.

Right. He should just crawl back into bed and get some sleep. He really should.

Except…

How many red Lamborghinis had hit a taxi in Paris that particular November?

AFTER TWO SCOTCHES TO BOLSTER HIMSELF, DANE called Henry Wagner's personal cell phone.

After three rings came Henry's sleep-heavy voice. "Hello, Dane. Is everything all right?"

"That depends. I need to verify something."

Henry yawned, but he didn't complain. He was a partner at Rosenbaum, McCracken, Wagner, and Associates. "Sure. Go ahead."

"My car accident in Paris. You handled it yourself, didn't you?"

"That's right, along with some associates from our firm in Paris." Henry didn't sound so sleepy anymore.

"Name or names of the people in the taxi. What were they?"

A slight pause. "I don't remember," Henry's tone was Teflon-smooth. "It was so long ago."

"Then remember by COB tomorrow and call me."

"The files are in storage in our Paris office. It's going to take at least a week or so to pull the information."

"Are you telling me it's not in a digital database?"

"That's right. I feel bad saying this, but I don't think I can help you if you need the information right now."

Did the lawyer think Dane was stupid? Henry had a memory like a bear trap—once information entered his brain, it never left.

"They were paid five million dollars, Henry," Dane said quietly. "It makes you sick to your stomach if you have to cough up five cents more than you have to. Are you telling me you honestly have no clue?"

"Sorry. Like I said, it was seven years ago."

Dane hung up, not interested in bullshit excuses.

Henry wouldn't have tossed five million bucks out there without an okay from somebody with a lot of monetary control in the family. Since Dane hadn't known about it, that left either Shirley or Salazar.

Dane started dialing his father's number, then stopped. If Henry was keeping quiet, it was due to a strict directive from someone in the family. The only person alive he'd obey like this was Salazar, and Salazar was the last one who'd tell Dane what he wanted to know.

He thought for a moment, chin in hand, then dialed Benjamin Clark. He needed a dossier on his accident ASAP, and nobody could get it faster than the family's PI. After the beep, Dane left specific instructions for the PI to follow.

Once he was finished, he pressed a corner of his phone against his temple. Then he noticed Sophia's purse and texted a few orders to the concierge service his family used.

It was already one o'clock; sleep was the next order of business. There was nothing more to do until Benjamin got back to him.

But he couldn't force himself to go back to bed. His muscles were too tense, and his nerves wouldn't settle. So many horrific possibilities were rattling around in his head. And no matter how he sliced and diced it, things didn't end well.

TWENTY-SIX

Sophia awoke, and opened her eyes blearily. The bedside clock glowed 03:10. She turned over...then realized Dane wasn't there. She reached out a hand; his side of the bed was cool.

For a moment, she'd thought he'd left, but this was his home. She shrugged into a robe she found in the master bathroom and went to the living room. The table was cleared of everything, and she frowned. Had Dane gotten up to clean up?

Then she heard it—a soft whirring and dull rhythmic slapping of rubber against rubber. Following the sound, she opened the door to another room. It was a home gym with a dark night view of Los Angeles. Dane was on a treadmill, facing the window and running. Sweat dripped down his bare torso in rivulets. Three empty sports drink bottles lay on the floor.

His motions were pure art, his biomechanics perfect. He would've made a great athlete if that had been his passion.

But his expression… It wasn't that of a man enjoying himself, or even someone merely focused on exercise. Desperation and something else she couldn't identify showed in his eyes.

He noticed her and stopped the machine. "What are you doing here, Sophia? Did the sound wake you up?"

She shook her head. "I just woke up." She handed him a towel from the built-in rack. "Why are you running at this hour? Didn't you say we have to get up early?"

"Sorry. Couldn't sleep."

His tone was too casual, too cool. Something must've been bothering him, but she couldn't begin to guess.

"Are you upset I said no to Paris?" she said, trying for levity. "Ask me again, and I just might say yes."

Just as she'd hoped, he smiled. "You don't have to go someplace you don't like just for me."

You shouldn't say such sweet things, she thought. It was harder to keep her heart locked if he wasn't even slightly selfish.

She held his hand. "Let's shower and go to bed."

"The two of us? I'm sweaty, but you seem okay."

"It'll save water, and I won't have to do it in the morning."

She gave him an impish smile as she pulled him toward the master bathroom. He didn't resist. Dumping their clothes on the tiled floor, they walked into a huge glass stall with multiple chrome showerheads, and soon warm water was cascading down their naked bodies. He poured some kind of green shampoo into his hands and washed her hair, massaging her scalp. She closed her eyes and moaned softly. It felt good…too good actually.

He rinsed her hair and washed her body this time, paying particular attention to her breasts. His soapy thumb brushed over her hardened nipple. She gasped as slick heat started pooling between her legs again.

"Bad boy," she murmured. "You're supposed to make yourself clean." She pumped body soap into her hands and rubbed it all over his hard body. A faint scent of pine and spices filled the stall. "I'm going to smell like your soap."

"I like that," he said against her wet neck, his tongue lapping at the water droplets.

"So do I." She reached down and fisted his hard cock.

A breath hissed out of him, and he pumped into her hand. She ran her thumb over the slit at the tip. The slick precum coated her skin. What would he be like in her mouth?

Almost instinctively, she dropped to her knees. The strong column of his neck worked as he looked down at her, his eyes bright.

She flicked her tongue over the bulbous head. "You know, I just realized I never got to taste you." Her hand wrapped around his shaft. It was so thick and long, she couldn't believe it fit her so perfectly. "And you got to have me twice." She dragged a fingernail along the underside of his cock. "Hardly seems fair."

She pulled the head into her mouth, working her tongue over it like a lollipop. He made a low guttural sound and wrapped her wet hair around his fist. She wondered for a moment if he was going to try to have her mouth at his pace, but he kept himself in check.

Humming her appreciation at his control, she took more of him until he filled her completely. He was salty with a hint of musk. The tight, flat muscles in his abs jerked as she hollowed her cheeks and sucked.

She palmed his balls and bobbed her head, desperate to make him feel as good as he'd made her when he'd gone down on her. She wanted him to forget whatever that had been bugging him enough to make him run so late at night. Rough breathing and the guttural groan rumbling in his chest urged her on.

"Make yourself feel good, Sophia," he said. "I want to feel you come with my dick in your mouth."

Heat sizzled along her spine. She put a hand between her legs. Her folds were already drenched.

She fingered herself, just the way he had. Her fingers curled, hitting the spot he'd hit with his cock earlier. Her lungs worked harder to drag in more air, and she increased the tempo of her mouth and hand. The tendons in his neck stood out as he clenched his teeth, and she knew he was very, very close.

And he'd never let go until she'd gotten off first.

"Come for me," he ordered, his voice harsh.

An orgasm crashed through her. As she rode one wave after another, he tightened his hold on her hair and pumped in and out, his pelvic muscles flexing. She felt his balls tighten, and at the final instant he pulled out, spurting all over her chest.

The warm water washed away his hot seed. He pulled her up and kissed her hard. "You drive me crazy," he said.

She smiled. "So do you."

He rested his forehead against hers. They breathed in each other's air for what felt like an eternity. Finally she pulled back and cut the water. "Think you can sleep now?"

He nodded. They dried each other and went back to bed. She curled around him, wishing she could heal his wounds so he'd never be compelled to run like that again.

SOPHIA GOT UP EARLY AS USUAL, THEN GRIMACED as she surveyed her clothes on the floor.

"What's wrong?" Dane murmured, still lying on his side of the bed.

"My clothes." She picked up her top and skirt. "They look so…wrinkled and worn."

He yawned. "Don't worry."

"Says the man with a closet full of fresh clothes."

"You've got some, too."

"I do?"

He sat up. "They should've delivered them by now."

He put on his robe and went to the entrance. She trailed after him. Sure enough, there were three boxes by the door, all with a gold-over-black logo that looked pricey. She didn't recognize the brand, but Dane had expensive tastes.

"There you go. That should take care of your problem."

"When did you order these?" she asked in awe.

"Last night." He picked them up and placed them on the coffee table. "See if they're acceptable. If not, I'll have another set delivered."

She opened them one by one. The first box held lingerie—a lacy white bra and matching panties... plus a garter belt that made her raise her eyebrows—and work clothes. A green silk blouse and a mustard skirt went surprisingly well together, and the material felt luxurious and soft against her skin. The second box had a pair of ballet flats, and the final box had a makeup kit.

"And everything the perfect size," she mused. "How did you know?"

"Well," he said, looking somewhat smug and self-satisfied, "I did touch you more or less everywhere."

She flushed. "Calibrated hands?"

"You could say that. Are they acceptable?"

"They're gorgeous. Thank you. You think of everything."

He dropped a kiss on her forehead. "They're nothing. Belated birthday present."

"Last night wasn't it?"

"I think I enjoyed myself too much to call it a present for you." He grinned.

It was so unexpectedly sweet and boyish that she almost couldn't breathe. *People are wrong about him*, she decided. He'd just never allowed himself to show his warm side. And why would he, when he'd been told he should never have been born by the one person who should've loved him the most?

She swallowed a small lump in her throat and smiled. "I'll make breakfast. Why don't you get ready?"

"We can just grab something on the way."

"I insist." She tiptoed and kissed him on the mouth before she could stop herself. "I can do a mean omelet."

DANE COULDN'T SAY NO TO AN OMELET, ESPECIALLY one that Sophia made. She puttered around in the kitchen, while he returned to the bedroom to get dressed.

As he put on his cufflinks, a small voice said it wasn't like him to enjoy a domestic scene. He hated it when women didn't get the hint and leave as soon as sex was over, and he always showered afterward so he could rest without any lingering remnant of them on himself.

But Sophia was different. He didn't want her to leave, and he didn't want to wash her away either. He held the bed-sheet to his nose. It smelled faintly of her. He should leave a note to housekeeping not to wash it.

Don't get stupidly sentimental. You don't know what Benjamin's going to say.

The cold reminder stopped him in his tracks. He pulled out his phone. Nothing from Benjamin yet. It had happened seven years ago. Sophia might have been mistaken about the other car being a red Lamborghini. After all, she'd said a lot of things were sort of hazy. She could've confused a Ferrari or something for a Lamborghini. And she'd said it had happened in the evening. Harder to see at dusk...

He rubbed his face. There was no reason to think the worst—and such pessimism wasn't like him. If Sophia had received five million dollars seven years ago, would she be in the dire financial situation she was now? Probably not. He should just wait and not spoil the happiness he'd found with her.

TWENTY-SEVEN

DANE WOULD'VE PREFERRED TO KEEP Sophia away from the family mansion, but she was worried about Roco. So after sushi for dinner later that day, he drove them back to Salazar's house.

"You know, Al's very good with dogs," Dane said.

"But Roco's my responsibility. I'm sure he misses his mommy."

Dane gave up. He wasn't going to win against her sense of responsibility, and it was cute and endearing that she took her dog-parenting so seriously.

"Did you ever have a pet growing up?" she asked.

"We weren't allowed."

"Was it because your mother was afraid that they might break something?"

"No. Dad didn't want any."

"Oh."

"There are a lot of things that he lets you do that we weren't allowed to do."

She was quiet for a moment. "Was that why you thought he and I were together?"

"Something like that. The Aston Martin you drove is very rare. Same model that Sean Connery's double-oh-seven drove. Iain, Mark and Shane would all give their left nuts to take it out for a spin."

"I had no idea."

"I know." He hadn't believed it before, but now he did.

By the time they reached the house, it was a little past nine. Al as usual was waiting for them, his back ramrod straight. The man could teach posture to ballet dancers.

"Sir, a special courier came by half an hour ago to deliver this." He handed Dane a brown envelope.

Dane glanced at the address. His heartbeat skittered.

Benjamin Clark.

Damn. That was fast.

Sweat dampened Dane's hands, but he gave Sophia a smile. "I need to review this."

He made a left turn to the family room with a few plushy armchairs and couches. After closing the door to make sure he was alone, he took a seat and ripped the envelope open. A slim report fell out.

This was it. The moment of truth.

He read it, his stomach in knots. The summary memo was succinct and to the point as usual.

November Seventh. Dane clenched his teeth at the date seven years past.

His Lamborghini had crashed into a taxi on its way to Charles de Gaulle airport. The other driver's identity was unknown. The Paris police didn't have a detailed record of the incident. All parties had settled amicably, or so the police claimed. The settlement amount was also unknown, but it had to have been significant. The cabbie had cut back on his hours after the accident, but was apparently still able to maintain his lifestyle.

The hospital that had treated the other driver had stated that in addition to the cabbie, there had been a young American woman. No name. She'd had injuries to her hip and dislocated a shoulder. The cab driver had suffered some trauma, although it wasn't specified.

A chill spread over Dane as he recalled what Sophia had said. Her shoulder wasn't normal anymore, and her hip had been injured. And those injuries were the reason her career had been cut short… seven years ago.

The hospital didn't have any patient info beyond that. The woman had elected to go to a medical facility in America for surgery. The hospital didn't know which one, and Benjamin had hit a dead end.

The same Parisian hospital had treated Dane as well, but he'd been in a different part of the building. A couple of days before the American woman's release, he'd been moved to Italy at his grandmother's request, to be treated by a private physician there. His records had gone with him.

The Italian physician had died two years ago, and

his practice had been sold soon after. The new office didn't have records for former patients.

Hands shaking, Dane shoved the file back into the envelope. He pulled up his phone and googled Sophia Reed. The Wikipedia entry should have the information about her competitive history. There it was. The final competition—The Trophée Éric Bompard. He clicked on it. His stomach dropped.

It had ended on November Seventh. Seven years ago.

Impossible that this was a coincidence.

Unable to sit still, he jumped to his feet and called Benjamin. The PI answered on the second ring.

"Got my report?" he said, voice as flat as usual.

"Yes. How much time would it take for you to find out about the American woman?"

"Maybe forever. The only reason I was able to dig up as much as I did was because I had the information you gave me. It's not just the other driver. The police didn't have your information either. So if the cabbie wants to find out who you are to squeeze more money out of you, he's shit outta luck. Somebody didn't want the details of the accident becoming public."

"I see. Thanks." Dane hung up.

It wasn't fear of some cab driver demanding more that had made his family erase the trail.

Dane thought back.

He'd been moved to Italy soon after the doctors in Paris had declared he was well enough to travel. Shirley hadn't wanted him in France.

"The lawyers will take care of everything," she'd said.

Five fucking million bucks could take care of a lot of things.

What could've made Shirley and Salazar go to this extreme length to ensure secrecy?

Clutching the report, Dane went into the hall. "Al!"

The butler appeared like a ghost. "Sir?"

"Where's my father?"

"In his study."

Of course. Dane rushed up the stairs, thinking of all the things he should say. He didn't want to betray himself, but the emotions churning inside him were too raw.

Without bothering to knock, he slammed the door open and walked inside the study.

Salazar was sipping scotch in a custom-tailored Italian shirt and slacks, while reading some documents. At the interruption, he put down the papers and looked at Dane. "You know, in my day people knew how to kno—"

"Whose idea was it to authorize the five million dollar settlement for my Paris accident?"

Something flickered in Salazar's gaze. "The Paris thing? Who said we paid that kind of money—?"

"Shirley."

"Oh." He shrugged. "Well, it was Shirley's call and I agreed. What about it?"

"Why did you offer so much?"

"Didn't want to make Americans look bad. The French already think we're assholes."

Dane clenched his hands. Benjamin's report crumpled in his grip. "You don't give a fuck about anyone. I'll ask again. Why?"

Salazar sat back with a sigh. "Because it was necessary."

"Who was the other party?"

"A taxi driver." Salazar rolled his eyes. "Obviously."

"He had a passenger."

"And? Why are you so curious about this all of a sudden? The money didn't even come out of your bank account. You should be grateful that I took care of it."

"Stop evading." Dane gathered himself. He couldn't unravel in front of Salazar. His father would enjoy the display too much. "Was it… Was it Sophia?"

Salazar met Dane's gaze levelly, then snorted out a laugh. "Sophia? Who told you that?"

"Henry," Dane lied.

The mirth vanished from Salazar's face. "Son of a bitch. He was supposed to keep his mouth shut."

Dane's chest hurt like a spear had gone through it. He'd hoped…he'd wished Shirley had been mistaken about the five million dollar payment. But this was far worse. Sophia had had to give up her dream… because of him.

"What the fuck is wrong with you?" Dane's voice shook.

"What the fuck's wrong with *me?* I'm not the one

who plowed two hundred thousand dollars' worth of car into a taxi."

"You thought five million would be enough?"

"Of course not! No Olympic gold medal's worth a mere five million, not to the athlete." Salazar sneered. "What? You didn't know she was favored to win? The girl was a machine, undefeated for eight competitions in a row."

Blood was rushing to his head, and Dane had to blink to clear the spots in his vision. Sophia had downplayed her accomplishments. He had no idea she'd been that good.

Salazar got up. "I did what was necessary, since you were a reckless idiot. What do you think Betsy would've done if she learned that my first-born had crippled her precious girl? She'd've held it over Geraldine, and your aunt suffered enough on that bitch's account."

"You don't even like Geraldine."

"What I like is irrelevant. It's what your grandmother wanted."

"You're lying! She would've never—"

"She would've done anything in her power to protect Geraldine! She was her favorite anyway. Rick and I had a discussion through our attorneys, and he was more than happy with five million bucks because the money was going to help him stay afloat. He didn't give a fuck about his daughter."

Bile rose, and Dane breathed harshly through his

nose. "You knew all that and you were still going to make her your mistress?"

"Who said anything about her being my mistress?" Salazar gestured violently with his hands. "I'm not interested in her that way."

"Then what? You took her in—"

"She asked for a place to stay!"

"—flaunted her in my face. What was your plan then?"

"I'm going to marry her."

Dane stared at his father, feeling like somebody had just delivered a kick to his head. "*Are you out of your mind?*"

Salazar gave him a dangerous smile. "No, not just yet. Sophia isn't the type to take my money. I already considered offering her some. But marriage....that would be different. Respectable. I'm old, and I'll probably die soon enough. That would leave her young and oh so rich. Unlike Rick, I've been judicious with my investments." Salazar placed both fists on his desk and leaned forward. "She'll be a *Pryce*, not that loser Rick's daughter. The name, even if she marries into it, will open a lot of doors for her. Especially combined with wealth, youth and beauty."

"That's your brilliant plan?" Dane was shaking so hard, he could barely get the words out. "How can you even *attempt* to say that you're doing it for her?"

"My plan's a hell of a lot better than yours. What are you going to do for her? Keep her in that dead-end job that pays like shit? Buy her things until you get bored of fucking her?" Salazar laughed. "Or are you going to marry her, now that you know? Do the *honorable* thing? That might work…except who's going to believe that *you*, Dane Pryce, Mr. Permafrost, Mr. Emotional Glacier, would be capable of caring enough for a woman to actually want to marry her?

"And when Sophia learns the truth—and she probably will, because the truth has a way of coming out—she'll hate you forever. Then *you* can see what it's like to go through the divorce of the century." He took a swig of scotch. "Hopefully, I'll be dead before that happens."

Dane clenched his hands, but still he couldn't stop the tremors running through him. Jesus. Fuck. *Fuck!* "I'd call you a son of a bitch, but that would be demeaning to your mother."

"Call me whatever makes you feel better. I'm not the one who shattered a young girl's lifelong dream trying to make a light!" Salazar spread his arms, then chugged down the rest of his scotch.

Dane's nails dug into his palms until it hurt. "Shut your fucking mouth! The only reason I haven't destroyed you is Shirley."

All the nasty mirth vanished from Salazar's face. "You already have…the moment you were conceived. It destroyed everything!"

Fury exploded in Dane's chest. He picked up a white porcelain ballerina and flung at his father. It shattered a foot away from the target. "You should've told her to abort me then! If no clinic would do the job, there were wire hangers!"

"Believe me, I regret not doing that every day of my life! If I had, I would've been happier, freer, without the woman who never wanted anything but my money. So yes, next time, I'm going to be with a woman I actually want to leave my fucking money to, even if it's your damn mistake I'm cleaning up!"

The report still clutched in his hand, Dane spun around and left the study. He had to get the hell out before he did something he'd regret. Like murder his own fa—

Sophia was in the hall. Her eyes were wide as she stared at him.

Apprehension slithered down his spine like an icy snake. "How much did you hear?" he asked, his lips barely moving.

"I..." Her throat worked. "Just...some yelling." But the glassy look in her eyes said she was lying.

He walked past her to Al, who was standing there, his face pale but impassive otherwise.

"Send my things to my penthouse," Dane said.

"Yes, sir."

Dane made his way down the stairs, wanting to rip the portraits from the walls, wanting to tear the bannister from the staircase and use it to beat his father to death. He couldn't stay in this house a moment longer.

"Dane!" Sophia called out. "Wait!"

He didn't stop. "Don't come to the office tomorrow," he yelled over a shoulder and jumped into his car.

The red Lamborghini. There to remind him, to punish him for what he'd done.

Anger bubbled inside. It was always there, seething in his belly.

He fucking hated everything. He hated life. He wished…

He wished he'd had the guts to kill himself way back when.

Some idiot eastern philosopher said life was suffering. He probably hadn't had a family like Dane's. If so, he would've known that some misery was too much to be endured.

Speed was the only thing that gave Dane any sense of freedom. He'd gotten one too many tickets, but he didn't give a damn. What good was money if he couldn't blow it on things that made him feel good?

Traffic in Paris sucked. He should've just stayed in Germany, driving the Autobahn, but Shirley had wanted to meet him here. She was the only one worth making a trip for.

He saw the light change. If he gunned it, he could probably make it. Sitting in traffic sucked, and he didn't want to do it any more than he had to. He stomped on the accelerator and felt the Lamborghini leap forward.

Just before he could cross the intersection, the light turned red. Shit.

He couldn't stop. Fuck it. Just go.

A taxi was suddenly in the intersection, the cabbie hunched forward, his eyes focused on the light that had just turned green.

"Fuck!"

His foot smashing the brake, Dane twisted the steering wheel so he wouldn't hit the driver, but it was too—

Metal crunched. The impact threw him forward; stars exploded in his vision. Something warm and sticky trickled down his face and dripped off his chin. Blood.

He tried to move. He didn't think he was that hurt, but his body wouldn't obey his commands. Loud French buzzed around him. He blinked as his vision dimmed for a moment…

Dane drove away, as fast as he could. His petulant lashing out hadn't just affected him. It affected everything.

TWENTY-EIGHT

Sophia shook. She couldn't believe how everything was suddenly, horrifically falling apart. Dane had barely glanced at her, and he didn't want her at the office. What was going on?

The ugly argument between Dane and Salazar still rang in her ears.

The moment you were conceived. It destroyed everything!

Not even her parents in their least paternal moments had said something that cruel.

"Miss," Al said quietly. "It's late."

She looked at him sharply. How could he speak in such a dulcet voice? He'd been standing outside the door longer and had heard more of the harsh words.

Or was this sort of thing so commonplace that it didn't bother him anymore?

"I need to borrow a car," she said.

"If you need to run an errand—"

"I'm going to see Dane."

"That would be unwise."

"Al, don't take this the wrong way. But I'm not asking for your approval."

The butler merely looked down at her.

She waited. "Do I have to call a taxi?"

A small sigh escaped his lips. "Very well. There's a Mercedes available for your use. I'll program the GPS with the address."

He led her to an enormous garage in the back. Dozens of valuable cars shone under the overhead lights.

"This one." He opened the door to a black sedan. When she got in, he gave her the fob and key and pressed a few keys on the GPS. "Are you quite sure you want to go?"

"Yes."

"Very well. Good luck, Miss. Do try to drive safely."

She pulled away from the Pryce family mansion and followed the GPS directions to Dane's place. With the hour being so late, traffic was light. She didn't spot the red Lamborghini on the way even though she sped down the highway. On the other hand, there was a shiny silvery Aston Martin with a Washington state license tag…

George, she thought.

Sweat beaded along her hairline as she pulled alongside the car…but the driver was an Asian man. She shook herself mentally. She was upset, and now she was getting paranoid. She had to calm down if she wanted to confront Dane.

She pulled up in front of the building and gave her key to the uniformed doorman, who recognized her.

"Is Dane Pryce in?" she asked.

"Yes, I think so. I saw him go up not too long ago."

She nodded. "I don't think I'll be here for long, but feel free to move the car if you need to."

"Will do." He tipped his hat.

She took the elevator to Dane's floor. As the digital display showed ever-rising numbers, her heart picked up its tempo. Sweat slickened her palms, and she wiped them on her skirt. She wasn't backing down. He couldn't shut her out over an argument he'd had with his father.

She knocked. When there was no answer, she said, "Dane, I know you're in there."

Still no answer. She banged her fists on the door. "Dane! Come on! We have to talk."

Silence.

"Fine. I'm not leaving until you come out!" She leaned against the door, arms crossed. "You can't stay inside forever."

Dane abandoned his glass and took a long swig from the bottle. The scotch burned, but he needed it to burn even worse.

Sophia's voice came from outside the door. "I'm not leaving until you come out! You can't stay inside forever."

He chuckled bitterly to himself. She was beyond naïve if she thought camping outside his door would give her what she wanted. He couldn't see her right now. He didn't deserve to see her, to be near her.

From a purely objective standpoint, five million dollars was acceptable compensation for what he'd done. She wasn't disabled. She wasn't scarred. She was still smart, brilliant and had her entire life ahead of her.

She'd marry some nice schmuck, have his babies and be disgustingly happy.

But this wasn't an objective situation. The fact that it was Sophia's dream he'd shattered with that careless decision in Paris made him want to vomit.

He dialed a private security firm he had on retainer for handling delicate situations.

"Mr. Pryce?" came a firm voice.

"I need a woman removed from outside my penthouse door. She refuses to go. You must show her every courtesy. Treat her the way you would've treated my grandmother," Dane said. They knew how much he'd adored Shirley.

"Yes, sir. We'll be there in ten."

"Fine." He hung up.

Shirley, Shirley, Shirley. She should've let Dane know the whole truth about the accident in Paris. Then perhaps he would've been more careful—even distanced himself from Sophia from the very beginning.

He shook his head. *No lying to yourself.* The truth was, he wouldn't have been able to stay away. She'd enthralled him the moment he'd laid his eyes on her in Mexico.

Holding the bottle by the neck, he mounted the treadmill and started walking. The liquor did very little to dull the pain in his gut.

Some moments later, he heard low male voices. Then Sophia's high-pitched yell pierced the silence on the floor. "Dane! Dane!"

He closed his eyes, willing himself to block it all out.

"Dane!"

The voice was cut abruptly.

Sophia was undoubtedly in the elevator now. The compulsion to go after her and hold her as tightly as he could throbbed in his head.

Go. It might not be too late. She doesn't have to know.

But *he* knew. And unlike some people he could name, he couldn't laugh and smile and lie his way through a relationship.

"*Aaaarrgh!*"

He jumped off the treadmill and threw the scotch bottle at the wall. Air sawed in and out of his lungs. He squeezed his head between his hands and shut his eyes.

Salazar had been right all along. Dane should've never been born.

TWENTY-NINE

SOPHIA LOOKED LIKE HELL THE NEXT MORNING, and felt worse. Thank god she was good with makeup. She covered the dark circles and unhappy lines around her eyes and mouth. When she forced herself to smile, she almost looked normal.

For once, Salazar wasn't there for breakfast. She didn't have much appetite, but forced a few bites down anyway. She refused to tragically waste away like some spurned gothic novel heroine. Injuries or no, she'd been a world champion and would be damned if she'd roll over.

Al appeared the moment she was finished. "Miss?"

"I'm going to work," she announced.

"Are you sure that's a good idea?" His voice was gentle. He'd probably learned what had happened at Dane's penthouse the night before. For a man who never seemed to leave the mansion, he somehow knew an awful lot.

"No. But it's the only idea. He can't kick me out of the office." Her chin trembled, but she firmed it with effort. "I work there."

"If I may… I have never seen young Mr. Pryce react so strongly before. Whatever is driving him, it must be deeply personal."

"I guess his veins aren't full of ice water after all."

"I would assume not. But he does have that reputation."

She forced a smile. "Thank you, Al. I'll be all right."

The drive felt incredibly long, but Sophia used the time to think things through. Whatever was the reason behind Dane's refusal to talk to her, it couldn't be anger or hate. The men who'd come to remove her from outside his penthouse had been courteous and polite, even as they had been forced to physically remove her. They'd almost seemed apologetic.

Dane had had a chance to calm down. Surely he'd realized by now how ridiculous and unfair it was for him to shut her out like this.

She held on to that thought as she rode the elevator up to the office and took her seat behind her desk. When the morning deliveryman came by to drop off a bouquet of cheery daisies, she saw the card signed *D* and smiled, tension leaving her. See? Everything was fine now. A couple minutes later, Dane stepped in. She gasped. Dark puffy half-circles were under his bloodshot eyes, and deep lines bracketed his mouth. His usually neat hair stuck up. The only thing that said he hadn't just rolled out of bed was his fresh suit.

His gaze sharpened at the sight of her, then at the daisies. He picked up the flowers and went inside his office.

Sophia followed him in and closed the door behind them.

"What are you doing here?" he said, not bothering to meet her gaze.

"I work here."

"I told you not to come in."

He tossed the bouquet in the trashcan with more force than necessary. Petals bruised and fell from the stems.

She dragged in a shaky breath. There went her theory that he wasn't upset anymore. Her eyes prickled, but she composed herself. "Did I do something?"

He stilled in the middle of getting out of his jacket.

"If I did, just tell me. This kind of stuff"—she gestured at the daisies—"isn't helping."

"You did nothing wrong, Sophia."

"Then why are you doing this?"

"Go home." His voice was harder and colder than it had been when she'd first met him at Elizabeth's function.

"No. I have a job to do here."

"You're wrong," he said. "You have nothing to do here. You work for me, and I gave you an instruction. Unless you want to be fired, you'll do as I say."

She stiffened. "Isn't that wrongful termination?"

"I don't give a shit. Sue me if you don't like it."

There was no getting through to him. He wouldn't even look at her, like he couldn't bear the sight of her.

"Fine. I'll go." She pressed her trembling lips together. She couldn't stop the bitter smile. "So this is what you mean by treating me fairly, huh? I should've known better than to trust that you'd keep your word if it involved some inconvenience for you."

"It's for your own good," Dane said between clenched teeth. "So go."

"For my own good." She looked up at the ceiling in disbelief. "Of course. Excuse me."

Sophia went to the garden and sat in the gazebo, staring at nothing in particular. She didn't want to go inside the mansion. Al's professionally reserved pity would be too much to bear, and in any case the thought of being around somebody right now was—

"There you are. Thought I saw your car."

She tensed at Salazar's voice. "I just want to be alone."

"Nah. No one wants to be alone when there's scotch." She turned, and he raised an unopened bottle and two glasses.

Unlike Dane, he looked fresh and well-rested. His complexion was lightly tanned and clear, with only a few wrinkles fanning out from the corners of his eyes.

The shirt and shorts he wore were freshly starched and pressed. It was unfair that he seemed fine while she and Dane weren't. She couldn't reconcile this nice Salazar, seen every morning, with the nasty one from the night before. She wanted to yell at him, but somehow she couldn't.

He sat across from her and poured the amber liquor all the way to the rim.

"I'm pretty sure that's not how you serve scotch," she said, looking away.

"Screw the rules. You look like you can use it."

She took the glass and had a swallow. It burned, but this time she didn't sputter.

"Good stuff, huh?" He sipped his.

She continued drinking without acknowledging him. A small smile curved his lips as he gazed at the pond beneath them.

Somehow she couldn't hold it back. He didn't get to smile after having played a part in the previous night's disaster. "Why did you say it?" she asked.

"Say what?"

"Those horrible things about Dane. That he destroyed everything, and that you wished your wife had aborted him. Not even my mother ever said that, and she's no candidate for sainthood."

"It doesn't concern you."

"But it does. Ever since you two talked, Dane's been treating me like he doesn't even want to be in the same building with me."

"Has he now?"

"Yeah. He sent me home from work today. Said there was nothing for me to do at the office."

Salazar had another sip. "It's more about him than you."

"Sure doesn't feel that way."

He laughed softly. "Jesus, you like him."

Was it that obvious? "Well…yes. I do."

"Bad idea. You'll only be miserable."

"It doesn't work that way."

Salazar lifted his glass like he was going to make a toast. "We seek out the things most likely to destroy us. Run to 'em, with open arms." He sighed and lowered the glass. "You hear about my divorce?"

She nodded.

"Ceinlys wouldn't have gotten a chance to divorce me if Dane hadn't come along when he did. I was going to divorce her all those years ago, but how could I? She was my newly wedded wife—not even a year had passed since our ceremony—and she was carrying my first child in her womb."

"*It wasn't his fault*," Sophia said, her voice tight.

"He's been her pawn the moment he was conceived. All those things he did to make sure I'd approve of him and his mother. Do you know what being with a woman who only wants you for your money does to a man?" He paused for a moment to pour more scotch. "Of course you don't, because you're not a man. But that's how it was in my family—every single one of our children was her pawn. So I did what I could to undermine their effect. I can play the game just as well as anybody."

Sophia shook her head. "It doesn't make any sense."

"What doesn't?"

"If that's all you were arguing about, why would Dane push me away? None of that has anything to do with me."

Salazar merely raised his eyebrows and drained his glass.

Sophia stood up. "He can't do this. I won't let him."

"You got a plan?" he asked, placing the empty glass on the stone table between them.

She raised her chin. "I'm going to fight."

"Nice sound bite, but it's really not worth it."

"He can't start something and then end it without an explanation. I'm not some toy he can just...*toss aside* at will." She'd already lost so much to the whims of fate. She wasn't going to let it happen again because of the whims of some man.

"If he won't even let you report for work—"

She raised a finger. "You asked me to come to the wedding with you and I said I'd think about it. Well, I've thought about it. I'll go."

He blinked. "As my date?"

"If that's how it has to be, yes."

A reluctant laugh tore from his chest. "God. You really know how to kill a man's ego. I've never had a woman tell me she wanted to be with me to get to my son."

She flushed. “I’m not doing this to hurt you.”

“I know, I know.” He waved his hand. “I just thought it was…funny.” He sobered. “It’s going to be a fairly fancy affair despite what Hilary thinks is going to happen. Got anything you can wear?”

“Well, ah…now that you mention it…”

“Why don’t you let me outfit you, then?” Salazar smiled. “It’ll be my pleasure.”

THIRTY

DANE DROVE TO HIS FAMILY'S ORANGE grove, where Mark and Hillary were having their wedding. Amazing that they wanted to get married there. It had been the scene of their first date, but that date hadn't turned out particularly well as he remembered.

However, Mark had been able to salvage things. Dane would never fix his situation with Sophia unless someone invented a time machine.

The memory of her trembling lips and tear-filled eyes gnawed at him, and he felt like his gut was full of broken glass.

His phone buzzed. *Vanessa.*

"Has the wedding been cancelled?" he said into the Bluetooth headset.

"Why would it be cancelled?"

"Why else would you be calling?"

She huffed. "The wedding is not being cancelled. I just wanted to know if you're bringing a date."

"What if I am?"

"I just wanted to gird myself. You always have the habit of dating the most unsuitable women. Like that blonde who called Hilary fat."

He drew a blank. "Who?"

"I don't know her name. But remember that time when Hilary and I went over to your place, and your plastic bimbo called her fat?"

"Vaguely," he lied. He didn't remember anything those girls did, and it annoyed him that Vanessa would put any weight on something one of them had said. Who gave a damn about those women anyway? "But you can relax; I'm dateless today. Are you already at the grove?"

"Uh-huh. I got here last night to help out with a few things."

"Amazing that Justin managed to find a flatbed big enough to cart you over on such short notice." He hung up.

Vanessa had spent entirely too much time and energy on Mark and Hilary's wedding. Maybe she wanted to live vicariously through them, since she herself had eloped. If she wanted, she could have a ceremony as grand as she desired. Her immensely rich husband Justin was whipped—for the time being, at least—and the curmudgeonly Barron Sterling, patriarch of that family, would give her anything she wanted because she was carrying his great-grandnephew.

Dane finally reached the grove. It'd been in his family for a few generations. Not because anybody farmed, but one of his ancestors had married a farmer's daughter and wanted to indulge her. Apparently he'd loved her.

Amazing that a Pryce man was capable of love.

Dane got out of the car and inhaled fresh air heavy with the scent of citrus. He looked over at the huge brick house that had originally come with the orchard. It stood like a monolith, blocky and imposing.

Salazar and Ceinlys had modified all their properties so that the master bedroom suite in each had a separate bedchamber for the mistress of the house. Dane didn't know why they'd bothered. It would've been easier just to get separated—certainly cheaper than going through all the renovation and re-furnishing.

Iain came out of the house, brows pinched and jaw tight. Dane shook his head inwardly. Iain didn't like conflict or getting involved in emotionally tense situations, and he should've stayed home if he'd wanted peace. Dane already regretted having come, even though he'd promised Hilary he'd attend. Eating takeout, drinking scotch and running would've been a more satisfying use of his time.

"What's wrong?" he asked, against his better judgment.

"Dude, everything." Iain took a long calming breath while pressing his fingertips together—some sort of yoga intervention, no doubt. "Mom's here."

"Obviously. Mark is her favorite."

"Aunt Geraldine, too."

"She was invited. Why is this a problem? Did she forget to RSVP?" That wouldn't surprise Dane one bit. Their aunt was notoriously flaky and self-absorbed at times.

"And *she*'s here."

Dane raised his eyebrows and waited.

"Dad's date." Iain gestured at the house. "*Sophia Reed.* Aunt Geraldine almost passed out at the sight of her."

Dane pressed his lips together, fighting not to betray a reaction. What the *hell* was Sophia doing there as Salazar's date? Was this some kind of fucked up revenge for the night before and the morning? "Is he drunk?"

"Nope. And Mom's being super extra-gracious. It's like they're back to their old selves—nice and polite to each other while…doing what they do best."

A spot behind Dane's right eyeball began to throb. "Where are they?"

Iain pointed at the house. "In the tea room. Man, I'm outta here. I need to…" He did the breathing thing again. "I gotta take a walk."

Dane took a moment for patience and control, then made his way to the tea room, which was ridiculously named since no one ever drank tea there—just various alcohols mixed with freshly squeezed orange juice.

The long hall to the room had numerous windows that faced south, opening onto the neat rows of citrus trees. There were a few limited-edition prints on the walls between them. Thankfully, Dane thought as he strode past, none of them were paintings Salazar had chosen.

As Dane got closer, he could hear his aunt's voice.

"I thought tonight's dinner was family only," Geraldine said loudly.

"You're mistaken. Even if you weren't, she *is* family," came Salazar's voice.

Dane stood by the open door and watched the scene unfold.

Despite her age, Geraldine was still stunning with her long jet-black hair and dark blue eyes. A flimsy sundress showed off her perfectly tanned-and-toned body as she crossed her arms in front of Salazar. Nobody would believe she was the mother of three grown-up children.

For his part, Salazar was dapper in a custom-tailored silk shirt and slacks. Sophia stood beside him, her back straight. A modest cream sheath dress and ballet flats made her look even younger and more radiant.

I shouldn't want her, Dane thought. Salazar was right. Dane had ruined everything she'd worked for, and there was nothing he could ever do to make up for that. Still, he couldn't keep himself from desiring her. His senses heightened until he thought he could almost smell her sweet feminine scent from the distance. What a stupid delusion. Obviously he needed some scotch.

Salazar put a hand on Sophia's shoulder. Dane clenched his jaw, stomping on an urge to rip the offending hand off Salazar's wrist. "Even if she weren't, it doesn't matter. She's here as my guest."

Geraldine gasped. "How can she be your *guest?* I thought you hadn't signed the papers yet. You're still a married man."

"Watch it, sis." The smile on his face cooled several degrees. "I'm not discussing my personal life with you."

"But you could be more sensitive."

"Could be, but why? I'm sure Ceinlys brought one of her man-toys. She seems to have one for every occasion."

"Salazar!"

Just then Sophia turned and her gaze locked with Dane's. It pulled at him like the current in a rushing river. A sizzle went down his spine. He hated himself for feeling it.

"Who's upsetting my favorite aunt?" he said, ensuring that his voice was casual but cold.

"Them." Geraldine gestured at Sophia and Salazar. "Did you know?"

"Yes. I would've told you, but I didn't think you were coming."

"I wasn't sure I would, but why not? Istanbul's really just a few connections from here—and I wanted to see everyone."

"Good." Dane put a hand on the small of Geraldine's back. "So don't let them ruin your time here."

"Fine, you're right. Let's eat. I'm starving," Geraldine said. "I hear the cook's outdone himself."

The cook always made a game effort, although Dane didn't know why. The man had seen how things unfolded at enough family gatherings. Nobody was going to eat. And even if they did, they wouldn't taste anything.

On the way to the dining room, he spotted his cousins Blake and Elizabeth. Blake mouthed, *Where's the liquor?* while Elizabeth pasted on a determined smile.

Even the start of the dinner was inauspicious. Salazar seated Sophia next to him. They were wearing matching cream-colored outfits. Ceinlys, on the other hand, had chosen a gray dress that was almost black and sat at the opposite end of the long table with Vanessa and Justin, who had also put on dark formal wear. If Dane hadn't known better, he would've thought they'd called ahead to color coordinate for maximum effect.

Justin's great-uncle Barron Sterling had showed up—and invited himself to the dinner, knowing full well nobody would deny him. The staff had already placed tea and a plate of freshly baked sugar cookies—his favorite—at his seat. Apparently oblivious to the tension, he beamed at the very pregnant Vanessa, while munching on the cookies.

At least somebody was happy. Perhaps everyone should start with dessert. See if that helped, since alcohol wasn't likely to.

The rest of the family spread out, and Dane ended up next to Sophia and across from Shane, who looked like he could use something stronger than wine. Shane's fiancée Ginger Maxwell had started drinking already. Smart woman.

Mark's best friend and best man Gavin Lloyd had an expression that reminded Dane of a wild tiger tossed into a cage. His dark hair was neat now, but it wouldn't be long before he'd start running his hands through it.

Dane had scotch and pretended not to see or hear Salazar and Sophia, which was damn impossible because his father wouldn't keep his mouth shut. Geraldine looked daggers at Sophia, which bothered the shit out of Dane, but he ignored that too. Sophia wasn't his problem—she was Salazar's date.

Dane signaled for more scotch. It was too bad he couldn't get drunk easily. He would've loved nothing more than to be so shit-faced that he didn't even remember being there.

"So which room is she"—Geraldine pointed at Sophia—"using? All my children are here for the wedding too, you know."

Blake tuned his mother out—Dane could tell from the way his eyes focused on a spot beyond her.

"All your children? I don't see Ryder," Salazar said.

"He'll be here. Sent his suitcases ahead." Geraldine made a face. "It's that worthless assistant of his messing up his calendar, undoubtedly. I told him he needs to get somebody more suitable. She's too large to be any good for his image."

Dane gritted his teeth and ignored his aunt's unfair and offensive assessment of the assistant. Ryder was probably distracted by some easy lay he'd spotted on his way to the grove. Who could blame him? If he was careful, nobody would find out. But that was like wishing turtles could fly. It would be all over the Internet in the next twenty-four hours, if not sooner. Ryder's exploits were legendary. Dane had heard there was an online support group for women he'd "humped and dumped."

Geraldine continued, "Anyway, everyone's going to be here soon. They're going to need their own suites."

"Sophia should stay in the mistress's chamber in the master suite in that case," Salazar said, taking a sip of wine. "Frees up one of the guest suites."

Dane coughed as his scotch went down the wrong way. Iain pounded his back with enough force to jar his lungs. Bastard. His brother probably still hadn't forgotten Dane's crack about his fiancée being a charity case.

"Not so hard, Iain," Ceinlys said. "For goodness's sake, be gentle with your brother."

"He won't break," Iain said, but he stopped.

Dane drew in air. "My back might," he muttered loud enough that only Iain could hear.

Geraldine plowed on. "That's ridiculous, Salazar. Consider Ceinlys's feelings."

Ceinlys raised an eyebrow. Dane shared the sentiment since Geraldine had always made it clear she'd never liked his sister-in-law.

"That's unnecessary," Sophia said. "I don't mind sharing a room with someone."

"Who?" Salazar waved his fork at his sons. "Dane's the only one single, and you don't want to share his room. He's an asshole. Just ask anyone."

"Father!" Vanessa said as Barron patted her hand.

God save him from family drama. Dane was going to need to mainline scotch at this rate. "Maybe Elizabeth can share hers."

"Absolutely *not!*" Geraldine said before Elizabeth could say a word. "I won't have *that woman's* daughter in the same room with mine!"

At the same time, Ceinlys said, "Stop this nonsense. I agree with Salazar," drawing a gasp from Vanessa.

Dane stared at his mother. "You do?"

"This is about Mark and Hilary's wedding. There's no point in creating inconvenience over appearances."

"Oh no, we can't have that," Salazar said, his eyes on Ceinlys, who smiled serenely at him.

"Don't be ridiculous. A hotel is perfectly acceptable for Sophia," Geraldine announced.

"I completely disagree." Salazar shook his head. "Logistical annoyance. What's wrong with the mistress's room anyway? It's totally separate from my bedroom."

"Except for the connecting door. And the fact that you'll be sharing a bathroom," Mark muttered under his breath as he reached for his drink. He'd barely touched his appetizer.

Thank you, Dane thought. "Just spit it out," he said, finally tired of the bullshit. "Are you signaling to everyone that she's going to replace Mom?"

Leave her a rich, young widow… That was the goal, or so Salazar had claimed.

Intellectually Dane knew that wasn't a horrible outcome for Sophia. She would never fulfill her Olympic dream, but she would have everything else she could want with the Pryce name and fortune. And Salazar hadn't been the one to ruin her lifelong dream, so even if she ever found out, it would be more palatable. Besides, he'd likely be dead by then.

But the idea of her and Salazar together turned Dane's stomach. The fact that he couldn't do anything about it made it a hundred times worse.

Much to his petty satisfaction, Salazar choked on his drink, while Sophia turned crimson. Hilary, Jane and Ginger looked like they wanted to be anywhere but there, except… Couldn't go anywhere, could they? Hilary's best friend and maid of honor Josephine just stared with unblinking brown eyes. Barron ate his soup, his attention entirely on the food. Vanessa buried her face in Justin's shoulder, while he downed his fourth drink. Elizabeth upgraded from wine to vodka.

As Salazar sputtered and coughed, Geraldine reached over and pounded his back with all her considerable might, honed from years of working out.

"I haven't even signed the papers yet," Salazar said between gasping breaths.

"Never stopped you before," Dane pointed out.

"Show some respect, Dane," Geraldine said.

"I am. If I weren't, I would've used far different language."

"Do you want to know if I'm sleeping with her?" Salazar asked, his voice hoarse from coughing. "If you do, say so."

Blake excused himself from the table. "Business call," he said.

Iain looked after him longingly.

Ceinlys sighed out loud, drawing everyone's attention. "Does it matter? The divorce is final. Everything else is just a formality."

Sophia jumped to her feet. "Excuse me. I need some air."

"Great idea. Take your time."

She paled at Dane's cold tone, then walked out, head held high like a foreign dignitary. And despite himself, his gaze followed her. Damn it.

Finally when she was out of the room, he turned his attention to Salazar. "Congratulations. Look what you've done."

"Me? You're the one who asked."

"I didn't." Dane bared his teeth in a nasty smile. "You did."

Salazar paused, then narrowed his eyes. "You're such an asshole."

"Thank you," Dane said coolly, tilting his scotch Salazar's way. "I learned from the best."

THIRTY-ONE

DANE ROLLED HIS SHOULDERS AS HE MADE his way to his suite. Two-plus hours of dinner, and there hadn't been a single toast to Mark and Hilary. The couple had been dying to get away.

They should've just skipped the farce from the beginning and eloped like Vanessa and Justin.

Speak of the devil... Dane scowled as a text from Vanessa came in. *Meet me in my room.*

Did she really want to spend more time with him? Or was she plotting something?

Dane went inside Vanessa and Justin's suite without a knock, then raised an eyebrow when he spotted Iain and Shane as well. Iain was sitting, his face unnaturally serene, probably in some kind of meditation so he wouldn't do something he'd regret later, while Shane was sprawled on a couch, nursing some scotch. Vanessa sat in an armchair with a glass of the family's orange juice. She was vibrating with energy.

If she hadn't been so heavily pregnant, she would've been pacing.

"Where's your husband?" Dane asked.

"Out," she said.

"Mark?"

"This is his *wedding*. I'm not going to bother him."

"What's the issue?" Dane took a seat.

"Is Dad going to sign?"

Iain and Shane's gazes swung Dane's way. He shrugged. "No idea."

"Weren't you at his place about that?" Shane asked.

"Not about that."

"But you were there."

"So? Have you ever known him to share his plans?"

Iain breathed audibly.

"Fine. How about if you had to guess?" Vanessa sucked down her juice.

Poor kid. For the kind of family bullshit they were all going through, she deserved a *real* drink. "I would say *probably*. Mom's right in that it's just a formality. The marriage is over."

Vanessa sighed, visibly deflating. "I can't believe it."

"Don't tell me you still have any romantic notions about the two of them," Dane said. "You're an attorney. Don't you know better?"

"They were in love when they got married."

"Shit happens, Vanessa. Love is not forever." Dane forced himself to stay relaxed. "And a miserable marriage will kill it every time."

Bitter cynicism curled in Dane's chest.

He remembered...

He lay in bed at night, waiting for Salazar to stop by to kiss him. He always kept his eyes closed and pretended to be asleep because then his father would linger a little longer.

Right on cue, Salazar entered the dark room and sat on the edge of the bed. A faint cologne and unfamiliar perfume came from him. His fingers caressed Dane's head, fluffing his hair.

"Sleeping without a worry in the world, while I'll never be free," Salazar murmured. "Never, not with more babies popping out of her all the time. If you'd just..." His hand stilled and there was a sigh. "You should've never been born."

The final words were whispered so softly that Dane almost hadn't heard them. An icy, paralyzing shock slammed through him. His eyes popped open, but his father wasn't looking at him anymore.

"Then I would've divorced your mother, and we would've both been happy. Away from each other. Now...it's too late."

Dane would never forget what he'd heard. Even if he'd wanted to, he couldn't.

"Love can last. You just have to find the right person," Iain said, jerking Dane's attention back to the present.

"Well apparently, our parents didn't." Dane's voice was much sharper than he intended, but he didn't give a damn.

"Like I said, I don't want to have to explain to this child," Vanessa rubbed her swollen belly, "why his grandmother is younger than his mom."

"Then just cut ties. It's not like he's your biological father," Dane said.

"Vanessa has a point, though," Shane said slowly. "I don't want to have that conversation with my kids either."

Vanessa gasped, then put a hand to her lips as tears shone in her eyes. "Is Ginger…?"

"No, no. But we're going to have one or two. Probably two. A couple of girls who look just like her." A goofy smile lit Shane's face.

"You just like the making part," Dane said coolly.

Vanessa scrunched her face. "Eww."

He leaned back and steepled his hands over his belly. "Stop over-thinking this. You all have a choice. You can have your children and deal with the fact that whoever Dad marries next is very likely going to be younger than we are. Or you can simply not have any kids and avoid the uncomfortable discussion. See how easy it is?"

"That's not a choice!"

"Only because you chose to do things out of order." He stared at her belly meaningfully. She'd gotten pregnant first, then married.

Vanessa turned crimson. "Are you quite finished?"

"Not at all. You should've known this would happen when the divorce came about. Dad is not good at being single. He'll re-marry soon enough, probably to a woman half your age. If that bothers you, you can wait a decade or two before starting a family. Or you can go ahead and teach your kids how the world really works."

His siblings gaped at him, their mouths hanging open like singularly stupid goldfish.

"Now I'm finished." Dane got up and left.

WORKING THINGS OUT WITH DANE AT THE WEDding might not have been the most brilliant idea. Sophia hadn't realized how hectic and crazy it was going to be at the grove. Then there were the unforeseen family issues. She should've known Geraldine would be attending.

The only people who seemed unaffected were Vanessa and Justin's great-uncle Barron, both of whom had eaten like everything was quite normal. But Sophia hadn't been able to manage more than a couple of bites, and most everyone else had consumed more alcohol than food from what she could tell.

At least the garden was quiet and peaceful. She needed the respite to think things through.

She spotted another person and stopped. The voluptuous silhouette made it clear who it was: Hilary.

The bride-to-be was alone. She was still in the deep magenta cocktail dress she'd had on at dinner. *This is a little weird.* Mark seemed so protective of his future wife. Sophia would've thought they'd have a walk together.

Should she say hello? Attending the wedding was starting to seem like a bad idea after all. The tension among some of the family members seemed to have intensified because of her, and she didn't want to upset the bride-to-be any more than she already had.

She'd just decided to slip away between trees when Hilary said, "Hey there."

All right. No choice now. "Hi."

"Recharging?"

"Sort of. Yeah." Sophia walked closer, then rolled her weight back and forth on the balls of her feet. "Sorry about being here and causing"—an awkward shrug—"the situation."

Hilary snorted. "It's not you. They would've found another reason to fight, especially with Ceinlys divorcing Salazar."

"Really? You think so?"

"Trust me. I know the family well enough now. You have to focus on what you want and pretend not to hear anything they say."

"Does that work?"

"Most of the time." Hilary gave her a rueful smile. "When Salazar told me he was going to bring you, I knew he had other motives."

"He's trying to help."

"He wants to help himself first." Hilary regarded Sophia thoughtfully. "I'd say he was trying to make Ceinlys jealous, but it only ended up putting you in a difficult situation with Dane."

"How did you guess?"

"You were at La Mer with him, right? Romantic dinner?"

"News travels fast aroun— Ohh, that's right. Mark..."

"...owns the restaurant. So which is it? Are you interested in Salazar or Dane?"

Sophia choked. "You're very blunt."

"You have to be in this family if you want to get what you want. Everyone is used to getting their way, and if you're timid, you know, they just roll right over you." Hilary shrugged. "You have to be fearless to get what you want in life, and if you're dealing with the Pryce family, you have to be doubly fearless. I almost let my doubts sabotage what I have with Mark, and that would've been awful. I hate to even think about it now."

"I can't imagine someone as self-assured as you having doubts."

"Ceinlys was against us being together. She didn't think it was good for Mark. She wanted him to have an 'emotionally comfortable relationship.'"

"Which is...what?"

"I know, right? But I guess it makes sense if you have a background like hers."

"I like Dane." Was "like" even a good word for what she felt toward him? *Frustrated with, crazy about, unable to forget...* Those might be better for her complicated emotions. Sophia sighed. "But he's so hot and cold. There are times when I think he doesn't even want to be around me, and then there are times he's amazingly sweet."

"He's always cold and direct. I've never seen him be nice to anybody, so if he's ever nice to you at all, then it's something. Everyone in the family thinks he's been…impervious to his parents' problems, but I think they've affected him the most. He's been with them the longest. Even if things were great in the beginning, it must've left scars. It did on Mark."

"Why are you telling me all this?"

"Because you're likable. It's obvious you didn't mean to create all this"—Hilary gestured around—"and…you remind me a little bit of myself when I was younger."

"Really? We can't be that far apart in age."

"No, but I can tell you've been kind of sheltered—no offense, okay?—and I had to grow up really fast. That created a lot of problems, and I was just…full of fear and doubts. I wasn't sure if I could overcome my past, have what I wanted. Then one day it hit me that only *I* could go after what I wanted. It was my responsibility, you know? And if I went at life half-assed, I wasn't going to get anything worthwhile. I had to pursue it a hundred percent, no holding back, even though I was scared inside."

Sophia could understand—and admire—that kind of drive and determination. "Looks like you got it."

"Yup." Hilary gave a small smile. "I heard about your parents and what they did. It's horrible, but you know what? It doesn't matter. You're smart and have everything you need to be successful in life." She cleared her throat, then laughed. "Anyway, enough blabbering."

"No, no. You've given me a lot to think about."

Hilary smiled. "I better go inside before another family drama breaks out. Good luck."

"Thanks. And you, too. I hope you have a fabulous marriage."

Sophia watched Hilary go, then stared at the night-blanketed grove. Had she been too timid? Spent too much time second-guessing herself?

She'd let Dane and Salazar control most of her situation. Granted, she hadn't had much option in the beginning—beggars couldn't be choosers and all that. But she didn't have to just stand by and let them decide all the major directions of her life.

The whole relationship thing was new to her. She'd never been in one, and didn't know how to act. She was scared she'd make a fool out of herself or get hurt.

But Hilary had reminded her of things she knew from her competitive years. Every time Sophia had been fearless, she'd won. Every time she started second-guessing herself, she'd bombed. How had she forgotten those lessons?

And what had her coach always said? "Don't be a wuss, Sophia. Go big or go home."

It was time she went big.

THIRTY-TWO

SOPHIA WENT UPSTAIRS. THE HOUSEKEEPER had kindly pointed out where Dane was staying. She wasn't going to let family issues get in the way of her objective. She hadn't come this far to be foiled. Once they left the grove, she'd never get another chance.

Go big or go home.

She was *not* a wuss.

Taking a deep calming breath, she went inside his suite without knocking. He wasn't in yet. The housekeeper had already unpacked his things.

Sophia hugged herself and paced like a tiger in the room. She went over all the possible scenarios, all the things she should say and do to get him to tell her what had changed.

Why can't relationships come with a coach?

The door opened, and Dane walked in. She spun around and faced him.

He froze. "What are you doing here?"

"Waiting for you."

"Get out."

"No." She put her hands on her hips. "You're going to talk to me."

"I said get out."

"And *I* said no. I'm not here as your employee, but as a wedding guest." When Dane turned around, she leaped and slammed her hand on the door. "You're not leaving," she gritted out between clenched teeth. Her hip hurt from the jump, but for once the pain was strangely welcome.

"Are you trying to make a scene?" He gave her an inscrutable look. "It's going to be embarrassing."

"You think embarrassment is a problem for me? It can't be more embarrassing than landing on my butt—in a skimpy dress—in front of tens of thousands of spectators and photographers. Or having photos of the moment plastered all over the Internet."

Muscles in his jaw worked. He gripped her wrist, and she pressed her entire body against the door.

"If you want to leave, fine. But I'm not going to make it easy for you, and you'll end up hurting me."

She waited for his next move, her heart thumping. What if…

"Damn it." Dane sighed, let go and backed away from her.

A small kernel of hope flared inside her. Despite it all, Dane didn't want to hurt her, and she had a chance to talk it over with him.

"This is ridiculous," he said. "Are you trying to spend the night here? It won't change anything."

"You're right, it won't. Not if you don't tell me what's wrong."

He looked away. "Not everything has a neat explanation. Sometimes things just are."

"No. You don't get to say that. I'm tired of people telling me how things 'just are.'" Those were the exact words everyone around her had told her three years ago, supposedly to console her. Screw that. She'd let them talk to her that way because it'd been easier for everyone involved. But she deserved better from Dane.

"It seems to me what you're really upset about is the lack of an easy orgasm." His body set in a tight line. His left eyelid twitched as he addressed her, even though he still refused to meet her gaze. "If so, there are plenty of dicks for you to choose from."

"I don't want some other dick. I want yours."

The cold mask slipped. Something dark and volatile seethed underneath, and she clung to it. It was the only sign that he wasn't as unaffected as he pretended to be.

"Still don't get it?" She pushed away from the door. "I want you."

He closed his eyes, his hands curling into fists.

"You can't block out the truth," she said.

"The truth." He gave a bitter laugh. "All right, fine." He took several big steps forward and shoved her against the wall. His large, hard body pressed against hers, and she moaned at how good it felt. He pushed his hands into her hair roughly, but she didn't care as his mouth crashed down on hers.

He kissed her like he wanted to consume her very soul. His lips, his tongue and his teeth engaged, demanding her complete compliance to his needs.

A small voice inside her head said sex wasn't the problem...or the answer. She knew that, but she was helpless to do anything other than respond as sparks shot through her body. But maybe the physical intimacy would lead him to open up afterward...

He moved his whole body against hers, his mouth plundering hers, one hand gripping her ass and another kneading one sensitive breast. She arched into him, tunneling her fingers into his hair. He pulled down her modest dress and bra until the breast popped free. Instantly he took the nipple between his fingers, and she bit her lower lip to contain a moan.

His fingers reached between her legs and pressed against her flesh through the flimsy fabric of her thong. "You're already soaked through."

"I told you I want you."

He took the hand away and shoved one of the wet fingers into her mouth. She'd never tasted herself like this before, but she didn't hesitate. She sucked it. The slick moisture on his skin was salty, the texture of his blunt fingertip rough. She flickered her tongue over it like it was the best candy she'd ever had. Cursing, he pulled her breast into his mouth and suckled hard.

Her nerve endings sizzled, and she could barely

stand as her legs shook. Heat pulsed through her, desire hot and achy between her thighs.

He pressed his lips to her ear. "How do you want it?"

"Hot. Fast. Hard." She put a hand behind his neck. "I don't care as long as it's you."

Fabric tore, and he tossed aside her ruined panties. In the blink of an eye, he undid his belt and dropped his pants and underwear. He pulled her up with his hands. She wrapped her legs around his waist and cried out when he plunged into her the same moment he let her drop.

His thick, hard cock impaled her to the hilt. She quivered, feeling impossibly full.

"This how you want it?" he whispered into her ear.

"Yes." She tightened her inner walls, clutching him.

He started moving, every stroke creating the most delicious friction. She arched her back and moved her hips as much as she could, trying to meet his thrusts. Heat incinerated the nerve endings all along her spine, and she bit her lower lip as an orgasm shattered through her.

Dane didn't give her even a second to catch her breath. He plunged in and out of her, his movements harder and faster. He adjusted the angle of her hips, and every time he thrust into her, he hit her clit. She fought to drag in air as another climax built. She wanted to prolong the moment, but he had other ideas as he rolled his pelvis and controlled the motion with ruthless determination and precision.

She came again, hard, the peak higher and more intense this time. Her inner muscles clenched around his cock, and he stopped, panting against her neck.

Finally when he could breathe more evenly, he pushed away from her. He was still hard and thick, slick with her juices.

Sophia watched him, her back against the wall for support. Her legs felt like jelly after such intense orgasms. "Your turn," she said, licking her lips.

He shook his head and wordlessly bent and pulled up his pants. He didn't look at her, not even once. "Now you got what you wanted. Hope you can sleep well tonight," he said in a low, deadened voice and walked out.

The heavy-limbed euphoria vanished like somebody had poured a bucket of ice water over her. Her chin trembled, and she pressed her lips together. Her eyes prickled. Gasping, she looked up at the ceiling, but the tears fell anyway.

Wiping her face, she grabbed her torn panties. Then gathering herself, she left the room.

She was through with this.

She'd never allow Dane to hurt her again.

FUCK, FUCK, FUCK.

Dane made his way to the manmade lake in the grove. The ducks were resting on the water, their soft murmurings soothing. There was a fair amount of moonlight, but he didn't need it. He knew the terrain from all those summers his family had spent there when his parents had been faking their happiness.

If he had it his way, he'd run, but going full speed with a dick hard enough to break a brick wouldn't be very smart.

Pulling away from Sophia had almost killed him, but he hadn't been able to continue. It wasn't even because she might win. Such trivial things had never concerned him. But he didn't want to give her false expectations.

He'd never, ever set incorrect expectations with anyone he dealt with.

"Dane."

He stopped at the voice.

Blake was reclining on a blanket spread on the grassy field. He'd changed his dress shirt and slacks for a casual t-shirt and shorts. He raised a bottle of bourbon and waggled an eyebrow. "Wanna join me?"

Not particularly. On the other hand, nothing else presented itself at the moment.

Dane plopped down next to his best friend and cousin and opened his palm.

Blake handed the bottle over, and Dane took a few swigs. "You should've taken the scotch. We have some good stuff."

"I was in a hurry. Grabbed the first bottle I saw."

Dane nodded. People had thought they'd bonded because they were cousins. Wrong. They'd bonded over the copious amount of alcohol consumed to escape the family circus.

"What's the deal?" Blake said. "You were pretty tense at dinner. Not like you."

"I was thinking about some…a hypothetical scenario."

"Like?"

"What would you do if somebody destroyed something you'd worked all your life for?"

"A hypothetical *revenge* scenario, eh? I like it." Blake pursed his lips. "Dunno. I guess it would depend on how badly I wanted it."

"How about something you wanted more than life itself?"

"Oh, I'd ruin the son of a bitch. By the time I was through, he'd wish murder was legal."

Of course. Dane would've done the same thing.

"What did Salazar do?"

"It's not him," Dane said. "It's me." He took the drink from Blake and swallowed another mouthful for courage. "I screwed up."

Dane then told Blake what had happened in Paris. How his family—Shirley and Salazar—had kept it quiet, along with cooperation from Rick. Blake listened, then shook his head.

"Five'll get you ten Rick blew the money. He was terrible with it."

"Probably," Dane said. "But that's not all. There's Mexico." He explained what had happened there as well in a few succinct sentences. "So it's…complicated."

"Tangled," Blake agreed, nodding judiciously. "Are you going to offer her money?"

"She won't take it." Dane didn't have to make the offer to know her response.

Blake regarded him. "I'd say you want her to take it…but you're also secretly glad she won't."

Dane said nothing. His friend knew him well.

"Since you gave me some good advice that time, I'll give you some now. You need to decide what you're going to do about this whole thing. She likes you. No idea why, since you can be a nasty bastard, but who knows what goes on in the female heart? Plus, I could tell from the way she was looking at you during dinner. As for her career, seven years is a long time. She should have gotten over it by now." Blake took a short draught from the bottle. "Figure skaters retire when they're young anyway. And there's the possibility that she'll never find out who was driving that red Italian number in Paris."

"But *I* know."

"Yeah, still…" Blake shrugged. "You're playing a game of what-ifs. What if you hadn't been speeding? What if you hadn't been there?"

Tension tightened Dane's jaw until his teeth hurt. "They're valid questions. If I hadn't been there, she wouldn't have been injured."

"But see, you don't know that. She could've slipped and fallen on an icy sidewalk and hurt herself the day before the big competition. A green Maserati could have come through at the next light and *killed* her. Besides, instead of focusing on what *you* could've done, what if her cab driver hadn't been speeding? What if he'd been more careful? Taken a different route?" Blake shrugged again. "On top of everything else, there's no guarantee that she would've won the Olympics anyway."

Dane shook his head. "Don't twist things for my convenience."

"I'm just saying." They lay there for a few moments, listening to the night. "You can push her away," Blake finally said, "but that'll have consequences."

No kidding. The hurt and devastation had shattered the blissful glow in her eyes when he'd walked out on her. He'd crushed a lot of people's hopes before without batting an eye—in his line of work, it was a weekly occurrence. But with Sophia, he felt like pond scum.

"If you want her and she wants you, don't be a martyr. It doesn't suit you. Make her happy if you really want to atone for Paris."

"A self-serving rationalization," Dane said, even as selfish hope stirred in his heart.

"No, it's a practical suggestion. The past can't be changed, but you can decide what you want for the future. But here you are, trying to ruin it over something that happened seven years ago. That isn't like you. It's sentimental…ridiculous, even. Serves no purpose." Blake plopped down on his back, staring at the sky. "Just think for a while, and you'll see that I'm right." He shot Dane a cocky grin. "As usual."

Dane swished the bottle. There was hardly any left. "Let's go back in and raid the bar. The seniors are off to bed."

The last thing he wanted to do was stay sober and think about what Blake had said about making Sophia happy to atone for the past.

SOPHIA WENT TO HER ROOM, THE RUINED PANTIES balled up in her hand. The stickiness between her legs had gone cold, and she grimaced the whole way. The recent orgasms still echoed through her body, but her heart felt like a rock in her chest.

The mistress's room had its own entrance. Maybe a couple having separate rooms was an old money thing. Her parents had shared a bed even when they'd disagreed over something. They'd rarely fought. Expending that much energy over each other had been regarded as pointless.

She tossed the underwear in a dark plastic bag to be thrown out when she returned to the city.

"So you made it back."

Yelping, she turned around. The doors to the

bathroom were open on both ends, and Salazar sat at the edge of his bed with a bottle of scotch. The top two buttons on his shirt were undone, and his hair lay messy, like he'd run his hand through it a few times.

"Why are you still up?" She forced a smile, hoping he hadn't seen what she'd been putting away. "Tomorrow's the big day."

"Ah, doesn't matter. Can't ever get to sleep before midnight anyway. Just the way I'm wired." Salazar lifted the bottle. "Want some?"

The gesture reminded her of how Dane had been in Mexico, sending a sharp pang through her heart. "Maybe just a sip," she said, coming over.

He poured her a full glass, almost to the rim. She sat next to him and sipped the drink, careful not to choke on the fiery liquid.

"It's good you missed the rest of the dinner," he said. "It was awful. Dane the Killjoy. And my sister… Jesus. She just won't shut up about anything." He took a long swallow straight from the bottle. "But nobody can make her keep her mouth closed since Geraldine's everyone's favorite. Not even Dane stops her because apparently my mother told him to be nice to her. Can you believe that? My own son ignores me, but not my shrilly old bat of a mother."

She ignored the insult. Salazar wasn't sober. "He must've liked her."

"They were a lot alike. Cold. Disapproving. Always thought everyone else was a disappointment." He sniffed. "It's no wonder Dane decided to send that girl Ginger to drag Shane back home from Thailand. Apparently he didn't trust us to do it." He snorted a laugh.

The sound was ugly and sloppy. How much had he drunk?

"Ceinlys looks young, doesn't she?" he asked abruptly.

She nodded. Not just young but dignified as she'd sat at the end of the table.

"That's how she is. Timeless." He sighed, his shoulders sagging. "Not like me. I've changed so much. Probably aged poorly."

"You look fine." Sophia cradled the glass in her hands, then took another sip as silence hung heavily between them. This was…awkward, but maybe Salazar needed somebody to talk to…even if it was somebody who didn't know him or his family situation all that well. With Mark getting married, he might be feeling nostalgic or something.

"Dane likes you," he said suddenly.

She choked on her scotch. "Salazar, really, the last thing I want to dis—

"He does," Salazar went on. "He thinks he's slick and can hide it from me, but I can tell. I'm his father, after all…even if he doesn't want it that way."

"I'm sure he respects you as a father." Even as she said those words, she knew Salazar might be right. After all, telling Dane he should've never been born probably had killed whatever love he might've had for his father.

"You're so sheltered, you have no idea what you're talking about. Mother disapproved of me, but adored him, saying he has all the right qualities to be the head of our illustrious family. Both of them made it clear how li'l they thought of me, while using the wealth that I"—he jumped to his feet, raising his hands—"created." He swayed unsteadily. "At least Ceinlys is hones' about what she saw in me—money! If I hadn't been trapped, I coulda started over. I met a woman I liked, you know. I'm not some unfeeling womanizing asshole!"

Sophia placed her more than half-full glass on the floor by the corner of the four-poster bed. "Why don't you sit back down? You might be a little drunk."

"This? Nah. This is nothing!"

"But—"

"You know what galls me? He's suc*cess*ful. Doesn't even need my damn money, which gives him moral superiority. But what he doesn't remember is that it's *my connections*"—he tapped his chest—"and this family name that gave him his start. He would've been nothin' without me." He slashed the air with his hand. "Nothin'!"

I should've declined the drink and shut the door and gone to sleep. What did she know about dealing with a drunken man who wanted to rant about his family? And despite what Salazar claimed, Dane was too smart and dominant to end up as "nothing," even if he hadn't had any special connections.

"Come on, Salazar. Sit down."

"No." He pulled back. "I'm def'nitely not drunk. Are you trying to treat me like an idiot too?"

"You know better than—"

"Do I? Do I? I'm a terrible judge of character, seems like. Screwed up so many things." He took another swig from the bottle.

The first thing to do was to get the bottle away from him. Sophia reached for it, and he raised his right arm. "Oh no, you don't!"

"Okay, well, I'm finished. I'm calling the housekeeper now to help you get undressed and go to bed." She hit the button by the bed for housekeeping.

"Now, why'd you hafta do that?" Salazar shoved the bottle to his mouth and chugged the rest, his throat working.

Sophia shook her head. He was acting like a temperamental child. Then again, the divorce probably wasn't all that amicable despite Ceinlys's serene appearance.

He dropped his empty bottle, then swayed a bit. "See? Perfectly sober."

"If you can count down from ten to one, I'll believe you."

"Ten. Nine. Eight," he began, then shook his head. "Maybe next is seven."

She sighed. That wasn't too bad. Maybe he wasn't as drunk as she'd thought.

He stumbled forward, losing his balance. She caught him, afraid he might hit his head on one of the bedposts. He was heavier than he looked, and he flailed, trying to regain his footing. It only managed to unbalance her, and they fell on the bed together with him on top.

A double knock sounded at the door, and it opened to reveal the housekeeper. "You called for...?" The rest of it died.

Sophia's skin prickled, and everything inside her froze at the sight of Dane's cold face behind the housekeeper. Cringing, she pushed Salazar off her. Dane must've been on his way to his suite. His gaze flickered to his father, who was laughing with a hand over his eyes, then to her. Her cheeks flamed.

Dane didn't say a word, but a corner of his mouth twisted into a sardonic smile. He turned away and walked past the housekeeper.

"Miss?" the housekeeper said in a normal voice, like this was an everyday scene.

"Can you please take care of him? He's drunk."

"Of course," she said at the same time Salazar muttered, "I'm rilly not."

"Just hush." Sophia got up and went to the hall. Dane was gone, probably already in his suite.

She dropped her head back, suddenly too tired to care. What did it matter what he thought? It was over anyway.

There was nothing between them anymore.

THIRTY-THREE

SOPHIA RUBBED GRITTY EYES AND GRIMACED at the bright morning light. That would teach her to stay up late with a glass of scotch.

She rolled out of bed and took a look at herself in the bathroom mirror. *Ugh.* At least she had the help of some excellent foundation and concealer. When she was finished, it looked like she'd had a good night's sleep. She went to Salazar's bathroom door and carefully put her ear to it.

Nothing from the other side.

Should she go wake him up? On the other hand, did she want another scene?

If he wasn't up in the next thirty minutes, she'd send housekeeping to check on him.

Her mind made up, she pulled her hair into a bun and put on a mint-green dress and matching flats. The shopper who'd brought the outfit had also thought of a pale cream-colored hat with a wide brim. Thank god.

The clock on the wall said thirty minutes had passed. Straightening her spine, she knocked on Salazar's door. When there was no response, she tried again, then waited a moment before opening it a crack.

The room was empty.

Huh. Guess he was up before I was.

She put the hat on and went outside. Normally she hated skipping breakfast, but eating would mean facing the Pryce family. She wouldn't be able to have more than a couple of bites anyway.

White ribbons and orchids formed an arch under which the couple was to stand. The rows of seats set up for the guests were all in a matching satin. A quartet tuned their instruments on a platform by the altar. A couple of staff were rolling out a thick, white carpet to create the virgin road.

Everything was classy and elegant. Sophia had never been to a wedding, but as she looked around she thought, *When I get married, I want one like this.*

Soon the quartet started playing music, and guests began to file in. Iain's fiancée Jane pulled Sophia over to the groom's side. A gorgeous burgundy raw silk dress hung from her delicate shoulders and ended a couple of inches above her knees. Unlike Sophia, Jane was wearing her curled brown hair down and had on a pair of stilettos.

"Love your shoes," she said.

Sophia smiled and ventured a "Thanks". Given how people had been the night before, she couldn't tell if Jane was being sincere or sarcastic.

"I'd kill for flats, but Josephine said I had to wear heels."

"Josephine?"

"Maid of Honor today and Fashion Gestapo every day. She despises flats." Jane sighed longingly. "She has to look good to maintain the image and all, but I'm a cook. You know what I mean?"

"Grass is always greener on the other side. I wish I could wear heels."

"Then why don't you?"

"Bad joints."

"Ooh, that's awful." Sympathy softened Jane's eyes.

Sophia smiled, the tension leaving her. "It's overwhelming, isn't it?" She gestured around.

"Can you believe it's only for the inner circle?"

Sophia raised her eyebrows at the expensively tuxedoed men and gowned women. "There has to be at least three hundred people."

Jane nodded. "And Hilary didn't even invite her family."

"Wow."

"Mine's going to be bigger, I think," Jane said. "I really want a small ceremony though."

"We can have a small one." Iain sat down next to Jane. The black tux fit him like a glove. "I'll drop-kick anyone who tries to crash."

Jane giggled, flipping her hair over a shoulder as she turned to face him. He kissed her knuckles. The gesture was so natural and innocent, but the look in his eyes made it almost too intimate for public consumption.

Sophia glanced away, then noticed Salazar sitting with Ceinlys. He looked great in his tux, but he didn't smile much. For a man who'd drunk so much scotch he'd almost passed out, he appeared perfectly fine. No trembling, no dark circles under his eyes. His mouth was set in a flat line, but it only made him appear solemn and distinguished rather than grim.

Ceinlys on the other hand sported a serene smile and wore a fitted deep blue dress that accentuated her feminine beauty. A dainty hat with netting sat over her dark hair. Her flawless makeup brought out her eyes, and juicy lip-gloss glistened on her lips. How could she be the mother to five full-grown children? Betsy was pretty too, but she was nothing compared to Ceinlys, who was far older but looked much more youthful and beautiful.

Nobody looking at them would suspect they were in the middle of an ugly divorce.

Mark and the officiant made their way to the front. In a perfectly tailored tuxedo, Mark looked stunning. The sun glinted on his onyx-dark hair. Anticipation seemed to bubble within him as he waited for his bride. At the officiant's request, everyone rose to their feet, and the orchestra started "Here Comes The Bride."

Hilary walked on Barron Sterling's arm. The Diamante crystals glittering in floral patterns, layers and layers of intricate lace and tulle created a dress fit for a fairy tale princess. Hilary's gaze didn't waver behind the thin veil, her step was sure, as she walked toward Mark, who looked at her like she was the only woman in the world.

Sophia sighed. What would it feel like to be the center of a man's universe like that?

A man slid into the seat next to her. "I can't believe he's getting married," he muttered.

She glanced over and blinked. It was Ryder, dressed in a tux and very dark sunglasses. No date, for once. "When did you get here?"

"Just before the bride made her grand entrance. Everyone was so busy staring at her that I was able to make it here almost undetected. It's almost impossible for someone like me to just sit down without causing a stir, you know." He looked around and sighed. "At least they saved me a seat."

She shrugged. Nobody had saved him a seat. There just happened to be an empty one next to her.

"Ah, Mark. I knew him, Horatio," Ryder said in a mock-grave voice. "He was supposed to be single forever. At least the bride's hot. Every one of my cousins has betrayed me, except for Dane. At least he'll be single forever."

Despite herself, she leaned closer. "He will? Why?"

"Are you kidding? What woman wants to marry an iceberg? He's cold, Sophia. Cold, cold, cold. Everywhere he shows up, the temperature drops. He's worse than Blake."

Just then the back of her neck tingled. She glanced over her shoulder and saw Dane watching.

Unlike her, he looked well-rested and calm. He seemed forbidding and inscrutable in his tux, which fit him precisely. His eyes were bluer than the deepest Arctic sea and—sure enough—just as cold.

Sophia's nerve endings prickled, and she turned away. So what if he was amazing in bed? He'd made it very clear how he felt about their relationship—if they'd ever had one. She was tired of his mind games. She'd always been good at playing them when she'd been competing, but this was something else. The rules were different, and the impacts left invisible wounds that oozed pain.

She focused on the couple. Was it her imagination or was Mark's chest puffed out like it was about to burst? His eyes shone with adoration. Even though he and Hilary were only holding hands, there was something so possessive and protective about the way he stood in front of her.

"I always thought life was like a puzzle," Mark began. "You never know how it's going to look, and the pieces you find as time passes surprise you. For the longest time I thought I had all the pieces, even though I always felt like something was missing. Then I saw you and I knew you were the final and the most vital piece. You make me believe I can be more than I thought I could ever be. With this ring I pledge my life and everything that I am to you. And I hope I can give you even half the joy and happiness you've given me."

That, Sophia thought fiercely. *That's what I deserve.*

She clenched her hands, doing her best to ignore Dane. She hadn't been throwing herself out there to be made to feel cheap and dirty. Now that she'd seen exactly what she wanted, she wasn't going to waste any more mental energy on a man who wouldn't give it to her.

She was going to go big on her own terms.

THIRTY-FOUR

SOPHIA DISAPPEARED INTO THE MILLING crowd. Mark and Hilary were on their fourth dance. They moved with grace, surety and a chemistry Sophia had seen from top ice-dancers who'd been together for over a decade.

It was just like Mark had said during his vow—Hilary was the final and most vital piece in the puzzle he called life.

Dane didn't dance, but he sought her out with his gaze. Her stomach jittered, but she ignored him. She wove in and out among the guests, evading him without looking like she was avoiding him. This was Mark and Hilary's moment, and Sophia didn't want any drama with Dane to mar the occasion.

"Are you going to dance or just walk around the perimeter?" Justin asked.

Sophia looked up at the man. His dark hair was slicked back, making him look roguish. Despite his keen gaze, the affable warmth on his finely chiseled face rendered him friendly.

"You know how to dance, don't you?"

"Of course I do." She'd taken ballet and hip-hop lessons to help with her skating.

"Great then." He put his hands on her and began to lead expertly.

Awfully presumptuous of him, but Sophia didn't argue. Dane would intimidate almost every guest at the wedding, but not Justin. Not only was he Vanessa's husband, but he was Barron Sterling's hand-picked heir. As ignorant of the business world as Sophia was, she'd still heard of Barron in conversations her father and George used to have.

At the thought of George, tension crept into her muscles. She forced herself to relax. He wasn't going to ruin her mood.

"Enjoying yourself?" Justin asked.

She nodded. "Too bad Vanessa can't dance."

"We danced until our feet hurt at our reception."

"I thought you eloped?"

"We did, but then we had a reception for family and friends."

Probably for the people on his side, since Sophia couldn't imagine anybody from the Pryces wanting another awkward family get-together. "I'm surprised you asked me to dance," she said, noticing Vanessa in her peripheral vision. The stunning redhead watched them over the rim of her OJ glass with a small frown. "I could've sworn she didn't like me."

Justin smiled, his eyes crinkling. Disarming—charming even—but there was a steel core in there that she could feel was dangerous. "She's over-protective at times and suspicious by nature. Makes her a great lawyer, but people often mistake it for hostility."

Diplomatically stated, but Sophia wasn't in the mood. "Which worries her more? That I might marry her father or date her brother?"

His eyes widened slightly…maybe at her bluntness. People probably minced words around him all the time. "All her brothers are taken."

"Dane's not."

He almost missed a step. "Dane? Are you kidding?"

"What's so incredible about that?"

"He doesn't like anybody."

Justin was wrong. Dane flipped between hot and cold too often for people to figure him out.

A thoughtful pause. "Vanessa doesn't know what to make of you. I, on the other hand, think you're all right."

"Is that so?"

"I like people who speak frankly."

"Then Dane must be your best friend."

Justin chuckled. "He's not bad for a brother-in-law, but I like my friendships a tad warmer."

The song ended, and the quartet started another. Before Justin and Sophia could part ways, Dane tapped Justin's shoulder and arched an eyebrow. "You've monopolized her long enough."

Sophia willed Justin to stay. The last thing she wanted was to dance with Dane.

But Vanessa's husband was apparently satisfied with the information he'd gathered so far; Sophia wasn't dumb enough to think he'd danced with her for no reason. He made a "be my guest" gesture with an open hand, smiled at her in a slightly conspiratorial way, and left.

Bastard.

As Dane put a hand around her waist, she pulled back. "Sorry. My hip's starting to hurt."

"Then I'll carry you to a chair." He bent, about to hook an arm behind her knees.

She made a small turn, deftly moving out of the way. "What are you doing?"

"Trying to carry you to a chair, unless you prefer to dance. I only need a few minutes of your time."

"Don't go out of your way on my account. I'm sure there are other women who are dying to dance with you."

He ignored her and put one hand on her hip and another around her hand. Sensations buzzed inside her, and she swallowed. *Cling to your anger, Sophia.* There was no way she was making another mistake with this man.

It was just one dance. Given how cold Dane was, he probably didn't know how to move. He'd drag her around in an attempt to lead—

But he was excellent.

She should've known. There seemed to be very little he didn't do well. He didn't try to hold her too close, signaled her perfectly with small pressures at the small of her back… Everything was textbook perfect.

She didn't want to dance like a corpse, so she followed. But her body stayed tense. It wasn't that difficult so long as she held on to her humiliation from the night before. "If you think this will change anything," she said in a low voice, "forget it. You cheapened what I offered and wanted from you."

"I'm sorry."

She blinked. For a moment, hesitation softened her posture, but then the tension came back, and her spine snapped straight. "Apology accepted. Now lead me off the floor."

He arched an eyebrow as though he couldn't believe what she'd said. If he'd assumed she'd roll over after what he'd done, he was in for a rude awakening. "I didn't realize you interpreted what I did as 'cheapening.' I had to go."

"Yes, because men do that all the time. Leave in the middle of sex without coming," she hissed in a voice only he could hear.

"I'm sorry for leaving you. I'm an asshole, Sophia, and I often do asshole things. I'm going to lay down what the future will hold if we do what you want." His voice held very little inflection, though something like pain was darkening his eyes. "If we stay together, one day I'll end up hurting you, and you'll hate me."

When he didn't continue, she said, "Aren't you also going to say you don't want me with Salazar? That's what everyone seems worried about."

"I've discovered that I'm a possessive bastard. The idea of somebody else having you makes me..." His hand tightened. "Let's just say it's a singularly ugly feeling. One I've never known before. You could be with Blake, who's my best friend, and I'd still feel it."

"But if you think you're going to end up hurting me—"

"Some selfish part of me thinks maybe...just maybe...I won't." His mouth closed in a line tighter than a clam's.

He wasn't telling her everything, but she knew this was as much as she'd get from him. "You've already hurt me, Dane," she said. "There are no guarantees in life. Have you ever considered that I might be the one to hurt you?"

He gazed into her eyes, holding the look for what seemed like forever. She felt like he was reaching inside and reading the book of her soul. "No. You would never do that on purpose."

"And you won't either."

He stroked her cheek, the touch feather-light and uncharacteristically tender. Her anger lost a bit of its steam as caramel-sugary warmth spread all over her. He pulled her closer now, and she let him. He dipped his head so he could whisper into her ear. "I don't just want sex. I want to take care of you, but...that's also selfish of me."

"You have it all wrong. It's sweet." Sighing, she laid her head on his chest. It felt perfect under her cheek, like it was made just for her. "Is it because of what Salazar said to you? I heard him say how things would've been better if you hadn't been born."

The muscles underneath her grew tight. "He's right."

"No." She lifted her face to look him in the eye. "It's unfair for him to blame his marital issues on you. Your parents' problems started before you were ever born."

He flexed his hands around her. "It's much more than that."

"Whatever. *I'm* glad you're here. But if we're going to do this, promise me you'll never shut me out like that again. I want you to be open and honest with me."

Old memories darkened his eyes. Probably all the bad ones he'd had with his father. Still, his voice was firm when he said, "All right. I promise."

SOPHIA HAD NO IDEA. AND COWARD THAT HE WAS, Dane couldn't tell her even as he promised. He didn't want her to find out. Ever.

If he kept his mouth shut, she wouldn't. The only other people who knew were Salazar—who wouldn't speak of it, given his role in maintaining the silence—and Henry, who would deflect her just as he'd deflected Dane.

After the dance, he took her to an empty seat so she could sit down and rest her hip. Guilt burned a hole in his heart like acid. Shirley had complained of pain in her pelvis, but she'd been in her sixties when the pain started. Sophia wasn't even thirty.

She grasped his hand. "Hey, what's wrong?"

"What?"

"You were frowning."

He looked at the crowd. Overflowing champagne and excellent food were keeping things lively. One thing Mark knew better than anybody was great food. "I was thinking we should leave after this." He turned to her, then added, "Unless you have other plans."

"We can go." She squeezed his hand. "I don't mind."

They went inside the house, into their separate rooms to pack.

Dane tossed everything into his suitcase with little care. If he missed something the housekeeper would forward it to him. He also texted Al to send all of Sophia's things to his penthouse, adding, *We're leaving now. Make sure to have them at my place* ASAP.

"Taking Sophia with you?" Salazar was leaning against the door, half-empty glass in one hand.

Dane looked away. The last thing he wanted to do was discuss things with his father.

"Did you tell her?"

"No."

Salazar nodded and took a drink. "She'll probably figure it out one day, you know."

It was suddenly hard to drag in air. It felt like there was a big, tight fist around his throat. Dane swung his gaze toward Sazalar. "Not unless you say something, she won't."

Salazar chuckled. "True. If I hadn't said anything, you would've never found out."

Dane froze, then narrowed his eyes. "Don't make an enemy out of me."

"Ah, don't worry. I won't be the one to tell her. After all, my hands aren't clean either." Salazar knocked back the rest of his drink. "But some day she'll find out, just like you did. And then what are you going to tell her? 'Sorry' will be a bit inadequate at that point." Something that could only be characterized as a smirk twisted his mouth. "Just remember how you reacted. And it wasn't even you who got hurt."

He pushed himself off the door and left.

Dane watched his father go. His hands began curling into fis—

Jesus, breathe and relax.

Dane rolled his shoulders and neck, then took a couple of deep breaths. The only reason he'd been able to put the pieces together was because Sophia had revealed the details of her accident, including the type of car that hit her. Unless he did the same, she didn't have the clues or means to put it together. So he was safe.

But somehow Salazar's words hung around his neck like a noose.

THIRTY-FIVE

"SO YOU FINALLY REALIZED YOU AREN'T WELcome here?"

Sophia faltered at Geraldine's derisive words. She stopped, setting her wheeled suitcase upright behind her.

"You should've never come here."

"Salazar asked me to come."

"*Salazar asked.* My brother has no brain when it comes to pretty young things. You're just like your mother."

Sophia felt her go-for-the-throat competitive instincts surface. *Betsy might not be the most maternal woman, but she's still my mother.* She took a half-step forward.

Hands on her hips, Geraldine straightened, her spine tight.

"Aunt, behave," came Dane's cold voice.

"I'm not the one misbehaving." Geraldine gestured at Sophia. "Just look at that trash, trying to insin—"

"*Enough*."

He didn't raise his voice, but it was so frigid Sophia couldn't help but shiver. Geraldine blanched. "How can you take that tone with me?"

"Easily. I'm restraining myself because I promised Grandma I'd be kind to you." Dane drew himself up to his full height. "*Do not push me*. And most importantly, do not treat Sophia with disrespect or my tone will be the least of your problems."

Geraldine's eyes widened, and she opened and closed her mouth a few times. Finally, she said, "You're going to break a promise to your grandmother over *her?*"

"Yes. Now, if you'll excuse us."

He put a hand to the small of Sophia's back and led her toward the parking lot.

"You didn't have to step in there. I had that," Sophia said. "And don't break your promise on my account."

"There were other promises. I've decided that some of them were more important than the one to be kind to Geraldine."

She looked around for his Lamborghini. "Where's your car?"

"Over there." He gestured at a brand new black Bentley, gleaming in the California sun.

"What happened to the Lamborghini?"

He shrugged. "I got bored with it." He opened the door. "Get in."

She climbed in. When he got behind the wheel

and started driving, she said, "Nobody gets bored with a Lamborghini."

"When you have as much money as I do, you do." He looked straight ahead. "Besides, I know you don't like it."

Her heart softened. "Is it because of what I said about the accident?" She laid her hand over his. "You shouldn't have. It's been seven years. It doesn't bother me." Not entirely true, but… She just couldn't wrap her mind around the gesture. "What are you going to do with your old car?"

"Don't know. It's not important."

"Not important? It's an expensive car."

"What would you do with it if it were yours?"

"I…don't know." She'd never had anything that valuable. Her father had liked to live rich, but he hadn't given her anything *that* extravagant. "Maybe you should sell it and donate the proceeds."

He snorted. "Have you been hanging around Elizabeth? You sound just like her." His long, blunt fingers tapped the steering wheel. "All right, what cause is most important to you?"

She grew quiet. What she wanted to do sounded so first-world, and she didn't want any negative judgment from him. Not when they'd finally moved past the ugliness.

"Well?"

She cleared her throat. "Okay, well… I was thinking…"

He looked over at her. "You asked me to be honest with you. Surely you plan to do the same in return."

Jeez. He had to hit the fair play button. "If it was my money, I would sponsor a promising young figure skater." The words tumbled out faster. "I was very lucky that I never had to worry about how to pay for all my training, costumes and skates and travel, but most skaters aren't rich, and most don't get rich either. It's not like football or basketball, you know? I don't want a talented skater to give up on their dream because of a lack of money."

There was an almost imperceptible tightening of his jaw. If she hadn't been watching him so closely, she wouldn't have noticed. She turned away.

He probably thought it was the most ridiculous idea ever, the way her father had. Rick had always said there were better ways to spend money, and it wasn't on her future rivals. She'd assumed he'd been worried about her, but now she knew better. It had been about maintaining his lifestyle.

"If that's what you want, that's what we'll do."

Her head swiveled Dane's way. "Really?"

He nodded. "You can oversee the whole thing. I wouldn't recognize talent or potential. Figure skating isn't my area."

If they hadn't been in a car, she would've thrown her arms around him. It was so sweet and unexpected. "Thank you." She squeezed her hand over his.

"Don't thank me, Sophia. For anything, ever."

SOPHIA'S EYEBROWS PINCHED, AND DANE KNEW HE shouldn't have said that. Thanking each other was a social norm, but fuck social norms. He couldn't just sit there and listen to her gush over a stupid car.

And if she'd had any idea what getting rid of the Lamborghini *really* meant, she wouldn't be so happy.

People thought he loved that car. Why wouldn't they? It was a status symbol. A public statement that "my dick is bigger than your dick."

But every time he got into it his chest tightened, and his stomach felt like somebody had dropped a nest of angry wasps inside. The red Lamborghini had always reminded him of what he'd done—how stupid he'd been.

Getting rid of it gave him some space away from that nasty feeling. And he didn't deserve the relief.

"You'll just have to get used to hearing it," Sophia said, her voice firm. "I'm not going to turn into some unsociable brat because it suits you."

"I'm not asking you to be rude to others. Just don't thank me."

"You know you're being really weird, right? Because when I thanked you before, you didn't object."

"Things are different now," he said. "I'm not a stranger you're imposing on. We're going to be living together."

"All the more reason for us to be nice to each other."

Rolling his eyes, he turned on the radio.

She crossed her arms. "Turning on the radio does not end the discussion in your favor."

Her sass brought a reluctant smile. The women he used to date would've interpreted his order as a carte-blanche invitation to grab whatever they wanted.

He looked at her dress. The color complimented her eyes…but it also looked very new. "Did Salazar buy you that?"

She nodded. "I didn't have anything to wear. I mean, I have a black dress, but that would've been sort of…funereal."

"When we get home, I want you to sort your things into two piles. Stuff you got from him, and everything else."

A wary gleam entered her eyes. "Why?"

"I'm going to burn everything he bought you."

"Dane! That's such a waste. I haven't even worn some of the stuff."

"Then we can donate it to some homeless woman."

"Is this some kind of father-son pissing contest?" She shook her head. "I know you two have an ugly history, but this is kind of extreme. It's not like I think about him just because I'm wearing something he bought. I think about you."

"It's not that simple. Just do as I say." Then he added, "Please," because he had a feeling that the word would persuade her.

Sure enough, she sighed. "Why? Give me one good reason."

"I don't want you to owe him anything." *I don't want him to provide for you because that's* my *job.* "He likes to flaunt his money, then act like he's some great enabler of his children's success. Did he brag about what he did when we turned twenty-one?"

She shook her head.

"He gave us fifty million bucks each for our twenty-first birthdays. The money was supposedly our legacy, so we could pursue our dreams and be happy." Dane snorted. "Because money can make up for everything in his world. When I was twenty-one and one day old, I gave mine back to him. I didn't need it, and I didn't want to give him the satisfaction of pretending that he'd done his paternal duty."

Something shifted in her expression. Maybe it was empathy that softened her face. "Okay. If you feel that strongly, we'll donate the clothes. I'd hate to… burn them."

"Thanks."

"Oh you get to thank me, even though I can't thank you?"

He didn't respond. It wasn't the same thing at all, but he couldn't explain it to her.

When he'd made the decision that he couldn't let her be with Salazar, even if things might end badly, he'd also decided that keeping one secret couldn't be that complicated. But he'd misjudged. It was like a pebble tossed into a lake, creating ripples that affected everything.

It didn't matter, he told himself. As long as Sophia didn't know, it didn't matter.

THIRTY-SIX

Sophia and Dane entered his master bedroom suite together. It felt like forever since he'd had her removed from the premises, although it'd really only been three days. Even though she'd been here before, this time felt special, like she was taking a step toward a possibility rather than a brief detour.

The huge walk-in closet was neatly divided into two sections—one for him and one for her. Dane had a surprising number of clothes, most of them business wear: pressed suits and dress shirts and slacks. Whoever had brought her things from the Pryce family mansion had also unpacked for her. His gaze skimmed over her rather meager outfits and four pairs of shoes—flats, heels and sneakers.

"That's all you have?" he asked, shock heavy in his tone.

She shrugged. "Yup. But it's really plenty." Four tops, five skirts, two pairs of slacks plus a black cocktail dress were enough to get her through until she could save some money for shopping.

His jaw slackened. "Did the creditors seize your things, too?"

"No, it wasn't like that." The ugliness of her departure from Seattle still had the power to make her heart tighten. "I could only, um, take one bag." Before he could probe, she added, "It's not easy to travel with a dog and a lot of suitcases."

"You need more things."

"I'm fine." Not that she disagreed with him. She hadn't been thinking clearly, and she'd forgotten to pack things she should have in her hurry to get out of the city. But she didn't have the money to buy anything until she got paid.

He snorted and pulled out his phone. From the arrogant set of his eyebrows and mouth, she knew he was going to ignore her. She put a hand over his mobile.

"Dane, I didn't agree to do this so you could buy me things. People are probably speculating by now."

"So? Let them talk."

"It'll bother me. If they're strangers, I would've tuned them out, but they're your family." Despite what he claimed, he cared about them.

"Fine. What are you going to wear to the opera?"

"What opera?"

"I have two tickets. Opening night."

She stepped back and regarded him. "Do you even like the opera?"

The smile he gave her was positively angelic. "I *love* the opera."

Like anyone was going to believe that. She didn't think he had any tickets either. But he might get a pair just to make a point.

And unfortunately, she didn't have anything that would be suitable, especially for an opening night. He'd undoubtedly put on a tux.

"Thought so," Dane said after a moment of silence. He lifted the phone and dialed. "Josephine. Can you spare about four hours tomorrow? Uh-huh. I know you have the time. Whatever you want. Of course. Excellent..."

While he made the arrangements, Sophia looked around the penthouse, trying to conceal her unease. She'd have to ask Josephine to stick to a realistic budget, so she could pay Dane back later. "Where's Roco?" she said when Dane was finished.

"I don't know." He checked his phone. His eyebrows snapped into a deep V. "Al says he's staying at the mansion overnight. He's been a bit fussy and difficult while you were gone, and Al wanted to keep him overnight. Is that acceptable?"

"Sure. I'll go get him tomorrow."

"No need. Al'll have him delivered." She opened her mouth, and he put a finger over it. "Don't argue."

The doorbell rang, and he tapped his phone. The door clicked open.

A uniformed deliveryman came in with two large insulated chests and put them next to the dining table.

Sophia watched in mild disbelief as he laid out lobster, ravioli, salad and three different desserts—tiramisu, pecan pie and vanilla chiffon cake. He also pulled out a bottle of chilled white wine.

"Is there anything else you need, sir?"

"No, thank you." Dane scrawled his signature on a slip, and the man left.

She stared at the stuff on the table. "When did you have time to order all this?"

"Before we left the grove. Thought you might be tired and want to stay in. Unless you want to go out."

And here she'd thought she'd done a good job of masking her fatigue. "No. Let's stay in."

Dane pulled out a chair for her and uncorked the wine. "How's your hip?" he asked as he poured a glass for her and took his seat.

It had been throbbing for a while, but she didn't want to dwell on it. It was nothing a warm soak couldn't fix. "It's fine." She stuffed ravioli into her mouth, not wanting to talk about it. The complex flavor of creamy sauce and cheesy mushroom stuffing burst on her tongue, making her close her eyes briefly in appreciation.

Dane, however, remained undeterred. "Sophia. Full truth."

"It's really not that bad. A heat pack should take care of it."

His fork and knife went still. Regret and something else far too complex to decipher flitted-through his gaze.

She reached out and patted his hand. "I was lucky. I could've been limping or worse. But look at me. Nobody can tell I even had an accident."

He glanced away, then got up and poured a scotch. She noticed he always reached for the drink whenever he was upset or needed to stay calm.

Why did it bother him so much? Most people didn't care that much about her injuries. The only person who felt deeply about them was Chad, but he considered himself partially responsible for what had happened to her. He thought he should've stayed behind and driven her to the airport. But that was nonsense. His sister had just been diagnosed with breast cancer, and she'd needed him. He'd had to leave on the earliest flight out of Paris. Sophia could never be upset over something like that.

She didn't want to dwell on her achy joints and ruin the moment. Pasting on a smile, she gestured at the dessert. "I want one of each."

"That's more than the entrée."

"What are you implying?" She patted her belly.

Finally, a small smile. "You can have as much as you want." He got up. "I'll start the bath for you."

Dane had to leave before he said something stupid to tip her off. After dumping some bath salts in the huge tub, he ran the hot water and perched on the edge.

His eyes focused on a spot far beyond the mirror as something he'd read some years ago surfaced in his mind: *Kindness is the beginning of cruelty*. He'd thought the sentence apt, smugly confident that he knew its full epigrammatic meaning. He'd seen it growing up in his family, but what Sophia was doing was a million times worse because she didn't have any ill intent. He hated himself for keeping quiet while listening to her trying to console him over her achy hip.

Brutal honesty had always been the foundation of how he dealt with everything and everyone. It saved tremendous amounts of time and angst. It also ensured he never wasted any mental energy on pleasing his father.

But honesty was the one thing that would put disgust and contempt in Sophia's eyes when she looked at him.

He'd never cared what people thought of him… until her.

Call it whatever you like, you're in love with her.

He gripped the edge of the tub and closed his eyes. Why couldn't he have fallen for one of the blondes he'd dated? It would've been so…uncomplicated. He would've been able to go on as before.

Then he felt Sophia's hand on his head, pulling him close. He inhaled her sweet scent and pressed his face against her chest.

"Come join me," she said.

He didn't have to open his eyes to know she was naked. Want thickened his blood, the frustrated, frustrating need from the night before pounding through him.

He stripped down, flinging his clothes on the floor.

She sank into the steaming water and let out a soft sigh. "Just perfect," she murmured, her eyes on him.

He settled down on the other side of the tub and found her foot under the water. Heat flushed her cheeks and creamy breasts. Unlike before she didn't protest, and he gently massaged the sole. How could she think anything attached to her wasn't beautiful?

Objectively speaking, her feet did show abuse. They weren't the softest or the smoothest. But they were more amazing for the marks they bore—the way an old Stradivarius was incredible compared to a shiny violin that had never left its velvet-lined case.

She moaned when he found a knot and worked it, then moved to the other foot. Meticulously and with care, he ran his hands over all of her slick legs. She spread them wider as he came closer to her thighs. Her eyes darkened with desire.

"Dane."

He put his hands on her hips and flexed. "Tell me where it hurts."

Her throat worked. "Not hurt. Empty." She took his hand and put it between her legs.

Fiery need slammed through him. Damn, she was so hot, so slick.

Under the water, hidden from view, his fingers explored her most intimate architecture. She let out a soft cry, and he covered her mouth with his.

He wanted everything she had to give, to store it

in his memory forever, so he would never, ever forget what she was like in a moment like this.

She parted her lips, and his tongue slipped inside. She met him boldly, their tongues probing and fencing for every texture, every taste. Her delicate hands covered his chest. She pinched his small, flat nipples. He groaned and felt her mouth curve underneath his.

Her back arching, she pressed against him, rocking, the hardened tips of her breasts rubbing against his chest. Using his free hand to adjust the angle of her hips, he slid two fingers into her while circling her clit. Air panted out of her, and her skin took on a deeper shade of rose. From the way her inner walls pulsed, she was damn close.

She wrapped her hand around his wrist. "Not like this. I don't want to do it alone. I want you with me."

"I am with you. Now. Always. Forever."

When she didn't let go, he used his free hand to cup her ass, gently stroking the crease, then probing further. A gasp tore from her. He curved his other fingers, rubbing against the sensitive spot inside her.

She gripped his shoulders, her eyes glazing with impending pleasure. Her pelvis moved, seeking more.

He gave it to her. He wanted to see her come undone. Hear her scream his name.

"Yes, yes, yes." Her inner muscles gripped his fingers as an orgasm barreled through her like a freight train. She clutched him harder. "Dane…"

He wanted to take her out of the tub, to the bedroom, but her injured hip needed the heat. She put a hand on his cheek and devoured his mouth like the orgasm had never happened—like she was still starving for him.

"I need you inside me so bad," she said finally when she came up for air.

His heart thundered in his chest, his cock swelling until he thought it might burst. His mouth fused again to hers, he fumbled in the hidden cabinet by the tub for a box of condoms. Anticipation glittered in her darkened eyes when she saw what he had in his hand.

Sitting at the edge of the tub, he took care of the protection. As soon as he was ready, she was on him, her primed body reaching for him with a desperation that matched his own.

Taking her hips in his hands, he plunged into her. Electric pleasure rushed along his spine. Her fingers dug into his shoulders, her beaded nipples rubbing against his chest with every hard drive of his pelvis.

His vision hazed and blood thickened. He was so damn close, but Sophia was going to come with him.

Dipping his head, he captured a beaded nipple in his mouth and sucked hard. She arched her back, her throaty moans echoing along the bathroom tiles.

He increased the tempo, changing the angle of his hips until he found the perfect position. She screamed, her ankles flexing and toes curling.

Only then did he let go and join her in mindless bliss.

Sophia relaxed on the bed as Dane ran a comb through her wet, tangled strands. Most people didn't have the patience to deal with her wavy hair when it was like this, and given how demanding he was, she doubted he would be patient. But he was doing a fine job, and she was too content to complain. After the bath and amazing sex, her muscles felt like warm wax.

"Starting tomorrow, you should really focus on continuing your college," he said, tugging the tight plastic teeth gently through a particularly messy section.

"Why do I sense you want me to quit working?"

"It will be awkward if you keep working for me. Most people can't separate their private and personal lives. And there's the matter of office gossip. It wouldn't bother me, but would probably hurt your feelings. The infighting can get pretty vicious, especially when it's directed at a woman. And it's not like we need your income."

She turned to face him. "It's important for me to find a way to be on my feet. There are people who already think I'm a gold-digger, and I don't want to give them any more reason to believe that."

"If you want to work, you can. There are other companies out there."

What he said made perfect sense. And she didn't want any unnecessary ugliness in their lives. "Okay." She faced forward again, and he resumed the combing. "You're surprisingly patient."

"You mean the hair?"

"Mm-hmm. Most people would've yanked on it at least once by now."

"It takes as long as it takes. Hurrying through would only make things worse." Then he added, "I recommend starting at UCLA next semester."

"UCLA? I'm pretty sure I've missed the deadline for transfer."

"It can be arranged," he said calmly. "I want you to finish your college education and think about your second dream."

"Dane, I appreciate the gesture. But I don't want you calling in favors on my behalf."

"Don't worry. One, I want to, and two, it'll be for multiple good causes." He gave her a light swat on the rear. "Now stop arguing. You'll never find out what you want to do with rest of your life if you don't expose yourself to different things. You didn't dream of becoming some ornery executive's assistant when you were five."

"I didn't dream of being with you like this when I was that age either, but here we are." The mild tingling on her bottom was more distracting than it should have been.

"Yes, here we are." Dropping the comb on the sheet, he pressed his lips against her nape and breathed her in. "Sophia, having you finish school would make me feel better. For any number of reasons."

His large hands flexed around her waist. *It's really generous and considerate of him*, she thought as she rolled over. She should be thrilled to be able to continue her education.

But somehow, she couldn't shake the feeling that he was preparing her for a future without him.

THIRTY-SEVEN

SOPHIA WOKE THE NEXT MORNING TO FIND Dane's side of the bed empty and cool. She dragged herself to the kitchen in a robe and discovered Dane in his suit.

He pushed a cup of tea her way, then took a long swallow of his coffee. "Yes, I need to go to the office. Some things just won't wait." He finished his coffee and kissed Sophia on the forehead.

"When are you going to be home?"

"Definitely by dinner, if not sooner. There's yogurt and fruit in the fridge. You'll want something more substantial for lunch, so call the concierge. Here's the number." He handed her a card.

Just as he was about to go, she grabbed the lapel of his suit and kissed him hard on the mouth. His eyes darkened.

"See you this evening," she said, her breath fanning against his lips.

"Count on it."

After he left, she ate her yogurt and changed into in a fitted t-shirt with a red "Vincero!" across the chest. It was funny how domestic the morning scene had been. But it didn't feel as awkward or…*staged* as when she'd been in Salazar's home. And she liked it that there weren't staff members tripping over each other to cater to her every whim. Although there was that concierge service.

Shaking her head, she settled down on the bed with her phone to read a suspense novel she'd bought before fleeing Seattle. As she thumbed through it, her phone rang. Libby's face popped up on the screen, her tongue sticking out. With a small grin, Sophia picked it up.

"So you *are* still alive! I called for your birthday, but you never got back to me. I would've called again, but then I had to travel to our D.C. office. I seriously thought you died or something."

"Oh my god, I'm so sorry." Sophia cringed. She'd refused to check voice mails or texts after she'd turned on her phone, in case George tried to contact her again. It hadn't even crossed her mind that Libby might have been trying to get in touch.

"And I can't believe you got invited to Mark Pryce's wedding and danced with Justin Sterling and *didn't tell me!*"

Geez, news travels fast. "How did you know?"

"Gossip sites. Officially there was no media there, but you know how it is with photographers these days and their telephoto lenses. Jerks."

"They aren't that bad," Sophia said, although she'd hated them with a passion when they'd published unflattering competition pictures of her. No one needed to know what she looked like in the middle of a triple lutz.

"The photos they took were nice, but I want to know what's going on with you. Are you avoiding me? It's not like you to be like this." Libby sounded hurt.

Yes. Because I still haven't figured out how to break the news that your brother tried to rape me. "I'm really sorry. I was planning to call, but things went sort of crazy here. It's a long story, but I had to leave Seattle."

"Why? Stalkers again?"

"Something like that."

"That's terrible! But you're okay, right?"

"Yeah, I'm fine."

"Okay, good. So where are you now?"

"L.A. But you can't tell anybody, not even George." *Especially not George.* "I don't have Chad anymore, so..." Sophia shrugged away the pain.

"What? Why not?"

"Well...Dad died broke, and Chad can't afford to work for free."

"So the rumors about your dad are true?"

Sophia frowned. Hadn't George told her? "Probably."

Libby sighed. "That's just awful. But you should totally call Chad."

"I can't."

"Why not? Look, I don't know what happened when you had to let him go, but he's pretty unhappy."

Sophia rubbed her forehead. *Damn it.* "That's why I can't call him." Things had already been awkward enough when he'd come to say goodbye, and she didn't want to create more discomfort by contacting him.

"What are you talking about? He's unhappy because you haven't called him!"

"What?"

"I ran into him last week. He was in town to see his sister. He asked me how you were doing, if you were okay. He said he's been hoping you'd call him once the whole thing about…you know…letting him go wore off. I got the feeling that he feels like you don't want to see him because you're embarrassed about something. Maybe he decided you were ashamed of your father's financial situation and didn't want to make it worse by calling first or whatever."

A realization sledgehammered Sophia at the base of her skull, making her feel dizzy. Why hadn't she thought of this before? Having Chad around would ruin George's plan to assault her. Whatever George might've told Chad, it was probably calculated to make Chad stay away.

"Sophia? Sophia, you there?"

"Yeah, I'm here," she said faintly. "I have to go."

"Okay. I'm going to be in L.A. sometime in the next few weeks. Let's meet up."

"Sure, I'd love that. Call me when you have firm dates."

"Will do."

Sophia hung up and dialed Chad, her fingers

shaking. When he answered on the fourth ring, she choked out, "Hello?"

"Sophia! Baby girl, how are you?" His voice was as warm and open as ever, as comforting as warm soft sand on a beach. "I was hoping you'd call. Took a while, huh?"

"I didn't know you were waiting." She sniffed. "I thought…" No. She wasn't going to waste their time talking about George. "What have you been up to?"

"Same old same old." He chuckled. "How about you? Staying with your mom and her new husband now?"

"Um…no. I didn't want to, you know, impose on them or any—"

Chad snorted. "Man. I shouldn't have asked. She didn't even bother to offer, did she?" He'd always been open about how he'd felt about her parents for neglecting her. "If you need a place to crash, you're welcome at my apartment. I still keep it, but I'm not there much. Mi casa es tu casa. You know that, right?"

"Of course. Thank you, Chad, but I'm all right for the moment."

They continued to chat. He told her all about his nephews and nieces, how his sister's cancer was still in remission, and how much he missed her. She told him about her stay in L.A. in a few large brush strokes, how she was going to finish her last two semesters of college at UCLA.

"So Mister Mexico Man wasn't a total washout after all," Chad said.

"He's really a good guy. I'm glad things are working out between us."

"Yeah, yeah that's good. Still… Geraldine Pryce's nephew? Insane. She hates your mother."

"He's not like Geraldine, and she has a good reason. I'd be angry if I were in her shoes."

"Yeah…" Chad sighed. "I'm not saying what your mom did was cool, but things could've been better."

"Things can always be better."

He laughed. "Forgot what a perfectionist you are! Anyway, listen up. You call me if you need anything, you understand? I'm always here for you. Doesn't matter if you can't pay my salary or whatever. I'll always come if you need me. Okay?"

A thick lump clogged her throat. "Okay," she managed. "Thank you."

After they hung up, she buried her face in the pillow. A complex mix of relief, affection and anger coursed through her, and hot tears stung her eyes. Chad wasn't upset with her, and she had another person who was wholly on her side.

A gentle hand rubbed her back. "What's wrong?"

Dane.

She wiped moisture from her cheeks. "When did you get back?"

"Just now." His eyebrows pinched together, and he searched her face. "What happened?"

"I just talked with Chad."

"Chad?" Confusion clouded his face for a moment, then cleared. "Your chaperon slash bodyguard."

"More than that. Like a parent." She sat up. "I thought he didn't want to talk to me after he was let go. I couldn't pay him, you know? But it turned out that he thought I didn't want to talk to him."

"How is that even possible?"

She shook her head. "Some miscommunication."

He put an arm around her and pulled her close. "I'm sorry." He pressed his lips on her head. "That's terrible."

Anger at George surged inside her. Before she could stop herself, she said, "No. Criminal. That's how it was. The rat bastard lied to Chad so he could try to rape me."

Dane went absolutely still. "What?" He turned her around so he could look her in the eye. "What happened?"

"When I learned my dad left me penniless… Geo—" She stopped. She couldn't reveal the name yet. Libby didn't know, and Dane certainly wouldn't sit on his hands if he knew. "Chad had to get another job. He cares for me, but the man has to eat and keep a roof over his head. But at the same time if he knew I was in danger, he'd come for me and make whoever hurt me sorry. So this asshole lied to Chad and made me feel guilty so we wouldn't contact each other. Then he tried to…you know."

Dane's knuckles whitened, while dark red flushed his cheeks. Fury burned hot in his eyes, but when he spoke, his voice was soft. Almost calm. "But you got away."

"He underestimated me. I'm a lot stronger than I look. All figure skaters are. So I smashed his head with a lamp."

"Good. Is he dead?" Asked in a completely matter-of-fact tone.

"He's not dead, but he won't bother me again." *Probably.*

"So that's the real reason you had to leave Seattle."

"Yes. I thought I was all alone. To know there was still somebody in my corner… I can't even describe what a relief that is." She sniffed. "I'm not alone."

"Chad isn't the only one you can rely on. I'm here for you." Dane rested his forehead on hers. "I'll always be here for you."

Many people had told her the same thing. Her coaches. Her skating friends. Her parents, even. But she'd known they hadn't really meant it. The real meaning was: *so long as the money keeps coming, so long as it's convenient* and *so long as it doesn't get in the way of my social calendar.*

But Dane's promise didn't come with an unspoken qualification. People thought he was cold because he was blunt and would never say anything nice just to sound nice. But there was a good side to his social tactlessness. When he said something, he meant it one hundred percent.

"I know." She tilted her mouth up. "Kiss me."

His lips brushed against hers, the touch feathery. He felt so warm, so sweet it made her chest ache. She pressed closer, deepening the kiss, and he fell slowly back on the bed, pulling her on top of him. She traced his lips with her tongue. She'd never taken the initiative, been so bold with him like this.

His mouth was surprisingly soft and full, his lower lip gently curved and plump. Somehow, she'd never noticed that before. He'd always seemed so unyielding and untouchable, like a frigid northern mountain.

When his tongue met hers, she moaned deeply in her throat. He kept his hands on the mattress, letting her control the depth and tempo of the kiss. Lying on him, the entire length of her body tingled with feral, elemental awareness. Hot blood pumped through her, her heart knocking hard against her ribs.

Almost without thinking she gripped his shoulder and put a hand behind his head. She felt like she was drowning in him, and she never wanted to come out of it. Desire pulsed in the slick emptiness between her thighs, and she deepened the kiss, pressing their bodies together until nothing separated them, and cradled his thick, hard length between her legs.

Her breasts felt pleasurably crushed against his chest, the nipples beading and aching for more. Their mouths still together, she rocked, determined to drive both of them insane with need.

He let out a low groan. His hot hands tunneled under her shirt, one roaming up along her back and the other going under the waistband of her skirt and panties to grab her ass. She gasped at how good it felt. How turned on she was.

"You're sensitive all over," he whispered into her ear. He licked and nibbled on her neck.

Shivers went through her. She clenched her inner muscles, the emptiness like a knife. His teeth nipped at her, and a sharp pleasure streaked from the spot on her collarbone all the way down to her dripping core.

"Please..."

He pushed her shirt out of the way, then her bra. Her breasts popped free, and he latched onto a nipple, pulling it into his mouth. His cheeks hollowed with the strength of his suction, and she tunneled her hands into his hair and arched her back, silently begging for more. She couldn't speak, not with the white heat pulsing through her.

The hand that was under her skirt circled around to her front. He ran a finger along her swollen lips and then began to gently rub her clit. She cried out, and his mouth was back on hers, swallowing the rest of the sound. She clutched him harder against her and rocked. Stars and colors burst behind her eyes, and pleasure curled at the base of her spine.

Suddenly he plunged two fingers into her. And they were enough to push her over.

She shuddered as an intense orgasm crashed through her body. Dane held her through it all, then stripped them both, throwing their clothes on the floor in a careless heap.

His taut, heavy body lay next to her, and he pulled her on top of him until she sat astride. The lean muscles on his belly tightened as she rolled a condom down his erection and positioned herself.

Placing her palms on his chest, she sank onto him, filling herself with his thick cock. Sweat beaded on his skin as she moved up and down. It was different being on top, controlling the angle and depth of the penetration. She leaned forward and ground herself against him. She was so full, and her clit felt amazing against his hard pubic bone. One shockwave after another swept through her as she moved, her gaze locked with his.

"Dane..."

"Sophia."

Sweet reverence shook his voice, and she clenched her teeth. She wanted to draw the moment out as long as possible, but she was so, so close. Pleasure as sharp as a blade seemed to split open her heart, and she suddenly knew that he'd always been meant for her, maybe from their time in Mexico. How else to explain this intense connection between them?

A low groan rumbled through his chest, and he put his feet flat on the mattress. He thrust into her, his powerful pelvis and ass flexing. She met him stroke for stroke. Air sawed in and out of her, the sound rough and uneven. His heart thundered underneath her palms, and she trembled on a precipice...

Another climax barreled through her, and she convulsed. "Dane...Dane..." She vaguely heard herself whimper as she fell from her peak.

He gripped her hips and plunged into her so hard she was surprised her bones didn't rattle. A guttural shout tore from his corded neck as his entire body bowed from the force of his orgasm.

He wrapped his arms around her and tucked her head in the crook of his neck, even as he fought to control his breathing.

They stayed like that, heart to heart, until she could barely hang onto consciousness. Her ear pressed against his chest, she relaxed, feeling safer than ever before.

Sophia felt almost boneless, but Dane knew she wasn't quite asleep. She was most likely in that blissful in-between state.

It was beyond him even as he held her. He stared at the ceiling. It infuriated him she'd been so alone and helpless. At least he knew what he'd done to deserve all the shit in his life—being born when he shouldn't have. What had she done?

She pressed her lips over his heart. "Thank you."

"Mmm? For what?"

"For being generous." She kissed the spot again. "And honest."

Bitterness and self-incrimination spread like poison in his veins. She had no idea how wrong she was. If he'd been honest…

His hands clutched her.

If he'd been honest, he would've lost her. It didn't matter what he'd done to make up for the past—if she found out, she would never forgive him.

"Remember what I said?" he said. "Don't ever thank me."

She snorted. "I can thank whoever I want, even if it's you. You'll just have to get used to people acknowledging you when you do something nice for them."

Each one of her words cut into him like a shard of glass. "Then promise you won't leave me."

"Why would I want to do that?" A bemused smile curved her lips. "I don't think I could even if I wanted to. Look how fate put us together again."

Fate. Maybe there was something to the idea. He hoped so. But their time together felt like that drawn out, ticking moment before a bomb exploded.

THIRTY-EIGHT

Sophia didn't want to go shopping with Josephine Martinez, but Dane refused to budge on the matter. "If I let you go alone, you're going to buy the cheapest things you can find off a clearance rack," he said, scarfing down a big plate of breakfast eggs and bacon.

"What's wrong with shopping at sales? Don't you like saving money?"

"Penny pinching." He shook his head. "It's cruelty to copper, you know."

"What?"

"Copper has feelings too. Just because it's strong and silent..."

"Seriously?"

"...can't blush, since it's already red..."

She laughed. "Did you dump some rum in your coffee?"

"It's for a good cause. Gives Josephine a job. Surely you don't object to that."

She sighed. This was a small battle not worth fighting over. The real one would be when she saw the fashion consultant and tried to set a strict budget.

"Don't worry. She has a great taste," Dane said.

"If by 'great' you mean 'expensive,' I agree. I've seen how Josephine dresses."

"I'll send you a driver at around ten."

"Does he know where we're supposed to meet?"

"She's going to text him the address. Preferably someplace exceptionally tasteful," Dane said, getting up to leave for work. "I'll see you for lunch."

Shaking her head, Sophia put on the simple sheath dress that Salazar had bought her for the wedding. Despite Dane's insistence, she hadn't gotten rid of it yet. She would've preferred to wear one of her old things, but she didn't want to embarrass Josephine by being turned away at the door of some fancy boutique. No *Pretty Woman* moments if she could avoid them.

Right at ten, a uniformed driver arrived with a black limo. Sophia stared. It was much too extravagant, but she bit her tongue. *Not the chauffeur's fault.*

It took a little less than an hour to reach their destination. Or...maybe not.

"Aren't I meeting Josephine Martinez?" she asked, staring at the two-story residential building outside as the limo engine died.

She'd figured they'd meet at a mall or somewhere similar. But this place was something between a house and a mansion complete with a garden. Double columns framed the main door. An elaborate bronze lion-head knocker shone in the sun. She couldn't imagine what kind of shopping could be done there.

"Yes, ma'am." The driver opened her door. "This is the address."

She got out and knocked.

A comfortably rounded middle-aged woman answered the door. She wore a white t-shirt and khaki shorts. If this was the kind of place you went to get a gown grand enough for the opening night at an opera, Sophia was the empress of China.

"Hello," the other woman said with a friendly smile. "You must be Sophia Reed. Please come in. Everyone's waiting for you."

Everyone?

The woman led Sophia down a long hall. A few interesting contemporary art pieces hung on the walls. The interior was bigger than it looked from the outside. At the end was a living room. Josephine was standing with her arms crossed. Just like at the grove, she was impeccable in a sea-green dress—the latest design from some famous brand undoubtedly. Sophia hadn't seen the woman in anything other than the most fashionable clothing. Josephine's thick dark hair hung loosely, a shaggy look that was emphasized by the way she was shaking her head.

"Absolutely not, Vanessa. That's the craziest idea I've ever heard."

"Oh for god's sake, I'm the client!"

"And I have a professional duty to stop you when

you're about to commit a fashion *faux pas*." Suddenly she turned. "Hey, there you are."

Vanessa swung her head so she could see Sophia over the back of her couch.

"Um… Hi." Sophia waved.

"Tell her, Sophia. Tell her she needs to listen to me unless she wants her newborn to wear the most hideous outfit ever," Josephine said.

"No, tell her the customer is always right."

Oh boy. "You should listen to the professional," Sophia said. "But at the same time"—she turned to Josephine—"you should select items that reflect the taste and sensibility of the client."

Vanessa blinked, then snickered. "Do you have any legal training?"

Ginger came in from the other side, bare feet slapping the hardwood floor. Unlike at the wedding, she wore a comfy tank top and denim shorts. The gorgeous blonde rolled her eyes and put her hands on her hips. "Are you guys finally finished arguing?"

"Sort of, with Sophia telling both of us to shut up and grow up."

Sophia cleared her throat. "I believe I was more diplomatic than that." She turned to Josephine. "So. Are you ready?"

Before the personal shopper and fashion consultant could respond, Vanessa said, "Not just yet. Please sit down. I asked her to bring you here because I wanted to check you out without Dane around." She cocked her head and regarded Sophia thoughtfully. "You're not dumb like the blondes he generally likes to date."

Ginger flushed. "Do you have to be rude?"

"Apparently yes!" came a response from the kitchen. Jane waved. A cheery apple-colored apron wrapped around her yellow sundress. "Heya! I'm making sandwiches for lunch. Hope you like them."

"I love sandwiches," Sophia said.

"But first, serve the apple pie. Junior wants some," Vanessa said. "Actually never mind. I won't fit into any of my maternity clothes at this rate."

"You're fine." Jane came back with a platter of warm, gooey apple pie, vanilla ice cream, and plates and silverware for everyone. She served Sophia first. "Vanessa wanted to talk, but then I decided that the least you deserve is some homemade pie and ice cream for us commandeering your time like this." Her smile held a tinge of apology. "I hope you don't mind."

"It's all right," Sophia said. It was impossible to stay upset with the sweet woman who served a slice of piping hot pie that smelled like heaven.

Jane then sent plates loaded with the pie and ice cream to everyone else.

Vanessa dug in and moaned. "This is amazing. Like, 'almost makes me forget what I was supposed to be doing next' amazing."

"I'm a pro." Jane beamed.

Sophia took a bite as well and joined the chorus of moans. Jane's pie was to die for. "It's probably the best pie I've ever had."

"Thank you."

"But I'm sure you didn't ask me here"—Sophia glanced briefly at Josephine—"to share a pie." She turned to Vanessa. Since this was her home, it seemed most logical that she was the one in charge. "Didn't Justin already tell you what you wanted to know after he danced with me at the wedding?"

"He did, but I just can't believe it. You like Dane? For real?"

"What's so unbelievable about that?"

"No, the question is, what's *believable* about it? Women don't like him, not the way you mean," Vanessa said. "I can't help but think you actually, you know…*really* like him. And Dad too! I'm trying to wrap my mind around it."

This was awkward, but at the same time this was Dane's family. "Salazar was the first person who offered to help me when I was down and almost out. I'm sure you know my father left me penniless. As for Dane… I like it that he doesn't treat me like some delicate breakable thing. He doesn't sugarcoat things, but he's surprisingly sensitive."

The other women's jaws dropped.

Ginger was the first to recover. "Sensitive? Does Dane have a long-lost twin?"

"Not that I know of," Vanessa said.

"What do you really want to know?" Sophia said. "Are you worried that I'm a gold digger?"

"No. That's what puzzles me. The women my brother tends to go for are all pretty easy to peg—the same for my dad—but not you. I—"

Just that moment, Dane burst in with the flustered housekeeper following him. "What the hell is the meaning of this, Josephine?" he demanded, his jaw tight.

Josephine blanched. "Dane, we—"

"I invited her over for lunch," Vanessa said, her chin tilted defiantly.

"This is *not* what I asked you to do," he said to Josephine, as though his sister hadn't spoken. "You'll hear from my lawyer." His voice was eerily quiet, but tension rolled off him in ominous waves. Then he turned to Vanessa and the other women. "If you want to have a *real* lunch with Sophia, great. I'll even pay for it. If you're aiming for an inquisition, get in touch with my lawyer. You aren't harassing her."

Sophia put a hand on his sleeve. "It's not like that. I'm fine."

He pulled his arm until her hand fell into his palm. "You may be fine, but I'm not. They'll show you the respect you deserve. And next time, contact me immediately when they pull this kind of stunt."

Vanessa blinked a few times. "You're actually serious."

"As a cardiac arrest. Otherwise I wouldn't be here. Don't test me, Vanessa. You know what an asshole I can be." His lips curled. "The only reason I'm not going to ruin you for this is because you're my family, and Shirley asked me to be nice. But not even her dying wish will keep you safe next time."

He led Sophia out, a protective hand on the small

of her back. When they got back outside, her chauffeur jumped to his feet. "Mr. Pryce."

"You're fired. Consider yourself lucky that's the only thing I'm doing."

She stopped. "Dane."

"He didn't do his job right. It's not his job to make things easier for my family to bully you." He opened the door to his car. "Get in. We're finished here."

She did, then turned to him as soon as he was inside as well. "How did you even know I was at your sister's?"

"The GPS system." He looked straight ahead, driving away from the house. "It texts me your location every time the car's parked."

The nerve! "You were *spying* on me?" She crossed her arms.

"No. I was making sure you didn't somehow convince Josephine to set a budget *you* were comfortable with."

"I highly doubt I would've been able to do that."

"You underestimate your powers of persuasion. Anyway, it was a good thing that I set it up. Otherwise who knows what those women would've done."

"Dane, those women are your *family*—or practically—and they're worried." She sighed, uncrossing her arms. "And how can you blame them? You thought the worst of the situation when I first showed up in the city."

His knuckles tightened. "Are you still upset about that?"

"Of course not. I'm just trying to show you how unreasonable you're being."

"You have no idea how patient and reasonable I am right now. You don't know what I wouldn't do to keep you protected."

IT DIDN'T MATTER WHAT SOPHIA DID, HOW MUCH she cajoled. Dane wouldn't discuss the incident. But she didn't believe he would really sic his lawyers on Josephine…would he?

The only thing he'd done was buy her more clothes than she could possibly wear. After taking her home, he had somebody come to the penthouse to get her measurements and deliver twenty boxes of clothes, underwear and shoes within three hours.

"If you tell me what you're going to do to Vanessa for real, I'll keep them," Sophia said, eyeing the piles with unease. They were excessive. On the other hand, he never did anything by half-measures. She should've expected this.

His expression remained bland. "If you don't keep the clothes, I'll sue my sister for sure."

"At least hire the driver back."

"Absolutely not. I don't pay people who can't complete their job to my satisfaction."

"It was an honest mistake. He probably had no idea what they were going to do and just took me to the address Josephine gave him."

"So you do admit it was her fault."

"*No!*"

"The discussion's over, Sophia. They knew what they were getting into."

She snapped her mouth shut. Knowing why he was doing this made it harder for her to stay angry with him for refusing to discuss it further. On the other hand… "You can't sue people every time you don't like what they do."

"Sure I can. Why else do you think I have a law firm on retainer?" He placed his credit card on the counter. "I have to go back to the office, so take this and treat yourself to something nice. A spa or massage or something. And sorry about my asshole family."

Her arms crossed, she glared at the credit card. Like she was actually in any mood for a spa treatment!

Maybe he'd be more amenable after work. If nothing else it'd give him some time to calm down.

But he remained impossible. Not even a fabulous Chinese dinner could change his mind.

"You're so unforgiving. Are you always like this?" she asked.

"When it involves you, yes."

"Argh!"

She plopped down on the couch and turned on her tablet. There was no point anymore. She was going to read and see if it helped her relax.

Dane didn't try to talk to her. Instead he reviewed work documents.

When she changed and crawled into bed a few

hours later and put her arm on his chest, Dane cocked an eyebrow.

"What?" she said.

"Sex isn't going to work."

She shook her head. "I wasn't planning on it. I want us to have sex because that's what we want, not for some…ulterior reason." She put a finger over his mouth as he moved to kiss her. "I'm not finished. Our bedroom shouldn't be a battleground. You're going to know when I'm upset with you or disagree with you, but I'm not going to turn that into some kind of fight here too. This should be our safe place."

Something eased in his gaze, and he pressed his lips against her finger. "Thank you."

"Now." She pulled the finger away, giving him a soft smile. "You may kiss me properly."

THIRTY-NINE

SOPHIA KEPT HERSELF BUSY FOR THE NEXT FEW weeks. She'd thought it'd be difficult without a full-time job, but doing all the paperwork she needed to start at UCLA kept her occupied. She didn't know what strings Dane had pulled, but somehow she was allowed to start from the next semester. Then there was the job search. She was determined to begin working as soon as possible.

Still… It was frustrating to look for a position when almost every listing she was interested in required a bachelor's degree. What mysteries of the universe was she going to learn in the final two semesters of college that would make her so much more qualified than she was now?

Since she didn't have to dress to be seen, she wore comfy clothes every day—loose t-shirts and cropped jeans. If Dane was in the mood to go out, he called her at least an hour in advance to let her know. The purported opera outing was beginning to take on a mythical quality, and she was starting to suspect that it had been a sham all along. Regardless, it was impossible to hold that against the man who made her feel like the luckiest woman in the world every day. She buried her nose in the bouquet of pale pink roses that had arrived earlier that morning and smiled.

Her phone rang. “Hey!” came Libby’s exuberant greeting. “Got a minute?”

“Sure. Nothing but time these days.”

“That sounds so weird coming from you. You were always so busy!”

“Well, you know… I’m not competing anymore.”

“Do you…uh…miss it?”

Sophia considered. “No. I mean, I did, but now there’s other stuff.” Like finishing college. A future with Dane. Although they’d never talked about it, she couldn’t help but think…

“That’s great. I’m so happy for you. So how’s Geraldine’s nephew treating you?”

“Oh my god, *fabulous*. He makes me feel so special. I can’t describe it. It’s like he really appreciates everything I am, not just the parts that are sort of convenient, or make him look good, you know?” She sighed.

“Was that a sigh? After describing The Perfect Man?”

“No. Well, it was, but—

“Yeah, I think it was. And it wasn’t a good sigh. Which is a little weird.”

“Well… I don’t know. You’ve had more experience with relationships, so maybe you can help.”

"Of course. Just tell me."

"There are times I feel like he's being a little strange."

"You mean, like…in bed?"

Sophia laughed despite herself. "Uh, *no*. All that's fine. Better than fine."

"Oooh, lucky girl. Okay, so strange how?"

Sophia searched for the right words. "Like, I feel this odd vibe of, I don't know…desperation or despair or something like that from him. It's hard to describe, but it's like he's expecting something horrible to happen."

"To him?"

"I guess. If I didn't know any better, I'd say he's afraid I'm going to leave him…except that's crazy."

"Maybe he thinks you're going to pull the same stunt he pulled on you in Mexico. Revenge. Tit for tat, right? But if that's the case I'd say he's not the right one for you. He should know you better by now."

"No, that's not it. If he thought that, we wouldn't be together." That much, Sophia was certain of.

"Then I don't know what to say. Why don't you, you know, ask him? Get a couple drinks in him first and make him talk."

She snorted. "He can drink like a fish. He could drink an ice rink full of liquor and still be sober."

"Then why don't you wait until we see each other in person? Bring him along so I can do the Best Friend Inspection. I'm in L.A. right now actually."

Sophia sat up straight. "Really? Awesome. When do you want to meet?"

"Don't know yet. I have to check with George. He's in the city, too."

The news hit Sophia like a brick. Sweat slickened her hands, and something sour flooded her mouth. She breathed through her nose audibly. "What's he doing here?"

"Some kind of a new business deal with a guy named Starling or something. I wasn't paying attention. He's been here for a couple of weeks."

"He doesn't have to come." There was no way Sophia was going to see Libby if George was tagging along.

"But he's going to want to see you, too."

"You know what? I really need to check with Dane. He's so busy, he's always got all these meetings and presentations and everything, but maybe he can find some time, you know?" Sophia clicked her mouth shut when she realized she was babbling.

"Sure! Text me with a time."

"Actually why don't you text me with a few time slots that are good for you and we can go from there?"

"Will do, this afternoon. Love ya!" Libby signed off with a loud kissy noise into the phone.

"Love you too."

Sophia tossed the phone on the counter and buried her face in her hands. It didn't matter where Libby was now. Sophia couldn't see her best friend, not when George was around. But she still didn't know how to tell Libby the truth without hurting her.

Someone started knocking at the door. Sophia jerked around, almost falling off the stool she was sitting on. Her heart hammered with a spike of adrenaline.

It's not George. He doesn't know where I am.

Fingering her necklace, she took a quick peek through the peephole and opened the door. On the other side was Vanessa. Her red hair fell around her face in loose curls. She'd gotten even bigger. The yellow maternity dress she had on made her look like she'd swallowed the sun.

"What are you doing here?" Sophia asked.

"I was in the neighborhood."

"Oh. Okay."

"Can I come in or are you going to make me stand out in the hall?" A small smile punctuated the question.

Sophia stepped aside. Vanessa walked in, her two-and-a-half-inch heels clacking on the hard floor. It was amazing she could still walk in those shoes.

"How far along are you?"

"Eight and a half months. Two more weeks!" A giant huff of breath. "God, I can't wait." Vanessa went to the couch and sat down with an audible sigh. Her ankles were thick, her feet visibly swollen.

"Want to put your feet up?"

"No." She put a hand to her back and bit her lower lip. "Actually, yes. If you don't mind."

Sophia put a cushion on the low coffee table. "There."

"Thanks." Vanessa sighed. "I used to have nice ankles and feet. Now they look like I'm part elephant."

"You should see mine. Skating is terrible on the feet."

"Nothing's worse than cankles."

"Yeah, but another month or two and you'll get your body back." Sophia gestured at the kitchen. "Want something to drink?"

"No, thanks. I can't even have a sip of water without having to run to the bathroom in ten minutes. I know, I know, TMI."

Sophia sat in an armchair. "I don't think it's that bad. At least you're honest."

Vanessa studied her. "That sounds awfully like something Dane would say."

"Maybe his good qualities are rubbing off me.

"Ha. This is the point where I think I'm supposed to give a hollow laugh."

"So, does Dane know that you're here to see me?" Before the redhead could get any wrong ideas, Sophia raised her hand. "I'm only asking to see if I want to keep your visit quiet or not. I don't want him trying to sue you or something."

"He doesn't know, but you don't have to worry. The last time we spoke was about a week ago. He called to let me know that he wasn't going to sue anybody. He said it was your idea. *Not* suing, that is."

"Well, that's a relief." She'd been worried, but it'd been impossible to bring the matter up again with Dane being so stubborn. He probably hadn't fired the driver either. "I'm glad. But it wasn't me. He wouldn't have done anything to hurt you."

"How can you be so sure?"

"It's obvious he cares deeply about you. Everyone criticizes the way he speaks, but nobody has pointed out what he'd done to help his family. He adored his grandmother, and he's the one who brought his youngest brother home."

Vanessa winced. "Shane's situation was different."

"That's not what I heard. Shane would still be in Thailand if Dane hadn't sent Ginger to bring him home." Sophia shifted in her seat. "I'm surprised you never noticed his kindness."

Vanessa blinked a few times, then shook her head. "You're entirely too optimistic when it comes to Dane. Anyway, I'm not here to talk about him. I'm here to say that I'm sorry about what happened last time. I just really wanted to know what kind of person you were, and…you were nothing like I expected. Then when Dane stormed into my place…" She laughed shakily. "It's just…not something I ever thought I would see. He generally doesn't care much about women he's with. Ice water in his veins and all that."

Jeez. Did everyone in the family believe that?

Vanessa continued. "It's not easy for me to be rational when it comes to my family. We've all had a difficult time growing up"—she flashed a sheepish smile—"which sounds ridiculous when we've had every material advantage. Our parents have always been rich, and we never lacked for anything…except affection and love. But I think Dane had it the hardest. He experienced what it could've been like. Our parents weren't always so stilted and awkward around each other. They were actually in love at one point. So he saw the kind of ideal family life we could've had, only to have it yanked away from him. The rest of us didn't have it quite that bad."

It finally clicked for Sophia—the source for Dane's anxiety. He thought what they had together would disappear, just like the lovely period from his childhood. She reached over and briefly laid her hand on the other woman's. "Vanessa, thank you for telling me this. Really." She smiled. "So does this mean you don't think I'm a gold-digger?"

Vanessa shifted. "Believe me, one thing I'm *not* worried about is some woman taking financial advantage of Dane." She shifted again, her eyebrows dipping into a V. Sweat beaded along her hairline.

Sophia peered at her. "Are you all right?"

"No. Or maybe yes. I don't know."

Vanessa was visibly panting now. Sophia put a hand on her shoulder, and Vanessa took it. "I think it's the baby."

"The…baby…?"

Vanessa nodded. "Yes. I think he's about to come. I've been…having contractions since late morning, but…didn't think…" She took several huffing breaths, then seemed to relax a bit. "I've had false alarms before. But I guess it's real this time. I think my water just broke."

Sophia's mouth dried. She had no idea what was

involved in child labor except what she'd seen on TV. "Tell me what to do. Who do I need to call?"

"Justin. But can you help me up first? I want to get to my car."

Sophia put her arms around Vanessa and pulled her up. Her skin was flushed and clammy with sweat, and she was panting again. Sophia squeezed Vanessa's hand and led her to the lobby.

"Where did you park?" Sophia asked.

"In the front. The concierge service downstairs has my keys."

Right on cue, the concierge rep appeared like an apparition. He took one look at Vanessa then turned to Sophia. "Miss Reed?"

"She's going into labor," Sophia said. "Can you help me?"

He jumped into action, carrying Vanessa to the car and depositing her on the passenger seat. "Anything else?"

Sophia glanced at Vanessa, who shook her head. "No, thank you." Sophia climbed behind the wheel.

"Call my husband. Please."

"What's the number?"

Vanessa groped blindly and pulled her phone from her purse. "Press one."

A couple of dial tones and a warm male voice said, "Hello, sweetheart. How are you feeling?"

"This is Sophia. Vanessa's going into labor *right now*. What hospital should I take her to?"

"*I'm not having my baby at the hospital!*" Vanessa bellowed, making Sophia jump.

"Ignore her," Justin's voice said in her ear. "I don't care that it's only two weeks early. I'm not taking any chances." He gave her the name and address of a private hospital. "You know where it is?"

Amazingly enough, she did. "Yes."

"Take her there. They'll have everything ready. I'm leaving right now. Sorry to impose on you, Sophia. I should've insisted on a chauffeur."

"I'm happy to help. Can you call the family and—?"

"I'll take care of everything else. Just get Vanessa to the hospital."

FORTY

THANKFULLY THE TRAFFIC WASN'T TOO BAD. Once they reached the hospital, everyone sprang into action, taking her and Vanessa to the private wing.

Even though Vanessa had complained about wanting to have the baby at home, she didn't put up a fight when the nurses wheeled her away. Justin arrived five minutes later and ran right past Sophia to reach his wife.

Sophia didn't blame the man. His hair stuck up like he'd run his hands through it during the drive to the hospital. Lines bracketed his mouth; he'd lost the tie he normally wore and undone the top two buttons on his shirt.

None of the rest of the family had arrived yet, so Sophia pulled out her phone and called Dane.

"Hello, Sophia. Is everything okay?"

"Of course. Why?"

"It's not like you to call during the day."

"Oh." She frowned. Maybe he was busy. "Am I interrupting anything?"

"Not at all. Always happy to hear your voice."

She flushed, warm pleasure unfurling inside her chest. Now that she thought about it, she *was* intruding on his day. His schedule was always packed.

"I have a surprise for you, so I'll be home a bit early today," Dane said.

"If it's something expensive, you should return it."

He laughed. "It's priceless, but you won't want me to return it."

She rolled her eyes, even though she couldn't stop smiling. "By the way, did you get a message from Justin?"

"No idea. I've been in meetings all morning. Why?"

"Vanessa's having her baby. Like, *now*. We're at the hospital." She told him the location.

"Isn't it early?"

"About two weeks, but I'm sure she and the baby will be fine."

"Okay. I'll be there soon." He hung up.

Sophia bought a bottle of water and waited. It didn't take long before Ceinlys arrived, her stilettos clicking on the hard hospital floor. Dressed in an elegant cream-colored one-piece, she looked like she was about to have lunch with the queen of England. Her perfectly coiffed hair didn't show the slightest hint of gray. A slim leather belt cinched around her waist accentuated her trim figure.

Feeling like a grubby urchin compared to the impeccably groomed woman, Sophia braced herself. Technically, she hadn't done anything while she'd been staying with Salazar. But appearances mattered, especially to families like the Pryces. Although Ceinlys had been courteous and gracious at the wedding, there was no social reason for her to restrain herself now.

"Sophia."

She swallowed. "Hi, Ceinlys."

"Thank you for taking care of Vanessa."

Oh. "It was nothing."

"Not nothing." Ceinlys shook her head. "No telling what would've happened if she'd been alone or, god forbid, driving. Justin should've gotten her a chauffeur weeks ago." Her mouth thinned.

"I don't think Vanessa wanted one. But her doctor's here now. I'm sure she and her baby will be fine."

"Vanessa has always been headstrong. But you're very kind." Ceinlys sat next to Sophia. "This may take a while. The first baby is always the most difficult. If you want to go home, I'll arrange for a car."

"It's all right. Dane's going to be here soon."

Ceinlys stared at her freshly manicured nails for a few moments, then uncrossed and recrossed her legs. "How are things with the two of you?"

"Wonderful. He's very sweet."

"I'm glad to hear that." Ceinlys smiled, but her eyes were still guarded. "Not many people think that about him."

"They don't understand that he says exactly what

he means." Sophia turned slightly toward her. "It's nice to be with someone whose intentions I don't have to second-guess."

"I suppose that's true." Ceinlys smiled again, this time with more warmth.

"And part of that is that he's very honest in his affection."

"Perhaps it's you who's showed him it's acceptable to express affection. Although he's still closed off and cold with other people."

Sophia laughed, and after a moment Ceinlys joined in. "Yeah," Sophia said. "I've noticed a bit of that here and there."

"Haven't we all." The older woman sighed. "None of my other children are that way. I don't know what happened with Dane."

"Is it because…" Sophia debated, but she had to know. It had been churning in her mind for a while now. She lowered her voice. "Is it because you and Salazar blamed him for being born and ruining your married life?"

Ceinlys drew back slightly. "What on earth are you talking about?"

"I thought…I mean, don't you feel the same way about it?" Sophia bit her lower lip, wondering if she'd misjudged the situation.

"About *what*, precisely?"

"I'm sorry. I shouldn't have said any—"

"You will tell me *exactly* what you're talking about, and you will tell me *now*."

Now I've done it. "I heard Dane and Salazar arguing, and your husband said that Dane ruined everything the moment he was conceived."

Ceinlys's mouth parted, the blood draining from her face. Not even the perfectly applied layers of makeup could hide the sudden pallor. "I…I had no idea. I thought it was some exaggerated anger on Dane's part." Ceinlys clutched her purse, her knuckles white. "I don't know why Salazar would think that or even say that to Dane. We'd been having issues even before I became pregnant for the first time. It had nothing to do with him. Nothing! I—"

Just then, Salazar arrived. He was dapper in his crisp button down shirt and dark slacks. His steps were light and springy as though he was dancing to a tune only he could hear.

Ceinlys rose to her feet. "Excuse me. I need to speak to my husband."

"I'm sorry I said anything. I shouldn't have," Sophia said.

"It's something I needed to know. I wish I'd known earlier." She gave Sophia a strained smile. "Thank you."

Her back stiff, she walked toward her husband.

CEINLYS WAS SHAKING INSIDE. SHE'D HAD NO IDEA Salazar had treated Dane with such cruelty. If she'd known… If she'd known, would it have made any difference?

Even with all the history between them, she couldn't deny Salazar could still make her heart flutter. Maybe it was because he could be dashing and romantic when he made the effort. Except those occasions had become increasingly rare as the years went by.

When he'd taken Sophia in, Ceinlys had assumed that he was having an affair with the girl. But it was apparent now that that wasn't the case. He genuinely wanted to help her, and that reminded Ceinlys of the man she'd fallen in love with. Still, what Sophia had revealed wasn't something Ceinlys could ignore. He had no right to blame Dane for their failures.

"Salazar. I doubted you'd come."

"Well, her real father's gone, and"—he shrugged and glanced away—"I'm the closest thing she has."

A knot in her heart tightened. Here was the good and kind Salazar again. "Can we talk for a moment?" A couple of nurses hurried by. "In private?"

"Yes. I was hoping to talk to you… Well, to you through your lawyer." His voice was as light as his step, but his eyes betrayed nothing. "But we can talk without the overpriced middlemen if you want."

She nodded and led the way.

The wing for Vanessa was private, with no other patients on the floor. The kind of comfort and luxury only people like the Sterlings could buy. When Ceinlys had had her children she'd had a private wing to herself, not because Salazar had cared, but because that was what Shirley had decided her grandchildren deserved.

At the end of the hall was an empty room, with a neatly made bed and some plastic flowers. Ceinlys walked inside, Salazar following closely.

She spun around to face him. "Is it true that you blamed Dane for our failing marriage?"

He tilted his head. "Who told you that?

"I have my sources."

He shrugged. "I never blamed Dane for the fact that our marriage failed. I blamed him for being born, and preventing me from leaving."

Semantics. "Why didn't you leave?

"I was planning to. But then you got pregnant. I couldn't leave the woman who just announced she was carrying my first child. So I stayed. I told my lawyers that it wouldn't be necessary to file for divorce."

Ceinlys pressed her shaking lips together. But the tremors didn't ease. They spread through her body until her knees were almost knocking against each other. She clasped her hands tightly. "You should've left me back then. We could have saved ourselves decades of pain."

"I agree. I should've known better, which is why I said I wanted to talk to you."

"So you're agreeing to the terms?"

Salazar shoved his hands into his pockets. "No. Your terms are unacceptable." He raised a hand, stopping her from speaking. "You're demanding fifty million. You can do better than that. You've given me four children, and I've given them each fifty million dollars. Surely you're worth more than that." He caressed her cheek, the touch feather soft. “The settlement is two hundred million dollars. Fifty per child.”

Ceinlys almost fell. Her vision dimmed for a moment, and she fought for air, unable to understand what he was saying. Two hundred million dollars? That was more than she ever wanted from him.

“That will ensure you’ll never have to do anything for money again. Life is short, Ceinlys. Especially for us at this point. Go do the things you really want to do.”

“I don’t understand.”

He looked away. “I know you married me for money, while I married you for love. I just wish I’d had the courage to leave as soon as I found out. Then we could’ve saved each other a lot of misery. And I would’ve never said those horrible things to Dane.” His mouth twisted. “Poor impulse control. Always has been a problem.”

“But what made you think that I married you for money?” She took a step forward. “Your money was never a consideration. I would’ve married you even if you had nothing.”

His jaw tightened. “Let’s not. You and I both know what happened.”

“I most certainly do not. I’ve never done anything to make you think that I married you for money. I want to know why you thought that. I deserve that much!”

Salazar’s cheeks turned dull red. “I heard you talking to Olivia. You were telling her you married me for money. I believe the exact quote was 'Money, of course, why else.'"

She shook. She remembered that moment. Her friend Olivia Fairchild had been nagging at her, mocking her for her sentimentality. And finally Ceinlys had gotten fed up and said that she'd married for money just to shut Olivia up. She'd always flaunted her old southern roots and made Ceinlys feel inferior about everything. But she'd had no idea Salazar had been listening to the phone conversation. "We wasted our lives over that?"

"What did you expect me to do? I wasn't going to confront you. I had my pride."

Of course. Salazar was a proud man. He would've never questioned her about what he'd heard because it would've made him appear weak and needy.

You should never have lied, not over something as pointless as Olivia's taunts.

"I hope you're happy with whatever you decide to do in the future," Salazar said. "We both deserve to be happy."

He pushed himself away from the bed. Ceinlys raised a hand, but it was shaking so hard she dropped her purse. He picked it up and handed it to her. When she didn't take it, he put it on the bed and started to walk away. She couldn't move even if she wanted to, and she couldn't speak even if she wanted to, not through the big lump lodged in her throat. Tears blurred her vision.

And she couldn't see Salazar anymore.

FORTY-ONE

VANESSA DELIVERED A HEALTHY BABY BOY after six hours of labor. Dane knew his sister was tough, but this was beyond his expectations. And he wasn't alone in his admiration. All the siblings, their significant others, several of the cousins and both sets of parents looked at her with pride and happiness. Then there was Barron, who puffed out his chest like he was single-handedly responsible for the baby.

Her sweaty hair stuck to her face, and her gown was wet as well. But he'd never seen her more beautiful or radiant. She held the infant boy carefully to her chest. Then, finally, she let Justin hold their baby as well.

In Dane's peripheral vision was Sophia. Tears glistened in her eyes, her hands over her mouth.

He put an arm around her waist. "What is it?" he murmured.

"The baby. He's so beautiful. I've never seen anything so perfect before."

"I take it you've never looked in a mirror. But yes, he's pretty close."

She smiled and laid her head on his shoulder, and he knew he'd said the right thing.

What would it be like for him and Sophia to have a child together?

He blinked at the thought, almost gasping at how suddenly it hit him. He'd never wanted a child. Experience had shown him that children were simply pawns in their parents' games, and beyond that, he'd just never understood the point.

Still, the idea wouldn't leave his mind. It drew a picture of Sophia with their baby. It would be red. All newborns were red, and they wailed in their thin reedy voices. But even in that state, the baby would look just like Sophia. Dane wanted it to inherit all her sweet temperament. He was too much of a bastard to give anything worthwhile to their child.

A fiery need surged through him, and he shifted slightly, making sure his sudden tumescence was hidden. Damn it, he felt like a perv. What the hell was he doing, thinking about impregnating Sophia and getting a hard-on while surrounded by the family to celebrate the birth of his nephew?

And there was always the monstrous, overhanging shadow of their relationship: Sophia didn't know the whole truth. She'd undoubtedly hate him if she learned what he'd done to her.

A baby could strengthen the bond between the two of you, an insidious voice whispered.

The more likely scenario—Sophia would leave him, ripping out his heart in the process, and take the baby too. It was that fear which had paralyzed him every time he thought about the future.

"You live too far away," Barron said, shifting another vase of flowers. Somehow the news had gotten out, and congratulatory gifts had been arriving steadily for the past few hours. "I'd like to spend at least a month with you, but Kerri's probably going to have her baby soon." Kerri was his granddaughter.

"You can come back anytime you want. It's not like you can't fly back and forth." Justin's tone was anything but sympathetic.

Vanessa licked her lips. "I'm thirsty. Is there any more water?"

"Hmm… Looks like we're out," Mark said.

"I'll get some," Sophia said. "Be right back."

"I'll go with you," Dane offered.

"I can carry a couple bottles of water. You stay here with Vanessa." She squeezed his hand and slipped out quietly.

It was all Dane could do to not go after her. He didn't want her out of his sight. He couldn't help but think that if she did, he would lose her forever. Guilt and foreboding gnawed at him, from a place deep in his gut.

He'd always thought lies hurt the people who were lied to. He'd never realized until now how they could hurt the ones who'd lied themselves.

SOPHIA WALKED TOWARD THE VENDING MACHINES at the end of the hall, her step light. Maybe this was why people called it the miracle of birth. The baby was so gorgeous. And the way Dane had looked at his nephew… Her heart pounded. She'd seen the sudden longing on his face, and she knew he wanted one too.

As the vending machine dropped the bottles of water, she fantasized briefly about the kind of child she and Dane could have together. Maybe the child would have Dane's determination, and his big generous heart, and maybe her artistic expressiveness…

She grabbed the water and headed back toward Vanessa's room, shaking her head at her own silliness. They might be living together at the moment, but they hadn't discussed anything concrete about their future. Talk about putting the cart before the hor—

She bumped into someone as she turned the corner. "Sorry." She glanced at the man's face and felt a surge of horror run up her spine.

George.

He seemed to have recovered from getting his head bashed with a lamp. His gaze was sharp, his complexion healthy. He wore a dark suit; a burgundy tie with golden diamond accents looked like a streak of old blood on his white shirt. There was a bouquet of yellow chrysanthemums in his hand.

She'd gone over a lot of scenarios involving what she'd do if she ever ran into him, but having it happen in a hospital after Vanessa had just delivered a baby boy wasn't one. Her brain seemed to turn into thick slush; everything went into slow motion.

"Hello, Sophia." His whisper crawled over her skin like a spider. He glanced around, then gripped her wrist hard enough to grind the bones together.

She dropped the bottles as her fingers went slack from the pain. She scratched his hand, but it only pissed him off. "Bitch!" he hissed and shook her.

Before she could draw in a breath to scream, he yanked her into a dark, empty patient room. He threw the flowers on the bed and shoved her toward it. She stumbled and crashed against the frame, her hip hurting from the impact.

Immediately he was upon her. He twisted her around so she was jack-knifed over the edge of the bed, face pressed down in the yellow blossoms. He pulled her arms behind her, his big hand crushed her small wrists together. His body trapped hers, and the smell of the flowers was suddenly overwhelming.

He dug his free hand into her hair, pulling at it painfully. "If you make a sound, I'll shove your face into the mattress until you suffocate," he spat. "I'm not making the same mistake twice."

A shudder ran through her, and she bit her lower lip, determined to master herself. Showing weakness would only embolden someone like him.

"Let me go," she said in a low voice. "You know I'm not going to say anything."

"I do?"

"For Libby's sake."

He leaned until his chest was flat against her back. "I'm doing this for her sake too," he whispered.

Nausea swept through Sophia as his breath brushed against her ear. The smell of old coffee and doughnuts mingled with the chrysanthemums.

He rocked against her butt, and she quailed. She could feel the swollen hardness against…

God. He was going to rape her right here in the hospital. And if he pushed her face into the mattress like he'd threatened, nobody would hear anything.

Distract him. Make him talk.

"How is this for Libby?" Sophia said.

"She would've wanted me to take care of you. Just like I took care of her."

"You…had sex with Libby?"

"Of course not, you sick fuck. She's my *sister*." The disgust in his voice was palpable. "But you're not my sister, now are you?"

"At least be honest. There's no 'taking care' of anyone here. You just want sex. No, you want to rape me."

"You want honesty? Okay. *Honestly*, I'm helping you out. I know who you really are—what you really are—and I'm still willing to take you."

"What the hell are you talking about?"

"You think anybody's going to want you if they know how fucked up you are? How damaged?"

"My injuries aren't a secret."

"Oh, right, your mangled hip." He chuckled,

running a hand over her in a horrifying caress, flank and the back of her upper thigh. "But I wonder if they know you're more fundamentally flawed."

"George, seriously, I have no idea what you're talking about. Get off m—"

"Didn't you ever wonder why your daddy started to act erratic? Appearing drunk in public, all that stuff?"

What the hell? "He was drinking." Or so she'd been told by everyone, including her mother.

"He had Huntington's disease."

"Hunting—what disease?"

"Huntington's. It's a genetic condition. Makes you unable to control your own body. That's why he always appeared drunk. Sadly, Huntington's disease is neither curable nor treatable. You degenerate over the years. You think your hip injuries are bad? Wait until Huntington's hits you."

"There's no guarantee I'm going to have it too." Biology hadn't been her best subject, but she knew hereditary traits weren't always passed on.

"You have a fifty percent chance of getting it. If you have the marker for the condition, you *will* get it." His voice dropped half an octave. "That's why *I* was going to step up and do the right thing. Do you honestly think anybody would want you if they knew? You can't even have kids—not unless you want them to get it, too."

She clenched her hands. There was no way she had any disease. George was making stuff up to justify what he'd done. "You're lying."

"Sorry, I'm not. Call Rick's doctor. He'll confirm everything."

"You're lying! Doctors make mistakes all the time!"

"Not with stuff like this." He leaned down, his lips next to her ear, creating a sickening intimacy. "But I would've taken care of you. After all, I'm not just your best friend's brother." The chrysanthemum petals crushed under her face as he pressed her head down. "I'm *your greatest fan*."

Oh god. He was the stalker!

She could feel the cool hospital air hit her thighs as he started working her skirt up. A fiery fury swept through her, giving her a burst of strength. She bucked, twisting. A wrist slipped out of his grip. She reached up behind her head and dug her nails into the flesh that she found there.

"Aagh!" He let go, putting a hand to his face. It came away smeared with blood. "Bitch! You're gonna pay for that."

She flipped over on her back, just as he raised a clenched fist. She held her hands out and screamed, her gaze darting around for anything she could use against him. She wasn't going down without—

The door crashed open; George spun around. There was a looming shadow for a quarter-second and then Dane's fist connected with George's nose with a loud crunch.

Blood dripped from his nostrils and stained his clothes as George reeled back. Dane wasn't done. He grabbed George by his suit lapels and hurled him into a wall, then followed up with a knee to the gut and another punch.

George collapsed, groaning.

Chad came into the room. Sophia thought, *Chad?* but then he was at her side, looking at her and cursing under his breath. "You all right?"

"Yeah." Her voice shook. She hugged herself. "He didn't really get to do anything. But how…why are you…?"

Chad jerked his chin at Dane. "He hired me."

Then it dawned on her. The "priceless" surprise Dane had mentioned…

Dane took a quick look at her messy hair and snarled, "Do you know this piece of shit?" He kicked George again.

She nodded.

"Is he the one who…?"

Dane didn't have to finish. She knew what he was asking. She hesitated for a moment, then nodded again. He'd find out sooner or later anyway.

"You son of a *bitch*." Dane was on George again, his fists brutal. George had gone fetal and was pleading for mercy.

"Dane, stop, *stop!* He's not worth it," she said. She looked desperately at Chad. "*Please*."

"Halfway agree with your man," Chad said, but he stepped over and pulled Dane off of George. "Come on. This asshole's done."

The lights came on in the room. Sophia flinched at the sudden brightness. Iain stood there, taking in the scene, his mouth hanging open. "What the...? Are you all crazy?"

Other members of the family appeared–Ceinlys, Salazar...even Barron, whose loud complaints about the lack of water died an abrupt death. Sophia pulled inward, hugging herself and stepping aside. It wasn't her fault that Dane and George were fighting, but if she hadn't been here, they wouldn't have. Or if she'd just let Dane come along with her to the vending machine...

Chad let Dane go and came over to her. "Hang in there, champ."

She nodded absent-mindedly, but she could barely register anything with all the adrenaline surging through her body.

"What's going on here? Who is this man?" Barron gestured with his hand. Confusion carved deep lines on his forehead.

"I'm George Grudin," he moaned. "I had an appointment with Justin Sterling earlier today."

"You have no idea what kind of trash that"—Dane gestured his bruised knuckles at George—"*thing* is. I'm going to make sure he never walks again."

"Okay, Dane, time to chill. He's not worth going to jail for," Iain said.

"You're wrong." Dane started for George again, but Iain put him in an arm-lock. "Let me go! He attacked Sophia."

Iain's head snapped Sophia's way, along with everyone else's—except George and Dane—and his gaze sharpened as he registered her state. "Oh."

"If that piece of shit had hurt Jane, you wouldn't be so calm."

A flush rose on Iain's face. "You're right…but I'd still want someone to pull me away."

"For heaven's sake, somebody get a nurse," Ceinlys said, but nobody moved.

George turned until he was lying on his back, then choked back a laugh. "'Dane'? You're Dane Pryce?" He looked at Sophia without waiting for a confirmation. "You're with *him?*"

"It's none of your business," Sophia said.

Amazingly, he began to laugh. "You stupid… This is the man who crippled you!"

FORTY-TWO

SOPHIA DIDN'T GET IT. EACH WORD OUT OF George's mouth made sense separately, but together…

George chortled hoarsely. "The accident you had in Paris. He paid your daddy five million bucks to keep his mouth shut."

The room seemed to tilt slightly. Dane couldn't be the driver from Paris. He simply couldn't. "You're lying." She turned to Dane, willing him to deny it. The muscles in his jaw tightened, but he said nothing. Salazar sighed and rolled his shoulders.

Suddenly her mother's words came back to her: *he owes us*.

Now everything made sense. She remembered Salazar's mild surprise at seeing her. Despite his off-hand explanation that he hadn't been taking calls, the more likely scenario was that Betsy had forgotten, but he hadn't let that minor detail get in the way. Not when he knew.

"What is this…person talking about?" Ceinlys said.

"There was a car accident in Paris seven years ago. It ended Sophia's figure skating career right before the Olympics," Dane explained, his voice wooden. He didn't look at anyone, his gaze fixed somewhere beyond the wall in front of him. "I was the driver who hit her."

"Why wasn't I told?" Ceinlys said.

"You didn't need to know," Salazar responded. "Sophia, Dane didn't know either. I was the one who dealt with the aftermath, and no one ever told him who the people in the other car were."

But he obviously learned at some point. "How long ago did you find out?" Sophia asked Dane, staring at his face.

His expression was as barren as a cliff. "A few days before the wedding."

She pieced the information together. "Is that why you were acting so strangely? Telling me not to come to work, then later getting me to transferred to UCLA?"

He said nothing.

Embarrassment and humiliation seared her face. She'd been so stupid. She'd thought what they had was real. But in reality, the only person who'd felt anything was her.

It made so much sense now. His excessive generosity. His insistence that she find another path to pursue. Even his unusual attentiveness in bed. It all had been…atonement.

"You should've told me," she said, her voice barely audible over the roaring in her head. If she'd known she wouldn't have given him her heart. She would've made sure to not take his gestures for anything more than what they were. "*You're despicable!*"

"Sophia..."

Chad put himself in front of her. "Don't even think about it."

"Step aside. I pay your salary," Dane snarled.

"To protect her. And I'm protecting her from you."

She breathed deeply for a moment to gather herself. It wouldn't do to break down in front of everyone.

But it was too late for excuses. There was nothing Dane could say.

She stalked out, her hands clenched by her sides. She didn't know where she was going or what she was going to do, but she knew she couldn't stay in the same room with Dane any longer. She couldn't be with a man who spent time with her out of guilt.

She was gone.

No. The precise assessment of the situation was—he'd lost her.

Dane had known all along she would never forgive him if she found out, but the reality choked him, paralyzing him like a viper's venom.

He squeezed his eyes shut. This had to be a nightmare. *It had to be.* In another second, he'd wake up with Sophia in his arms like always. She'd continue to sleep peacefully, and he'd lie there in a cold sweat and stare at the ceiling until his heart slowed.

George's grating laughter snapped him out of it. "I'm going to make you pay. I'm pressing charges."

"Oh for god's sake!" Barron stepped up spryly and gave George a soccer-kick in the ribs. "There. Why don't you press charges against me while you're at it?"

George groaned. "Mr. Sterling!"

"You're a disgrace. *I* am going to press charges against *you* for being trash because your particular flavor of trash is so offensive it's got to be illegal." Barron then turned and smacked Dane on the shoulder. "And you: stop standing around! Go get your girl while I take care of this…garbage." Then he bellowed, "And somebody get Vanessa some water!"

Dane pulled himself together. What the hell was he doing? He had to come up with a game plan fast. But the first priority was to stop Sophia. If she left, he might never get her back.

He ran out into the hall. The elevator doors at the end of the long corridor were closing with a soft chime. "Shit."

He charged down the corridor. Sophia was on that elevator. Another one opened, and he got in and pressed the close and L buttons repeatedly. "Come on. Come on!"

Before it shut, Ceinlys slipped inside.

"You should stay with Vanessa," Dane said.

"She has an army of people." Ceinlys squeezed his forearm. "You need at least one person by your side."

He stared at her hand. "You think I'm going to fail."

"What do *you* think?"

He looked away. He'd never, ever done something knowing his chances of success were low. His financial empire was built on careful planning and—as far as possible—risk avoidance. But Sophia wasn't an empire to be built. He'd never win her by being careful. He had to lay it all down.

They finally came to a stop at the lobby. He hit the button for Vanessa's floor and ran out. "Don't follow me," he called back to Ceinlys.

Sophia wasn't anywhere to be found, not that he'd expected her to linger. He went outside. Gray, more gray and some trees and lawns. Cars. Uniformed nurses on a break.

Come on. She couldn't have gone that far.

There!

Sophia was marching down the sidewalk with Chad behind her. Her fists pumped. Tension had pulled her shoulders together, raising them until they almost brushed her gold hoop earrings. She hadn't even taken her purse.

Dane ran after her. "Wait!"

She took one look over her shoulder and picked up speed so she was power-walking.

Chad stopped and took a solid stance as Dane neared. Why the hell had he ever thought it was a good idea to hire the man?

Because you were terrified for her—that someone might hurt her again when you weren't around.

"Get out of the way. You have no idea what you're dealing with," Dane said.

"You firing me?"

"No. Just give me a minute of privacy with her. You know I'd never hurt her. Otherwise I wouldn't have hired you."

Chad gave him a very hard stare, but finally nodded and stepped aside. "Fine. You better not make her cry though."

Dane rushed toward her as guilt plowed through him. She couldn't run because of him.

"Sophia." His hand closed around her wrist. He made sure to be extra gentle. She needed that after the ordeal she'd gone through with that piece of trash upstairs.

"Let me go."

He did so, but stood in her way. She wouldn't look at him, and it was flaying him alive. "Listen to me."

"I've already heard enough." Her chin trembled, and she bit her lower lip. "There's nothing you can say."

"Sophia…" For once he didn't know how to fix it. He almost always knew exactly what to say—the unvarnished truth. But now it was too late.

"You had plenty of chances to be honest with me," she said. " But you preferred to keep the secret. Was it fun for you, playing games with some penniless waif you'd picked up? Did it help you sleep better at night, giving crumbs to a girl whose lifelong dream you ruined?" Tears started to roll down her cheeks, and she covered her face best as she could with her free hand. "You've done enough. I don't want to see you ever again."

Desperation dug its claws into him, and the wall around his heart cracked. There was a vise around his chest that tightened until he couldn't draw in another breath.

One part of him wanted to let her go as she wished, while another whispered he should beg her to stay with him. Then another part of him—the one that had made him successful—demanded that he *make* her stay with him. He always did what he wanted. Why should this be any different?

And he hated himself for even thinking of forcing her to do something. After all that had happened, how could he even consider it?

His father had been right all along. He should've never been born.

He breathed out long and steady. He dug into his pocket and pulled out his keys. "Here. Take these. Take my car and stay at the penthouse. I'll check into a hotel."

She stared at the offering like it were a rattlesnake. "I'd rather sleep under a bridge."

"Preposterous. I won't let you sleep under anything other than a proper roof," Ceinlys said, approaching them. She handed Sophia a handkerchief but looked at Dane. "Staying at your place is an insensitive idea." She turned to Sophia. "Enough with all this lodging with Pryce men. You will stay at my place and that's that. And I won't hear of you speak of sleeping under a bridge ever again. Understood?"

Her voice was as hard as ice. Dane ground his teeth. Sophia needed empathy, not someone trying to boss her around. "Mother, this really does not con—"

"You know what? I like that idea, Ceinlys," Sophia said, cutting him off. She still didn't look at his face, her eyes focused somewhere around his sternum. "I'm staying with your mother while I figure out my next step. Don't even think about contacting me. We're through."

Chad gave him an indecipherable look, and the three of them turned and walked away. Dane stood there on the sidewalk, watching them go and feeling like his heart had been ripped from his chest.

FORTY-THREE

SOPHIA HAD ASSUMED CEINLYS WOULD HAVE A place much like Salazar's or Dane's, but her condo was spacious and surprisingly homey. The tall ceilings and bright colors made the place look bigger and airier than it was. A couple of contemporary art pieces hung on the walls. Despite having only a few pieces of furniture, the place didn't look barren. It had a minimalist elegance that Sophia found comforting.

"I'll get the guest bedrooms ready," Ceinlys said. "Let me know if you need anything."

Sophia perched on the edge of a couch and buried her face in her hands. Her eyes stung like they were full of sand. Time passed slowly, or felt that way. She didn't know how long she'd been sitting there when her phone rang…again. She'd been ignoring it since she'd gotten inside Ceinlys's car.

"You want me to shut it off?" Chad asked, his voice gentle.

She shook her head. Just in case it was the UCLA people calling her back about her application, she glanced at it. *Libby* flashing across the screen made her gut clench. Had she heard about what happened? Or maybe—hopefully—she was calling to meet like they'd talked about earlier…

"Hello?"

"Oh my god, Sophia!" Panic edged Libby's usually bubbly voice. "Tell me it's not true."

"What?" she said, but her heart was already sinking.

"I just got a call from George's lawyer. He's in jail for assaulting somebody at a hospital. He's saying it was you."

"Libby…" So the Pryce family had decided not to let it go. It might not have been their decision. Justin must've been furious at the incident marring what was supposed to be one of the most joyous moments in his and Vanessa's life.

"It's a mistake, right? George would never do such a thing. Can you call the police and tell them?"

Sophia glanced down. Bruises bloomed on her wrists like ugly flowers. "I'm sorry, Libby, but it's true. He did attack me."

"What?" That single syllable, whispered, so full of tremor and confusion… It felt like it was going to change her life.

Sophia rubbed her forehead. "Libby… He… attacked me at the hospital." She didn't mention him being one of her stalkers. It was already bad enough.

"But why? Did you say something to him?"

"No!" Sophia bit her lower lip. "It…wasn't the first time he'd tried to hurt me."

"What are you talking about?"

"He attacked me before. In Sea—"

"Sophia, no! No way!"

"Libby, listen to me. The real reason I had to leave Seattle in such a hurry was George. He…" Sophia looked for words to soften the blow, but there was nothing she could do. "He tried to rape me."

"No…no…" Libby sobbed. "You have to be mistaken."

Sophia laughed hollowly. "I'm really sorry…but there's no mistake. I managed to get away by hitting him on the head. But otherwise…" Sophia swallowed. She didn't have to finish.

"Why didn't you say something?"

"I just…couldn't. I didn't know how to tell you."

"What am I going to do?"

"Libby, I don't… I guess just…leave it up to his lawyer." Sophia hesitated. "I'm sorry."

"Why are you sorry? My brother tried to…*hurt* you." Libby cried harder. "I can't believe this. I had no idea."

Sophia closed her eyes as her friend's sobs rang in her ear. She'd been deluding herself. The real reason she hadn't said a word wasn't because she didn't know how. Seeing her friend hurt felt terrible, and there wasn't a thing she could do to lessen Libby's pain.

She let the tears fall as her heart ached all over again.

"WELL, WELL. WHO WOULD'VE THOUGHT?" Ceinlys's droll voice came from the office door.

Dane glanced at her. "You don't have an appointment."

"I'm your mother."

He should toss her out. He never allowed people to drop by unannounced. On the other hand, this was a special case; she might have some news about Sophia.

It had been two weeks. Sophia had cut all communication with him, and every day something inside him withered a little bit more.

"I have to admire your restraint." Ceinlys took a seat. "Mark made a national spectacle of himself to woo Hilary. Iain bribed André from Éternité for a chance to talk to Jane. Shane apparently had some sort of physical altercation with Ginger's brother to win her back—although I'm not quite clear on how that proved his love for her. But you! I understand you've made hundreds of millions more since Vanessa had her baby."

"You understood wrong. Sixty-two million," he said, hating her presence and blithe tone.

Ignoring him, she crossed her legs. "During the welcome home dinner for Shane—which you missed—Vanessa said that Shane was the most perfect of my sons. Apparently you, Iain and Mark were practice tries." Amusement lit her eyes. "But you proved her wrong. You are the most perfect one."

He ground his teeth. "Would you prefer that I drown myself in scotch? I have people depending on me. Like the employees you just passed by when you invaded my office so rudely."

He rose and walked around the desk to kick her out. His mother had worn out her welcome the moment she'd opened the door. His knees popped and ached, abused from miles and miles of running every night. He should let them rest and heal, but he couldn't stop. It was that or drinking, and he didn't think Sophia would approve of him getting shit-faced.

Or kicking his mother out.

Sighing, he rubbed his face. "You need to go. I have an appointment."

Ceinlys stood and put her hands on his cheeks. "You have to take better care of yourself. You think you can pretend, fake your way through this, but I can see what's happening. You've lost weight. Your complexion's awful. Are you sleeping at night?"

"Worry about your divorce. Finalize everything before Salazar changes his mind."

"I'm not worried about the divorce. Be kind to yourself, Dane. Everyone makes mistakes."

"Tripping and falling is a mistake. Playing roulette is a mistake. Ruining somebody's lifelong dream is not."

"So prickly. So proud. Do you know why your father's and my marriage failed? It wasn't because we didn't love each other. We simply couldn't bear to make ourselves vulnerable. And I don't know if you've ever been that way with Sophia. Just feeling love for someone isn't enough if it doesn't come with action. One of my…friends told me that love requires the merging of two souls in order to be complete. But how can you merge them if they're encased in stiff, stony shells of pride?"

"If you know so much, why can't you fix your marriage?"

"Because it's too late. I lie at night thinking about why I was so foolish. Why Salazar and I let our pride and fear get in the way of true happiness. I wish I could go back in time. I wish I'd been braver and we could start over, but your father and I have done and said too much at this point. But it's not too late for you and Sophia." She took one of his hands in both of hers and looked up into his eyes. "She's in a very, very vulnerable position, Dane. I know it's difficult—even frightening—but if you don't take the leap, you'll lose her forever. Don't end up like your parents."

He said nothing.

"Now, I really must go. You're not the only one with appointments to keep." One final hand laid gently on his cheek, and then she left, the door shutting with a click behind her.

Dane sat heavily in his seat, dropping his head back. Did his mother think he hadn't done anything? He'd called. Texted. Sent letters. Sophia wouldn't respond to anything from him. It was difficult to "merge souls" when one of them wouldn't agree to meet. He was running out of options, but he also knew he couldn't continue like this.

As he spun around in his chair, a fancy white envelope on his desk caught his eyes. The delicate loopy handwriting on the outside meant it came from Elizabeth. Probably hitting him up for more mon—

The donation!

He jumped to his feet. God, why hadn't he thought of it earlier?

So much time wasted.

He dialed Mark. Time to call in a favor.

"FAVOR MY ASS," MARK SAID ON THE PHONE. "THAT was an act of sabotage."

"You would have preferred Hilary to get in a car with somebody like Ryder instead?" Dane arched an eyebrow.

"Of course not."

"I drove her back to L.A. safe and sound from the grove. You owe me."

"No. If I do this for you, *you* owe *me* because there never was a debt between us."

"Is that what Hilary thinks?"

A long pause. "Fine, you can borrow André. Jeez. He's going to filet my face for this. Can I ask what you want him for?"

"A date at my penthouse. Very private. Very romantic."

"Oh." Disapproval came through strong and clear. "You found a blonde you like?"

"Something like that," Dane said. He wasn't telling his brother he was in love with Sophia when he hadn't told her yet.

"Fine. But it can't be on a weekend. A Monday would be best."

"Don't worry. I'll let you know the time and date."

FORTY-FOUR

SUCCESS IS THE BEST REVENGE.

Sophia repeated it to herself as she forced down a breakfast of scrambled eggs and yogurt under Chad's watchful eye. Even if she had no appetite, she shouldn't neglect her health. It was practically all she had left.

Until Huntington's disease got her.

No. Not going to think like that. The disease might not even manifest itself. She had a fifty percent chance. Given all that had gone wrong in her life, surely she was due for a break.

Except the universe didn't care about fair.

She pushed the thought away. The possibility of a debilitating disease wasn't going to stop her from living her life the way she wanted to live it. She wouldn't give anything that much power. She was going to pretend she was all right until she knew otherwise.

Still, it wasn't easy to fake it, not when there was a big gaping hole in her heart.

It'd been three weeks since she'd walked out on Dane. She should feel fine by now. She told herself she was all right, but the hole wouldn't close, not even a little. If anything it'd gotten bigger. But how could that be?

At least she had plenty of things to fill up her time. She'd started a new job at Omega Wealth Management, and that kept her quite busy. Apparently there had been an opening for an assistant, and Hilary had passed along Sophia's name to HR. She'd learned how to manage five ultra-busy associates' calendars and make killer coffee.

"If you want to climb the ladder fast, you have to make the best coffee in the office," Hilary had said. "Every person at OWM can do important things well. Bosses appreciate subordinates who can do everything—even the mundane stuff—well."

"Are the eggs not to your liking, my dear?" Ceinlys asked, walking in. As usual she was dressed elegantly; today it was in a cream tunic and a skirt. Sophia had never seen her less than immaculate.

"No, they're fine. Thank you."

Chad gave Sophia a meaningful look that said, *Then eat, champ.*

The older woman took her coffee and had a sip. "I saw Dane last week."

"Oh?" Sophia couldn't choke down the eggs. Suddenly, they tasted like sawdust.

Chad got up, mumbling something about needing more coffee, and disappeared into the kitchen.

"How was he?" Sophia tried for a polite curiosity, even though her heart had picked up its pace.

"Quite well, apparently. He made a few million dollars."

Bitterness coursed through Sophia. "Good for him." So it was business as usual for Dane. But then it made sense. All he'd ever felt for her was guilt, so without her around to constantly remind him of what he'd done, it was inevitable he'd go back to the way things had been.

"And whatever diet he's on seems quite effective," Ceinlys continued. "He's lost at least fifteen pounds."

Sophia's fork clattered on the plate. "*Fifteen pounds?*" He'd never had an ounce of fat to spare.

Ceinlys nodded. "At the rate things are going, he'll have to get his clothes altered." She set her coffee cup neatly in front of her. "I know he's been calling you. You should at least hear what he has to say. That way, you won't have any regrets down the line."

"Ceinlys…I know you mean well, but it's too late. He should've told me the truth when he found out."

"Do you know why people hide the truth?"

Sophia wanted to squirm under the older woman's gaze. "For their own convenience? Because they're horrible?"

"Fear." A long sigh. "Dane was never afraid of the truth. It was his bluntness that often caused friction with the people around him. The fact that everything he said was true upset them more because they had nothing to fight back with, so they complained that he wasn't kind enough."

Sophia stared at Ceinlys. "I know that."

"So think about what sort of fear could make a man like that act the way he has."

Loud knocks came, sounding like gunshots. Ceinlys frowned. "What on earth could be so urgent at this hour?" She got up and went toward the door.

Sophia moved the scrambled eggs around on her plate. To imagine a man like Dane having any kind of fear was ludicrous. He'd always been driven, focused, cutting through everything like a shark's fin across a lake.

But maybe he was afraid of hurting you…the way you were with Libby.

Sophia hadn't been able to say anything to her best friend…even though she herself had been the victim. And Dane had *caused* the accident in Paris. It must've been a hundred times worse for him.

But even if she could forgive him for withholding the truth, she wasn't okay with the situation. She pushed herself away from the table. She'd thought he cared for her. That what they had was genuine and real and affectionate even if he didn't love her quite yet.

A dark scowl marred Ceinlys's forehead as she came back with an envelope.

"It's for you."

"Me?"

"You're being served."

DANE KEPT GLANCING AT HIS PHONE WHILE reviewing a report on the latest business idea he'd backed. He'd laid the slim unit on his desk to make sure he didn't miss it when it buzzed.

Eight o'clock.

She should be calling by now.

Come on. Come on.

Sighing roughly, he turned a page. Had Ceinlys interfered? He ground his teeth. It was quite possible. He could just imagine his mother telling Sophia, "Here's my lawyer's number. Have her take care of the matter."

Damn it.

His phone buzzed, and he almost jumped. He almost snarled when he saw Blake's name on it. "What do you want?"

"Hello to you too. Who moved your chee—?"

"I don't have time for this."

"I was going to ask you to—"

Another call. Sophia. His heart slammed against his chest. "Can't talk." He killed the line with Blake on it, then breathed in through his mouth. "Hello, Sophia."

"*What is the meaning of this?*"

He couldn't help but smile. Her voice sounded glorious, even in anger. He closed his eyes, savoring it. "The meaning of what?"

"You're *suing* me? Along with Elizabeth and her foundation?"

"Ah. That."

"*Yes*. Ah. That."

He opened his eyes. "You owe me a date which you refuse to honor—by failing to return my calls or texts to set up a time—despite the fact that I've upheld my end of the bargain by writing Elizabeth's foundation a check for five hundred thousand dollars... which she has cashed. I was misled and defrauded."

"Misled and defrauded? We've had all those dinners and outings together."

"And? You never said any of them was the date you owed me for the bachelorette auction."

"You. Are. Unbelievable."

"But not unreasonable. I'm willing to drop it. All you have to do is agree to a date with me. Alone." He wasn't about to have Chad hanging around in the background.

"Or what?"

"'Or what' is, presumably, in your hand right now. There will be no settlement. I want my money back, plus interest and attorney's fees."

"Interest and attorney's fees? Are you insane?"

He went on like she hadn't spoken. "Every penny Elizabeth uses to defend herself and her foundation means one fewer penny for feeding hungry children and building schools for them." He paused for dramatic effect. "A tragic outcome."

He could almost hear her jaw creaking with anger. "Fine," she said. "Lunch. Today. One hour."

"Don't be absurd. For half a million dollars, I deserve at least four hours of your time. And it's going to be dinner, not some lousy lunch."

"Absolutely not. I'm a working woman now. I can't stay out late."

"Don't tell me OWM insists on a curfew now."

"Of course not, bu—"

"We can do it on this Thursday. I'll send you a car."

"I don't need a car."

"Of course you do. You've been carpooling with Hilary. Now, stop fighting me on this." He softened his tone. This battle wasn't about defeating her. It was about both of them winning. "I want at least two hours of your time. If I bore you to death, you can leave afterward. The lawsuit gets dropped, and we can all pat ourselves on the back for doing our part to help the children."

There was a long pause. "Do you know how ludicrous this is?"

"No, but I'm sure you'll tell me on Thursday."

"I want your promise in writing."

"Done. Expect it by COB today."

"What am I supposed to wear?"

"Dress comfortably. Be yourself." He hung up before she could argue further, trying to find a way to foil him. He pressed the rounded corner of his phone against his forehead and let out a shuddering breath.

Step one was accomplished. Time for step two.

André stared at Mark, one hand still on the cutting board in Éternité's kitchen. "Romance?" he said, continuing to hold a huge knife in the other.

Mark made a face. "Yes, if you can imagine Dane actually worrying about something like ambiance. It has to be the most romantic dinner ever."

"Of course I can do romance. The most romantic romance! I am French. But why must I go to your brother's place?"

"Because it's my brother who needs the romance."

The chef shook his head. "It is a joke, *n'est-ce pas?* 'E is romantic like…like…"—he rolled a thick wrist toward a slab of pork belly—"like the pig's belly!" He paused for a moment. "But of course, I can make even the belly of a swine romantic."

Mark almost rolled his eyes. "Yes, I can tell. Please can you do this for me on Thursday? Then I can finally tell Dane to go to hell next time he tries to squeeze a favor out of me."

"Eh? What is it you owe 'im?"

"He got Hilary out of an unpleasant situation once."

"I like your wife. Very well, I will do zis."

"*Merci.* And since he's paying for the ingredients, you should buy the most expensive stuff. I insist."

"*Mais bien sur.* Cheap cannot be romantic. After I am through"—André pointed the tip of his knife at Mark—"'e will feel as though 'e owes *you.*"

FORTY-FIVE

HALF AN INCH TO THE RIGHT. A QUARTER OF an inch forward.

Dane tilted his head. *Still doesn't look good.* How many nudges did it take to place a vase just right?

Maybe he should've chosen something other than calla lilies as the centerpiece. They looked sort of boring, which was surprising because they'd seemed okay until about half an hour before. Pale lavender orchids might have been better with the five hundred scented candles he'd lit in the penthouse.

The living room had the most impressive flower arrangements, made with roses and a few other flowers he didn't recognize. Was it him or did they clash with the calla lilies on the table?

André set plate after plate of the most gorgeously prepared food on the table. "They really ought to be served in courses," he muttered.

"But I don't want a server," Dane said again, doing his best not to snap at André, lest he spit in the food.

"*Oui, oui*. Romance. I understand. Still." The stocky Frenchman sighed. "At least you have good wine. And I have outdone even myself on the duck."

Dane looked at the thinly sliced duck in some sort of dark, glossy wine sauce. If it tasted half as good as it smelled, it was going to be amazing. Assuming he could choke it down past the big fluttering lump in his chest.

After the chef left, Dane paced, unable to sit still. Excess energy jittered inside him like soft Jell-O. One more minute and Sophia would be here.

Right on cue, a firm knock sounded.

Taking a deep, calming breath, he opened the door. Sophia stood on the other side in a fitted black dress—the same one she'd worn to Elizabeth's function all those months ago. Unlike that time, she'd put on a pair of flats, and her loose hair curled around her delicate face.

"You've lost weight," he said, hating that he was the cause.

"So have you. Your mother was impressed with your diet."

He allowed himself a small reluctant smile. It was like his mother to say something like that. "Come on in."

"I thought you were taking me out." Sophia bit her lower lip. "I don't know if it's a good idea for me to come in."

"Nothing's going to happen unless you want it to."

She rolled on the balls of her feet, then nodded. "Of course."

She crossed the threshold, and he let out a breath he hadn't realized he'd been holding.

Finally.

He shut the door.

SOPHIA CLUTCHED HER PURSE AS SHE TOOK STOCK of the penthouse. This wasn't just a dinner. Candlelight cast a warm glow around the huge space, and every nook and cranny had flowers in it. Where Dane had gotten the food was anyone's guess, but it smelled incredible. Despite her nerves, her mouth started watering.

"André—the chef de cuisine from Éternité—prepared everything himself," Dane said as though he'd sensed the direction of her thoughts.

"Wow. Does he often cook for private parties?"

"Never, but I called in some favors."

He raised a hand like he wanted to touch her, then dropped it. The gesture sent a sharp pang through her heart. They used to be more openly affectionate and physical. Now they couldn't even touch each other without feeling awkward.

For a moment, she wished she didn't know the truth. Then she would've been able to continue to live a sweet fantasy.

He pulled out a chair for her, and she sat down at the beautifully set table. "They're lovely," she said, looking at the calla lilies.

He flashed her a quick smile. "I'm glad to hear that. Wine?"

She shook her head. "If you have some ginger ale…"

"Got it."

With the methodical efficiency of a waiter at an upscale restaurant, he served her ice-cold ginger ale and followed up by giving her the best pieces of food from the platters set out on the table.

Finally when he sat down, she took a bite of some poultry on her plate. The meat was tender with a nice texture, but she couldn't taste anything. Sweat slickened her palms, and she tightened her grip on her silverware. "It's good."

"Thanks." A piece of food quivered on the end of his fork. He hadn't eaten anything. He put down the utensil and drank some wine. "I don't even know why I insisted on a minimum two hours. What I'm about to say won't take much time at all."

Her mouth dried. "You don't have to say anything. I'm not here to listen to you apologize about what happened in Paris." She didn't think she would be able to stand it if he did. She couldn't bear to hear him tell her every happy moment between them was just him working on his guilty conscience.

"I didn't ask you here to apologize about the accident, although I am…inexpressibly sorry that I took so much from you. I was angry, rebellious and impulsive back then."

"Dane—"

He raised his hands, palms facing forward. "Hear me out. Just...let me talk. Please."

She settled back and nodded.

"I was attracted to you from the beginning—when we first met in Mexico. But you weren't like most of the women I preferred to date. You saw too much." He dragged in a shaky breath. "I didn't want to leave myself that vulnerable to someone. When you're vulnerable like that, you get used." His forefinger followed the delicate line of his wine glass stem. "Become a pawn in someone else's game." He met her gaze. "I couldn't let myself believe you might be different. People with power always want to use the ones without it...and then discard them."

She hurt for the life he must've led. She knew "people with power" didn't mean what most would think of as the powerful and influential, like politicians and wealthy people. He was talking about his parents—the people who had inflicted pain on him with their carelessness or out of pure blindness to what he needed.

"When you popped back into my life," he continued, "I couldn't help but assign the worst possible scenario because that was easier than believing that maybe I was getting another chance. Then I got to know you and I realized you were nothing like I imagined."

"What made you change your mind?"

"When you beat me at the rink." A smile ghosted over his lips. "I saw how good you were, how effortlessly you moved across the ice. Skill like that doesn't come without a great deal of sacrifice and years of hard work. So I knew you weren't the kind of woman looking for an easy, pampered existence." He poured himself more wine. "Once I accepted that, I started to open my heart to you without realizing it myself at first. You started to fill the emptiness in my life little by little, and we fit so naturally that it was too late by the time I learned about my role in destroying your dream. Honestly, I wanted to push you away. I didn't deserve the happiness you gave me, but imagining you with anybody else, especially my father, just…made me sick."

"Dane, Salazar and I—"

"He was going to marry you. He told me so when I confronted him about covering up the accident."

Her jaw dropped. "*What?*"

"He's old and will die at some point in the not-too-distant future, which would leave you a rich widow. Then you could do whatever you wanted with the rest of your life. You would also have become a Pryce, which would've conferred quite a bit of influence."

"Dane…" She fought for words. She had no idea Salazar had planned to go to such an extreme. Not doing anything by half-measures must be hereditary in their family.

"I couldn't let him do it," Dane continued. "Even if I didn't deserve it, I wanted to be the one to make you happy."

Her stomach fluttered, a thousand tiny birds trapped within.

"I love you, Sophia. You're the only woman I've ever loved, and you're the only woman I will ever love."

Tears blurred her vision. Unable to stop herself, she sniffed and got up.

Dane jumped to his feet. "I'm not finished," he said, desperation and the fight for control sharpening his voice. "I want to marry you. I want to spend my life with you. I understand if you can't forgive me right now, but I want a chance to earn your forgiveness."

Shaking her head, she buried her face in her hands. "I can't. It's impossible."

"Nothing is impossible." His voice shook with tension. "There's always a way."

"I'm not talking about forgiving you for the accident. I'd already done that, even before I knew that the driver was you. I had to, in order to be able to move on. My only disappointment had been—" She stopped. If she let him know she loved him back, he might shrug off what she had to say. "There's a fifty percent chance I may have Huntington's disease. George dropped that bombshell at the hospital before you found us." She wiped the tears away. Mascara streaked her palms.

"I'm sorry to hear that, but it's not a guarantee.

We can find a specialist. We treat cancer these days, surely we can—"

"It's incurable and untreatable. I don't even know when it's going to show. It may hit me when I'm fifty. Or maybe I'll succumb to it when I'm thirty. You need..." She squeezed her eyes against the pain. "You need to find someone who loves you back and not burden you the way I might."

His warm hands cradled her face, his forehead against hers. "I don't care how many healthy days you have left. If we only have twenty-four hours left to share, then we'll simply have to cram a lifetime of love into one day. I'm not letting anything get in the way of loving you."

"How am I going to do the right thing if you say things like that?" A sob wracked her body. "I saw how you looked at Vanessa's baby. If I have the disease, I may never be able to give you children."

"If all I cared about was children, any of the women I've dated would have been acceptable. My love isn't contingent upon you giving me children. It is you, only you that I want. If we can have them, great. If not, I have four siblings who are sure to have nephews and nieces for us to spoil." His thumb brushed away tears at the edge of her eye. "I love you, Sophia. Will you give us a chance?"

She nodded. "I'm too selfish to say no."

A soft sigh escaped between his parted lips, his shoulders finally relaxing. "Thank you."

"And just so we're clear, I love you, too, Dane."

His eyes blazed, and he swooped down for a hard kiss. She wrapped her hands around his wrists and allowed herself to be lost in the moment. Need pulsed through her like liquid gold. It wasn't just heat, but something infinitely sweet and precious.

"Promise me you'll make an honest man out of me," he whispered against her mouth.

She nipped his lower lip. "First things first." Then linking her fingers with his, she dragged him to the bedroom.

FORTY-SIX

SOPHIA TAPPED HER FEET ON THE COOL LINOleum floor, then curled her hands so she didn't start biting her nails again. The waiting felt like forever, even though the clock said only ten minutes had passed.

Dane put a hand over hers. "Hey. It's going to be all right."

She nodded, forcing a smile. Six months had passed since the dinner, and it'd been like a dream. It did indeed feel like they were trying to cram a lifetime of love into every single day.

And that was what had given her the courage to seek the answer—to see if she carried the genetic marker or not. Otherwise she wasn't being fair to him…or to herself.

Dane had asked her a few times to marry him, but she'd demurred. She hadn't wanted to make the decision without knowing. He'd understood her hesitation, but had kept asking anyway. It only made her love him more.

"I'm just nervous that I might have it." She pressed her legs together to stop the foot tapping. "It's so silly because knowing is probably better than not knowing so I can plan for it, but..." She sighed heavily.

"You're going to feel silly when you find out you don't have it."

She chuckled weakly at how confident he sounded. Gratitude filled her like warm honey. He'd been so patient, so strong by her side. "Are you going to dole it out?"

"It?"

"Love. If I don't have it, you'll have a lifetime to love me."

"No. I'm still going to give it my all every day." He kissed her on the forehead. "You're worth it."

Finally the nurse called her name, and she got up and held out a hand. "Come on."

"You sure?" Dane said.

She nodded. "We should be together."

He took her cold, clammy hand. "Okay. Let's do it."

The doctor's office was at the end of the hall. It wasn't a big room, but it was enough to fit three people comfortably.

Dr. Brown was fairly young, in his mid-thirties. The soft lines on his face made him look boyish although there were a few premature gray streaks in his golden hair.

He smiled as Sophia and Dane entered together. That was a good sign, right? Surely he wouldn't have smiled if the result was bad…

"Please sit down," Dr. Brown said. He flipped through some papers.

Nervous energy burst through her like a cloud of wasps. He spoke, but she couldn't hear anything over the buzzing in her head. His mouth moved in slow motion, the light in the office dimmed and—

"Sophia? Sophia!" Dane was shaking her. "Are you all right?"

"Yes." She blinked a few times. "What happened?"

"You went pale so fast, we thought you might faint," Dr. Brown said, concern in his dark eyes. "Did you hear what I said?"

"I don't… No." She looked at Dane.

"The tests came back negative. You're fine."

She let out a breath. *She didn't have it!*

"Congratulations." Dr. Brown smiled.

"For real? There's no chance of error?" she asked.

"Well… Nothing is absolute, but the chances are virtually zero."

She clasped her hands together. "Thank you, thank you, thank you."

The doctor laughed. "So happy for you, Sophia. And you too, Dane."

Her legs shook so hard, she could barely walk on her own. When she stumbled in the hall, Dane scooped her up and started carrying her.

"Oh my god, put me down!" she squealed.

"I think I'm entitled to carry my woman, especially after such great news." He smiled. "I knew it."

"How?" she asked, wrapping her arms around him.

"We were due for some good fortune in our lives."

When they reached the lobby, he let her down. Her body glided along his, and she inhaled sharply at the contact. It was insane how much she wanted him still. She'd always thought the heat between them would wane as they stayed together longer, but it only seemed to grow more intense.

"So. Are you going to give me my answer?" Dane asked as they walked out of the medical center together.

She stopped and unlinked her arm from his. When he cocked an eyebrow, she extended her hand. "You may put the ring on my finger."

"Finally!"

He grinned and pulled out the familiar velvet box. He popped it open to reveal a beautiful sapphire ring—an heirloom from his grandmother. It fit perfectly on Sophia's finger. The huge blue stone sparkled under the bright sun.

"It suits you." He kissed her knuckles. "You just made me the happiest man in the world."

"And you just made me the luckiest woman in the world. I love you, Dane."

With a broad smile, he picked her up and spun with her until they were both breathless. Then touching his lips to hers, he said, "I love you, too."

FORTY-SEVEN

Two and a half years later

"ABSOLUTELY NOT," DANE SAID, TAPPING A finger twice on the report on his desk. "Tell him to get his act together. He has a week."

"Yes, sir."

Quiet knocks at the door, then it opened, and Sophia poked her head in. "Sorry, I hope I'm not interrupting."

"You aren't." Dane grinned.

The meeting was supposed to continue for another half an hour, but his employees knew better than to object. There were only two types of people in Dane's world now: his wife and everyone else.

The men got up and left, nodding at Sophia. "Ma'am."

On the other side of the open door was Chad, who nodded at Dane once, but otherwise remained impassive. He stared at the men one by one as they walked past.

When the door closed, she smiled sheepishly. "I definitely interrupted. I shouldn't have come without an appointment."

"Don't be ridiculous. My wife does not need an appointment to see me." He got up and kissed her. "I'd love to think that you came by because you missed me, but it's only been four hours since I had you coming in my arms."

She giggled, her cheeks turning red. "You're so naughty. What if someone hears you?"

"Men will hate me, and women will envy you. See if I care." He perched on the edge of his desk and pulled her closer, turning her until her ass cradled his hardening cock.

"You're incorrigible. Anyway, you're right. I do have some good news. I have to share now or I'm going to burst."

He laughed at her enthusiasm and rested his chin on her shoulder. "All right. Go on."

She ran her hands over his. "You remember Jillian Lim?"

"The young figure skater?" Sophia had started to sponsor some promising skaters who needed financial help. At first Dane had been concerned, worried she might feel depressed or resentful about her broken dreams. But the work seemed to energize her, connecting her to the world she loved so much.

"Right. She won the regional!"

"That's fantastic. So is she going to the national championships?"

Sophia shook her head. Her loose hair tickled Dane's nose, and he inhaled her intoxicating scent. "She needs to do well at the sectional first, but I'm sure she will. She's amazing."

"Congratulations, honey."

"Jillian's mom sent me an email and a link to a video. If you want, we can watch it later."

"I'd love to. Want to have lunch to celebrate?" Jillian was the first skater Sophia had sponsored.

"Wait. There's more."

He arched an eyebrow.

She turned so she could face him. "You're going to be a father."

Warmth spread from the center of his heart until his entire body tingled. His mouth parted, and he could feel it curving into the goofiest and happiest smile. "How far along are you?"

"Five weeks and five days. Hold on. I have a picture." She dug into her purse and pulled out an envelope. Inside was a black and white photo of what appeared to be a squishy dot. "He's really small. Still sesame seed-sized."

"But the most amazing and wonderful baby ever." He dropped to his knees and pressed his ear against her flat belly. "I can tell."

Sophia laughed, the gentle sound rippling over his soul. "You can't hear anything yet."

"I don't need to." He turned his face and looked up at her. A lump in his throat thickened his voice. "Our baby's going to be as perfect as its mother." He kissed her stomach. "Thank you for this incredible gift."

"You're welcome, love."

Her fingers brushed through his hair, stroking him. He closed his eyes as sweet contentment spread through him.

He was exactly where he belonged forever.

Thank you for reading *The Billionaire's Forbidden Desire*. I hope you enjoyed it.

Would you like to know when my next book is available? Send a blank message to new-from-nadia@aweber.com or go to my website at www.nadialee.net to sign up for my new release alert.

Thank you for being a part of the Pryce family. But you don't have to say goodbye! You'll see your favorite familiar faces and meet some new ones in *A Hollywood Deal*, the first book in Billionaires' Brides of Convenience series, featuring the Pryce cousins.

A Hollywood Deal (Billionaires' Brides of Convenience Book 1)

Paige Johnson is used to cleaning up after her boss,

Hollywood superstar bad boy Ryder Pryce-Reed. Nothing can shock her—not the countless "humped and dumped" women or the wreckage in the wake of his wild ways—until he asks her to marry him for a year.

Billionaire actor Ryder needs to marry for a year to claim his beloved grandfather's painting. Who better to help out than his big and beautiful assistant Paige? The rules are simple: give everyone a good show while keeping it strictly professional. But what happens when he can't keep his hands off his sassy, luscious "wife"?

ABOUT NADIA LEE

New York Times and *USA Today* bestselling author Nadia Lee writes sexy, emotional contemporary romance. Born with a love for excellent food, travel and adventure, she has lived in four different countries, kissed stingrays, been bitten by a shark, ridden an elephant and petted tigers.

Currently, she shares a condo overlooking a small river and sakura trees in Japan with her husband and son. When she's not writing, she can be found reading books by her favorite authors or planning another trip.

To learn more about Nadia and her projects, please visit www.nadialee.net. To receive updates about upcoming works from Nadia, please visit www.nadialee.net to subscribe to her new release alert.